KETTLE OF FISH

KETTLE OF FISH

NIGEL TRANTER

EDINBURGH
B&W PUBLISHING
1995

Copyright © Nigel Tranter
First published 1961
This edition published 1994
by B&W Publishing
Edinburgh
ISBN 1 873631 46 6

British Library Cataloguing in Publication Data:
A catalogue record for this book is available from
the British Library

Cover illustration: Detail from *The Herring Fleet
Leaving the Dee, Aberdeen* (1888)
by David Farquharson
Photograph by kind permission
of Aberdeen Art Gallery & Museums.

Printed by Werner Söderström

AUTHOR'S FOREWORD

This is entirely a work of fiction. Not only are no living persons referred to herein, but no existing institutions, companies or offices, in Berwick-on-Tweed or elsewhere, are represented. Even the Tweed Commissioners, that excellent if somewhat amorphous body of gentlemen, are not to be taken as being blamed for being what they are—proprietors of river fishings of over a certain annual value, or their nominees—or for carrying out their statutory duties under the terms of the Act that appointed them.

I have merely taken what seemed to me a potentially explosive situation, and fictionally exploded it. I am no lawyer, and my interpretation of the Tweed Fisheries Act of 1857, Amended 1859, may well be far from legally accurate, and my suggested methods of reform not only quite impracticable but thoroughly scandalous. I hope and pray, therefore, that no foolish fisherman or other may be tempted to put my methods and theories to the test of action—not without specifically absolving me of all responsibility first, at any rate.

And yet . . . !

Can Parliament continue to contravene the International Convention of the Sea—of which Britain is a signatory—and the international three-mile limit with impunity? The Tweed Act does, you know. What would the Icelanders, for instance, say if they knew?

There are two sides to every problem, of course, and this tale deals very blatantly with one side only—for it is not a text book but purely an adventure story.

NIGEL TRANTER
Aberlady 1960

I

THE new schoolmaster strolled out over the big cobble-stones of the long pier that stretched, curving like a great fish-hook, into the heaving darkness of the North Sea, a hook inadequately baited with the red gleam of the harbour light at its point. He did not hurry; indeed he could not, for the April night was dark and the going underfoot rough. Not everyone would have chosen that pier for a walk before turning in; the new schoolmaster, however, had been wrestling all evening with a problem far removed from the rock-girt Berwick coast-line, and he judged the fresh salt easterly breeze off the sea as the best means of clearing his head for a night's sleep. And even the benighted pier was less likely to be lethal to the uninitiated walker, he imagined, than any clamber up the steep cliffs that hemmed in the little fishing-village of Airdmouth, or dizzy cliff-top scramble thereafter. Airdmouth, situated as it was, could not be bountifully provided with comfortably gentle walks.

As he strolled further along the pier, Adam Horsburgh was glad of the faint glow that came from across the bay, where somebody had left their car's headlights burning. They were more than half a mile away, but, shining directly across the black water, served to show up and outline the bumps and inequalities of the pier's stonework—which was a convenience.

He had just reached the bend, where the pier curved round to its hook-like finish, when it happened. The draw and surge of the tide against the rocks deadened any sound that might have warned him. Abruptly, a man was standing in front of him, close; a big man, arms akimbo, barring his way.

The new schoolmaster halted, with a gasp of breath. The newcomer appeared to have risen out of the very ground. Since that consisted, however, of moderately level and very solid stone, another solution had to be sought. The only alternative was descent from above. Along the seaward side of that pier,

1

as further protection against the great seas that pounded this coastline, there ran a stout thick wall, of about the height of a man. It could only have been from the top of this that the fellow had jumped.

They stared at each other in the gloom. The big man had any advantage that there was, as far as light went, with his broad back to the headlamps' beam. Not that Horsburgh, who was still very much of a stranger here, would have been apt to recognise him anyway.

Not a word was spoken. The newcomer jerked head and thumb in the most obvious gesture of dismissal, authoritative, almost threatening.

Horsburgh parted his lips to speak. Then he thought better of it. He did not normally swallow threats readily—but he had been made very much aware of being a newcomer since arriving at Airdmouth, and as such was walking warily, metaphorically if not actually. Moreover, there are more ways of entering a house than by smashing the door in with your fist— military service had taught him that, at least. He swallowed, therefore, gave a single nod of the head, and turning about, walked back whence he had come. Only the "Damn!" that was jerked out of him as he tripped over a particularly uneven stone spoiled the pregnant silence of the entire encounter.

Whatever the appearances to the contrary, the new schoolmaster was not really a discreet nor yet an incurious individual, however. Walking back along that pier, his mind was very busy. What had the incident meant? What was that fellow doing up there on the wall? Why had he thought it necessary to jump down and confront a stroller? Would he really have used violence to turn him back, as had been the impression given? If so, what was behind it all? What, in fact, went on behind that sea-wall?

The headlights from across Airdmouth Bay were still shining. Somebody over there who was not worried about his batteries. Looking back, Adam Horsburgh could see no sign of the man whom he had left—nor any detail save the red pier-head lamp. Choosing a spot where the deck-house and mast of one of the fishing-boats moored to the pier might be expected to cast some sort of shadow from those headlamps, he crossed to the wall. It was built of the same rough masonry, providing ample toeholds. Gripping the top, he hoisted himself up, to peer over.

It was darker on this seaward flank, difficult to see anything at all, save that the pier slanted down in a sort of ramp at this side. The tide was barely half-full, and much of the weed-grown slope was uncovered. Nothing else was apparent, except the white-laced edge of the hissing swell.

Easing himself back, Horsburgh continued unhurriedly with his walking. But at the end of the pier, instead of proceeding along the one-sided village street of huddled whitewashed cottages to his own lonely schoolhouse, after a swift look round he turned and clambered down the seaward side of the pier to the seething water's edge. He began to make his way back again.

It made slow going, for the bank was steep and the seaweed was slippery. Time and again the man slipped, only saving himself from the water by inches. Soon he was going almost wholly on hands and knees.

It seemed much further back to the bend in the pier, this way. He kept looking up, watching the top of the sea-wall. From down here, it was fairly clearly outlined by the diffused glow of the far-away car's lights. Presently the dark bulky figure of a man was silhouetted, sitting up there. He appeared to be doing nothing—just sitting.

Then Horsburgh saw the boat. Or rather, it was the phosphorescence of oars dipping into sea-water that he saw; the dark outline of the boat itself only materialised after more peering.

It was not far out, and being rowed pierwards. By four oars apparently. Just below the man on the wall.

Adam Horsburgh crouched still, while the boat drew in. He was seeing things a little more clearly now. He thought that he could just discern more men, who reached out from the ramp to pull the boat in. Certainly he saw the man up on the wall wave his hand—a most evident all-clear sign.

3

So that was what the fellow meant, at least! He was a look-out, to ensure that the people below were not disturbed, and placed where any signals that he might make could be seen in good time, silhouetted against the glow. Which meant that the car across the bay was in this thing too; it was no accident that its lights had been left on to shine this way. There was organisation here.

The watcher moved a little closer, the better to see what went on. It became obvious that the men on the bank were not just hauling in the boat. The boat was stationary—but the men were still pulling, he thought. It must be a net. A salmon-net? Salmon fishing. Poaching? Could one poach salmon in the sea? Horsburgh did not know. But why the secrecy and precautions otherwise?

The pulling in of the net seemed to take a long time. But at length the greenish flash and glimmer of phosphorescent scales gleamed brighter than any water, and there was much activity amongst the men. They were in to fish. Something of the excitement of the moment communicated itself to the watcher. He rose up to get a better view, slipped on the weed, and fell with a crash. And what was worse, with a splash—for a leg and an arm struck the edge of the water.

No doubt it was the splash rather than the crash that caught the look-out's attention, however painful the latter to the recipient, taking the noise of the waves into account. At any rate, in a moment the man up on the wall was on to his feet, pointing and shouting.

Thereafter everything happened in a rush. Acting almost entirely instinctively, Adam Horsburgh scrambled to his feet again, turned, and started to run. Unfortunately he could not run very fast or steadily, what with the weed-hung slope of the stones underfoot and the fact that he had jarred his hip unpleasantly in his fall. Whereas, it was very evident that the big man up on the wall had no such drawbacks to contend with. Fully a yard wide, the flat top of that wall made a much better running-track. It took only a few moments for the runner above to reach and pass the one below. A few yards further,

4

and the former flung himself down, to drop over the side of the pier on to the weed in front of the fugitive, blocking his way.

There were shouts, and the heavy hollow thud of rubber boots, sounding from behind.

The new schoolmaster was suddenly very angry. He did not reason out the fact that he was doing nothing wrong, that this was a public place and that he had every right to walk along the pier day or night, that he was not even doing these people any harm. Nothing like that. He merely knew a great wrath that he should be threatened and harried like this, and made to feel a fool. Possibly even his main source of ire was at the thought of himself running away like this—and being outrun. At any rate, without the least hesitation he hurled himself headlong at the large character who had the temerity and insolence to bar his way this second time, fists clenched.

It was a poor uneven fight from the start. Not merely on account of size and weight, for Horsburgh was no puny feeble figure but a stocky sturdy youngish man in his early thirties, who had played rugby for Heriot's for not a few years; but everything was against him that night—a dizzy head from his fall as well as his aching hip, ordinary leather-soled shoes on slimy weed, and recognition that he was outnumbered and his retreat cut off.

Indeed, he all but came to grief before ever he reached his immediate opponent, by tripping and stumbling only a yard or so from the big fellow, so that he perforce made his attack butting head first in a floundering scramble. The other had only to stand still and receive it, one shoulder propped firmly against the walling of the pier. He did so, and at the same time swung a mighty swipe at his assailant—which caught the tottering Horsburgh on neck and shoulder, very adequately completing his downfall.

Heriot's playing-fields are a hard training-ground, however, and their graduates are taught not only how to fall, but to do so profitably. Even in this angry predicament, training was not entirely wasted. As he went down, the smaller man flung out his arms and locked them around the other's knees. No stance of seaweed was sufficient for that sort of thing. Feet flying from under him, sea-boots or none, the big fellow crashed heavily.

Though only approximately half of him fell on top of Horsburgh, the weight of him did not do a lot for the latter's wind.

Vigorously the two of them struggled there, now one, now the other almost in the sea. Adam, a modicum of wisdom come to him, concentrated on seeking to break away from his opponent's grip before the others could come up—that and trying to recover his breath.

It was hopeless, of course. The big man knew that all that he had to do was to hang on until his colleagues arrived. Circumstances permitted him to do that most ably.

Four more men came thudding up, to lay vehement hands upon the struggling schoolmaster. Whatever Horsburgh may have said, between them the others uttered never a word.

They pulled him upright and held him so, ungently. The big man got to his feet, considering the prisoner. Then glancing at the others, who seemed to await his command, he nodded, and jerked his eloquent thumb over his shoulder. Seawards he jerked it.

As with one accord, the other four took the schoolmaster by arms and legs, and threw him into the waves.

The shock of receiving such treatment was almost greater than the shock of the cold water to Adam Horsburgh. Indignation and fury, rather than sea-water, blinded him as he went under—and unfortunately had the effect of opening his mouth in gasping protest. A large mouthful of salt water had a remarkably swift and sobering effect, however, promptly engendering a more practical view of the situation. The air in his clothing served to buoy him up, at first, and after that original and unpleasant plunge under, he struck out for the pier again forthwith, spluttering more sea-water than profanity. The men ashore seemed to be watching him with a detached interest—though one of them was in process of taking off the second of his long thigh-boots.

The North Sea swell was surging up and down the sloping

stones of that ramp quite dauntingly, as seen from this angle, and Adam had difficulty in obtaining a grip and drawing himself up. At his second attempt, men stooped down, reaching out towards him. The schoolmaster mouthed watery curses at them, but presently he realised that hands were reaching out to grab him and draw him in, not to thrust him back. Surprised as he was, he forbore to thank his rescuers for this service.

Horsburgh's chittered protests brought forth no apologies, no answer of any sort. Strong hands gripped his shoulders again, and propelled him into motion. Not shorewards either, but back along the pier. He went, reluctantly, tripping and stumbling, half-carried indeed.

Reaching the spot where the gleaming silver of great fish shone from amongst the dark folds of heaped nets, and where the boat still dipped and swung a yard or two out, with one man aboard, they halted. Horsburgh's captors seemed to be extraordinarily effective at action without discussion or words of any sort thereon. The boat was beckoned closer, and another man climbed inboard. He then turned to receive the dripping prisoner, who was more or less lifted bodily down to him. It was the same large man as before.

Adam, still making at least token protest, was thrust into the wide stern, where he was sat down upon a pile of wet net. It was a roomy black boat of the typical coble build, of broad beam, shallow draft, upturning prow and flat stern. The two fishermen got out the long narrow-bladed oars, and without any evident instructions or farewells from the others, started to pull outwards, seawards.

"What's . . . what's the meaning of this? Where are you going?" Adam demanded. "Where are you taking me?"

There was no answer from the rowers. Obviously he would be as well to save his breath for chittering with.

They rowed steadily, stolidly out, the boat heaving to the lively swell. Quickly the pier faded and merged into the general gloom. Only its red light glowed, unwinking.

After a while it became apparent that they were, in fact, swinging round that light. Soon it was actually behind them, and Horsburgh realised that they must be crossing Airdmouth Bay. The car's headlights from the other side no longer shone.

The half-mile row passed in silence, save for the slap and gurgle of the water, and the faint creak of the oars on their pin-rowlocks. Adam noted that these last appeared to be muffled in cloth and no doubt greased. Nothing seemed to have been overlooked, nothing left to chance, in this affair.

The darker loom of the land bulked before them again, accompanied by the steady sigh of breaking waves. At a stretch of shingly beach, the oarsmen drove the coble directly ashore—a manoeuvre for which, in fact, its flat bottom was designed. As the pebbles crunched under them, and the craft came to an abrupt stop, the big man gestured with that thumb of his. The new schoolmaster, on principle, sat still. Shipping the oars, the two fishermen unhurriedly rose and advanced on him over the thwarts. Gripping him by the shoulders, they heaved him up and over. Adam's principles did not insist that he struggled. He *wanted* to get ashore and away, didn't he?

He found himself wading in a couple of feet of swirling water, on pebbles that rolled beneath his feet at the tug of the tide. By the time he won clear of the waves, and looked back, the coble was already disappearing into the night.

Almost, the victim of it all was more irate than ever, at that sight. It was all so calmly assured and authoritative, so blatantly terse and damned superior. He might have been a naughty child, one of his own pupils, caught poking his nose in where it was not wanted and should not be, given a fright and taught a lesson—but not allowed to get into any serious danger, of course—fished out, dumped on a far-away shore to cool his temper whilst he scurried home bedraggled and humiliated. Dealt with, dumped, abandoned.

Not for a long time had Adam Horsburgh felt so angry and helpless. Helpless meantime, anyway—though that did not mean that he would remain that way, by God!

Anger, however righteous, was of little use to him there and then, nevertheless. He had, he reckoned, almost two miles to walk home—and over rough ground, for there was no road along the shore this side of the bay.

That thought brought to mind the car. If there was no road down here, then it must have been parked up on the cliff-top. The cliffs certainly were much lower at this southern end. That would be the way for him, then. Try to get up the cliffs. Even going after that, if a car could get there. Better than miles of stumbling over rock and reef and seaweed along this iron-bound shore in the darkness.

A veil can be drawn over Adam Horsburgh's homecoming that night. Suffice it to say that it was difficult, protracted, and productive of considerable frustration—plus a few scrapes and grazes. The new schoolmaster's bump of locality turned out to be rather less effective than he had thought. It was well past midnight before he reached the door of his darkened school-house on its little peninsula, his clothes almost dried upon him. Not a light shone in the village, not so much as a cat moved abroad. Even the gulls had stopped their incessant screeching.

Something white on the doorstep caught the man's eye. It was a parcel, roughly wrapped in newspaper. Two parcels actually, a smaller one within quite a large one. This last, heavy and solid-feeling, contained half of a fair-sized salmon—six pounds at least, Horsburgh calculated. In the smaller one was a little two-gill flask, half full. Only the merest sniff was required to establish that it held whisky—a generous dose.

The schoolmaster stood there in his barely furnished kitchen with these two tokens before him, while the tension drained out of him and the frown faded from his brow. Then he laughed, a short bark of a laugh. And any vague thoughts of official complaint or informing the police went the way of tension and frown.

That is not to say, however, that Adam Horsburgh went to bed that night in any way determined to forget the whole affair, comforting warm glow inside him notwithstanding. He was not that sort of man.

9

II

THE schoolmaster was not really a drinking man at all, and his visit to the little bar of The Fishers' Tryst early the following evening was his first. Facing the pier-head, it was no more than a low-browed whitewashed cottage without, and a low-ceilinged, wall-boarded and once-varnished establishment within, with some battered tin advertisements, shining brass beer-pump handles and a number of dark-green glass floats hanging from the ceiling in nets—presumably for reasons aesthetic, since all customers of more than very medium height were forced to continual ducking to avoid them. Eyeing these, Adam wondered whether perhaps they were there as a warning to the thirsty on the perils of impaired ducking faculties?

Only one individual patronised the hostelry so far, a middle-aged man in the inevitable blue jersey, faded overalls, tweed cap and sea-boots turned down below the knee. Not that this could be looked upon as of any significance, for apart from letting accommodation for summer visitors, sea fishing was Airdmouth's only industry—though a few of its young women travelled the three miles daily to work in Berwick-on-Tweed.

This man, sitting at a little glass-topped table in the window, eyed Adam with dispassionate calm, and in answer to the newcomer's greeting, nodded, said that it was a fine night, and thereupon stared out of the window and far away. Adam's follow-up about a touch of rain sank without ripple into a pool of silence.

The proprietor, who himself looked more fisherman than hotel-keeper, materialised, served the new customer with a pint of export ale, remarked that aye it was a fine night, and sighing, withdrew to some inner sanctum.

Adam raised his glass mug, said cheers vaguely to the back of the fisherman's head, received no comment, and sipped thoughtfully.

Two more men came in, both in jerseys and stained canvas jerkins, glanced at the schoolmaster, and brushing the film of fine rain from their sleeves, remarked that it was a fine night. They nodded to the other fisherman, and were served with small whiskies and half-pints of beer, which they drained in successive and businesslike gulps. Thereafter they sighed and contemplated infinity through the cracked mirror behind the bar. They were men of about Adam's own age, and one of them had a distinct bruise on his weather-beaten cheekbone.

Adam cleared his throat. "Good catches?" he asked politely. "At the fishing?"

There was a few moments' silence. Then one of the newcomers muttered, "Och, well," and stared hard into his froth-lined mug.

"I'ph'mmm," his companion agreed, and raised his voice a little. "Two more, Jock."

The proprietor emerged, sighing, served two further whiskies and beers, and retired. Taking up their drinks, the pair moved over to sit beside the first fisherman, backs rather noticeably to the room.

Adam tried again. "Prices keeping up?" he wondered. "Not much point in good catches if the price drops away."

Nobody actually denied that.

"In-shore fishing most of you will go in for, here? Flounders, rock-cod, and so on? The odd salmon, or two?"

"Hech, aye. Och, dearie me. Man, man," the middle-aged fisherman mentioned, addressing the low brown-patched ceiling. It would have taken a clever man to say for certain whether that was in answer to Adam's questions, any sort of commentary on what had gone before, or an entirely new and independent pronouncement.

"Ooh, aye. Uh-huh." One of his colleagues spat accurately into a convenient spittoon.

"Just that," the other observed, and downed whisky and beer.

Adam Horsburgh could be a determined man, even obstinate at times, but this was a tide that he could not swim against. Biting his lip, he applied himself to his beer—until he realised that he had almost finished it. Not wishing to have to swallow another dose, even a half-pint, and hoping still for some opportunity to achieve what he had come for, he sipped daintily, spinning out the meagre residue.

There was barely a spoonful left in his mug when the door opened to admit two more customers. One of these was small and elderly and grizzled, and walked with a limp. Now, while Adam had not consciously noted anything of the sort at the time, it came to him quite distinctly now that one of his assailants of the night before *had* limped. At some moment, somehow, a part of his mind must have noticed the fact. Moreover, the second man was not only very tall, but heavily made, seeming to bulk very large indeed in that low-ceilinged room, and having to dodge the hanging glass floats at every second step—though with an accustomed ease that bespoke much practice. This big fellow had a shock of sandy hair, tufted sandy brows, and, still more noticeable, prominent sandy eyelashes fringing very blue eyes. The twin Logan girls in Adam's own class at school were notable in exactly the same fashion—and a handful they were, too. The schoolmaster drew a long breath.

The new arrivals showed no hint of discomfort at sight of the company in the bar. Their unhurried greeting, though brief, was easy, and comprehended all present, including Horsburgh. That man, who had been prepared almost to shout aloud if anybody else announced that it was a fine night, raining as it now was, swallowed the formalised Lowland Scots greeting along with the rest, in his quickened interest.

The big man came up to the counter actually close alongside Adam, ordered the usual nip and chaser, and then, noting the state of the schoolmaster's mug, quite casually offered to fill this up too.

"Er . . . no. No thank you," Adam said—to add hurriedly, lest this refusal seemed too curt, "I've had quite enough, thanks." He swallowed, realising that this last must sound either priggish or quite absurd. "I was, h'm, just going," he ended up. Which was not what he had intended to say, at all.

The other nodded his sandy head unconcernedly, and tossed a remark over to one of the men in the window.

Adam felt the need to assert himself, somehow. "You are Mr Logan, I shouldn't wonder?" he jerked.

"Aye, I am that. Though I don't often get Mister. Sandy Logan, that's me," the other answered.

"Yes, I thought I recognised you." A brief pause. "From the resemblance, of course—to the two Logan girls. At school."

"Aye, poor lassies—it's no' fair, is it! You'll be the teacher, then? The new man at the school."

"Yes."

"Aye, then. Well, you belt the holy hell oot o' those two if they give you any cheek, mind! I'm feart for them myself." The big man smiled gently. "Canna do a thing wi' them. Eh, Dand?"

The grizzled man grunted non-committally, and applied himself to his liquor.

Adam eyed his empty mug. "You are a fisherman?" he said. It may have sounded just a little bit like an accusation.

"Aye," Logan agreed. "You could call me that."

"Perhaps, then, you could tell me what I want to know. You see, I'm rather interested in . . . salmon."

There was a distinct pause. Nobody in that bar actually looked at anyone else.

Except for Sandy Logan, that is. He turned directly to consider Adam, as though with kindly interest. "Salmon, is it?" he repeated, after a moment or two. "Och, salmon is a special kind o' fish, man. It takes special fishing, too. Not for the likes o' us, at all. No, no."

"Indeed? How do you mean—not for the likes of you?"

"Och, well. There's folks that can fish for salmon—and folks that canna. That's us."

"You mean—legally?"

"That's right. What other way would I mean?" That was entirely mild.

"Well, I suppose that there is probably quite a bit of, h'm,

13

poaching goes on?"

There was a shocked hush. The man Dand swallowed his chaser fast and audibly, and banged on the counter loudly for more. A strong clearing of throats came from over at the window table. The proprietor reappeared, shaking his head portentously. The new schoolmaster was made to perceive, with entire clarity, that decent respectable folk did not discuss such things—and certainly not in public.

Adam looked at Sandy Logan.

"Poaching is it, you say?" The big man shook his head. "Och, now—that's no' a thing that the likes o' us can tell you aboot. You could try the polis, maybe. Or the Berwick Salmon Fisheries."

"There *is* no policeman in Airdmouth."

"That's a fact. It would have to be Berwick, maybe. Aye, Berwick's the place for you, right enough."

"I wonder! I thought that I might possibly get more, er, first-hand information, nearer here."

"I doubt it, man—I doubt it. Och, the Tweed's the place for the salmon, and Berwick's on the Tweed."

"What's a body wanting to ken all this aboot the salmon for, anyway?" the grizzled man Dand wondered of the room at large.

There was a faint murmur of agreement.

"The fact is, I'm rather partial to salmon," Adam explained carefully. "I happened to come by a bit, yesterday. A very nice bit. And now I'd like another piece to send home to my parents in Edinburgh. They're very partial to salmon, too, you see."

"Is that so? Well, you just try Wilson's shop in the Castlegate o' Berwick, and you'll get as nice a bit o' salmon as any place I know," the big man declared. He tossed off the remainder of his beer. "Goodnight to you. Coming, Dand? Aye, Tosh. Aye, boys." Weaving his way expertly amongst the floats, he made for the door, the grizzled man at his heels.

There was a scraping of chairs, as one after another of the customers followed him out.

The hotel-keeper and Adam were left looking at each other.

14

Or, more accurately, the former looked significantly and a trifle sourly from the latter to his empty mug.

Adam coughed, said goodnight, and retired abashed, the aura of defeat heavy about him.

The new schoolmaster was not quite defeated yet, however. There was only one man in the village of Airdmouth with whom he had established anything of a friendly relationship in the months that he had been here—not that he had tried very hard to do anything of the sort, for such was not the purpose of his coming. This man was the Reverend Malcolm Fraser, a Highlandman and incumbent of the local Presbyterian church. It was typical of the quite crazy situation of this village nearly three miles north of the Tweed that, while it was theoretically part of the English county of Northumberland, its only church was a Scots one—just as the blood, background and way of life of practically every one of its three hundred inhabitants was also Scots.

Adam went to call on the Reverend Mr Fraser. A widower, he was a man now in his mid-sixties, of a dry humour and with a liking for books. Sitting before the minister's fire of driftwood from the shore, Adam did not take long to work round the conversation to approximately where he wanted it.

"Those two Logan twins are quite a handful," he mentioned. "Just high spirits, of course. No harm in them. What sort of a background have they? What sort of a man is their father?"

"Sandy Logan? Och, Sandy's quite a character. A big man. . . ."

"I know that much. I've seen him."

"Aye. But Sandy's big in more ways than one, maybe."

"A bit of a scamp, is he? Something of a problem—like his daughters?"

The older man looked surprised. "Mercy, Mr Horsburgh—what makes you think that? It's a strange way to speak of Sandy Logan. He is the most go-ahead man in Airdmouth. He's skipper-owner of the *Bluebell*. That's the biggest and most modern fishing-craft in the harbour. And he's one of the leading elders of my kirk."

Adam stared. He bit his lip. "Look," he said, after a moment or two, "we're talking about the same man, are we? A great tall fellow, with a lot of sandy hair and very blue eyes?"

"There's only the one Sandy Logan," the minister nodded. "And you've described him. What's the trouble, Mr Horsburgh? Don't say that you've fallen foul of Sandy? He's not at all a quarrelsome type of man."

Adam thought fast. Complications rose up and marshalled themselves before his mind's eye in serried ranks. He had to live in this village for the next year or so, at least—and it behoved him to do so, as schoolmaster, with some dignity and at least an appearance of discretion. Moreover, he had deliberately come here, from Edinburgh, for peace and quiet. All in all, it seemed at least common sensible to watch his step. He coughed.

"Not at all," he said. "Nothing like that. I barely met the man. Just had a word with him down in the pub. Interested, because of the two girls. Extraordinary resemblance. I probably got quite a wrong impression. I thought that he might be a bit of a lad—that's all. He was with a queer-looking older man, with a limp. Dand, he called him. . . ."

"Andrew Fairgrieve, that is. Skipper of the *Ladybird*. Another pillar of the kirk."

"Indeed." Another thoughtful frown. "Both skippers of boats. These are the large fishing-vessels, I take it—not small craft?"

"Oh, yes—they're quite substantial boats. Twelve tons. Five men of a crew. That sort of thing."

"And what do they fish for? Is it deep-sea fishing? Or line fishing? Or salmon, perhaps?"

"Not salmon, no. They're seine-netters, mainly—but they do some line fishing too."

"You say no salmon fishing. Why is that?"

"Well, it's not allowed. Actually, it's rather a sore point around here. Salmon fishing is restricted, you see, ostensibly for the benefit of the salmon themselves, but in fact for the

16

advantage of the angling interests on the River Tweed and the commercial fisheries at Berwick."

"But how can that be, up here on the open sea?"

"Quite easily, unfortunately. By an Act of Parliament defining the mouth of the Tweed as extending to ten miles north and south of Berwick, and five miles out to sea?"

"Good gracious! You mean to say that all that, ten by five miles—fifty square miles of the open sea—is included in the River Tweed?"

"For the purpose of salmon fishing, yes. In all that area, no one may fish for salmon without the permission of the Tweed Commissioners—who are, in fact, proprietors of fishing-beats on the river above a certain annual value. A very nice piece of legislation—for them! Passed a long time ago. But not so nice perhaps for the fishermen of the coast here, who may not fish for salmon in their own waters, off their own shore. It is a sore point, as I say."

"I see, I see," Adam said slowly. "I don't wonder, either! It seems grossly unfair, to me, I must say. This puts rather a different complexion on . . . on, well, on the whole fishing situation! I always understood that the open sea was free for all to fish—though I realised that you had to buy some sort of a licence to fish for salmon. Can nothing be done about it?"

The minister relit his pipe. "It's rather strange that you should ask that, Mr Horsburgh. Actually, I've written to Sir John Scott, the local Member, about it. Quite recently—for, of course, the new salmon-fishing season has just started. I'd written before, of course, to no effect. But this time, Sir John has promised to come to discuss the thing with the fishermen here at Airdmouth. As well he might, for he hasn't been here for years, the man. Not that I'm very hopeful of results, mind you."

"You mean, there's not a lot that Scott can do?"

"Can do—or will do? You see, Sir John's own estate of Linburndean borders the Tweed for fully a mile and a half. Which makes him one of the Tweed Commissioners himself!"

"I see."

"Still, it's something to have got him to agree to come at all. His majority was very low at the recent election, of course—perhaps that has something to do with it!" Mr Fraser sighed, shaking his grey head. "I'm afraid that I may be turning into something of a cynic in my old age—which will never do, for a minister of the Gospel, will it? Have another droppie, Mr Horsburgh?"

"Thank you—no. I have disturbed you, sir, for quite long enough. And I've a lot of work awaiting me back in the schoolhouse."

"A lot of work . . . for such a small school? I think that you must take your duties very seriously, Mr Horsburgh? We don't see you out and about nearly enough. In fact, if I may be so presumptuous as to mention it, you hardly seem to be the type to bury yourself in a place like this, anyway? A young and obviously intelligent man, in a remote little two-teacher school like Airdmouth. It doesn't seem to fit, somehow."

Adam stood up. "You yourself refute your own contention, sir," he said, smiling. "A small remote parish, on the very edge of Scotland. Just over the edge, in fact! Yet good enough for the Reverend Malcolm Fraser, Master of Arts and Bachelor of Divinity!"

The other shook his head again. "I am an old done man," he said. "I came here ten years ago, from a big city church, when my wife died. It seemed . . . necessary, at the time. I was a coward, perhaps—possibly something of a deserter, even. Though a pastor's flock is not to be measured in terms of numbers and prominence."

"I am sorry," Adam said. "I . . . well, I'm sorry. Since you've been so candid and sincere, I can hardly be less so. The fact is, I took this job in order to gain a year or two of peace and quiet—to write a book in. A novel. Or, rather, I fear it will work out into three novels—a trilogy. It's something that has been working away inside me for a while. But in Edinburgh, in a big school, I just could not get down to it. There were too many incidental activities, too many distractions altogether. So I applied for this small out-of-the-way job when Donaldson

18

died. . . ."

"My dear fellow—I'm delighted to hear it!" The minister took Adam's arm. "A novel? A trilogy? Splendid! I had no idea that we had a literary man come amongst us."

"You haven't, I can assure you!" the younger man told him. "Nothing remotely like a literary man. It's just a story, that I've got to get out of my system, somehow. It's been on my mind for years, worming away. I've got to get it off, if I'm to go on living with myself. That's all. Nothing literary about it. But . . . I'll be obliged, sir, if you will keep this to yourself. I seem to be a difficult enough pill for the locals to swallow already, without adding to it!"

"Very well, young man—it's your secret, and it's safe with me. Though I think the people here might well be almost as pleased as I am to hear what you're doing. Still, that's your affair."

"Yes. You will understand why I don't go about a lot, why perhaps I make a bit of a hermit of myself? There's an awful lot of writing to be done. . . ."

"Yes. Yes, I see. Though shutting yourself up too much with yourself could have ill effects on your writing too, you know. At least, if all we read is true. But, look—come to this meeting with the MP, at any rate. It should be interesting. And important for the people here. It's to be on Friday evening, in the village hall. I had expected it just to be a private discussion with a few of the fishermen, but Sir John evidently is going to make a public meeting of it. Something to do with future votes, no doubt! You come."

"Very well. I'll do that, Mr Fraser. Goodnight—and thank you."

III

ADAM HORSBURGH sat at the back of the hall, and listened. It is to be feared that he did not listen very hard, for the meeting was a disappointment. Nothing had been said about salmon fishing at all—in fact, from the start it had just been an ordinary political meeting. Political meetings were not Adam's cup of tea—and the honourable Member for Coldinghamshire and the Tweed Burghs was no more than usually engrossing in his speech. The schoolmaster indeed, with his mind on his novel, might well have slipped out quietly ere this, but for two things; the fact that he *was* the school-master, and such behaviour might be noted and held against him—and the fact that there was a young woman sitting, like himself, away by herself at one side of the hall, who kept drawing his gaze. He had never seen her before. She was no village girl, clearly. Well-dressed, well-groomed, she had a great shock of chestnut hair—and that confident but casual natural carriage which is an instinctive challenge to most men. Not that she was sitting in any sort of challenging fashion in Airdmouth village hall. Adam could not see much of her face, downbent as it was, but her profile was clear-cut and piquant. If that was not enough, she was paying even less attention to the speaker than he was; she was in fact reading steadily and unabashedly through a paper-backed novel. These various attributes and indications made quite an impression on the schoolmaster, despite, or perhaps because of, his potential authorship; he was that sort of young man.

Sir John Scott humphed and hawed and puffed his way on, the audience sat woodenly, a strong and virile aroma of fish, tarred rope and black twist tobacco arising from it, the girl steadily and unhurriedly turned page after page, and Adam considered many things, in a fleeting and irresponsible sort of fashion.

Abruptly the speaker wound up and sat down—to everybody's mildly dazed surprise. There was quite a large attendance for Airdmouth, and for a political meeting, though there were remarkably few women present. The chairman, whom Sir John had brought with him and whom nobody knew, announced heavily that the speaker was prepared to answer questions, provided that they were relevant and brief.

For a while there was silence, and the Member was beginning to gather his papers together, trying not to look relieved, when from amongst a solid phalanx of blue jerseys and overalls in front of Adam a voice spoke.

"The man hasna said anything aboot the bluidy salmon fishing!"

There was a murmur of agreement from the company, and a brief silvery cascade of laughter from the girl over at the side, who had at last glanced up from her book.

The chairman looked hard at the group from which the voice had spoken. "That is, h'm, not a question," he pointed out. "Ah . . . anything else?"

Sir John looked at the ceiling.

Slowly the Reverend Mr Fraser rose from his seat at the front of the hall. "I had not intended to speak, to take part in anything that might seem controversial," he said. "Many people think that the Church should steer clear of political matters altogether. But I must say that I had expected Sir John to deal, at least in some measure, with this matter of the salmon. In fact, I had understood that that was the main object of the meeting. You have been very informative on the Government's attitude in many other matters, sir. Could you not have devoted just a little time to this subject which so much concerns this community?"

"Hear, hear!"

The chairman looked at Sir John, and raised his eyebrows. "That is not really a question, either. . . ."

"If that's the way of it—what's the speaker going to *do* aboot it, then?" Sandy Logan asked, quite mildly, getting to his feet. "Aboot the salmon. That's a question, sir—and we'd be

21

obliged by an answer."

"Hear, hear!"

"You've said it, Sandy!"

With every appearance of reluctance, the Member rose to his feet. "With the best will in the world, my friends, I can't give you the moon," he said. "I did not say anything about salmon fishing for the very good reason that there is nothing that I *can* usefully say. It is a very complex and difficult subject, as you very well know. Unfortunately, I can neither affect the salmon's habits, not alter the laws that govern the catching of them!" He laughed then, and shot a quick glance over to the far side of the hall where the young woman sat, isolated. He aroused no answering mirth therefrom.

Adam Horsburgh decided that she must be a reporter, for the MP to be concerned about his effect on her.

"*We* ken fine you're no' the Lord Goad!" a young man announced, from near Logan. "But it's the MPs make the laws, is it no'? They can damned well unmake them, too, can they no'?"

"Not single-handed they can't, my good man, I assure you."

"Have you tried yet, man?"

There was some laughter now, but the chairman was not smiling. He rapped on his table. "I cannot have the speaker hectored," he asserted. "And I will not allow disrespectful language. . . ."

"It's all right, Major—I can handle this fellow," Sir John said. "I've met his kind before. You, my man, must realise that Parliament exists to make laws for and to look after the interests of the people as a whole—not for any special little group . . ."

"Like the Tweed Commissioners!" the young man ended for him. He was a dark and saturnine type, poker-faced and unsmiling. There was more laughter, led by the girl with the book. Horsburgh was beginning to enjoy the meeting.

"Not at all. That remark was quite uncalled for. I tell you, Parliament must legislate for the many, not the few. That is democracy."

"Aye, then. And how many Tweed Commissioners are there? Beyond yoursel'? Twenty? Thirty, maybe? And how many fishermen in fishing-villages up and doon the Berwickshire and Northumberland coast that canna fish for salmon in their own sea because a bluidy Act o' Parliament says the mouth o' the Tweed runs for ten mile north and south o' Berwick, and the right to fish for salmon in the Tweed belongs only to you Tweed Commissioners? What is the few and what is the many, eh? Where's the democracy? Tell me that."

"You are making a speech," the chairman announced sternly. "I will have no speeches. This is question time."

"It's no' a speech—it's a question. I canna make it shorter."

"You are talking nonsense, sir, anyway!" the Member declared. "If it wasn't for the ban imposed by the Tweed Commissioners, on indiscriminate fishing at the mouth of the Tweed, there would be no salmon left for anybody to fish."

The dark man was beginning to answer that, hotly, when Sandy Logan signed to him, and stood up.

"There may be something in that, sir," the big fellow said reasonably. "That may be right enough for the river itsel'. But no' for the open sea, surely? The sea's free, is it no'? Anybody can fish for salmon in the sea, can they no'? Other places. Why no' here?"

"Hear, hear!"

"Because, sir, Parliament in its wisdom has decided otherwise."

"Ooh, aye?" The dark young man was not to be silenced. "*I'd* say because the bluidy Tweed Commissioners—who are the owners o' salmon fishings worth £30 and more along the banks o' the river—want the profits to themsel's! Aye, and there was plenty profit, too—I read that last year they took 17,000 salmon and 12,000 grilse frae the mouth o' the Tweed! No' bad, wi' the fish fetching ten bob a pound!"

There was a buzz of comment and indignation. The chairman banged the table. "This is disgraceful!" he cried. "Sit down! I'll have no more from you. Not another word. You'd better be careful what you say in public, young man, or you'll find yourself in trouble. In serious trouble, believe me. Do you realise that your are as good as accusing our honoured and respected Member of corruption? No, sir—sit down! I insist. If there is any more out of you, I close the meeting. That is a promise! And if there are to be any more questions, they'll have to be of a very different sort, I assure you all!"

Into the muttering and shuffling, the Reverend Mr Fraser spoke. "I am sure that George did not intend to imply any sort of dishonesty on the part of Sir John," he said. "Or of the other Tweed Commissioners. Nobody suggests that. I think his point was that the Act does in fact seem to work very much in their favour, and not at all in favour of the coastal fishermen. I don't think Sir John will disagree with that?"

The Member shrugged. "That is a matter of opinion. The Commissioners may benefit, as owners and lessees of fishings. But they have corresponding liabilities and responsibilities. Anyway, *I* did not make up the Tweed Act—and I can't unmake it. I am afraid that I have nothing more that I can usefully say on the matter."

An uneasy pause followed. Three or four fishermen got up and walked out of the hall. Others looked as though they might follow them. The chairman did nothing to stop them. Then Sandy Logan rose once more.

"There's another thing that maybe the Member can tell us," he mentioned, almost gently. "Will Sir John say how the Fishery cruisers'll let foreign fishermen take salmon oot there beyond the three-mile limit, and yet prosecute us and take oor gear if we do the same thing. It doesna seem just sensible."

There was a hollow stamping of rubber boots on the flooring.

"H'mmm. Yes, it may seem a little bit strange that, I admit. But it is quite simple, really," the Member answered. "The mouth of the Tweed, for the purposes of the Act, goes five miles out to sea as well as ten miles up and down the coast. But, of course, there's the international three-mile limit, and the Government would not want to enforce the five-mile ban on foreigners in this particular locality only. It would be a bit difficult. So . . . well, there it is."

"Aye, there it is, a' right!" the dark young man George cried. "So the cruisers'll swipe us, their ain folk, and let the damned foreigners be! You ca' that fair? More democracy! Crazy, *I* ca' it!"

"Oh, well—just one of those things, my friend. The national aspect must necessarily come before the local. With all this Iceland trouble, we obviously can't start trying to impose a ban on foreign fishermen for the extra two miles."

"But you'll keep the bluidy ban on *us*!"

"*I'm* not keeping any ban on anybody. . . ."

"But you're no' going to do anything aboot it?"

"I didn't say that. But I don't see that there is much I can do. I can go and see the Ministry, of course—but I can't honestly hold out much hope of anything resulting from that. The law is the law. . . ."

"And you're damned if you're going to try and change it!"

"Silence!" the chairman ordered. "I'll have no more of this."

"I think you've probably said enough, George!" the minister called back from his front seat.

Sir John, after a quick glance over towards the young woman, went on. "Parliament is grossly overworked, as you must all know. Even if I was convinced that it was in the general interest that the Tweed Act should be amended, the chances of getting Parliament to consider the matter are remote indeed. I am sorry, but that is the situation."

"If we got up a petition? A petition to Parliament," Sandy Logan suggested. "Would that no' help to get something done, sir?"

"A petition? I can't really advise you that a petition would do much good. The only times that a petition is of much effect is when a great public outcry is produced. It is that that has the effect, not the petition itself. And I don't see you stirring up the general public of Britain wildly over your salmon, you know!"

"But if we did get up a petition, sir—you would present it to Parliament for us?"

"As your elected representative, it would be my duty to do

so—provided that it was in the proper form. Respectfully and loyally worded, and so on. But you may as well know that the manner of presenting a petition to Parliament is merely to pop it quietly into a black bag behind the Speaker's Chair, with no more fuss than posting a letter. That is all that happens. I don't see what good that would do."

A heavy silence followed. Men looked at each other hopelessly, gloomily. The chairman caught the Member's eye, nodded, and made to rise.

"You have not considered the law of Scotland in this matter? That parts of this Tweed Act may be contrary to the law of Scotland? It is a point that might be worth looking into, sir. The right of the subject by common law, in Scotland."

Adam Horsburgh was almost shocked to realise that the voice speaking was his own. Only after the words were out did he rise uncertainly to his feet. He had become so interested in the thrust and parry and hidden implications of the discussion that he had spoken up practically involuntarily. As a newcomer, and only too well aware of the suspicion with which rural communities regarded newcomers, he certainly had no intention of taking any public part in this controversy.

If he was surprised at himself, he was not the only one. Heads turned round, all over the hall, to stare. The chairman frowned, and looked at the Member. Sir John, perhaps noting the change of accent and the inferences of education, mustered a bland smile.

"I'm afraid that I do not understand you, sir," he said. "I do not see, at the moment, what the law of Scotland has to do with the matter."

"I think that it may have quite a lot to do with it," Adam answered. Having started this, he had to go on with it, at least for the moment. "And it is rather different to English law, in many respects, as you are no doubt aware."

"That may be so, my friend. But what has this to do with the case? However much some people may wish it otherwise, this area for three miles north of Berwick and the Tweed is not in Scotland. Has not been for a long time. It is a detached portion

26

of the County of Northumberland, and has been since 1929, if I remember rightly. As such it is part of England, and is subject to English law."

"Shame!" came from somewhere in the middle of the hall. "Berwick for Berwickshire!"

"Aye—Berwick for Scotland!"

There was applause and some laughter. Even Sir John Scott was prepared to smile a little at that sort of nonsense.

"Quite, sir," Horsburgh agreed quietly. He told himself that he should be sitting down, leaving the thing. This was nothing to do with him. But something forced him to carry on. "Whatever the rights and wrongs of *that* matter, it is not the land that we are talking about—in this area or any other. It is the water. The sea. And the Tweed is Scottish water. Recent litigation has brought it out very clearly in the Press that any fishing disputes in the River Tweed are to be judged according to Scots law— even if they relate to the English bank or tributaries flowing through English soil."

"M'mmm," said the Member, fingering his tie.

Adam was aware of the suddenly increased interest and tension around him. Also that the young woman at the side had turned and was looking directly at him. Part of his mind noted that full face she more than lived up to the promise of her profile.

"As I see it," he went on, shrugging, "you can't have it both ways. If, legally, the mouth of the Tweed extends for ten miles along the coast and five miles out to sea, then legally that area is Scottish water and English law does not apply. And Scots law, relating to tidal waters for instance, is different from the English—that I do know. Relating to salmon fishing too, I think."

"Indeed. Are you a lawyer, then, sir?"

"No, I'm not. I'm a schoolmaster. But my father was a solicitor, and I have some smatterings of law—Scots law, of course."

"Very interesting, I'm sure. But I still do not see that it affects the issue. If Parliament has passed a law giving

27

jurisdiction over the mouth of the Tweed to the Tweed Commissioners, then the authority is theirs, whatever legal code they use. It makes no difference."

"It could do. If a Scots court found that part of your Act was contrary to Scots common law."

The other frowned. "My dear sir—we are governed by Parliament, not by Scots common law."

"Are you so sure, sir? Have you forgotten Clause Ten of the Treaty of Union?"

"Eh? The *what*?"

"The Treaty of Union. Between England and Scotland. Of 1707. The document that regulates relations between the two kingdoms. Clause Ten safeguards the integrity of the Scots legal system and code for all time. I may not be a lawyer, but I know a little bit about history!"

"My God—we're getting back to 1707 now! Look here, my good man—all this legal hair-splitting is quite beyond me. Beyond everybody here, I'd say. We'll leave it to the lawyers to argue about. Personally, I'm prepared to put my trust in the Acts of Her Majesty's Parliament." Sir John consulted his watch elaborately. "I'm afraid I've overstepped my time, as it is. I'm sorry, but we'll have to be moving on. Eh, Major?"

"Ah . . . yes. Yes, of course. Definitely. Well, then—that closes the meeting, I think, ladies and gentlemen. In the circumstances, I am sure no formal vote of thanks is required. I will just say thank you to Sir John on your behalf, for coming and expounding the Government's programme to us so thoroughly and lucidly. . . ."

As they all streamed out, thereafter, Adam Horsburgh received friendlier glances than had been his lot since he arrived in Airdmouth. Nobody spoke to him, however—until he found himself at the outer door, curiously enough almost side by side with the young woman with the chestnut hair. He had not exactly arranged it that way—merely held back a little until their courses were likely to converge.

"Good work," she mentioned to him, smiling a little. "You shook them—you certainly shook them."

"Er . . . thanks," he acknowledged. He thought of a lot more things than that to say to her, too—but it was not just then that he thought of them.

He went out behind her into the dark April night. A thin smirr of cold rain blew in their faces from off the North Sea. The rough cobblestones of the pier gleamed in the light from the hall windows, and the masts of the three or four fishing-boats swayed dimly to the tide. A large and expensive-looking car was drawn up there on the cobbles. In the back of it, the glow of a petrol-lighter revealed Sir John Scott already ensconced, lighting cigars for the Major and himself. Into the front of this equipage the girl climbed, eased into the driving-seat with the gleam of long legs, and started up the engine. The headlamps blazed on, to light up all the huddle of low-browed whitewashed cottages that crouched beneath the black barrier of tall cliffs. Then smoothly, with a quiet purr, the big car moved forward to take the climbing cliff road.

Somewhat bemused, the schoolmaster returned to his darkened schoolhouse that stood on its own little foreland of grass and rocks thrusting into the restless sea.

It was much later that night, with Adam Horsburgh wrestling less than successfully with what he felt must assuredly be the dullest hero yet to drag through the pages of any embryo novel, when a knock sounded at the schoolhouse door. Surprised, he went to answer it. It was black dark outside, but he could just distinguish three figures standing there. And whatever the obscurity, the size and bulk of one of them loomed large enough to leave little doubt as to identity.

"It's a fine night, Mr Horsburgh," the deeply gentle voice of Sandy Logan said easily. "Och, we saw your light shining, and we thought that maybe we'd no' be disturbing you? The fact is, I happened to come by a wee bit salmon—just a chance, from a friend in the trade, as you might say. We minded you said you liked a bite o' salmon noo and then. Here it's."

A newspaper parcel was held out, extraordinarily like that other that had graced the schoolhouse doorstep those few days before.

"Oh. I . . . er . . . that's very kind of you," Adam said. "Too good, altogether. Very thoughtful. I much appreciate it. I will, h'm, pay for it, of course. How much? It feels a nice piece. . . ."

"Wheesht, man—wheesht!"

"But I can't just accept a large piece, like this, from you. . . ."

"Och, goodness—what's a wee bit fish! Anyway, we canna sell salmon, man—it's no' legal for the likes o' us."

"Ummm," Adam said. "Well . . . look—would you care to step inside? I'm afraid I can't offer you anything very interesting to drink. I don't go in for company much. But maybe a cup of coffee . . . ?"

The big man leading, the three visitors stepped over the threshold with noticeable alacrity, and clumped straight into the untidy sitting-room without any symptoms of hesitation.

"Take a seat," Horsburgh invited, and the newcomers promptly lowered themselves on to the extreme edges of three chairs. One of them was the grizzled skipper Andrew Fairgrieve, and the third was the dark and angry young man who had harried the platform party at the meeting, whom the minister had referred to as George. Logan however introduced him as Tosh Hogg.

"Make yourselves comfortable," Adam said. "I'll just put the coffee on."

"Och, well—I wouldna bother," the big man said earnestly. His companions made urgent agreement noises. They were eyeing the jumble of open books and scattered papers that littered the table. Sandy Logan shook his head. "Man, it must be a right hard life, the teacher's," he observed sympathetically. "Working a' the hours into the night. I couldna be doing wi' it, mysel'."

"You occasionally put in a little night work yourself, I imagine?" their host said. "Fishing I mean, of course!" Then he noticed their gaze at the papers. He cleared his throat. "You mustn't take all that mess too seriously. That's not all actual lessons. The schoolmaster's life does have its compensations. . . ."

"Ooh, aye." The big man looked directly at him. "You said

some right interesting things at the meeting the night, Mr Horsburgh."

"Oh, well—nothing much really. Just a few inexpert suggestions. Shooting my neck out a bit, I suppose. I hadn't intended to say a word, of course—but that man Scott's mixture of smug superiority and dodging the issue made me forget myself."

"I'm right glad it did. You talked good sense to me."

"That's right," Dand Fairgrieve nodded. "Yon bit aboot Scots law was real interesting."

"Well, it was a shot in the dark, really. I'm pretty vague about it all. But at the back of my mind there was something— something wrong with the whole business. Something that doesn't fit. I don't mean about the unfairness of it all—that's obvious. Something on the legal side."

"Aye, then. We'd like to think you were right, Mr Horsburgh," Logan agreed. "We would so. For sure you had yon man Scott worried a wee."

"D'you reckon he was stalling, on the petition idea?" the younger man Hogg put in. "He wriggled oot o' that, pretty quick."

"Well, no," Adam said. "In that matter alone I think I tend to agree with Scott. I'm not against petitions to Parliament in principle, of course. But in this case I don't think it would achieve much. Parliament itself couldn't be less interested, I'd imagine. It's only when the signatures to a petition get up into the millions, and the Press gets worked up about it, I'd say, that it achieves anything. It's the publicity that does—not the petition itself. A few thousand signatures aren't a threat to anybody, these days. Still, there'd be no harm in having a petition to back up anything else you might do."

"Anything else we might do," Sandy Logan repeated. "Such as, Mr Horsburgh?"

"Oh, well—I hadn't really thought out anything very definite, you know. It's not actually my business, is it? I mean. . . ."

"You had something in mind, just, did you no'? Even if no' all worked oot? Just an idea?"

"Something to do wi' Scots law, was it no'?" the dark Tosh prompted.

Adam smoothed his chin between thumb and forefinger. "Just how serious are you all about this?" he asked, slowly. "I mean, how much does it mean to you? Is it a bit of sport you're after—so that you can indulge your taste for a bite of salmon without, h'm, having to do it at dead of night when nobody's looking? Or is it a pleasant little addition to your ordinary fishing? Something to add a little to the catch? Or is it just a sense of grievance, genuine grievance which you wish to right?"

"Look," Logan said seriously, sitting forward. "We used to be herring fishers around here, all doon this coast. But the deep-sea trawlers ruined the spawning-beds, and the herring shoals just dinna come to these waters any more. There's just the white fish and the flat fish left to us—but the trawlers havena done *them* any good, neither. Small craft like oorsel's canna compete wi' the big boys, wi' their refrigeration plants and their organised transport and markets. There's only the leavings o' the local market left to us—and that's cheaper supplied by the fish trains frae Hull and Grimsby and Aberdeen. Each year the number o' small boats working frae the fishing-villages hereaboots goes doon. The young lads see no future in it—and awa' they go. And there's nothing else for them here. Another few years o' this . . . !"

"That's right. That's the way o' it," Dand Fairgrieve agreed.

"The salmon would make a' the difference," Tosh Hogg put in. "You market them by the pound, no' the ton. Local market, too. We'd sell a' we could catch, easy. There's money in it. Big money. Thousands."

"This is no bit sport, for us, Mr Horsburgh," Logan assured. "It's serious. It could be the end o' Airdmouth."

"I see," Adam nodded slowly. "I had not realised that it added up so large. The stakes are higher than I thought. But it would make the risks more worth taking." He looked up. "Are you *willing* to take some risks, over this business? Real risks?" He smiled a little. "I think you have already done so, haven't you? Risks of more kinds than one! Including technical assault!

But what I'm suggesting is rather different. Though, if you were prepared to take the one kind of risk, possibly you'd be prepared to take the other. Openly. Are you prepared to meet trouble—to seek it, in fact? To risk fines, confiscation of gear, maybe—possibly prison?"

The others stared at him.

"Just what are you getting at?" the big man asked, heavily.

"Just this. I think the only way effectively to solve your problem is to challenge the validity of the Tweed Act. In law. Scots law. If you can get a Scottish court to uphold your rights under common law against it, then the Act will *have* to be amended. So the obvious thing is to go ahead, openly, and fish for the salmon where you believe you've a right to do so. Try to get charged, in fact. Then fight the case. Fight it right up through the courts, if need be. If you win, the Act is proved unworkable. If you lose, at least you will have got major publicity as to the unfairness of the thing—and I'd say, won a lot of public sympathy. Something to make your petition worth launching. A campaign of deliberate infringing of the Tweed Act, and fighting it, is what I'm suggesting."

"Whe-e-w!"

"Jings!" Tosh Hogg exclaimed. "You're no' suggesting much, are you, man!"

"It's a big thing, I admit," the schoolmaster agreed. "But then, it's a big issue. One that's never been taken up before. It may well be *too* big for you, I quite realise."

"We're no' saying that, either—no' just yet, anyway," Logan told him. "But we'd have to be pretty sure o' our case before we got into that sort o' thing, Mr Horsburgh."

"Of course. We'd . . . h'm . . . *you'd* have to get proper legal advice first. Counsel's Opinion—that sort of thing. My own notions are far too vague and sketchy to go on."

"Aye—an' just what *are* your ideas aboot this being against the Scots law?" Dand Fairgrieve asked. "We havena heard them yet."

"There are a few points that I've got ideas about—but most of them I'm pretty vague over. We'll need to look into them.

33

But one thing I'm fairly sure of—that all salmon fishing in the sea, in Scotland, is a Crown right. That is not the case in England, I think. But the Crown's rights go out only for *one* mile beyond low-water mark. Not three—and certainly not five. If Scots common law applies after that mile, then I'd say that the Tweed Act is infringing the law of Scotland over forty square miles of sea."

"Well, now!" Sandy Logan said, blinking. "Just fancy that!"

"But if bluidy Parliament says it's five miles . . . ?" Hogg objected.

"Parliament can be challenged. It's made bloomers before this, and had to put them right. The Treaty of Union clauses were 'for all time coming'—that is what's called the Entrenched Clauses. The one about safeguarding the integrity of Scots law is in that class."

"Then you're suggesting we should fish for salmon, openly, anywhere oot beyond one mile frae low water—and see what happens?" the big man summed up.

"Exactly—if you're prepared for trouble. And prepared to go ahead and fight the thing all the way."

There was silence in that room for a little. Then Tosh Hogg spoke up.

"It's all right for you, Mister. *You* don't risk nothing—no fines, or getting your gear confiscated, or maybe going to the jail!"

"Och, tut, man Tosh . . . !" Logan began.

"I don't run the same risks, admittedly," Adam agreed. "But I would be running some. If you do this thing, I'd want to be included in the campaign—come out with you. I'd expect to. Then I'd be at least an accessory after the fact. I'd take my share of the risks."

"Och, we wouldna want you to do that, Mr Horsburgh," Logan disclaimed. "No, no."

"But, yes . . ."

"A' this—taking the thing to law, fighting it in the courts, getting this Counsel's Opeenion—would take a deal o' money, would it no'?" Fairgrieve intervened. "Hundreds o' pounds, likely. Lawyers ken how to charge! Whoever wins, they do! Where's the money coming frae?"

"Where from but from the obvious source? From the salmon. With the stuff fetching ten shillings a pound, you ought to do quite well. Pay it all into a Fighting Fund, at this stage. Let everybody know that you're doing that, too—that you're not just pocketing the proceeds. That ought to do quite a lot of good with public opinion and the Press—and help to tie the hands of the authorities, too. Make the salmon pay for the salmon!"

Abruptly, without warning, Sandy Logan slapped his great knee resoundingly. "By Jove!" he said. The others exchanged glances.

"We'll have to do some thinking aboot a' this," Dand Fairgrieve said, rubbing his bristly chin.

"Jings, we will!" Tosh Hogg cried. "Plenties!"

"Of course you will," Adam agreed. "So will I, for that matter! It's all just a very rough idea, at the moment."

"Just that,"the big man nodded."But, man, it's the cheeriest rough idea I've heard tell o' for a long time! It is that!"

"Well. . . ." The schoolmaster glanced around him. "Mercy—I never got the coffee put on!"

With remarkable unanimity the three visitors were on their feet.

"Och, it's gey late, Mr Horsburgh—time we were awa'," Logan asserted.

"That's so, aye."

"But it wouldn't take a minute."

"No, no. . . ."

"We havena the time, see. . . ."

"Nae coffee!" Tosh Hogg said flatly, heading out of the sitting-room.

As the door closed behind the three fishermen, Adam Horsburgh turned to look ruefully at the scattered papers and open books on his table. What had he done to the novel that had brought him to Airdmouth? What had he done, in the name of goodness?

IV

THE *Bluebell*, 30 feet long, of 12 tons, powered by a sturdy 22-hp 4-cylinder semi-diesel engine, skipper Alexander Logan, gleaming pridefully in yellow varnish and polished brass, set sail from Airdmouth's harbour of a bright but chilly April morning, and turned her upthrusting broad bows due east, dipping them confidently into the long swell. A large crowd saw her off, with resounding cheers—for of course there had been no secret made of this challenge to Parliament; quite the reverse. Crews of the other fishing-boats in the harbour stood by as though rather aggressively disinterested—for with so much at stake and confiscation of the boats themselves possible, it had been decided that more than one craft at a time should not be risked, or Airdmouth could be crippled. Not all of the other crews stayed sourly behind, however, for there had been great competition to get aboard the *Bluebell*, and Logan's boat was sailing with fully twice her normal complement. Included in the crowd aboard were Adam Horsburgh and Dand Fairgrieve. Tosh Hogg, who was *Bluebell's* mate, declared that the boatload of them was nothing but a damned shambles.

A short distance out they turned a little south of east, so that the vessel began to roll as well as dip, in a sort of corkscrew motion. Adam was thankful that he was a reasonably good sailor. He steadied himself against the doorway of the little square wheelhouse aft, and spoke to Sandy Logan at the wheel. He had to raise his voice against the throb and snort of the powerful engine.

"You know where you're going, then? I mean, this turn southwards. You're not just heading for anywhere out there, beyond the mile limit?"

"Och, fine I ken where I'm going. The sea's no' just a great dish o' water where every bit's the same as every other. Especially for fishing—and salmon most of all. I'm making for a bit called the Doo's Bed. It's a shoal, aboot two mile oot, on a line that the salmon take. It brings them up shallow enough for oor net, see. We canna go deep."

"You say a line the salmon take? Do you mean that they have certain actual lines they follow? Routes, in the sea?"

"Aye. Into the Tweed. There's lines o' them coming in frae a' sides. Like spokes to a wheel."

"All the time? You mean that there are salmon heading in to the Tweed all the time? Every day? You'd think the river would be stiff with fish, if that's so."

"Och, well—they're no' going *up* a' the time. Up the river. The fish are running, as we say, for aboot four hours at a time—two hours on the ebb to low water, and two hours at the start o' the flood. But it's no' every day they're actually going up the river. They need a bit spate, you see—plenty water coming doon, for to get swimming up over the caulds and weirs and that. So they have to wait oot here, till the river rises—wi' rain up in the hills."

"I see. That accounts for the emphasis these Tweed Commissioners place on the *mouth* of the river. It makes more sense."

"Ooh, aye—they ken what side *their* bread's buttered on, those ones."

"And how do you find these salmon lines? One of which, presumably, goes quite close inshore—round the end of Airdmouth pier, in fact!" Adam grinned.

"Och, well," the skipper said mildly. "Aboot finding the lines—oor forefathers hae kenned aboot them for centuries. We a' ken them. . . ."

"I meant finding your way to them, actually. As now. Knowing when you've reached one?"

"You can place them by the chart, or by landmarks. This Doo's Bed's easy. We'll soon be there. D'you see yon row o' trees marching ower the crest o' the hill, there? Aye—well, when you can see the cairn on the top o' Hyndlaw bang in the middle o' those trees, you're ower the Doo's Bed."

"I see." The schoolmaster gazed around him. "Not a lot of

shipping about yet." Two fishing-boats of the same sort as themselves could be seen some distance to the north, presumably out from Burnmouth or Eyemouth, apparently heading directly seawards. A large tanker, its upper works gleaming white in the morning sunlight, was steaming north, four or five miles out, making for the Forth estuary. Away to the south, almost hull-down, an old-fashioned coaster was trailing a long plume of black smoke from its high thin stack. "It looks as though we won't be spied upon for a bit, at least."

"It's no' from the sea we'll be spied on," the big man said. He pointed south by west, "Yonder's Berwick pier—no' three miles away. There's four coastguard stations along this bit coast—it's a tricky one for shipping. Anybody wi' a glass can see what we're doing."

"They couldn't be sure that it is *salmon* you're fishing for, though, could they? It might be something else, quite legal?"

"I'ph'mmm. Maybe. But anybody who kens anything aboot fishing'd wonder for why we're using a drift-net here! I'd say they wouldna need three thinks, either!"

"Coming up to the Doo's Bed noo, Sandy," Tosh Hogg called from forward. "Maybe you canna see for a' these bluidy passengers!"

"Aye, aye, Tosh. Fine that."

"I dinna like a' these jellyfishes," Dand Fairgrieve announced, spitting expertly well to leeward. "They're a right plague."

"D'you mean they can be a nuisance? In fishing?"

"They can clog up the nets," Sandy Logan explained. "Weigh them doon. And sting like the devil when they've got to be cleared. Sting the fish, too." He began to swing the wheel round. "I'm putting her before the wind, to shoot the nets," he said.

The *Bluebell* turned in a fairly tight semicircle until the easterly wind was blowing directly astern. Then eager hands forward began to pay out, swiftly but carefully, the nets so orderly heaped and coiled in the bows. A nylon drift net was being used. There seemed to be a great amount of it, to Adam's inexperienced eye. It was not one net, in fact, but a series of up

38

to a dozen, each of which when stretched, was about fifty yards long, attached one after another to a single long line. These, it appeared, hung vertically in the water, to form a long rectangular curtain, the upper edge, supported by yellow spherical floats, being about twelve feet below the surface, the net itself hanging down for over sixty feet, weighted at its base by lead sinkers. The entire contraption was attached to the boat by a long cable called the messenger. The shooting of this elaborate collection of ropes, netting, sinkers and floats was an intricate business that in inexpert hands could have resulted in a hopeless tangle in a matter of seconds. The watcher wondered and admired.

The net all out, the craft was brought round head into wind again, and a red mizzen sail run up on the rearmost mast, and the engine switched off.

In the sudden replacement of noise by sounds—the sounds of the hiss and slap of the seas, the creak of timbers, and the cries of the seabirds which followed the boat like an escort—Adam was soon asking questions. What was the sail for? How did the whole thing work? How were the salmon caught? How could they be sure that there were any salmon there? And so on.

Lying to the nets, the skipper had time to explain; indeed everybody now, after the burst of activity, had time on their hands. Drift-nets meant just that—boat and nets drifting with the tide. The sail was to keep the craft bows on to the wind, and therefore manageable. The nets, now represented only by a long line of yellow floats stretching away from them for over a quarter of a mile, were like a high wall of mesh erected across the hoped-for line of the salmon's route, into which it was hoped that the fish would swim and get entangled in the meshes. These meshes, by law, must not be less than one and three-quarters of an inch square, so that immature and part-grown fish were not caught. Salmon did not swim in shoals like lesser fish, Logan pointed out, so that the echo-sounders which they used to locate herrings and so on were of little use here. They just had to spread their barrier of net where they hoped it would do most good, and keep it at the height where they thought the salmon would be likely to swim—and leave the rest to tide and luck. It was no question of scooping in a net and drawing up fish, but of patiently laying a long trap for individual fish to swim into. They would give it a couple of hours, and then haul in and have a look.

Those were a trying couple of hours for Adam Horsburgh—though not, obviously, for his companions, some of whom promptly disappeared into the tiny fo'c'sle forward, or disposed themselves in sheltered spots, and went to sleep. For one thing, Adam found the drifting rolling sway of the vessel much more unsettling on his stomach than when she had been making a forward progress. Also, he was keyed up all the time, by the feeling of tension, of defying authority, and he was forever scanning the seascape for craft coming to demand an explanation—especially from the direction of Berwick harbour. Admittedly they were deliberately trailing their coats, asking to be caught and charged, challenging the Act which said that what they were doing was forbidden—but every instinct nevertheless made him dread the appearance of opposition, and hope that they might escape unquestioned, this first time at least.

Nobody came near them, however. They might have been the most law-abiding and ordinary fishing-boat in the North Sea, and their position on the water entirely innocuous. Rocking and heaving to the swell, they lay on the blue-green white-flecked sea utterly ignored, completely inactive—but somehow naked, vulnerable.

To try to distract his mind from both his stomach and his guilt complex, Adam fixed his gaze on the line of the coast, two miles away, seeking to establish all the landmarks and to relate them to the stormy history that their names conjured up. For that sun-bathed vista, all spouting wave-lashed rock-bound coves, towering purple-brown cliffs and green rolling hills slashed with the raw red of tilth or watercourse, bore a more savage and bloodstained past than almost any other strip of land in these islands. Over it, that no-man's-land of the Border, had swept the tides of invasion, pillage and ravishment, times without number, back and forward, century after century. When it was not the nations themselves that set it aflame, its own warlike inhabitants and their near neighbours maintained the tradition—feud and foray, raid and reiving, heroism and shocking cruelty, blazing patriotism, crazy chivalry and barbarous excess, made romantic by haunting ballad and stirring folk-song. Adam's eyes slid from the lift of Brankston Hill and Flodden Field and the hollow of Norham, across the Merse to Hume Castle, to Halidon Hill and Lamberton, to St Abb's Head and Fast Castle and Lammermuir. Over that far-flung landscape every acre had been fought over, every village sacked and church burned, every burn had run blood. Yet there it lay, bathed in the forenoon sunlight, fair, placid and at peace at last. And here he was, seeking to involve it in still another battle, however bloodless, another struggle, further controversy.

The man frowned.

Was he being a fool in all this, he asked himself? Was it not only crazy to implicate himself in what was really no concern of his, but wrong, irresponsible, to egg on and advise these others to revolt, to defy not exactly the law but the lawful authorities? Their cause was just, yes—but what were its chances of success? He could not honestly answer that. No man could, at this stage—though by no means everyone would be optimistic. So much depended upon imponderables— niceties of the law, the reactions of others, the effect on public opinion, political repercussions. The whole thing was a gamble, as Adam's legal friends in Edinburgh had pointed out to him with considerable unanimity when he had gone to consult them a day or two before. He had tried hard to get an eminent QC of his acquaintance to make an authoritative statement on the question, without success, and had had to fall back upon the not too coherent opinion of a young and lively advocate with no reputation to lose. Patrick Raeburn had declared that they certainly had a case—though whether that case could be steered successfully through the Scottish courts

41

was another matter altogether. The Crown's rights, he said, in salmon fishing, undoubtedly extended from low-water mark for only one mile seawards, under the *regalia minora*, and thereafter coastal waters seemed to be held in trust for the public use under the *regalia majora* up to the three-mile limit, the Crown only acting as the people's guardian. Beyond that the seas were ownerless under Scots law. The Tweed Act's 'enclosure' of *five* miles out to sea, therefore, on the face of it ran counter to this interpretation of common law, he thought. All would depend on the Scottish court's willingness or otherwise to counter the pernicious doctrine, English doctrine be it said, of the sovereignty of Parliament and its powers to override the common law and ignore the binding provisions of the Treaty of Union. All a bit tricky, Pat Raeburn agreed—but though Parliament might be able to steamroller its way over common law rights, it did not follow that it would find it expedient or politic to do so, especially in view of the resentful state of Scottish political opinion anyway. Therefore, he believed that they had a case worth fighting, based as it was on the effect on public opinion and the sense of justice, rather than on mere legalities. Further even Raeburn would not go. A number of Adam's solicitor friends had more or less agreed. His efforts to get someone more senior to back this up with a written Counsel's Opinion had failed, not only the QC shying off. But back at Airdmouth, the will to fight that he had implanted in these fishermen had taken root and burgeoned into a vigorous determination. No sticklers for legal hair-splitting, they had been content that a trained advocate believed that they had a case, and a chance of winning, and would hear of no craven backsliding now, despite the schoolmaster's somewhat belated reminders of the value of caution. So here they were. The die was cast, and the fight on.

Even two anxious hours will pass. At last Sandy Logan gave the order to haul nets. The *Bluebell* came to life. The automatic hauling-gear, like a small powered winch, was switched on, and the long messenger warp began to come in, to be coiled neatly by a man in a compartment of the hold, ready for re-shooting, the boat heeling over to the drag of it, so that Adam had difficulty in keeping his feet. Another fisherman, called the cast-off, deftly disconnected the nets from the warp, while a third handled the floats and lines as they came in. Normally it fell to the remaining crew-member, aided by the skipper, to shake out the fish, herring usually, from the streaming nets themselves into the hold—but today there were many hands to assist. As well that there were, for the nets were almost solid—not with salmon, unfortunately, but with jellyfish. Almost every other mesh seemed to be clogged with the slimy brutes with their trailing tentacles. Not every jellyfish stings, but those that do make up for the others. Sandy Logan called out that there were gloves in the wheelhouse locker for those who wanted them, but his offer was ignored. Men went to work with batons and scoops and their bare hands to clear the messy cloying creatures, cursing comprehensively as they did so. Adam, following Dand Fairgrieve's example, grabbed a wooden fish-scoop and strove to shovel some portion of the wobbly unpleasant mass overboard—with only partial success. Soon his hands were tingling as though beaten by the most virulent spring nettles.

There was much more than jellyfish caught in those nets, of course—Adam saw starfish, crayfish, eels, squids and other things that he could not identify, entangled in the meshes, as well as much seaweed—but nothing that looked like a salmon in the first net. It was not until the second one was well in that he espied two firm-bodied lashing things amongst the wrack, caught by their gills, so much more silvery and substantial than the rest—but no monsters for all that. He pointed them out with some excitement—but his cries were lost in the incessant clamour of the gulls which had now descended upon vessel and nets in a diving, flapping, raucous and quarrelsome throng, buffeting men's faces with their urgent wings in their efforts to get at the fish. Adam's companions dealt with these two salmon with no corresponding excitement or even comment.

The nets continued to come in inexorably. There was no moment's pause in the heavy labour, no respite while the mechanical hauler rotated. The third net contained no salmon at all, but the fourth held a good-sized fish and three smaller ones. Adam found that he was breathless, arms aching, soaked with water sprayed from the nets, bruised by being knocked against hard things by the lurching and much-canted boat, and that his red-blue hands had achieved the seemingly impossible by being at the same time numb and stiff with cold, and burning hot but equally stiff with stings. As the last two nets came inboard, his panting efforts were flagging noticeably; he was prepared to accede that there was something to be said for the life of a schoolmaster as compared with that of a sea fisherman.

There was one smallish salmon in one of those nets, and nothing in the last.

Adam was so relieved when the hauler was eventually switched off, and the urgency of the labour slackened away, that he was disinclined to be critical of the catch. Not so his companions. Clearly they were much disappointed in the haul. Seven fish in all—and only one of them of a respectable size. This last might be a twelve-pounder, Sandy judged, but the rest would not add up to more than twenty-five pounds between them. Less than forty pounds in all.

"We'd do a sight better off the pier back home!" Tosh Hogg declared, disgustedly. "This is nae use!"

There was growled agreement.

"I'd say it was not too bad," Adam put in. "After all, forty pounds at ten shillings a pound means up to £20. Not too bad for one haul, surely?"

"*We* don't get ten bob a bluidy pound for it, man!" the mate exclaimed. "We'll no get more'n five or six bob, clean weight. Yon's *shop* price. Clean weight, we'll be lucky if we get £10 for this lot. No' much for a' this shower o' men's day's work, the engine's fuel, and a' the rest o' it. Jings, no!"

"Och, we'll stick to the shore o' a night, wi' a coble and bag-net," somebody backed him up. "There's no' that much salmon oot here, anyway—I said it frae the first. Too far oot."

"Aye, that's right, Jock. The brutes keep closer in. . . ."

"But don't you see—that's not the point!" Adam cried. He had to shout, to be heard above the screaming of the gulls that still squabbled round the *Bluebell*. "You may get more salmon by poaching close inshore, at night—but you're not going to challenge the Tweed Act that way. That's *only* poaching—against the law of Scotland as much as of England. That's no use for your fight. Not only because you aren't *seen* doing it—you could do it by day, I suppose—but because it doesn't give you any case to fight when you're charged. The whole point of the thing is that the Crown's rights to salmon fishing go out only for a mile in Scottish waters—and these are Scottish waters according to the Act. So you've got to do your fishing at least a mile out."

"And if there's no damned fish in it? Eh? Do we sit oot here catching jellyfish?"

Sandy Logan intervened. "That's enough oot o' you, Tosh," he said, genially firm. "We'll maybe have to do both—fish oot here in daylight, to get oorsel's charged, and poach by night to make enough cash to fight oor case! We're going to be right busy! But, see—maybe we were no' in just the best spot, here. Nobody's come bothering us yet. We could try another bit shot, further in a wee. This Doo's Bed runs in for near half a mile."

This was agreed, if without enthusiasm. Adam was unsure whether to cheer or groan.

The *Bluebell's* engine was started up again, and she moved some small way nearer to Berwick, south by west. Then the manoeuvre for shooting nets was gone through once more, and they settled down to another spell of waiting. It would not be for the two full hours, this time, for the hauling in had taken fully thirty minutes, and the fishermen seemed to be convinced that the salmon would only 'run' during the period of two hours on either side of low water and that there was little use in drift-netting them at any other time.

Fairly soon after they were settled in their new position, a sea-going fishing-boat, somewhat larger than their own, rounded the head of Berwick's long Queen Elizabeth Pier, a mile and a half away, and came out approximately in their direction. A stir of anticipation ran down the length of the *Bluebell*.

Sandy Logan put his glasses on her. "It's the *Spittal Queen*," he reported. "A seine-netter—a herring boat. I canna see more than just her crew aboard—but, och, it's hard to tell."

"The authorities—the water bailiffs or the police or whoever represents the Tweed Commissioners—would they come out in a craft like that?" Adam asked. "Not in something more official-looking?"

"Och, aye—any boat that was handy. They'll no' have a craft o' their own lying by for this sort o' thing—for there's never been any o' it before. This is something new we're doing. There's plenty poaching goes on at Berwick, my goodness—but it's no' oot here in the open sea. The bailiffs can do their work on shore or in a coble."

"Yes—of course. Who is going to, to . . . well, do the talking, when they arrive?"

Logan shrugged. "I'm the skipper," he mentioned easily. "But if you're keen for a bit word, Mr Horsburgh—nobody's stopping you."

"M'mmm." Adam frowned. "You know, I wish you would stop calling me Mister," he complained, almost irritably. "It makes me feel an awful outsider. Horsburgh's good enough—though Adam would be better. That goes for everyone."

Non-committal grunts were the only answer to that plea. All eyes were firmly fixed on the oncoming boat.

As the other vessel drew nearer, five men only could be seen in her, three of them dressed in the bright yellow oilskins that seemed to betoken deep-sea work. She came to within about three hundred yards of them, and then, without hailing the *Bluebell*, put over her helm a little and swung off on a new tack to starboard, heading now due east as for the open sea. A man leaned out of the wheelhouse with its nodding radio whip-mast, and waved to them—a friendly-seeming gesture with nothing ominous about it.

Sandy waved back. "Just Fred Spowart wondering what we're up to," he interpreted. "Having a wee look on his way oot . . . but ower shy to ask questions!"

Adam knew himself to be much relieved—and immediately took himself to task therefore. They had come out here to challenge and be challenged, hadn't they? Then why jib at the business—why hope to put it off? Unreasonable—that is what it was. A kind of cowardice. A fine defier of the law he made . . . !

No further incident occurred before Logan, seeming to sense the hour and state of the tide without resort to a watch, declared that the run would be over and they might as well haul in.

Once more the heavy wet labour commenced. There were fewer jellyfish this time—but fewer salmon also. Four was the total haul, and it was not until the very last net was drawn in that any one of substance appeared. This proved to be a fine fish of almost twenty pounds that, lashing wildly, all but escaped from the net as it came inboard. Indeed, it had Tosh Hogg next to overboard, as he flung himself bodily upon it, and wrestling man and fish and netting were dragged in, a heaving soaking heap. Amidst much shouted advice and humorous comment the combatants were finally extricated from the enveloping meshes—which still of course continued to come in on the automatic hauler—and the fish was eventually dispatched.

This incident put everyone into a good humour for the trip home—though there was no blinking the fact that the day's fishing was still far from a financial success—for the other three fish would not make more than a dozen pounds between them. That did not represent economics for a boat and its crew.

On their way home, Sandy Logan appeared to be somewhat preoccupied with the view ahead, frequently training his glasses towards Airdmouth and its harbour. Presently they drew near enough for Adam to see with the naked eye that there was some sort of gathering congregated at the pier. There had been that, of course, when they left—but that was nearly six hours ago, and they could hardly expect the folk to have waited; moreover, the other fishermen in the remainder of the village's boats would have gone off to the normal fishing-grounds hours ago.

"What do you make of it?" Adam wondered. "You don't think . . . ?"

The big man shrugged again. "We have oor registration number painted in big white letters on oor bows," he pointed out. "Anybody wi' a telescope could have made them oot frae Berwick. Easy enough to ken who we are and where we come frae. They didna *need* to come oot for us in a boat."

"I see. But they wouldn't be catching us red-handed, this way."

"No need for that either, is there, Mr . . . Adam? They can just demand for to see oor catch."

"You could refuse?"

"Oh, aye—I could that. But it would look gey suspicious. Would you have me do that?"

"Yes, I think so. It doesn't matter how suspicious it looks, after all. It will merely mean that they will have to catch you red-handed another time. That gives us a little longer. If you let them see the salmon, they'd have the right to confiscate them. So you'd lose your first £20 worth of Fighting Fund. They might even try to hold the boat. No use letting them get away with anything the easy way."

"Right you are, Adam man—whatever you say." The skipper raised his glasses again. "Though, mind you, I misdoubt if yon's the bailiffs after a'." He smiled. "I think I can just make oot two tow-heided wee deevils capering up on top o' yon sea-wall, fair asking to be falling in! In school hours, too. . . "

Sure enough, the reception committee that awaited the *Bluebell* as she chugged into harbour consisted not of the indignant authorities from Berwick but of the entire roll and muster of Airdmouth's little school, including the motherly Mrs Paxton, Adam's sole assistant. The youngsters, she explained cheerfully to her superior when they had berthed, just would not apply themselves to their lessons with all this excitement going on, trying to look out of the schoolroom windows all the time to see whether the fishery cruisers were after the *Bluebell* yet. With so many of their fathers and brothers involved, not to mention their own headmaster, could you blame them, she asked? She couldn't control the two classes properly single-handed, anyway—so she just declared a sort of half-holiday, and here they were to count the salmon . . . and maybe call it Natural History. . . .

Somewhat guiltily, Adam agreed that he quite understood—and hoped fervently that the Director of Education had no spies located in Airdmouth.

So amidst vociferous squeals of excitement and acclaim, headed up and amplified by Sandy Logan's twin daughters, the adult miscreants were welcomed home—though it is possible that even greater satisfaction would have been engendered had they managed to get themselves arrested. Sandy, for the sake of communal morale, had the salmon laid out on wooden sleds that were used for carrying nets, giving the big fish a sled to itself. Men bearing these like stretchers, with the children running and shouting alongside, the first salmon caught and exhibited openly in Airdmouth for a hundred years were carried up over the rough cobbles of the village street. The womenfolk gathered in doorways to laugh and wave and jeer a little, as women will. The Reverend Malcolm Fraser came from the Manse to meet them, binoculars still hanging round his neck, and after admiring the catch judiciously, displayed the Kirk's solidarity by insisting that the place for the fish was in the old crypt under the church, once the burying-ground of Lamberton lairds but now surely the nearest thing to an ice-house in Airdmouth.

Thereafter, as Adam moved off in the direction of his school on its little green promontory, not a student was to be seen, curiously enough, not a youthful voice was upraised, to compete with the gulls, in all Airdmouth. Almost as rapidly and effectively the fishermen melted away likewise, though probably in a more consistent direction—even though the front door of The Fishers' Tryst remained firmly closed, of course, the licensing laws being what they are.

The first blow had been struck—to what purpose remained to be seen.

49

V

THE next morning Adam watched from the schoolroom window with mixed feelings—and with a certain amount of surreptitious competition from his students—as the *Ladybird*, Dand Fairgrieve skipper, drew away from the harbour mouth a good hour later than the *Bluebell* had done the day before. The other fishing-craft, *Bluebell* amongst them, had sailed for their usual fishing-grounds three hours or so previously; it was the *Ladybird's* turn to try for salmon today, and according to the theory of the four-hour run of fish, there had been no point in an earlier start, the tide being an hour later each day.

It was a dull grey morning, with occasional smirrs of fine rain filming the windows—not conditions in which the school-master could have anticipated with pleasure spending six hours in an open boat, with net-hauling and jellyfish scraping as occupational highlights. His hands and wrists still tingled fiercely from yesterday's stings, badly enough to have seriously disturbed his night's sleep. Yet he watched that craft, neither so large nor so spick-and-span as *Bluebell*, sail out with real feelings of regret. He ought to have been aboard—little use as he had felt himself to be the day before. He was largely responsible for the fact that she *was* heading out there looking for trouble, and he should have been with her to meet it. But he had his job to do here; he could not leave the school day after day. He had more responsibilities than one.

Throughout the forenoon the man's attention was as far from concentrated on teaching as was his pupils' on learning. Visibility did not extend for much more than half a mile most of the time—but that did not prevent Adam from making frequent moves to the window to peer out. Jeannie and Janet Logan were at the height of their powers throughout.

As well, perhaps, that the Easter vacation loomed ahead.

Towards midday the weather cleared sufficiently to give a

50

normal horizon. Try as he would, Adam could not find the *Ladybird* out there. During the night there had been a gusty wind and a fair sea was running, making it very difficult to pick out small craft at any distance. Now and again he thought that he discerned an occasional fishing-boat, but these seemed to be further to the north and further out altogether than he would have expected *Ladybird* to lie. Dand Fairgrieve had talked about trying another area off the Tweed's mouth, that he called Sim's Shelf. Possibly this was too far south to be seen beyond the southern headland of Airdmouth Bay. One of his scholars might have enlightened him had he been rash enough to ask. If this sort of thing went on, he might find himself investing in a powerful pair of binoculars.

At least there was no sign of grey-painted fishery cruisers or any other official-looking craft off their stretch of coast, as far as he could see.

There was still nothing to be seen of the salmon fishers when afternoon school broke up at three-thirty, and the scholars shot out of the building like a barrage of ballistic missiles, sound effects included.

It was just a little embarrassing for their tutor when, a few minutes later, for the sake of fresh air, he took a very casual stroll, and his feet happened to lead him in the direction of the harbour, to find the entire school already congregated there on the pier, including Mrs Paxton, gazing seawards.

Ladybird eventually materialised, slipping round the headland to the south fairly close inshore, about half an hour later. No signs of either excitement or elation were evident about her as she entered harbour, her crew studiously ignoring the presence of watchers on the pier, and going about their berthing operations with the most trying deliberation. Even the children's enthusiasm wilted under this, and there was comparative silence as the fishermen climbed up on to the pier one by one and stalked off moodily homewards, disinclined most obviously for idle chatter. Dand Fairgrieve came last, a single sagging sack over his shoulder, far from burdensome as regards mere weight at least. He spat.

"Two damned skittery wee fish!" he reported sourly, to Adam. "*Two*, I tell you. Died o' fright at the sight o' the net, I shouldna wonder! We near threw them back. Two salmon—and a few wee trouties. This is nae use, man."

"I'm sorry," Adam said. "That's bad luck. Disappointing, I realise. You were at this new place? Sim's Shelf?"

"For the first haul, aye. We got nothing in that, at a'—but the trouts and jellyfish. We moved right close in, then—no' much more than a mile off the Spittal beach—for the second try. And got these!" He spat again.

"M'mmm. And nobody came out after you? Even when you were close in, like that?"

"No' a soul. No' a cheep oot o' anybody. Seems like they couldna care less where we fished—and I dinna blame them! It's a mug's game."

Frowning, Adam shook his head. "I'm sorry . . . but it's not, you know. I'm sure it's not. Not taking the long view. They're bound to care—the authorities, the Tweed Commissioners. They can't just go on letting the Act be flouted, shrug it off—the Act which gives them their monopoly, the entire authority for their existence. If you get away with it, others will start. . . ."

"And a lot o' good it'll do them! They're welcome to the lot, frae me!"

"But, look—you always wanted to be allowed to fish out there. That was what your complaint was about. You *thought* the salmon were there. They used to be there. The Commissioners thought they were there when they inserted that bit   in the Act. Perhaps you've just not gone about the job properly . . . ?"

"Maybe—aye, maybe. But I canna afford much finding oot, Mister Horsburgh. No' at this price. It costs us near £40, in wages and the boat and fuel, to do what we did today."

"As much as that! That's bad. I'd no idea. . . ."

"Aye, then," Dand Fairgrieve said, and set off up the pier. Even the ever-present gulls winged heavily away.

It was late that night, with Adam immersed in his novel—

though not so deeply as he would have liked—when Sandy Logan called. He was alone.

In the chronically untidy sitting-room, Adam faced him. "Well," he said, heavily. "Have you come to call the whole thing off, then?"

The other raised his sandy eyebrows. "Eh? Call it off? Och, man Adam—what for would I do the likes o' that?"

The younger man paused. He was not quite sure whether he was relieved or weakly sorry to hear this. "I just thought . . . after the *Ladybird's* bad day. Dand Fairgrieve was telling me what it cost. . . ."

"Och, aye. We havena mastered the right way o' fishing for salmon oot there in the open sea, that's clear, But it's early days yet. Gie us time."

"Yes—but that's what you can't have, apparently. Fairgrieve was saying that he'd had enough. Your own mate Hogg was talking the same way. . . "

"Man, you don't have to take yon too seriously. Let them have their grumble. Tosh'll do as I say. Dand, too." The big man yawned cavernously. "O-o-ooh, aye. We've more'n grumbles to worry us, Adam."

"You mean . . . something else is wrong?"

"Well, no' just *wrong*, maybe. But difficult, a wee. You see, we're having trouble selling the fish."

"*Selling* it? But I thought there was a ready market for salmon? That's what you all said."

"Aye. That was true enough. But that was just the odd fish or two. We could ay sell them for a good price to local hotels and farms and the like, round the countryside. There's folk always good for a pound or two o' salmon, and no questions asked. But . . . well, doing it on a bigger scale, it's different."

"It's a bit early to be moaning about that, isn't it? You *aren't* doing it on a bigger scale yet. That's the whole trouble, isn't it?"

"Aye. I'ph'mmm." Sandy eyed the ceiling. "Just so. In the open sea, that is. But, och, some o' us were oot last night. Just here and there, you ken, along the shore. Wi' the cobles and the wear-shot nets. We did no' so badly, a' things considered."

"Poaching, you mean!"

"Och, yon's a word sensible folk dinna much use, Adam. It gives a wrong impression, sort of. We were just fishing in the sea again—but frae the shore."

"It comes to the same thing, whatever you call it, man. It's illegal, by Scots law, unless you have a Crown charter or grant. It could wreck your . . . our whole case if you were caught at it."

"Tut, man—we had plenty look-outs."

"I see. But . . . oh, well—leave that, just now. You did quite well, you say?"

"Forty-eight fish," Sandy admitted modestly. "No' bad. Aboot four hundred pounds weight, altogether."

"Good Lord! Four hundred pounds! Forty-eight salmon! That's . . ."

"There were four crews at it, mind. Here and there, as I say."

"Four crews? Of half a dozen men each? And plenty of look-outs, you say? That must have been practically every man in the village!"

"Och, well—barring yoursel' and the Minister, maybe . . ."

"Well, I'm damned!" Adam stared at his visitor. "And here have I been wasting my sympathy on you all! On Fairgrieve especially, for his wasted day. And all the time . . . ! No wonder he and his crew thought two fish from the open sea were small beer after that! And him grumbling like . . ."

"Tired he'd be. Dand is ay grouchy when he's needing his sleep." The big man yawned again. "I didna get that much sleep mysel'. The tide was right for it frae aboot midnight on, you see.

"I'm not weeping any tears over you either! I can't say I approve of all this. But . . . well, now you've run into a disposal problem? Of the fish?"

"Aye. Oor own bit private market's no use for this lot. And it'll no' keep all that long."

"You'll have to try the town, then. Berwick."

54

"That's no' so easy, either. A couple o' the boys have been to Berwick this afternoon. They got rid of a few o' the fish— but no' many. There's plenty salmon frae the legal fisheries, there. It's an offence to buy poached salmon, mind. Big fines. And everybody kens us frae Airdmouth, and that we havena a legal right to take salmon. It's no' that the folk are hot against poaching—there's plenty poachers in Berwick itsel' and always has been. But what wi' the legal fish, and their own poached fish, to get rid o', it's no' easy for us to find buyers."

"You'll just have to sell on the wholesale market, then. Send the fish south, where it's wanted. Through the fish salesmen."

"They're no' supposed to handle poached salmon either. They're linked to the legal fisheries, at Berwick itsel' and up the river. They ken we're frae Airdmouth—they ken us a'." Logan leaned forward. "But, now . . . if somebody was going to them wi' an offer o' fish, somebody they *didna* ken, and who looked and sounded sort o' respectable. . . ."

Adam looked hard at his visitor.

"I mean, a gentleman wi' a sort o' educated voice. There's one or two would likely ask no questions. They'd take it he was one o' the lairds or their agents, frae up the river, likely. Or frae one o' the angling syndicates. It's no' that they're against poached salmon, you see—it's just that it shouldna be *obvious*."

"You're trying to suggest that *I* should go to Berwick to sell your poached salmon for you?"

"Well . . . in a kind o' a way, yes. Nobody kens *you* there. You look real respectable. And you've a car. You said yoursel' that we've got to get that Fighting Fund built up, some way."

"But that isn't the sort of thing I could do, at all. I've never sold a fish in my life. . . ."

"You came oot in the boat wi' us yesterday, You'd never done that before either, Adam man. If you could do that, take that risk, what's the difference?"

"Ummm."

"I'd give you two-three names to call on. One o' the boys would follow you wi' an old van, wi' the fish. There'd be nothing to it. If the salesmen werena interested, you'd just breeze oot. It's worth a try—for we canna pay lawyers withoot the money. You said it yoursel'."

The schoolmaster scowled. "Confound you, Sandy Logan—you're a menace! All right—I'll try it. But I shouldn't think I'll be any more successful than the others."

"Och, never say that. Tomorrow afternoon, then, after the school skails? Tosh'll drive the van—and let you have the names and addresses." The skipper stood up, stretching. "Well, I'm off, Adam. Good luck."

"Well . . . I suppose so. Who's out tomorrow? Fishing for the salmon? In the open sea, I mean. That's the main thing, mind. We've got to keep that up. To force them to do something about us."

"Ooh, aye. Me it is again, tomorrow. The *Bluebell*. I'm taking it every second day. *Ladybird* and the *Partan Lassie* every fourth day. I'll hold them to that." He yawned once more. "Goodnight, then."

"Goodnight. Off to your bed, Sandy—you sound as though you need it."

"Aye—in three-four hours. Fine that."

"Why? You don't mean . . . ?"

"Och, there's a few lads oot wi' the cobles and nets again, the now. I'll away and give them a bit hand."

"Again! But this is too much! You'll be exhausted, man. Anyway, it's just asking for trouble, to do it so often. The wrong kind of trouble. Somebody's bound to stumble on you, one night."

"The only man ever stumbled on us ended up in the sea, mind!" The other grinned. "Och, it's no' a great place for stumblers o' a night, Airdmouth! Goodnight, Adam. . . ."

Feeling extraordinarily guilty and furtive, Adam parked his car in the grey climbing Hidehill of Berwick-on-Tweed, not far from the massive ancient walls, and with a glance left and right, made for the mouth of a narrow entry, a vennel or alley barely living up to its imposing name of Quality Street. Some distance behind him, an old and decrepit van, once painted green, drew up with a prolonged screeching of brakes that ought to have riveted the attention of all Berwick on the vicinity. Tosh Hogg waved cheerfully to the retiring schoolmaster from the cab.

Frowning, Adam hurried along the dark cobbled lane, resentfully eyeing a couple of inoffensive ladies discussing current events from open windows in upper floors at either side of the street. He was looking for Number 17. Between an empty-seeming shop and an apparently blank house door decorated with a bill against posting bills, numbered 15 and 19 respectively, opened a black archway. Down this stone-flagged tunnel the man plunged.

It gave on to quite a wide courtyard, cobbled, and flanked on all sides by lean-to sheds and buildings. Three or four large hand-carts were parked here, together with some enormous bottles cased in wickerwork and a few old barrels; neither sign nor smell of fish was evident. From what seemed to be a little office across the yard a wan light shone. Inside, a fat man in shirt sleeves was reading a newspaper. A cat came and rubbed round Adam's legs.

"Er . . . I'm looking for one John Sinton," he announced at the open door. "A fish salesman, actually. Number 17. Can you guide me?"

"I'm Sinton, aye. What can I do for you, sir?"

Adam was surprised. "Do you buy fish?"

The other heaved himself up, and emerged from his den. "Aye—whiles I do. Depends on the fish, sir."

"Oh, well . . . I have some salmon for sale. Er . . . quite a lot." That was not the way that he had meant to put it, at all.

"Salmon, eh?"

"Yes. You buy salmon?"

The fat man looked his visitor up and down. "Well, now. I do and I don't, as you might say. Salmon is one of them things, sir. What sort of salmon were you thinking of?"

"What sort . . . ? Why ordinary salmon, of course, first-class fish, fresh caught and in good condition. Varying sizes of fish."

"Indeed. Is that a fact, sir? Uh-huh. Well, now." The fellow

57

seemed to be exceedingly vague about his business. But there was nothing in the least vague about his suddenly darted demand. "Where are they from, sir—the salmon?"

"H'mm." It was Adam's turn to be vague. "From a fishery up there, in which I am interested." He gave a comprehensive wave of his arm that might have included any or all of the territory of southern Scotland. "A fishing syndicate, I suppose you'd call it."

"Ah," the fat man said. "A syndicate. Uh-huh. Up river?"

Adam frowned, and summoned what he hoped were his most authoritative tones. "Look, my friend—I'm not trying to sell you the fishery!" he said. "It's just the fish."

"Just so, sir. How much?"

"Eh? You mean how much weight? Oh, say two or three hundredweights."

The other's thick lips pursed into a brief soundless whistle. "You've had good sport, sir!"

"It's not sport, it's business," Adam assured him. "Are you interested?"

"Well . . . what sort o' price are you looking for, sir?"

"A fair price, naturally. The standard wholesale price, or near it."

"Uh-huh. I see. Well, now—a pity, I havena really a market for all that salmon today, I doubt. Sorry, sir."

"Then some part of it, perhaps?"

"Ah . . . I'm afraid not, sir."

Adam bit his lip. "Very well. Sorry to have troubled you. Good-day to you."

"If you like to leave me your name and address, sir, I could maybe let you know if I should happen to hear of a buyer for you . . . ?"

"Thank you—that will not be necessary." Rather precipitately Adam turned about and hurried back down the pend.

The next place that he tried, along to the end of Quality Street, round a corner, through an archway under the ramparts and down towards the river, was a very different establishment, consisting of a large concrete-floored modern shed, recently

58

hosed down, surrounded by large sinks, cutting-boards, scales, ice-bins and piles of fish-boxes. This at least looked and smelled as though connected with the fish trade. Only there was nobody to be seen therein.

Adam wandered about, poking his head round doors, into offices and stores, clearing his throat loudly and eventually calling out for attention. Nobody materialised. He wandered out, to the riverside. Two or three fishing-boats were moored to the wharf there, very similar to the Airdmouth craft—but only great gulls, standing about in contemplative dignity, seemed to be in charge. He moved back indoors. Stepping over to the heaped fish-boxes, he opened the lid of one. Two nice salmon lay glistening therein, packed in ice. He was trying to assess their weight when a voice spoke coldly, close behind him.

"Anything especial you want, sir?"

Dropping the lid rather abruptly, Adam jerked round. A woman stood there, eyeing him as though he might be some-thing that would normally be thrown back into the sea. She looked extremely like a particularly efficient lady-doctor, in spotless white coat and glasses. Where she had sprung from was a mystery—though possibly the noise of plumbing from somewhere near by accounted for much.

"I was just, er, looking round," he explained. "I didn't see you. I mean, before. I called out. I was just having a look at these fish . . ."

"Quite," the clinical lady said, with exemplary patience.

Her eyes seemed to reflect the surrounding ice—though that may only have been her glasses.

"Yes. Well, I've got some salmon to sell. Quite a lot. You, you buy salmon here?"

The woman stepped briskly across to a desk, opened it, and drew out an invoice book with carbon paper. She also whipped out a ballpoint pen which she held poised. "Name of fishery?" she said, tonelessly.

"Eh? Oh, well . . . h'm . . . a bit soon for details, isn't it? I mean, to start writing things down like that before we've decided on anything. The price, and all that . . ." Adam played for time, urgently.

"If we are to buy fish, sir, details are necessary," he was told coldly. "The price, obviously, is the current market price."

"Yes, but . . . well, one thing at a time, eh?" He produced a rather hollow laugh—which was not echoed. "We have two or three hundred pounds to sell, you see. And more to come."

The lady waited, pen hovering, ready.

"I mean . . . are you prepared to purchase that sort of amount?" He could think of nothing else to say.

"Naturally. We are wholesale fish salesmen. That is what we are for. There is nothing wrong with this fish, I take it?"

"Oh, no. Nothing like that. Not at all. Excellent fish. Fresh caught. Fine condition." Adam stopped abruptly. He must not gabble, never gabble.

"Quite. Name of fishery, owner or lessee? To be delivered here, or sent for? Average size of fish?"

The man moistened his lips. "Oh, we can deliver them here. We are just a group, you see. Not any special commercial fishery. More or less a syndicate. . . ."

She raised slender eyebrows. "Two or three hundred pounds—and more to come. A successful syndicate! I suppose that your own name and address must serve, then, Mr . . . ?"

Adam coughed. "I *can* give you my own name and address, of course," he temporised desperately. "But as a matter of principle, I don't see what that has to do with the matter. It is purely a commercial exchange. I represent a syndicate with so much prime fish for sale. You buy them, on their merits as fish. I can bring them here . . . in a few minutes. What my personal name and address has to do with it, I can't quite see." The sentiments sounded less lofty, even in his own ears, than intended.

The other's pale lips seemed to become a thin line, and her nostrils pinched in. "Salmon is a game fish," she declared, as thinly. "A licence is required to deal in it. Just as presumably you are aware, sir, that there are restrictions on catching it! There are certain regulations to be observed, to comply with the law. If you are not prepared to abide by these

60

regulations . . . ?"

"No, no—I don't say that, of course. But it's a lot of red tape. Making unnecessary work. However. . . ." Adam, faced with complete stalemate, fell back on a weak and quite unworthy subterfuge. "I suppose the best thing to do is just to go and bring you some of the fish. Let you see it. Then we can talk business more—er—profitably. It's not far away. I'll go now. Right away. Thank you."

Without risking any further converse, he touched his cap sketchily, and retired from that lady and from the establishment at a pace little short of a run. He did not look round, even when he got out into the street. Neither did he head for the vicinity in which Tosh Hogg had drawn up the van and was presumably waiting patiently; rather he sought to lose himself in the maze of narrow streets that climbed the hill towards the upper town.

No amount of striding and dodging, however, served to lose him his sense of feebleness and frustration, almost his shame. Why on earth had he taken on this ghastly job? Why had he let himself be talked into it? He was not the man for this sort of thing, at all. It was quite hopeless, anyway, obviously. He had two other names in his pocket—but he was damned if he was going to call on them, and get involved in more wretched shifts and evasions of this sort. The sooner that he got out of Berwick-on-Tweed the better!

Nevertheless, something, some reluctance to be beaten, some misplaced sense of duty, drew his steps eventually in the direction of East Street, where the third of his addresses was situated. This proved to be a small and low-browed shop in a steeply climbing street, with nothing whatsoever in either window save a sleeping cat. Inside, he could see a great deal of coiled rope and twine, some square tin cans stacked up, and a dark bundle in one corner that he took to be netting—visibility was not very good, what with the narrow dark street, the cloudiness of the day, and the unwashed state of the windows. There seemed to be an inner door with a glass panel through which artificial light gleamed as from a distance. The entire place looked just vaguely furtive enough to be slightly hopeful. Nothing clinically efficient about it, at any rate. Taking a deep breath, Adam reached for the door handle.

The door was locked, light within or none. He knocked— and elicited no reply. He knocked again, more loudly, and rattled the door. The cat looked up balefully, yawned, and curled tighter.

There was another of the pends or archways, of which Berwick seemed so fond, adjoining the shop, which presumably led into the back premises. This one however, was barred by a wooden gate. He tried the handle. This also was locked. But it was not very a high gate. With no great exercise of agility he could climb over it. Peering through, Adam could just make out, down the pend, a door that must lead into the back-shop. It stood half-open. There was a hand-cart in the pend, of the same type as he had seen in the first place—no doubt for wheeling up fish from the wharves. He put both hands and one foot on the gate, and took a quick look up and down the street, before climbing over.

A policeman was watching him from further up, hands behind his back, one booted toe tapping the cobblestones, with every appearance of interest.

Adam blinked rapidly. Then he shook the gate. He also raised his voice, to ask into the pend if anybody was there. He did not wait overlong for an answer to that, however. Instead, shrugging elaborate shoulders, and sighing as loudly as he could, he set off down the street at a determined pace. He took the first lane that turned off to the left, with expedition.

It was with considerable relief that the man emerged on to the busy modern High Street a short while thereafter, that was thronged with people with whom he could mingle anonymously. He had the fourth and last address still in his pocket—but it could stay there. Nothing, neither conscience nor hope nor the reproaches of his colleagues, was going to take him in search of it. He had had enough. Some other method of disposing of salmon would have to be found—but not by him.

Adam reached this decision without a great deal of debate, staring unseeing into another shop window—but a busy and perfectly open and normal shop this time. It was just as he realised that it was a fish-shop at which he had subconsciously paused, and that he was in fact gazing into the glazed and disillusioned eye of a large if truncated salmon, that a voice spoke close behind him.

"Still preoccupied with salmon?" it asked—a cool and feminine voice.

Adam spun round.

VI

IT was not the clinical fish-lady at all—the quality of the voice should have told Adam that. It was the young woman with the chestnut hair and the profile, who had been at the meeting that night in Airdmouth, and had driven away with Sir John Scott. The man had no difficulty in recognising her again; she was not the sort that a man like himself forgot with any rapidity. She was smiling now. In his relief, he grinned back widely, opened his mouth to declare his pleasure—then shut it again, on second thoughts.

"Ah. M'mmm. Good-afternoon," he said instead, warily.

"I thought it was you," she told him, easily. "I thought that you were looking a little anxious, too—as though that salmon might be going to bite you!"

"Not at all," he said. "I mean, I was just thinking. About something else altogether."

"Dear me—not salmon, at all! I'm disappointed. I was rather hoping that you might be thinking of little else, these days! I had high hopes for you, you know—after your stirring intervention the other night. And in view of, shall we say, current developments!"

"Developments?" He caught her eye, and looked away quickly. "Have there been . . . developments?"

She laughed, and she had a pleasant tinkling sort of laugh, musical and spontaneous-seeming—though with a woman that might have been a rash assumption. "Don't pretend to complete innocence—that you Airdmouth people know nothing about what's going on, Mr . . . er . . . ?"

"Horsburgh," he muttered. "Adam Horsburgh."

"Well, Adam Horsburgh, schoolmaster and public agitator—don't tell *me* that your educatory agitation hasn't borne quite surprisingly ripe fruit!"

Adam cleared his throat. "I don't know what you mean, I'm

afraid."

Again she laughed. "You make a most unconvincing liar, Mr Horsburgh! But I suppose that I should honour you the more for that? You know what I mean very well. You're not going to deny that these last few days Airdmouth boats have been quite openly fishing for salmon off Berwick, well within the limits of the Tweed Act, in broad daylight. In fact, there is one at it out there at this moment! Don't tell me that you didn't know that—after you more or less challenged the validity of the said Act at that meeting!"

Adam looked up and down the busy street. Why had he ever come to Berwick this day! "You're . . . you're rather jumping to conclusions, aren't you?" he suggested, heavily. "I mean, connecting boats out there with me, or with Airdmouth for that matter. It's not illegal to fish from a boat out there, or anywhere else in the open sea, provided you use the right nets. How do you know they're fishing for salmon? And why are you so sure that they are Airdmouth boats . . . ?"

"My dear man—be your age!" she requested. "I shouldn't think that there is any town in the British Isles better provided with telescopes and field-glasses than Berwick-on-Tweed—or more interested in salmon, one way or another! Your boats' registration marks are perfectly clear to any decent telescope. Also the fact that they are using drift-nets in spots where only salmon could be expected to be worth catching. You don't get herring-shoals a mile off Berwick pier or Spittal sands! Everybody in Berwick, and further afield, knows what's happening out there. That fishermen from Airdmouth are openly defying the law."

Adam stroked his chin, quite thankful that the noisy passage of a heavy lorry up the High Street gave him a moment or two to marshal his thoughts. "The authorities . . ." he said. "The authorities don't seem to be taking quite such a dramatic view of all this as you do? Otherwise, wouldn't they be doing something about it? Taking some steps to stop this fishing that you speak of?"

"They would, I've no doubt—if they were a bit more sure

of their position! The authorities, or some of them at least—my father for one—are not just too happy at the moment about their own legal position, I think. Thanks to your little lecture, the other day, perhaps. My father has been very busy consulting learned gentlemen in wigs. . . ."

"Your father . . . ?"

"Yes. The arch-enemy. Sir John Scott. I'm Hazel Scott. Didn't you know? Oh, I'm sorry—that ought to have been made clear, perhaps. But don't look so shocked, Mr Horsburgh—I'm on your side, you know. Have been from the first. I thought I indicated that to you, after the meeting?"

"I'm . . . I'm glad to hear it," Adam said, with only moderate conviction.

"Yes. So it's all right, you see. You're quite safe with me. No need to be so cagey." She glanced about her. "But, look—don't you think we might go somewhere just a little more private, to discuss all this? All the shouting makes me quite hoarse. I had never realised before just what a place for traffic Berwick was. A cup of tea, perhaps?"

Adam's doubt, however ungallant, was not to be hidden. "That would be very nice, I'm sure, Miss . . . er . . . Scott," he mumbled. "But, well—have we all that much to discuss? I don't . . ."

"Of course we have! I want to hear all about it—how you're getting on, what luck you're having with the salmon, what your plans are. I'm most interested. I may even be able to give you some quite useful advice, too—for I know some of the weaknesses of the other side, you see. I know what they're worried about. And you're going to need all the good advice you can get, I think Mr Horsburgh. Daddy's no fool, you know—even though he gives that impression quite frequently. And you have powerful forces ranged against you."

"I know that. I never thought Sir John was a fool. Only a—a . . . well, skip that!" The man eyed her directly. "Why are you doing all this, Miss Scott?" he demanded. "I mean, why should you be on *our* side? *For* the fishermen and against your own interests? Against your father?"

"Why are *you* for the fishermen?" she countered. "You're a schoolmaster—and not just the usual kind for a small country school either, if I may say so! You're obviously not of fishing-stock, and with no real interest in salmon, as such, I suspect. I should think I'm concerned for much the same reasons as you are—because I like to see justice done, and I tend to have a soft spot for the underdog, every time. Also, I like a good-going fight and for folk to show some spirit. Or don't you believe me?"

The man made a gesture of conventional protest.

"You can trust me, you know," Hazel Scott added, quietly.

Adam was lost, of course. For a man of his make-up to deny a good-looking and charming young woman anything was difficult enough; when she challenged his belief in her, it was less possible still; and when her arguments made good sense into the bargain, the issue was settled. He capitulated with as good grace as he might.

"Let's have that cup of tea," he said. "To tell you the truth, I could do with one, myself. I've had a rather trying afternoon, what with one thing and another. Where shall we go?"

"Cairns' is just a few doors up. I can recommend their scones. Good Scots fare—nothing anglicised about it! I rather gather that will appeal to you?"

As they moved up the street together, Adam considered sidelong the girl's expensive-looking tan suede and sheepskin coat, stylishly cut tweed skirt, and general air of well-groomed prosperity. "As well that I have on my best suit," he mentioned. "I was trying to be taken for a gentleman, this afternoon—not with a great deal of success, I fear!"

The girl got almost the whole story out of him, of course—though not the extent of the night-time coble-and-net poaching; he had just sufficient discretion to withhold that. She made a good listener—and there seemed to be no doubt as to where her sympathies lay. She had an eagerness and enthusiasm, apparently natural and spontaneous, that was for ever breaking through the well-bred and flippant veneer—which was quite

67

potently disarming. Moreover, owing to Adam's rather ridiculous preoccupation with secrecy and caution in that tearoom, so that he kept his voice down to little more than a throaty whisper, their heads had to be pretty close together much of the time—which was not without its own effect, on the secret-revealer, at any rate.

"So you are here to sell the fish for them," she commented, at length. "I think that idea of putting the money into a Fighting Fund is good. Once that gets known, it ought to do your cause a lot of good. And you're going to need it all, anyway—for I think that's one of the things that the other side are banking on, that you won't be able to afford to fight the legal battle very far, if it comes to court. I mean, fight it right up to the highest courts, to the House of Lords, if necessary. Pretty big money is needed for that sort of thing. I'm glad you're making a start, at any rate."

Adam drew a hand over his mouth. "Well," he said. "It's a bit of a false start, so far. And looks like staying that way, unfortunately."

"What do you mean—a false start?"

"Just that I haven't managed to sell a single fish, so far! I haven't found anybody who will touch the fish with a barge-pole!"

She stared at him. "You mean, because it's *you* that's selling it? Because of where the fish come from?"

"That's the whole point—because I can't *tell* them where the fish come from!"

"But if you're doing this fishing out there openly—asking to get caught and charged—why try to hide where they come from? Tell the dealers."

"Because for the moment, they are *poached* salmon. And it seems there is as heavy a penalty for dealing in poached salmon as for catching them. The Airdmouth fishermen are known here, and anyone buying from them would know that they were buying illegally caught fish. We'd hoped that if *I* seemed fairly respectable looking, and nobody knowing me here, the buyers might accept them from me, asking no questions. But it

68

seems that's out. The first thing they ask is the fishery the salmon came from, or, at the very least, my name and address. I can't give them that, without giving the game away—so we're sunk. There's a whole van-load of poached salmon, four hundredweight of it, down in Hidehill, waiting." Adam belatedly remembered poor Tosh Hogg, sitting on his guilty cargo, and knew an access of remorse.

"Four hundredweight!" she repeated. "That's a lot of salmon! Goodness, at current market prices that's worth over £100! You people have been pretty lucky with your fishing!

"H'mmmm," the man said. "Well . . . you could call it luck! But it won't be worth that sort of money for long—or any money at all. Even in ice. It'll go wrong on us."

"What are you going to do, then?"

"I don't see anything else for it, but to take it back to Airdmouth."

"Not on your life!" Hazel Scott exclaimed. She got to her feet. "You'll never build up a Fighting Fund that way. We'll just go down to Quality Street right now."

"Eh . . . ? Quality Street? You mean—Sinton's?"

"Yes. John Sinton. That's who we deal with. He buys all our fish, from Linburndean."

"But I've been to him. He was the first I tried. It's no good. He wouldn't touch our salmon. Said he'd no market for it."

"No market! He sends a truck load of iced salmon every second day to Manchester, throughout the season! He may take a rather different view of the business if I'm with you," the girl suggested. "We'll go down and see."

"But, look here," Adam protested. "I can't have you doing this—getting mixed up in it. It's kind of you—but not only is it nothing to do with you, but you might get into trouble, serious trouble. They're still poached fish we're trying to sell."

"Fiddlesticks!" his companion said. "Look—are you paying for this tea, or am I . . . ?"

So, in a smart open cream sports car a few minutes later, Adam once more found himself at the mouth of the dark entry to John Sinton's modest premises. Neither very happily nor hopefully he followed his determined companion up the pend.

The stout man was talking to what looked like a commercial traveller, in the centre of his little courtyard, as they came up. But at sight of the new visitors, this unfortunate might not have existed. In mid-sentence John Sinton dropped him, and actually achieved a bow, approximately from his substantial middle.

"Afternoon, Miss Scott," he greeted effusively. "This is a pleasure, indeed. No' a bad day, for the time o' the year. We havena seen you in for a bittie. How is everything at Linburndean, Miss? How's Sir John?"

"He's not so bad—though he'd be better if he drank less!" the young woman answered, casually frank. "Look here, Sinton—my friend Adam here tells me that you're no longer interested in buying salmon. Is this true? Does it mean that we've got to find somebody else to sell to, this season?"

"No, no, no—och, nothing o' the sort, Miss Scott! Mercy me, no." The fat man cast a wary eye on Horsburgh. "It was just . . . I was sort of unsure of the market at the time, you see. . . ."

"What's happened to the market? Don't tell me that Manchester has suddenly lost interest in fresh salmon?"

"No, no. It was just that I didna ken . . . I didn't know, Miss Scott, just the way the demand was going, if you see what I mean. And the ruling price. Just sort of temporary lack of information, if you take me." Sinton, though smiling deferentially to the young woman, was making somewhat urgent gestures with one plump hand, half behind his back, to the man with whom he had been talking. That individual humbly and promptly effaced himself by sidling towards the pend and away.

"Indeed," the girl commented. "I've never heard you complain of lack of market information before. I hope it isn't general? I mean, if we go now to one of the other fish people here, they're not going to suffer from it, too? Dawson and Kennedy's, perhaps? We might have to get in touch with some of the Manchester wholesalers direct, in that case . . . ?"

"Oh, no. That won't be necessary, Miss Scott—no need for that," the other told her earnestly. "It was just temporary, as I said—very temporary indeed. I have the information, now. Och, yes. The phone, you know. Real convenient. Yes, yes. It's all right now. Prices fair enough—not bad, at all."

"Good. So you'll buy our salmon now, will you?" There was just the faintest emphasis on the our.

"Naturally, Miss Scott. Of course. Delighted. If . . . if the gentleman had just sort of mentioned your name. . . ."

"I don't see what that's got to do with it, Sinton?"

"No, no. But . . . och, well—I might have got the information for him. Quicker. Got it on the phone, you see. To, er, Manchester. Aye. Och, but never mind that, now. . . ."

"No," Hazel Scott agreed. She turned to her companion. "I think, if you just go and bring the fish, Adam . . . ? I'll wait here for you. You won't be long?"

"Not five minutes," that man assured her. "This is, h'm, more like it." He turned, and trying not to hurry, headed for the street.

He found Tosh Hogg where he had left him, fast asleep in the green van, apparently quite unconcerned over either the delay or the fact that he had been left sitting in public on what might be likened to a load of dynamite. Adam made his apologies brief, therefore. He did not go into details of the selling arrangements, beyond mentioning that it had all been a little difficult. He suggested that Tosh should not appear along at Sinton's place; he himself would drive the van along and bring it back here afterwards, when the mate could pick it up again. The other was quite agreeable.

Adam arrived back in the courtyard to find Miss Scott discoursing apparently on social scandals to Sinton, who was sniggering appreciatively.

"Sinton's very hard-hearted about the price, Adam," she mentioned, turning. "The best he'll offer is six-and-threepence a pound. D'you think we should accept that?"

Adam gulped. He had not dared hope for more than five shillings, for such doubtful fish—and would have accepted three-and-sixpence. "Er . . . well, I suppose so," he muttered. "We don't want to haggle, do we? Especially as I think there's rather more of it than I, er, suggested. I mentioned to Mr Sinton, I believe, that there was between two and three hundredweights. Looking at it now, I'd say there's probably more. Maybe four hundredweights."

"Oh, that won't matter—will it, Sinton? All the better. All goes the same way—to Manchester."

The fat man blinked a little. "Well . . . provided it's first-quality fish, Miss. . . ."

"Naturally. Come on, then. Let's get it over with."

They went out through the pend, Sinton pushing one of the hand-carts. He looked at the decrepit van somewhat doubtfully, but made no comment. Adam helped him pull out the fish-boxes filled with salmon and ice, and load them on to the barrow. There were twelve of them, and it took three trips to get them all in.

The weighing-machine was in one of the lean-to sheds, lit unexpectedly by strong fluorescent strip-lighting. Under this Sinton examined each fish carefully, before weighing it, peering especially at head and gills.

"All netted fish," he remarked. "Uh-huh. Just so. Oh, aye."

"Of course," the young woman answered. "You didn't think they'd been caught with a cleek, did you? Or dynamite?"

The other laughed loudly. "Hardly that, Miss Scott—hardly! No, no. Some nice fish here, though—very nice."

"Quite. That big fellow's a beauty. Twenty pounds, I'd say?"

"Eighteen and a half, just," the fat man announced. "Aye, a bonny fish. Just where did you get this one, sir?"

"Oh, some distance up," Adam answered vaguely. "In deep water, if I remember rightly."

"Aye, so. Uh-huh. Quite."

When the weighing and inspection was finished, Sinton, apparently an expert in mental arithmetic, announced four hundred and eight pounds in all, of total value one hundred and twenty-seven pounds ten shillings. How would they like payment?

"Cash," the girl replied, promptly. "Easiest for everybody, don't you think? Best for you, certainly, Sinton? Unless, for Income Tax purposes, you would prefer to write out a cheque?"

The other did not answer that. He thrust his hand into his evidently capacious trousers' pocket, and brought out a great fistful of crumpled notes, Scots, Treasury and fivers. Puffing heavily he counted them out—and though it took time, no more than half of the heap was eventually handed to Adam. The rest was thrust back whence it came.

"You'll not need an account, likely, sir?" he suggested.

"Well . . . perhaps not," Adam acceded, taking the untidy collection of paper a little uncertainly.

"Well, that's fine," Hazel Scott said. "Everybody satisfied. Thanks, Sinton. I'll give Daddy your good wishes. I'll remind him about the matter of the railway charges, too. No doubt he'll know who to speak to. Well, bye-bye. I expect Adam here will be bringing you another lot, one of these days."

"Surely, surely. Any time, sir. Though I can't always guarantee six-and-three, mind . . . !"

"You great robber, you, Sinton! I bet you get eight-and-six at least for it, in Manchester! You're all the same, you middlemen! Utterly heartless . . . !"

As they walked out together to the vehicles, Adam found it hard adequately to express his feelings. Indeed, it was the other who spoke first.

"Sorry," she observed, going down the pend, "about all that too-familiar Adam-business. I had to call you something, and the surname would have been risky."

"Lord—as though that mattered!" he said. "Only thing you could do, anyway. Look—I don't know how to begin to say how grateful I am! You did that magnificently. And getting that price—six-and-threepence! I'd have taken half. All that money! I don't know what to say."

"Nothing to be said," she assured. "There was little enough to it, as you could see. Owing to my father spending so much of his time at Westminster, a lot of the estate-management falls to me. So Sinton knows me fairly well. Likewise, he knows very well on which side his bread is buttered—especially where the Inland Revenue is concerned! So it was all plain sailing." She eased herself expertly into her car. "If there is anything else that I can do, you can always get me on the end of the phone."

He frowned. "Thanks. I'm very grateful, as I say. But I'm not too happy about all this, you know. I mean, you going against your father, like this. It's all right for us—very nice. But it's not so nice for him. It's bound to make trouble between you. Family trouble. I wouldn't like . . ."

"I wouldn't worry about that, if I were you," she said. "Daddy knows that I disapprove of his attitude on this subject. As on some others. He knows too, that when I disapprove enough about anything, I'm apt to do something about it! It's happened before! We understand each other, just the same. So don't let it trouble you, Mr Horsburgh."

"M'mmm. Well. . . ."

"*Au revoir*," she said, smiling, and pressed the self-starter. "And thanks for the tea. Ladykirk 290 is the number." A slim hand waved farewell, and the sports car shot off, its throaty roar resounding in the narrow street.

Despite various satisfactions, the man still frowned a little as he gazed after her. It seemed a pity to have reverted to the Mister Horsburgh again after the Adam.

Driving the van back into Hidehill, he handed it over to the lounging Tosh.

"Your girlfriend's a right high-stepper, is she no'," the latter mentioned, grinning. "Specially getting into yon wee white slug o' a car. The pity I was away back here . . . !"

The frown returned. "She's not my girlfriend. She's . . . well, never mind. But instead of making cracks, Hogg, you should be mighty grateful to that young woman. We've got a Fighting Fund started, because of her—and *only* because of her. One hundred and twenty-seven pounds ten of a Fighting Fund. Here you are." Adam thrust the bundle of miscellaneous notes at the fisherman. "Give you those to Sandy Logan—and tell him to thank his lucky stars that there was somebody more effective than me at selling salmon in Berwick this day!"

"Jings!" Tosh Hogg exclaimed. "Crickety-bluidy-Jings!"

VII

THERE was no very good reason why Adam Horsburgh should have been standing there on the stony beach beneath the cliff that drizzling wet night. In theory, he disapproved of any of them being there. He was not really being very useful, however helpful his intentions, and the others would have been just as well without him. Sandy Logan had indeed tried to dissuade him from coming.

Nevertheless, he had insisted on taking part this time. He had argued against this night-time poaching, and lost. It was not that his moral sense was seriously outraged by the principle of the thing; indeed he could not see anything very basically wrong with what they were doing. It was undoubtedly contrary to the law of Scotland, however—and that meant that it could seriously weaken, probably shatter, their case if they were caught at it. He had not failed to point this out to his fishermen colleagues on numerous occasions—but to a greater or lesser degree they had been doing it all their lives and saw no point in stopping it now when the money was needed, not selfishly, but in the cause of reform. The salmon fishing out at sea, too, was continuing to be unproductive of worthwhile catches—so it was all the more necessary to bring up the bag by this coble-and-net poaching at night. The tide, an hour different every day, made it most hopeful to fish tonight for the two hours before and after midnight. Adam's determination to come along stemmed in some obscure way from the fact that he had been instrumental in *selling* the fish, most of it poached, and so felt some vague responsibility to be deeper in still. A foolish reaction, undoubtedly.

There were two teams out tonight, one under Jamesy Pringle of the *Partan Lassie* somewhat nearer in to the village, and their own under Sandy Logan here near the southern headland of the bay—not far in fact from where Adam had been landed

76

unceremoniously that first night of his investigations. There were also three look-outs stationed at strategic points in the vicinity.

Sandy's lot had made two casts already. The first had been a complete failure, and the second had produced only two small fish, one a blacktail as it was called, an immature fish of little more than a pound's weight, and late for the season, which had been thrown back as both law and common sense required. The rest had been the inevitable jellyfishes which were plaguing the coast this year. The men were blaming the wind for these poor results, backing south from west; apparently the wind had a lot to do with the route and the times in which the fish ran. Wind off the land, it was best to fish thus with the making tide; wind off the sea, to wait until after high water. Why this should affect the salmon was not explained to the schoolmaster. The others were arguing now as to whether it was worth-while going on here, moving to another spot, or giving up altogether for the night.

"We'll try one more shot," Sandy decided. "Here. It's as good a bit as any, the way the wind is. If it's no good, we'll just awa' hame."

This was agreed—Logan usually getting his own way, even though the six men with him now were not all of his own crew.

Tosh Hogg and a second man climbed into the almost flat-bottomed black coble, with most of the net piled neatly in a great heap on the broad stern board but its end anchored on the beach. They pulled out directly seawards, with slow regular strokes of the long oars, paying out the folds of the net behind them, cork floats keeping it upright in the water. They went perhaps two hundred yards out, and then began to turn in a fairly wide semicircle, before rowing their way back to the shore on a parallel course. They brought the final warp of the net back with them.

After a short wait, and a quick smoke, with three men at each end, the pulling in of the net commenced.

It was slow toilsome work, for net and ropes seemed very heavy in the water. The men pulled rhythmically, in unison, with the foremost pair, in their long thigh-boots, well above their knees in the water. The third man of each side saw that the wet folds and coils were arranged as neatly behind him on the stony beach as might be.

Whatever else this shot was going to produce, the crop of jellyfish clearly was once again going to be heavy. The brutes were a major nuisance, clogging up the meshes, weighting everything down, and on occasion stinging viciously. Adam's vocabulary was considerably enriched as he laboured alongside the incensed fishermen.

As the net came in, the two horns of it were drawn closer together until both sets of men were standing near each other.

A leaping lashing crescent of silver in the foaming shallows proclaimed their first decent-sized fish, when, of a sudden, into the appreciative shouted comments, Sandy Logan's voice rapped out a command, loud and clear.

"Quiet! Quiet, all o' you! Listen!"

Every man stiffened up, abruptly motionless, the net held. Only the salmon continued to cavort in the shallows.

They strained their ears. The beat and draw of the waves on the shingle sounded from all along the shore. Curlew were calling sadly from high ground behind the cliff-tops, and somewhere a duck was quacking steadily. Apart from these, no other sounds reached them.

"I thought I heard a whistle," the big man said, after a moment or two.

"A whaup, likely, up there, Sandy?"

"No. It wasna that. It was . . ."

"Look!" Tosh Hogg cried. "Up yonder." He pointed back, northwards, towards the village.

In the darkness, a yellow point of light was blinking on and off. How far away it was would be hard to say; it was high up, not at shore-level—on the cliff-top obviously.

"Yon'll be Dod, signalling . . ." somebody began, when he was interrupted by the high shrilling note of a whistle, in a series of long blasts. The light was extinguished abruptly.

"The polis!" Sandy exclaimed. "Yon's a polis whistle, for

sure."

"Jings! What are they doing here? Whae put *them* on to us . . . ?"

"Maybe it's no', Sandy. Maybe it's just some wee laddies?"

"It's the polis, all right," Logan reiterated. "Blowing yon way. They've been tipped off, somehow. Look, now—get this net in, quick! In wi' it. We'll maybe have to act right lively."

The words were hardly out of his mouth when light returned to the scene—but not that small yellow pinpoint, as before. Now two great double beams of white blazed out, some little distance apart. One of them appeared to be approximately where the earlier gleam had shown, the other somewhat nearer; but both were high up, and though not at the same angle, both shining out to sea.

"Headlamps!" Tosh declared. "Powerfu' ones, too! Bluidy polis-cars! They got them right to the edge o' the cliff, some way."

"Quick! Forget them!" Logan commanded. "Get these nets in—never mind how. Clear oor feet."

There was little need to urge them on. Nets were expensive, and would undoubtedly be confiscated if found. Energetically they tugged and hauled, cursing those jellyfish. One man flung himself upon the salmon, knocked it on the head, and tossed it into the boat—a nice fish of a dozen pounds or so.

Now, of course, they were into a catch at last. As the folds of the net came in, jumping silvery fish kept appearing, each one holding up the dragging process while it was extricated from the clutching meshes.

"Leave them in," Sandy ordered, at length. "We canna wait." He kept glancing round to the north. The headlight beams up there were continually on the move, seemingly manoeuvring. Though they pointed seawards in various directions, in the main they appeared to be concentrating on a limited area fairly directly in front of them. The manoeuvring almost certainly represented attempts to get the beams sufficiently depressed, to get the cars into such positions that the headlights would shine downwards in some measure on to the beach below and not straight out to sea.

"It's no us they're after," Logan declared, after a minute or two. "It's Jamesy's boys. They're concentrating there—right above the Earl's Cove, where Jamesy is. They'll no' ken we're here. Damn it—we'll have to give Jamesy a hand, some way."

"How?" Adam demanded, panting, as he hauled on that wet, heavy and seemingly endless net.

"Distract their attention, some way," the other answered. "See if we can bring them along this way a bit, maybe. Take the pressure off Jamesy. I've got one torch, here. Say—how many o' you boys got torches wi' you?"

Adam had one, and two of the others likewise. Taking them, the skipper switched them all on, laying three on the rocks, pointing northwards, and waving and blinking his own, as though signalling. Whether this would attract attention their way was doubtful, admittedly.

At last the net was all in, a black heaving untidy bundle on the beach, with not a few salmon still entangled in its folds— not to mention jellyfish innumerable.

"Into the coble wi' it," Sandy directed. "Any way. Hear yon whistle again? Maybe that's aboot our lights?"

They piled the hopeless tangle of net into the well of the boat, splashing about up to their middles in the waves—all having long been wet through anyway.

The job done, and all ready for them to make a discreet getaway by sea, there was still no indication of what might be happening further along the shore, or whether their torches were having the effect of drawing any of the presumed chase this way. Sandy Logan rubbed his massive chin.

"Have to do something better than this," he said.

"Row oot in the boat," Tosh Hogg suggested. "Get into the light frae their cars. So's they see us. Maybe draw some o' the heat off Jamesy that way."

The big man shook his head. "Take ower long, Tosh. Anyway, it's no' likely the polis'll have a boat—unless they've captured Jamesy's. So they couldna do anything aboot us, on the water. They'd just leave us alone, I reckon, and concentrate

80

on the others. We'd be no better off. No—we'll have to go along the beach, just. On foot. Wi' the torches. Let them see us coming. Then they'll maybe leave Jamesy alone, and come at us."

"Jings!" Tosh said.

Adam rather agreed with that terse comment. It seemed a very drastic measure to take. He recognised, of course, that for the authorities to get their hands on Jamesy Pringle's crew, in the act of poaching, would be just as serious in its consequences as if they themselves were caught. The effect on the entire cause would be disastrous. On the other hand, Pringle's people might have managed to get away in time, in which case there was no point of them running their heads into a noose. He said as much—with a certain amount of support from others.

"No," Logan insisted. "We canna just leave Jamesy to it— and this is the only move that might do him some good. He's sort o' sandwiched in there, under those big cliffs. If they get doon to him while his coble was out shooting the net, he wouldna could get away by sea. If they've caught him, though, they'll no' get him and the boys up yon cliff easy, as prisoners. They'd take them along the shore, I'd say, to the village. Then'd be our chance."

"Look—we don't want any fighting with the police!" Adam protested. "No rough stuff. That would just about be the end of our campaign, whatever else happened!"

"Who said anything aboot fighting and rough stuff, Adam man? We just want to distract them. Draw them back here after us—then into the coble wi' us, and away. But, see—we canna stand here arguing aboot it a' night. If we're to do any good, we'll have to do it quick. You coming?"

One man was left behind with the coble, to have it all ready for a swift departure—the oldest and least agile man. The rest of the party, in a bunch, set off to trudge along the rocky beach northwards.

"Keep the torches on," Sandy directed. "We want them to see us coming. And mind, if they come after us, gie yoursel's

81

time to get back to the coble. You ken this beach better'n they do—but you'll maybe no' run as fast as them, wi' these heavy sea-boots on."

It felt very strange indeed to be tramping along over the stones and shingle and reefs of that dark shore towards those ominously pointing beams of light, proclaiming their presence by their own lesser lights, every sense alert for the first hint, sign or sound of other men. There was no talking, now; even the hollow clump-clump of rubber thigh-boots sounded too loud on the night.

Adam, who had no sea-boots and was wearing his oldest pair of shoes, wondered even at that how much more quickly he might run over this slippery and uneven ground than, say, one of the younger and more agile members of the Berwick Constabulary. Every step that they took meant that they had further to run back to the boat. How far apart had the two poaching crews been operating? Something between quarter and half a mile, probably, At least there was no risk of them losing their way in the dark, going or coming—for the cliffs towered blackly, overwhelmingly, on their left, and the tide foamed whitely on their right, with no more than a hundred yards of space between the two.

Adam was somewhat preoccupied with that frowning barrier of cliff. At this southern end of the bay it was much lower and broken down than at the other end. He had clambered up it that other night of sad memory, and worked his devious way along the top, eventually back to Airdmouth. Moving close to Logan, he expressed his fears.

"We could be cut off," he said. "Seeing our lights, if they've any folk left up above there, at the cars, they could send them along the top this way, to climb down behind us. It's quite possible to get down the cliff along here—I climbed up it that night. Then they'd be between us and the boat."

The other frowned. "They could, aye. But why should they? They're no' to ken that we'll be moving back to a boat."

"They might just want to get somebody behind us, to cut us off if we bolted. If they've got enough men to spare. We don't know how many there may be. Anyway they're not necessarily fools! They'll likely guess that if there are people along here, we've been poaching likewise. So we're sure to have a coble—and that's a useful thing to get back to if one's dodging police!"

"M'mmm." The big man halted. "Something in that, Adam." He stared up at the indistinct line of the cliff-top. In the drizzle of rain it provided no useful silhouette against the night sky. "I dinna see what we can do aboot it, just the same."

"One of us should be up there. With a torch, to signal down if there's any sign of them. Give you warning. Maybe it had better be me. Easier for me, in shoes, climbing up, than those great sea-boots. And I won't be much use to you in the boat, anyway."

"Well . . . maybe. You'd be the best, likely, right enough." The skipper looked forward along the shore again. "They're keeping gey quiet. And no lights showing. Doon by the water, I mean. You'd think, if they were having a stramash wi' Jamesy's boys, there'd be lights. . . ."

"Maybe Jamesy got away, Sandy," somebody suggested. "Away in their coble. And now the polis are just lying quiet, watching *oor* lights and waiting for us? I reckon this is bluidy daft! We'd have been better in the coble."

"All right," Sandy acceded. "We'll do both. Away back, Peter, to the boat. You and Kenny row it along here, as close inshore as you can, so's the rest o' us can get oot to it quick, if need be. That'll be the best thing. . . ."

"Aye, that's mair like it. . . ."

"And you, Adam, up the cliff. . . ."

"Yes. I'd better hurry. It might be too late, already—though it's not so bad if the coble's coming along after you. Look—when I'm up there, if I see any sign of them moving along the top or trying to get behind you, I'll shine my torch in a series of three short blinks—dot-dot-dot. And if I should be able to see them down below here, in front of you, I'll warn you by two long flashes—dash-dash. Okay?"

"Aye. And good luck wi' your climbing, Adam. I wouldna like creeping up yon cliff in the dark. . . ."

Adam Horsburgh did not like it very much either, there-after—even though he had done a bit of mountaineering in his day, and the cliff, of course, was nothing like perpendicular hereabouts. But finding the best route, in the darkness, was not easy—and obviously he had not come to as good a spot for climbing as he had stumbled on before. The ascent went up, apparently, in three rough stages, with a couple of broken terraces or shelves in between, far from level but where grass could grow nevertheless.

Adam reached the first of these without much difficulty—and then came to a full stop. The next section of the cliff seemed not only to be steeper, but actually to bulge out and overhang, just here. He cast about, but found no route up. How far this overhang might stretch, laterally, he could neither see nor guess.

There were three things that he might do. He could edge along this terrace to the right or to the left, hoping for a break in the overhang, or he could climb down whence he had come, to try somewhere else. Being the man he was, going down again would be the last resort; also, he was very much aware of the need for haste if he was going to be of any use to his friends down below. Which way to edge along, then—right or left? In the darkness, one was as doubtful as the other. Then he thought of using the only light available on that benighted scene to aid him—the glow of the cars' headlamps away to the north. By placing his head almost against the rock-face, he was just able to outline some part of the cliff, in that direction, against this diffused glow. It did not look good, at all.

Adam took the third alternative, for want of a better, and began to move sideways along to the left, southwards.

Whether it was, in fact, the wisest thing to do, he had no means of knowing. But presently he came to a sort of cleft in the face of the cliff, down which water ran in a recognisable flow. Whether this was a permanent burn, from the high ground, or mere rainwater draining off the cliff-top, at least the fact that it ran, rather than fell or cascaded, seemed hopeful. He could hear no actual splatter from above, as he would have expected if it had been falling sheer higher up. He decided to try to use this as a stepladder.

It was a wet business, of course—but then he was wet through already. He soon came to the conclusion that it was a permanent stream, for the stone around it seemed water-worn and very firm, as though all the rotted stuff had been washed away—good hand-holds being thus provided. Hand over hand the man went up, occasionally having to use his knees also. He made good time of it, now.

He must have passed the second grassy shelf without noticing it, for quite suddenly and before he expected it, he found the cliff opening out and levelling off around him, and perceived that he had reached the top.

Soaked, and panting, Adam turned and hurried along northwards.

The broken state of the escarpment meant that there was no clear edge to the cliff, no convenient cornice along which he could move, keeping the beach below always in sight. Quite frequently he had to be quite some distance back from the drop.

His friends, or at least the lights of their torches, were therefore only intermittently visible, now of course some distance ahead. He could distinguish no details down on the shore, at all—though the white edge of the tide was fairly clear, and the sea beyond seemed not really paler than the land but less solid, with the hint of luminosity about it.

It was on one of his inevitable detours to avoid a gap in the cliff-top, that Adam realised that he had stumbled upon a path—a path running parallel with the edge but some little way inland, here at any rate. The discovery gave him an idea. The rain had made the track muddy—he could feel that under his feet. Shielding his torch carefully within his wet jacket, he knelt down and shone the light on to the surface of the path.

Most clearly imprinted thereon were the marks of at least two pairs of boots, one Commando-soled rubber, the other plain tackets. Both were obviously freshly made, not blurred by the rain, and pointing back in the direction that he had come,

85

southwards.

Adam bit his lip. So he *was* too late. Two of them, at least, were already along behind them. There was no sign of any footprints returning this way.

He hurried down to the edge of the cliff, and began to blink his torch in the agreed series of three dots, pointing it downwards and along. He hoped that the fishermen would have the sense to keep an eye open this way, behind them—also that other folk, up here, would be less keen-eyed. He was partially relieved, at any rate, when quite quickly he perceived an answering dot-dot-dot signal from down below. At least they were warned, now. To try to let them know that the opposition were already south of them, he made a few careful gestures with his torch in that direction, sweeping it the full length of his reach and switching it off each time on the backwards swing. Somebody made an answering wave, which he took to imply comprehension. Switching off, he turned, went back to the path, and turned along it southwards, following those footsteps.

Adam did not hurry so much now. He went heedfully, peering into the gloom ahead, every faculty alert. He had no idea as to how far along those two walkers might have gone, nor whether they intended to climb down—and if so, whether they might have done so yet. They might not be coming back, even, or they might be standing waiting somewhere. He did not like his task, at all. He was not very happy about his back, either; if two had come along here, others might follow them. He could just distinguish the path before him in the gloom— but of course could not see tracks thereon; so every now and again he stooped down, shielding his torch, and confirmed that the footprints still led on. He also frequently glanced behind him. The cluster of lights down on the beach were now motionless, as far as he could judge; presumably the fishermen were prudently waiting for their coble to catch up with them.

It was as well for Adam that the wind was south-westerly, otherwise he might well have walked straight into the men whom he was seeking to stalk. As well also that his quarry had found something to exclaim about and to hold their attention elsewhere. A voice, quite close at hand, came to him on the wind.

"D'you no' see it, man? Look—close in. It's a boat."

"Where? I see nothing. Which way . . . ?"

Adam froze in his tracks, and then slowly lowered himself to his knees. Stare as he would, he could see no sign of men ahead—which must mean that they were down in a slight hollow of the cliff-top directly in front of him, where they would not stand out against the sky. They could be only a few yards away.

"There!" the first voice said, hoarsely. "It's rowing along—I can see the splash o' the oars. No distance out. Just below us, now. Damn it—you policemen wouldna be much use as bailiffs if you canna see that! Now, what the hell are they up to?"

"Which way is it going?"

"This way. Same as those fellows down on the shore, wi' the lights. I wonder . . . ?"

"Aye—aye, I see it now. It's close in, right enough. . . ."

"Look—I reckon that's for these boys to escape in. The ones walking along the shore there. They're barging along, pretending to be looking for trouble. But they're no' so bold as they seem! They've got this boat as a back door open for a quick bolt out to sea. Same as the others did. Canna be anything else. It's just a bluff, Andrews."

"Aye, maybe," the other said, sounding a little doubtful.

"See—you hurry back along to the Inspector. Tell him these chaps have a boat tailing them. Tell him it's a bluff—they're not wanting a fight. Tell him to warn his men down on the shore to lie low, to hide, see. To let these fellows past, then to move in behind them. Between them and their boat. That way he'll cut them off, and get some o' them, for sure. Leave some o' his men in front, to halt them and make a fuss. Then they'll bolt back, sure thing. Into *our* net for a change! Got it?"

"Aye. And you, Mr Hogarth?"

"I'll try and get down this damned cliff, somehow. Further along. It gets easier there, I know. I'll move along behind

87

them—stop any bolting back this way. I'll show a light—to panic them. Right—quick, now. Off wi' you, man. We havena much time."

"Uh-huh. Okay, then."

Adam threw himself flat on the wet grass, and rolled away as far as he could from the path, as a bulky figure loomed up out of the hollow. The man passed only a few yards away—and made just sufficient silhouette against the night sky to reveal the flat-topped cap and short cape of the County Constabulary.

The schoolmaster's mind raced. He had been right about the authorities not necessarily being fools. This man Hogarth who had given the orders—he sounded like one of the Tweed bailiffs, almost certainly—knew what he was doing. The moment that he spotted the coble, tailing along, he had tumbled to the weakness of the fishermen's position. Sandy and his crew were in real danger, now. And only he could do anything about it.

But, what? How could he warn them? The signals that he had arranged, the dots and dashes, did not apply to this situation. Other vague wavings of a torch would only confuse—and anyway would likely be taken for the enemy. Shouts from the cliff-top would never be heard against the noise of the waves. He certainly could not climb down again, in time. There was only the one solution left to him. . . .

Adam was on his feet, and hurrying back along that slippery path, by the time that his reasoning had reached this conclusion. Presumably his instinct had worked more swiftly. But even though his body was obeying his instinct, his mind was not consciously accepting instinctive decisions. He still hurried on in the wake of the policeman, nevertheless.

The fact was, of course, that what the situation demanded was that the constable in front be stopped from reaching his Inspector with his news. As a course of action from a reasonable and responsible citizen, needless to say, this was not even to be considered. Adam did not really consider it, as such. But

88

he ran on—and some more elemental and independent portion of his mind occupied itself with possible ways and means.

The obvious method, of course, was simple, physical and drastic—to waylay the man violently. Adam conceivably might be able to achieve this, given the element of surprise—possibly the rugby-tackle methods that he had once used effectively on Sandy Logan, not a mile from this spot. But that would be only the beginning of it. The policeman would have to be detained, as well as brought low—and he had seemed to be a big man, bigger than Adam Horsburgh. Short of using some sort of blunt instrument on him, this line of procedure did not spell probable success even to the most elementary and primitive part of the schoolmaster's mind. Something a little more comprehensive and effective seemed to be required.

The policeman was visible again in front of Adam now. Evidently he was not hurrying quite so hard as was his pursuer. From the conversation overheard, Adam had not got the impression that he was a mighty intelligent specimen. So much the better.

Adam's urgent feet had already taken him off the path, striking away to the left, inland. The terrain here was rough pasture, dotted with gorse bushes, the land rising gradually, with sheep scattered over it. Actually, the springy turf, though tussocky, made better going than the wet slippery path. Adam was running hard now, and drawing away from the track, in what was intended to be a wide arc. Though this, theoretically, should be a longer route, he hoped that, taking into account the indentations of the cliff line which the path more or less followed, if he went at his fastest, he ought to be able to get in front of the constable.

As he ran, he had little fear of the other seeing him, against the dark slope of the hill. How far to the west of the path he went, he could not tell; but the policeman, when his eyes were not on the track ahead, would be apt to look eastwards, probably, down towards the beach where events were taking place.

Slipping occasionally on the uneven ground, stumbling over

tussocky grass, dodging the gorse and scattering affrighted flouncing sheep, the schoolmaster pounded on. He himself, though he kept glancing down to his right, saw no sign of the other man—which made it difficult to decide when he might have gone far enough, when he might risk going down to the path again. He had all too little ground to play with, as it was, with those police-cars, represented by the blazing headlights, certainly a lot less than half a mile ahead. He must not get too near those.

Puffing and panting, he all too soon decided that he dare not go much further and began to slant down to the path again. Surely, at the rate the other had been going, he would not be this far yet . . . ?

At the track, he paused for a moment or two, staring back, and seeking to control his breathing. No sign of the fellow, yet. He glanced down. The lights of the fishermen's torches were almost directly below him here. They appeared to be stationary for the time being. Sandy Logan was being more cautious, it seemed—as well he might be. Possibly a scout had been sent out . . . ?

Subconsciously squaring his shoulders, Adam started to walk back southwards along the path.

He had not gone a score of paces before he glimpsed the dark figure coming hurrying towards him, outlined momentarily against the sky. He started into a heavy run again, at once. He waved his hand, too, and raised his voice to shout.

"Andrews!" he called. "That you—Constable Andrews?" He hoped that he was right about the rank. The fellow would never be a sergeant; surely, if he had been, the other man, Hogarth, would have called him that, would hardly have spoken to him as he had done?

As they came up with each other, Adam did not give the other time to ask any awkward questions. "Constable Andrews," he said, assuming the most authoritative voice of which he was capable, however breathless. "A new situation's developed. The Inspector's having to change his plans. These men down there—they've got a boat with them. Coming along

90

behind. Almost certainly it's all a bluff—they aren't looking for a fight, at all. Just a ruse to distract us. They won't know that the other poachers got away. The Inspector'll have to lie low—coax them on. Then get between them and the boat. Cut them off. Capture some of them. You and Hogarth are to get down on to the beach as quickly as you can. Come back along behind them. In case any bolt that way. You've got it?" He hoped that he might sound sufficiently authentic, official, informed, so that even though the policeman did not know him he would not think to question his *bona fides*, and assume him to be some sort of representative of higher authority.

The other stared. "That's . . . that's just what I was coming along to tell the Inspector, sir," he panted. "Mr Hogarth sent me. We saw the boat, too. . . ."

"Yes, yes. Well, we'll have to move fast. All of us. We haven't any time to lose. Away back with you, Andrews. To Hogarth. Then down to the beach, wherever you can find a way down. But be careful, for Heaven's sake! These cliffs can be dangerous. Don't break your necks. These confounded fellows aren't worth that! Further along it gets easier. Good luck!"

"Aye. Och, well. Right-o, sir." And meek as any lamb, the constable turned about and went hurrying off into the gloom whence he had come.

Adam Horsburgh let out a long if somewhat tremulous sigh of relief.

His task was not finished yet, however. Letting the policeman get only a little way off, he hurried down to the very lip of the cliff. Unfortunately the fishermen below had started to move on again, still northwards, slowly, but their torches still challenging attention. They could be little more than three hundred yards from the line of those headlights now. Cursing, Adam hurried after them, along the cliff-top some way. Finding a bluff which would shield his own light from the north, he got out his torch and began to blink his dot-dot-dot signal.

Almost immediately there was an acknowledgment flashed

91

from below. At least they were well on the alert down there.

Adam wondered whether he should try shouting—but decided that it was of no use. Not only on account of the noise of the waves; but that it might well be heard, carried on this south-west wind, along at the cars. Nothing for it but to signal—since he could not get down this high steep cliff to them. He had known the Morse Code once, in his Boy Scout days. Could he remember it—or enough to serve . . . ?

Without waiting for a conscious effort of memory, he began to switch his torch off and on, off and on. S and C and R and A and M, he blinked down at them. That was easy. It had to be brief, concise, with the fewer risks of error and confusion. He repeated SCRAM while he teased other letters out of his memory. He could not remember J. P, then. P-R-I-N-G-L-E G-O-N-E, he signalled. Then, since Q eluded him—F-A-S-T. He could not recollect K, so he ended A-W-A-R-E B-O-A-T. It was the best that he could do.

When he was finished, back blinked a light saying O-Something-A-Y. Again, O-Something-A-Y. That must be OKAY. Thankfully he waved his torch in a cross-cross sign, and switched off.

Adam, blessedly, now had only himself to look after. Since it was distinctly possible that other people along that beach might have observed his signals and warned others up at the cars, it behoved him to get away from this area just as quickly and discreetly as he might. He could not wait to see the fishermen embark. The thing to do, he decided, was to head straight inland, up the hill, through the gorse-bushes to the high farmland beyond. The railway threaded this, in a cutting, some way below the main road. If he was to slip down on to the line, and head along it northwards for perhaps half a mile, he would reach the side-road linking Airdmouth with the A1. That was the way home for him.

He followed this programme, in fact, without let or hindrance—if with one or two false alarms and starts occasioned by inoffensive livestock. He did not, however, enter Airdmouth by the road, recognising that it might well be under

92

careful watch for returning malefactors. Instead, just where the road began to descend the cliff to the village, he slipped away to the northwards on a little path that he had discovered led to the shore on that side. He reached his darkened schoolhouse therefore, eventually, from the opposite direction to the trouble spot, via the shore and without incident. Nor was he sorry to be home.

No light shone in all Airdmouth, no hint of life or movement or tension showed. The schoolmaster did nothing to break this calm. He stripped off his wet clothes and gave himself a bath in the dark, and found his way to bed in the same fashion. He would dearly have liked to know how the others had got on—but any attempt to find out, that night, would have been dangerous for all concerned.

Despite all his sins, no bad conscience kept him awake thereafter.

VIII

IT was Sandy Logan's turn again at the drift-netting demonstration, next morning, and, it being Saturday, Adam had arranged to go along. In the circumstances, he was prepared to find the trip cancelled—if indeed Logan was in any position to take his boat to sea. Sleeping late, however—having failed to set his alarm clock in the obscurity of his bed-going—Adam wakened to broad sunshine, to find the village going about its affairs apparently in entire normalcy, and fishermen already laying out the long drift-nets aboard the *Bluebell.*

Swallowing a hasty breakfast, the schoolmaster hurried along to the harbour—only just in time. Sandy Logan was just preparing to cast off, vocally aided by his twin daughters from the pier. Amongst those standing around, in the seemingly timeless manner of fisherfolk, was Jamesy Pringle. No hint or sign of anything out of the usual pervaded the scene. Adam's arrival, however, aroused an ironical cheer aboard *Bluebell.*

"Man, Adam," the skipper called out genially, "we were near away withoot you. We peeked in your window a whilie back, but hadna the hert to disturb your long lie!"

"Hang it—do you people *never* sleep?" Adam demanded, jumping aboard.

"Och, there's times for sleeping and times for doing other things, man. We'll get forty winks while we're lying to the nets, oot there."

"You should see us in the kirk, the morn!" somebody put in.

"Might as well be in oor beds for a' the good *this* trip'll do us, anyway!" Tosh Hogg declared. "It's a bluidy . . ." The rest was drowned in the noise of the diesels, as the skipper revved up.

As they chugged away from the pier, Sandy raised his great voice. "We'll pick up the cobles on the way back, Jamesy," he called.

"Aye then, Sandy."

"Where are they? The cobles?" Adam asked.

"Och, they're in a wee bit haven we ca' The Bield, a couple o' miles up the coast. We put in there wi' them last night, and walked hame. One by one, sort of. We found Jamesy there, when we put in. A handy wee place, yon. Used to be two-three houses—but it's deserted, noo." The big man smiled "Thanks for your bit ploy last night, Adam. Yon was real nice."

"Fancy a guy like you kenning the Morse Code!" Tosh added. "Leastways, sort of!"

Somebody else standing by the wheelhouse growled some similar acknowledgment.

Adam felt absurdly embarrassed. He knew how difficult it was for these men to express conventional admiration or gratitude. Almost anything came easier to them. "Straight out of 'Scouting for Boys'!" he said lightly. "In fact, the whole thing was pretty much Boy Scout stuff. I stalked a big-footed copper and a chap I took to be a bailiff—Hogarth by name— up on the cliff-top, overheard what they said about spotting your coble coming along behind you, and waylaid the copper as he went along to warn the Inspector in charge. I gathered that Pringle's lot had got away. Then I had to warn *you*. Tricky, when I'd forgotten practically all the Morse Code except the vowels!"

"Man, I hope you didna hurt the poor polisman that much!" Sandy said, shaking his head. "We canna have a' this violence! Tut, no! The rest o' us didna touch a hair o' their heads!"

"Well, I'm damned . . . !"

"George Hogarth's the name o' one o' the Tweed bailiffs, aye," Tosh Hogg confirmed. "You said there was an Inspector in it, too? Would yon be the polis, or the head bummer o' the bailiffs? They ca' him an Inspector, too. Either way, it looks like it was a right expedition against us, last night."

"Yes. It certainly does. Goodness knows how many men were involved. It strikes me that we were mighty lucky to get away with it unscathed."

"No' just unscathed, maybe," Logan amended. "Jamesy

had to cut his nets and run for it. He'd just shot them, when the polis showed up. Couldna do anything else. They were right on top o' him. He and his boys got away in their coble, but the polis got the net. It's a big loss—£25 these wear-nets cost."

"The first charge on the Fighting Fund! That's bad, though. Still, compared with what might have been . . ." Adam shook his head. "I was a bit worried about the police maybe catching people as they came back home, afterwards. I made a pretty cautious homecoming, myself, I can tell you! They must have been fairly sure that it was Airdmouth folk. Even if they couldn't catch us red-handed."

"Aye—that's why we came back one at a time," the skipper said. "They were watching the village, right enough. I seen two o' them, mysel'—but they didna see me! Jamesy and two others had to spend the night in the net loft! No' that the polis could of done much, mind, by then. They need to be getting us in the act, like."

"You didn't have the salmon with you?"

"No, no. The fish are still in boxes under water at The Bield. No' a bad haul, considering, either. Sixty pounds weight, all told, maybe. It'll aye help."

"Yes. But it's not worth it, just the same. This poaching, I mean. All this bears out what I've said from the start. It's too risky. If even one of us had been caught, from Airdmouth, it could have played the devil with our case. *They* know that, too. That's why they staged this raid—on such a large scale. . . ."

"Aye, maybe they do ken it," Tosh Hogg interrupted. "But tell me this—hoo do they ken aboot the poaching, at a'? Tell me that. Hoo did they ken we'd be oot last night?"

A little surprised at the way that was directed at himself, Adam blinked. "I don't know," he said. "I've no idea. Unless they just took a chance."

"No' them. Yon was a well organised raid. They didna do a' that on chance. They kenn't a' right. What *I* want to ken is who tell't them?"

"Why should anybody have told them? After all, they're

quite capable of putting two and two together. They possibly think that we're not likely to get all the amount of fish we are getting, out at sea. So the only other thing is that we're poaching it."

"Hoo do they ken hoo much fish we're getting?"

"They may have ways of finding out. I suppose Sinton may have gone to them—though I wouldn't think it likely."

"Me neither. If Sinton reckoned the fish were frae Airdmouth, and talked, he'd be getting hissel' into trouble right away for buying them. No, it's no' Sinton. It's yon girlfriend o' yours I'm worried aboot!"

Adam frowned. "Don't be absurd, Hogg," he jerked. "You know very well that it's thanks to Miss Scott that we managed to sell our salmon at all. She did a big thing for us—because she sympathised with our cause. She made herself an accomplice after the fact, for us. After that, would she turn round and betray us?" He coughed. "And, for the second time, she's no girlfriend of mine. I never saw her before that night of the meeting."

"Ooh, aye. Fine, that. But, look—what if they just used her as a trap? Eh? She got that first haul sold for us, aye—but you'd hae to tell her a good bittie first, I reckon? Did you no'? You couldna get her to dae what she did withoot telling her?"

"No. Naturally not. But I was careful what I said. I hardly mentioned the poaching. . . ."

"*Hardly*, eh? But any mention o' it would be enough, man. Maybe she just hardly mentioned it, too—to her dad! That'd be enough—aye, plenty. She's Sir John Bluidy Scott's daughter and that's plenty for *me*!"

"You're wrong, Hogg—I'm perfectly sure you're wrong. And I don't altogether like your manner, I may say!"

"My manner doesna matter a damn, man! What matters is that the polis are on to us—and you'll no' tell me they havena been *put* on to us."

"I don't think that necessarily follows. But anyway, there are plenty of other people who could have talked. The whole of Airdmouth knows about the poaching. Anybody could have talked—not deliberately perhaps. . . ."

"Nobody's ever talked before—and we've been taking fish a' oor days. Just noo, it is—a couple o' days after you tell't yon lassie—that the polis are on to us."

"Confound it, man . . . !"

Sandy Logan intervened. He had seemed to be concentrating all this while on steering the *Bluebell* out over the sun-kissed jabbly waters. "Och, you don't want to mind Tosh overmuch, Adam," he declared now, easily. "He's got a right coorse way wi' him, sometimes. No' but what there may be something in what he says, mind. Maybe Sir John Scott's daughter's no' just the safest one to be sort o' mixed up wi', in this."

Hot words sprang to Adam's lips, but he choked them back. "I think my judgment, in that, is as good as anyone's," he said, quietly.

"Maybe you're right. You did a fine job, Adam, getting a' that money frae Sinton—and if it was maistly Miss Scott's doing, as you say, we're grateful. Aye. But she might of let something oot, just the same—by mistake, you ken. It's easy done, especially in her ain family. Och, I think it would be safer, maybe, to sort o' leave her oot o' it, in future, Adam."

"I think you've got the wrong end of the stick, altogether."

"Maybe we have. But we canna take too many risks, can we?"

"Apply that to your night-poaching, then! That's where the real risks are being taken."

"Ooh, aye. I'ph'mm. Tosh—take the wheel a wee. I'll need to be having a right look at the chart and the sounder, for this bit. . . ."

Adam bit his lip, and turned away.

They were almost directly off Berwick now—and much nearer to the actual pier and harbour mouth than they had risked hitherto. Theoretically, the closer in to the mouth of the river they went, the more likely they were to catch salmon. Moreover, since the authorities had at last made a move against them at Airdmouth, it seemed probable that things would come to a head here also. So, this being possibly their last gesture in these troubled waters, they decided that they might as well make the most of it. Today they were going to flaunt their challenge on the Tweed Commissioners' very door-step.

Sandy spread a battered and stained chart over the steel top of the echo-sounder charging-box, and worked a pair of dividers over it. He glanced keenly at landmarks, and the sounder's depth readings, and nodded. "Another couple o' hundred yards or so, and we're dead on the mile frae the Queen Elizabeth Pier-head," he decided. "Wi' this wind against the tide, we'll no drift far." He thrust his head out of the wheel-house. "Right boys—we'll shoot here, and be damned to them!"

So once again *Bluebell* was brought round stern into the wind, south-westerly this time, and the long series of nets and floats and sinkers were paid out. Then, the dark sail was hoisted, and swinging round they lay heaving and dipping to their nets, so close to Berwick and Tweedmouth that they could watch individual walkers on the seafront.

"Noo, we'll see what happens," Sandy said.

They had more than an hour to wait, in fact, before anything happened at all—by which time the *Bluebell's* crew were fast asleep in various curious attitudes and corners. It was left to Adam, therefore, first to spy the motor-launch that rounded the long sickle of Berwick's great pier and breakwater, and came heading directly for them.

"Sandy," he called, almost with relief that at length the tense waiting was in sight of its end. "I think we're going to have visitors."

The skipper was wide awake immediately. "Aye, then—this is it boys. We've shamed them into it, this time!"

The launch, a powerful if clumsy craft of the converted cabin-cruiser type, came out fast, straight for them, its well seemingly tight-packed with men. Readily distinguished amongst them was the dark figure of a police-officer, with silver braid on the peak of his cap.

"You'd of thought they'd have risen to an admiral, Jings!"

99

Tosh Hogg jeered. "Yon's your pal Hogarth, Adam—the bailiff. The one wi' the black oilskins."

The launch swung round to windward of *Bluebell*, and throttled back her motor at about twenty yards' distance.

Sandy Logan got in the first salvo. "Fine day, aye," he called. "You for the fishing? Keep your distance, will you? I wouldna want you fouling my nets."

It was the bailiff Hogarth who answered, as the two boats lay stationary, within easy speaking distance. "You're Alexander Logan, Airdmouth," he asserted, rather than asked. "I suppose you know what you're doing, man?"

"Aye. I'm drifting for salmon."

"Then you're breaking the law, man. And you know it."

"I ken nothing o' the sort."

"Then you ought to. You Airdmouth people know the Tweed regulations as well as anybody else. There's no use playing the daft laddie, Logan. You're flagrantly breaking the law, and it's got to stop."

"Which law are you talking aboot, Mr Hogarth? The law o' Scotland, by any chance?"

"Don't come that stuff with me, Logan," the other jerked. "The regulations concerning salmon fishing at the mouth o' the Tweed are perfectly plain, as laid down by Act o' Parliament. You are deliberately breaking these, now—and have been for days. We've been very patient with you . . ."

"Why?" That was Adam Horsburgh speaking, and the single word came out like a whip-crack.

The bailiff paused, peering at Adam. "Eh . . . ?" he said, a little less certainly.

"I said why? Why be patient with us, if you are so sure of the law? Surely, assuming that you have any authority in the matter at all, your duty is to enforce the law, not to make exceptions to it, in the name of patience or anything else? If you think these regulations you speak of are enforceable, why haven't you enforced them before this?"

The authoritative confident tones, as much as the unexpected line of approach, undoubtedly shook the spokesman of the other side—a man of middle years and strong features, dressed in Lovat tweed and a black oilskin coat. He turned to look at the police-officer and at another man in uniform, both of whom frowned heavily but did not undertake any of the burden of discussion.

"I don't know who *you* are, sir?" Hogarth went on, recovering himself. "But I assure you that the regulations are clear and precise. And enforceable. All laid down by the Act. As are the penalties for doing what you *are* doing! Heavy fines, of up to £500. Confiscation of boats, nets and gear . . ."

"I don't think that you have come out here to confiscate us, just the same!" Adam interrupted, strongly, taking a chance. "Have you?"

Hogarth cleared his throat. "That depends . . ."

"Quite! It depends on what you think you can get away with, doesn't it?"

"My God—who is it that's trying to get away with it! Of all the damned nerve . . . !"

"We seem to be talking at cross purposes," Adam went on steadily. "The reason for that is perfectly plain, too. We are talking about two different things, entirely. You are talking about regulations, and we're talking about law. The law of Scotland—under which all issues relating to the Tweed fall to be decided. And regulations, as you should know, even statutory ones, take second place to the law. They must abide by the law of the land—otherwise they're invalid. Yours don't."

That was not quite so accurate a statement as it sounded, nor so simple, but it might pass.

The bailiff did not answer for a moment or two. The *Bluebell's* crew, taking the keenest interest in this exchange, took the opportunity to support Adam with far from *sotto voce* encouragements. Many heads seemed to be put together on the launch.

Hogarth returned to the attack. "This sea-lawyer's talk will get you nowhere," he asserted heavily. "The Tweed Act was passed in 1857. These regulations have stood for a hundred years. You needn't think . . ."

"That's because they've never been challenged. In a court of law. Challenged as to validity. Well—we're doing that now. Challenging them. Are you going to take us to court?"

"Damn it, man—you don't know what you're saying! You can't fish for salmon, like you can for other fish—by the law o' Scotland more especially. It's stronger on that than the law o' England, in fact."

"Because of the Crown's rights, only. And the Crown's rights in salmon fishing go out only for one mile beyond low-water. That's the law of it. And we are, at the moment, just a hundred yards or so outside that mile. You can do nothing about it."

"You're . . . you're talking nonsense."

"You wouldn't say that if you were a lawyer, Mr . . . er . . . Hogarth, is it? You didn't take the precaution of seeking Counsel's Opinion before you came out here this morning, did you? We did, you see. Which puts you at rather a disadvantage, doesn't it? Hard on you. I advise you to go back to Berwick, go to Edinburgh, in fact, and seek Counsel's Opinion, before you try to interfere with other citizens exercising their legal rights on the high seas—which is an offence in itself, you know!"

The bailiff all but choked. His colleagues looked at the sky, the sea, anywhere but at each other. The police-officer particularly, seemed as though he felt that he really ought to be somewhere else.

When Hogarth found his voice again, it was evident that he had lost something else—his self-control. "Damn you!" he shouted. "Of all the blasted cheek! You—a collection of dirty poachers! Crooks! Don't think, because you got away with it last night, you will again! We'll get you, all right! We know you. Just damned poaching riff-raff you are—for all your high talk! You watch yourselves . . . !"

"Mr Hogarth—are you accusing me—or any one of us—of poaching! Here, in public? In front of witnesses? Including an officer of police? That is a grave charge, I'd remind you. Have you any proof of your accusation? If not, then I'd advise you to take it back—at once!"

"We've got your nets, confound you!"

"Whose nets? If you have some nets or other, can you say whose they are? They are certainly not mine—nor anyone's here. We've lost no nets. Officer—I think, for his own sake, that you ought to restrain Mr Hogarth. He has already made at least one actionable statement."

The policeman, an inspector apparently, coughed. He turned a shoulder to the *Bluebell* and spoke in Hogarth's ear. A second man at the other side did likewise. Something of a discussion developed, with the bailiff seemingly fighting a rearguard action. Then suddenly the water at the stern of the launch began to churn whitely, as, without warning, she surged ahead. Round, south-about, she swung away. Back over the growing gap between the two craft Hogarth's angry voice came unevenly.

"We'll be back!" he shouted. "Don't think you're getting away wi' anything. You're bluffing—we know that! We'll get you, all right. You'll be sorry for this, I tell you. . . ."

The rest was lost in the delighted chorus of acclaim and triumph from the *Bluebell's* complement.

"Jings, Adam—you were bluidy marvellous!" Tosh cried. "You fair ca'd the feet frae under yon stinker! Did you see the polisman's face?"

Adam would have disclaimed modestly if he could—as well as issuing necessary and solemn warning. But Sandy Logan had slapped him on the back, with his great hand and major force, and the schoolmaster was utterly silent. Not before time, perhaps.

Thereafter, as they waited, drifting to their long line of nets, Adam was less successful in convincing the fishermen of the probably very temporary nature of their victory, plus some of the inherent weaknesses of their position, than he had been in upsetting the Berwick party. He pointed out that Hogarth and the others were only the minions of the people whom they were really fighting, not the principals. Talking them out of

103

countenance was one thing; defeating their long-established and highly placed masters was quite another.

Certainly it seemed that the authorities were not too sure of themselves. They had put off taking this straightforward action for as long as they could; they had preferred to try to catch out their challengers as it were by the back door, at the poaching; and fairly clearly, when at last they had been forced to act, Hogarth had been told to frighten the offenders, warn them off, threaten them, rather than to take the obvious but drastic line of arrest and confiscation. He could have done this, under the Act; he did not require the police to be present, or to do it for him. Bailiffs had powers equal to the constabulary, to apprehend and take in charge, within the Tweed Act area. The fact that he had brought the police inspector with him might be significant or might not. It might have meant that he had been afraid of violent resistance—or again, merely that it could be a help to overawe the fishermen.

The main point was, however, that though Adam's exchange with the bailiff had sounded stirring and strong and assured, it would not have sounded so well had there been a lawyer in the other boat. He had made a lot of large statements, some of them distinctly debatable. So much depended on the question of whether the other side would decide to risk making a stand on the doctrine of the sovereignty of Parliament—a doctrine not implicit in Scots law . . .

This, needless to say, was quite beyond the crew of the *Bluebell*. They saw the position much more simply; realistically too. They had won the first round—that was undeniable; won a round that they had not expected to win. That was cause for cheers, surely—not gloomy fears about the future?

Adam had to admit that, eventually. But he insisted, when it came to the real and final showdown, that he would much prefer it to take place on a rather different battleground—out beyond the three-mile limit. There, he felt, they could really force the issue, infallibility of Parliament or none—for of course Parliament was equally committed to the wider support of the international three-mile limit; more so. And, in view of

104

the Icelandic dispute, to fight for this curious five-mile ban here would be embarrassing to the legislators in the extreme.

Nobody disagreed with that.

This rather one-sided and unsatisfactory discussion was cut short by the skipper's decision to haul nets, a good two hours having elapsed since they were shot. Adam promptly became the least important and disregarded member of the company.

This time, they were spared the jellyfish. Congratulations on that score, however, were premature. In the second net to come in was a fair-sized salmon—but its appearance aroused no cheers from the fishermen; cut cleanly out of its silver back were two large red bites, each fully a hand's breadth across. One had severed the backbone, so that the fish hung crookedly in the mesh.

"Bluidy seals!" Tosh cried. "Look what the brutes have done! Five quid gone—in twa bites!"

"Seals . . . ?" Adam panted, snatching weed and starfish from the moving net. "Are there seals here? Would seals do that . . . ?"

"Aye, they would. They're deevils, the brutes—a right menace. Robbing the nets. They come frae the Farne Islands."

"But so close in as this . . . ?"

"Aye, it's seals all right," Sandy Logan confirmed. "They ken where the salmon lie, the critturs. The Berwick boys sometimes get them right inshore. This could be bad. . . ."

It was bad. As the next net appeared above the surface, it was seen that no fewer than four salmon had been caught in its meshes. But of these only one small fish was intact; of the others, one had only the head remaining, held in the mesh by the gills, one was only half a fish, and the last had a single large bite out of its belly.

A wrathful chorus arose from the boat. More than one seal was involved in this.

Before the fourth net appeared above water, heavings and convulsions were visible to all. Not even Adam required to be told what that meant. They had caught more than salmon, this time.

Sandy shouted out warnings and instruction. Men grabbed boat-hooks and batons. The turmoil in the water grew.

Sandy ordered the mechanical hauler to be cut out, and switched on the diesels. He manoeuvred *Bluebell* round slowly, carefully, until she lay almost alongside their streaming line of nets instead of bows-on to it—risky work, lest the least tendril of the meshes or float-ropes should foul the screw. Then, the engine shut off again, boat-hooks reached out to draw the heaving net close.

The seal was quite easily seen now, plunging and twisting, grey-brown and mottled, and much larger than Adam had anticipated—eight or nine feet long at least.

"Canny, noo—watch it! Watch it!" Sandy called, "Dinna frighten the brute mair'n you can help till you get it close. It's an auld bull—you can see its ears. Pity we didna bring the rifle."

"You're going to kill it? Must you?"

"Aye, we must," Logan answered grimly. "Better if we could of shot it dead before it could do any mair damage."

"It's the way nature made it, isn't it? And aren't seals protected by law?"

"Maybe they are. But look, Adam man—yon brute'll kill twenty salmon in a day, easy. Just bites oot o' each. And what aboot my nets? There's near half-a-ton o' wickedness there, thrashing aboot. It'll have made a bonny mess o' my net, if I'm no' mistaken—and'll make mair yet before we're through wi' it. Tosh—you right?"

"Aye, aye, Sandy."

Adam took one look at the big round eyes and old-man face of that seal, and then looked away. The clubbing to death of the creature was not a pretty business, and he wanted no part in it. Yet the fishermen's point of view could not be dismissed. When at length it lay still, and the difficult process of disentangling the bloody carcase from the meshes went forward, that point of view became the more evident. Lengths of the net were dragged aboard ripped and torn, and by the time that the body at last sank away into the depths, all knew that the nylon net

106

was a write-off.

"There's another £30 gone, then," Sandy Logan said heavily. "I'm no' that keen on killing things, Adam, but . . . we'll bring the rifle another time! We couldna have got it oot that net alive, anyway."

"They're a right pest," Tosh declared, washing his blood-stained hands. "And so are the mimsy-mamsy city folk who winna have them kill't. They dinna cost *them* anything! Every year the numbers o' them increase in yon Farnes. There's bluidy thousands o' them, now. They're spreading right up the coast to the Tay, they tell me. They'll kill mair salmon than a' the fishermen put thegether."

Adam did not attempt to argue that.

The two remaining nets were brought in, and produced only one undamaged salmon out of six—another blacktail, or immature fish. Clearly the seals went for the best fish. Clearly too, they had been on a good line for the salmon, here.

Arising out of these two facts, discussion developed as to what to do now. To try another shot, or not? If that had been the only seal, they might yet do well. If not, then they were only asking for further loss.

Sandy, whose nets were at stake, eventually decided upon a compromise. To go home now, he felt, might look from the shore as though the bailiff's visit had in fact scared them off early. Which would never do. Assuming that the seals were operating fairly close inshore, where the salmon could be expected to be thickest, they would go a bit further out—perhaps half a mile—and shoot their nets once more.

That they did—but only five nets now, instead of six.

They had not been lying in their new position long when a boat rounded Berwick's pier-head again, and came out towards them. It was not the same launch, this time, but a fishing-boat roughly similar to their own, only larger. Various were the suggestions as to her purpose.

As she drew closer, Sandy frowned, and reached for his glasses. "Tosh—d'you see that?" he said. "They've got sacks hung over their registration number. I wonder, noo, what's the meaning o' that?"

"Maybe some boys just feeling friendly—but dinna want the bailiffs to ken who they are?"

"Maybe coming to dae a bit o' fishing on their ain . . . ?"

"Aye—competition!"

The big man shook his head.

The newcomer did not slow down as she approached *Bluebell*. She did not come too near, either. She passed approximately a hundred yards south of them—and the only man of her crew evident was anonymous in yellow oilskin and sou'wester. Then, almost a cable's length beyond them, she suddenly ported her helm and swung round in a tight curve behind *Bluebell*—and kept on turning.

"Jings—she's heading straight for oor bluidy nets!" Tosh cried. "Damn it—she'll foul them!"

"The right stupid fools . . . !"

"Curse them—they're crazy!"

Sure enough, the other craft was bearing down directly, at full speed, on the centre of the line of five nets, plainly marked as they were by the yellow floats and the marker-buoy and flag.

Bluebell's crew began to shout and wave and point. Sandy Logan said nothing, but his great hands showed white at the knuckles as he gripped the wheelhouse door.

Two splashes astern of the newcomer caught everyone's attention. Sandy's breath came out in a long sigh.

"Aye," he said. "So that's it. Grapnels!"

"Eh?" Adam stared. "What d'you mean—grapnels?"

"Simple!" the other said, raspingly. "They're towing a couple o' hooks behind them. Right ower and through my nets!"

"But . . . but, Good Lord—you mean they're going to deliberately damage the nets?"

"Just that. Damage is maybe no' just the word to use, either!"

Logan's other colleagues did not require these explanations. Their shouts rose to a crescendo of rage, and pointing hands changed into clenched and shaking fists.

108

The other craft however went on, unheeding. Right across the line of yellow floats it went, and a moment or two later the watchers saw that line abruptly convulse and jerk and disintegrate. Immediately the boat pulled round, away from them, and went off parallel to the line, its grapnels dragging and tearing behind it. Right to the end of the line, past the marker-buoy, it went, and then turned and came back on its tracks, towards *Bluebell*. It was only too clear, now, what it was doing. Its grapnels would not sever the strong messenger-warp on which the nets were strung, so it was dragging its hooks up and down the line, below that level, to shatter the nylon meshes below.

Only the skipper was silent aboard *Bluebell*. Adam had to shout too, to make himself heard. "This is unbelievable—utterly devilish!" he cried. "Is there nothing you can do?"

The other shook his head. "No' a thing. We're tied doon to these nets. If we cast adrift frae them, chewed up like yon, wi' a' the floats jiggered, we'll lose them. Or what's left o' them. Anyway, we'd never catch up wi' yon craft—she can sail faster'n we can. A couple o' knots faster. Man . . . if I could only get my hands on them! If I could only get my two hands on them!"

"Sandy—cut the bluidy nets loose, and after them!" Tosh exclaimed, having difficulty in getting words out, and white with anger. "Ram the baistards! The stinking dirty low-doon baistards!"

"No use," the skipper jerked. "She's got the heels o' us. Or she wouldna be doing it. She'd make rings roond us."

"Goad, man—why didna you bring your rifle!"

It was maddening, infuriating, to stand there and watch, helpless. With the utmost deliberation the anonymous boat went about its business of destruction. Having come two-thirds of the way back towards *Bluebell*, it turned seawards again, seemed as though it was going to disengage, and then swung back to resume the process, men busy at her stern. They had done something to the cables towing the grapnels—short-ened them, Sandy said between clenched teeth, in order to make a new line of tearing, slightly higher up. These people paid not the least heed to the savage yells and challenges from *Bluebell*—indeed they seemed determined not even to look in the direction of their victims.

It was all over in a remarkably short time. On its second return beat, the craft, when it pulled away seawards, just continued on in that direction, dragging in its grapnels. One obviously would not come, so that rope was running out as the boat moved further away. They saw a man pick up an axe and cut through this rope at the gunwale. The other grapnel came inboard, long streamers of netting still attached to its hooks. The craft swung away round behind *Bluebell* in a wide arc, and headed back towards Berwick.

For a time, on the Airdmouth boat, only the incoherent expression of wrath prevailed—though its owner remained almost wholly silent. Then abruptly he smote the side of the wheelhouse with his open hand, a blow that made the timbers shake.

"Quiet!" he roared. "Quiet! A' the lot o' you. No' another word. Get these nets in. Switch on the hauler."

Eyeing him askance, the men went to work in sudden silence. Adam himself moved just a pace or two further from the big man—a wholly instinctive move of which he was scarcely aware. The quietly genial Sandy Logan, at that moment, was quietly terrifying.

The first net came in undamaged, with even a small salmon caught in it—the other boat had not risked coming near enough *Bluebell* to reach this. But all the further half of the second one was torn into ribbons. The third was no more than a tangled mass of loose ends and trailing strands. In the fourth, the jettisoned grapnel itself was still held amongst the ruin, its prongs wound round with tattered nylon. Of the fifth, there was hardly anything left at all; being the end net, it had been torn almost right off.

In silence the fishermen brought in the residue of the floats and ropes, and coiled in the messenger-warp. Before they had finished, Logan had the diesels started up and the *Bluebell's* prow swinging round to the north.

"Are you no' going into Berwick?" Tosh burst out. "Are you no' going in there to create bluidy hell, man?"

"No," his skipper said, shortly.

"But, Sandy—we're no' taking this lying doon? There's two hundred quid's worth o' damage done there! You're no' standing for that, Jings? Let's awa' in to bluidy Berwick, and tear the toon apart!"

"Isna that just what they want us to do?" the other snapped. "Put oorsel's in the wrong? Use your head, Tosh, instead o' your big mouth, for a change!"

"But, man . . . !"

"Quiet, I say!"

After a little, Tosh, greatly venturing, spoke again—but he addressed his remarks carefully to Adam Horsburgh. "Did you see yon guy in the wheelhoose, wi' the helmsman? He never came oot. In black oilies and a black sou'wester. Yon was George Hogarth, I'll be bound."

"Surely not," Adam said. "I can't believe that. Not Hogarth—not one of the official bailiffs. Official people would never stoop to this sort of thing."

"Would they no'? No' officially, maybe—but this wasna done officially. Yon was Hogarth, I'm willing to bet. Who else would dae the likes o' that, anyway?"

"Some of the Berwick fishermen, perhaps? The salmon fishers themselves? Resentful at us fishing in their waters."

"No' them. They wouldna dae a thing like that, to other fishermen. Would they, boys?"

There was a chorus of agreement on this point. All seemed convinced that it was authority that had acted thus, under the cloak of anonymity.

"If they canna get us the one way, they'll get us the other!" Tosh summed up. "I ken them. We should of gone right in to Berwick, and showed them two can play dirt, if it's dirt they want!"

Into the murmur of support for this view. Sandy Logan spoke. "We'd have ended up in jail, then, this day. Much good

111

that would have done oor case. They darena charge us and take us to court for fishing there—and they ken *we* darena charge them wi' what they did, for we couldna prove who did it. Anyway, *this* is no' the case we want to go to court on. We've got to swallow this, the way they had to swallow Adam's bit talk—if we're going ahead wi' oor fight."

"I hate to say it," Adam nodded. "But I fear you're right."

IX

ADAM saw practically all his associates in the salmon-taking venture, both legitimate and otherwise, in church the following forenoon. Fishermen have usually been amongst the most forthright practitioners of religion, from Galilean days onwards. Not for them the elaborate or casual luxuries of doubt and reservation; people whose life is spent at close grips with coastal seas tend to come to certain fairly definite conclusions on eternal verities quite early on.

The Reverend Fraser preached simply but vigorously on the possibility of hating sin but still managing to love one's fellow sinners. Never had Adam heard more lusty and mainly masculine hymn-singing. Sandy Logan was officiating as an elder with every appearance of normalcy.

After the service, most of the men, unnatural-looking in navy-blue suits, collars and ties, and tweed caps still in sharp enough folds to seem flat and new-bought, strolled down to the harbour. Caught up in conversation, Adam found himself there also. He was interested, and not a little concerned, as to popular reaction to yesterday's troubles.

If he had anticipated any mood of defeat, of hopelessness, even of a suggestion for going slow in their campaign, such fears were quickly dispelled. The general demand seemed to be rather for a quickening of the tempo of the fight, a peeling off of kid gloves, a striking of retaliatory blows forthwith.

The making good of Sandy Logan's losses out of the Fighting Fund was taken for granted, and the need to build up the Fund swiftly, substantially, was the more apparent. Adam did not contest this; indeed he perceived that if legal fees and possible fines were to be forthcoming from it, as had been the original intention, there would have to be very considerable replenishment, otherwise replacement of damaged or confiscated gear was going to swallow the lot.

113

How this was to be done was where they differed, of course. The fishermen were unanimous that it must be done, could only be done, by further and more profitable night poaching. Adam, still firmly against this policy—less on ethical grounds admittedly, than that it was too risky, too dangerous—advocated other methods of raising money, *any* other methods. He was on weak ground here, however, since he had no practical suggestions as to how sufficient cash could be produced in the short time, alternatively.

He was distinctly surprised when, arising out of this discussion, Tosh Hogg announced that there was another van-load of salmon waiting to be sold. Would Adam take it to the man Sinton the following afternoon? There should be almost another two hundred pound's worth in it, at the least.

The schoolmaster stared. "How can that be?" he demanded. "We haven't done well enough recently, for that. There was about sixty pounds' weight, wasn't there, from our interrupted poaching? And we didn't get enough, yesterday, with those wretched seals, to make so much difference to that . . . ?"

Tosh grinned. "Some o' us had a bit ploy last night, see you, Adam. A kind o' profitable ploy, too!"

"You mean you've been out poaching again! Last night? Confound it, man—this is crazy! It's just asking for trouble, for a complete finish to all our efforts. They'll be watching this place like hawks, now—you can be certain. I should think there's a patrol or picket of some sort permanently stationed round about Airdmouth, each night. . . ."

"Och, aye—we ken that. But it wasna near here we were operating, see. We went along to Berwick."

"Good Lord—to Berwick! You mean, poaching there? After dark? And after the Saturday evening close-time?"

"Just that. Why no'? We've got sort o' accounts to settle wi' bluidy Berwick, mind!"

"But that was just thrusting your heads into a noose! Berwick, of all places . . . !"

"No' us. The safest bit we could be, likely. They'd never look for us, there, on their ain doorstep. We reckoned it was

114

the best thing to do. It's the best place for the salmon, too—right at the mouth o' the Tweed. And don't thae Berwickers ken it! We proved it, too—we got fifty-four fish in three shots. Near five hundred pounds' weight! Yon's the place, a' right. Just behind the pier, we were, nicely oot o' sight. It was a fine dark night."

"You . . . you weren't seen? There was no trouble?"

"No' a cheep. It was a long row doon, wi' the coble—but och, it was worth it. Yon'll help to pay for Sandy's nets."

"May be. But . . . was Sandy in it, too?"

"No' me, Adam." Logan had joined the group, coming down late from his vestry duties after the service. "I didna ken anything aboot it. Tosh's idea, it was."

"And a damned risky idea, too! It may have come off once, but . . ."

"It's no' mair risky poaching there, Adam, than here. Less, I'd say—for they arena' looking for us there. And sort o' . . . what's the word? Poetic justice?" The big man shrugged, "Mind, I don't say I'd of said that a couple o' days ago. But things are different, noo. It's war to the knife, is it no'? We canna go on, withoot nets—as well they ken. We need money, big money, to buy new nets. It was in the interests o' the legal salmon fisheries o' Berwick that oor nets were destroyed. Right, then—let the same boys provide the salmon for new nets! They can well afford it."

"Aye, Sandy."

"Jings, yes!"

Adam perceived that he might as well save his breath. Besides, of course, he recognised that there was something in what they said. There was an inevitability about the entire campaign, which seemed to militate against half-measures. Presumably, if he had not been prepared to go all the way, he ought never to have started it. There was no withdrawal for him now, anyway—that was obvious. Though if he could have foreseen all this. . . .

"Well, we'll see about that," he said, rather feebly. He shifted his ground. "So I've to be the hawker of the poached fish again, have I?" He was deliberately sour, "*I've* got to lug the stuff into Berwick each time, and haggle over it. Despite the fact that you don't trust my judgment over Miss Scott . . . !"

"Sinton kens you, noo," Tosh pointed out.

"Just this once mair, Adam," Sandy said. "We wouldna want you to be troubled wi' it, other times. But we canna send any other man wi' it to Sinton. Who'd we say it's frae? You didna give him your name, mind. We couldna say it's frae Miss Scott. Besides, Sinton kens us Airdmouth chaps by sight, well enough. Most o' us, anyhow."

"He'll know, too, very well, where the fish are coming from. Who's behind it," Adam declared. "After yesterday, everybody in Berwick will know that."

"Aye—but it's a different thing kenning, and having to do something aboot it! When he's making a big profit oot o' it. So long as he can say he has no knowledge that the folk selling the salmon come frae Airdmouth. . . . Look, Adam—I've been thinking. If we send Dod Elliot wi' you, this time, so's Sinton gets to ken him—then *he* could do it after this. Dod's sort o' new to Airdmouth—he came frae Dunbar. Folk in Berwick dinna ken him yet. And he could drive the van."

"Well—if you like. . . ."

So on Monday afternoon, the day before the start of the Easter vacation, Adam hurried from afternoon school once again to Berwick-on-Tweed, sitting in the old green van this time, with Dod Elliot—a stolid middle-aged fisherman with practically nothing to say for himself, and a powerfully smelling pipe.

They drew up with the usual unnervingly loud squealing of ancient brakes outside the pend in Quality Street. Adam felt more than a little bit doubtful about the business, despite the good terms on which he had last parted from Sinton. Whilst he had no fears whatsoever that Hazel Scott might have informed the authorities about the Airdmouth poaching, it seemed probable that somebody had done so, deliberately or inadvertently. And Sinton could not be ruled out, for outside Airdmouth he was theoretically the only person in a position to talk, other than the girl. Admittedly it did not seem likely that he would have done so, in view of his own financial involvement; but nothing was certain. He need not necessarily have initiated any move himself; the police might have come and interrogated him. That woman in the white coat might well have gone to the police, and they could have made a round of the other fish-salesmen. In which case, what would John Sinton's attitude be now? What sort of a reception was he running into?

The fat man, in fact, received them affably enough, and plunged straight into talk about Miss Scott and her father. Great was his admiration for Sir John, and of course his daughter, it seemed. Fine people. Settled at Linburndean for centuries. None of the jumped-up kind. Public figure, Sir John, too. Never actually in the Government—but close to it, close. Pity there was no son. But Miss Hazel, of course, was a fine young woman. Able. Vigorous. Mind of her own. Ran the estate as well as any man. Good head on her shoulders. . . .

Adam tried once or twice to stem this tide, without success. His efforts in that direction, however, became more determined and urgent when the other began to interlard his panegyric on the Scott family with questions as to how they were, whether his caller was seeing much of them, whether perhaps he might be a relative, and so on.

"Look, Mr Sinton," he managed to say, during a long-overdue pause for breath on the salesman's part. "I agree with you about Miss Scott. And, of course, her father. I don't see a great deal of them, however. But . . . to business. I have brought you another load of salmon. Good stuff, again, and quite a lot of it. Do I take it that you are still in the market for it? As you indicated last time?"

"Ooh, aye. Uh-huh. Well, maybe, Mr . . . er? Maybe, aye. More salmon, eh?"

"Yes. About five hundredweight, actually."

"Five, eh? Man, you've been busy! Five hundredweight's a lot o' salmon."

"Too much for your market, Mr Sinton?"

"Och, I'm no' saying that. No. I wouldn't just say that. But

117

it maybe complicates the selling a wee bit, mind. Och aye, it's a complication."

"What is? The amount, you mean?"

"Just that. Aye, the amount, Mr . . . ?"

"Do you want it, then? You said any time, when we were here before. Do you want me to take it elsewhere?" Adam tried to sound suitably confident.

"I'm no' saying that, either, sir—no, no. If we can agree on a price, that is. Aye, that's the rub. The market's touchy, you see—for a big weight o' fish like that." The fat man was pinching his chin, and not looking at Adam at all.

"I would have thought that the larger the amount, the more stable the price? You gave me six-and-threepence, last time."

The other sighed. "Aye—I miscalculated yon time. I was ower generous for my ain pocket, sir. Much. I canna offer you that sort o' money for this lot, I doubt."

"Indeed. M'mmm—I'm sorry to hear that. What *do* you offer, then?"

"Och, well—four shillings is the best I can do."

"*Four* shillings! But . . . that's a ridiculous drop! That's . . . that's a forty per cent reduction, man."

"I'ph'mm. Aye, well—but fish is aye a tricky market. Fluctuating, if you see what I mean. Depending on supply and demand. If the demand goes down, see you, for any reason— like doubts about the origins o' the fish, maybe . . . and the supply goes up maybe, because o' new suppliers coming in wi' big hauls . . . well . . . !" The other darted a swift look at his callers. "Have you seen the papers, Mr . . . ? *The Scotsman*, maybe?"

Adam had been frowning. "Eh? What d'you mean—the papers?" He had not yet had time for more than a glance at his daily *Scotsman's* headlines.

"This illegal fishing. This poaching, sir. Trouble, they're having." Sinton's voice grated a little. "A bad thing. For the trade. Bound to affect prices. Bound to." Again the quick darted glance.

To gain time, Adam stalled. "I haven't seen all this. In the paper," he said. He cleared his throat. "Who's doing it? This illegal fishing?"

"It doesna just say. Some folk up the coast. But . . . it's bound to bring down the price o' salmon, you'll understand."

"In Manchester?"

"In Berwick! Here!" That was almost snapped out.

Adam thought hard and quickly. The situation was perfectly obvious. It could not be called blackmail perhaps, but it was the same sort of thing. Sinton knew very well where the salmon was coming from. He was not averse to handling it—but he was going to put on the pressure as regards price. It was nonsense to suggest that the coming of an extra few hundred-weights into the Berwick salmon trade, one of the largest in the country, would bring the market prices down by forty per cent—bring it down at all. But, on the other hand, if the matter had got into the papers, then any attempt by strangers to unload fairly large quantities of salmon most obviously would be suspect. Probably none of the more reputable salesmen would touch it. Sinton would know that very well. He had them in a cleft stick. Hazel Scott might possibly have argued the matter—played Sinton at his own game. But the fishermen wanted nothing more to do with her—and anyway, Adam would have been loth to go running to her, involving her further.

He swallowed. "Well, I suppose you know trade conditions best," he said. "It seems a very poor price to me. But if that is the state of the market just now, I suppose that I must just accept it."

"Aye. Uh-huh. That's the sensible way o' looking at it, sir," the other commended. "No getting away from supply and demand, man. Well, then—if you like to bring it in, sir, we'll see how much it comes to. . . ."

A short time later, then, Adam and the silent Dod Elliot were on their way home to Airdmouth with an empty van and another pocketful of creased and crumpled notes. These, however, added up to only £112 this time—less than for the much smaller previous consignment.

There were going to be some hard words spoken in The Fishers' Tryst that night.

Later, over a lonely meal of cold salmon, Adam read his *Scotsman*. He found the item that he looked for, on Page 5.

UNAUTHORISED SALMON-FISHING OFF
BERWICK-ON-TWEED

On a number of occasions recently unauthorised vessels have been observed apparently fishing for salmon with nets in coastal waters off Berwick-on-Tweed. These waters, under the Tweed Fisheries Act of 1857, Amended 1859, are declared to constitute part of the mouth of the River Tweed, and salmon fishing there is prohibited save by permission of the Tweed Commissioners and their lessees. The Tweed Commissioners are proprietors of salmon fisheries and rights on the river itself. This present display of defiance of the Act's provisions is causing concern to the authorities, who point out that unless there are restrictions of this sort, over-fishing at the mouth of the Tweed would have most damaging effects on the number of salmon coming up the river to spawn. This, it is claimed, might well ruin the Tweed as a salmon river.

The authorities concerned say that they have been very patient in this matter, recognising the perhaps natural instincts of certain coastal fishermen towards taking the occasional fish. But recent activities have become so blatant and frequent that official action has become necessary, according to these authorities. On Saturday a boat was actually lying to a line of nets fully four hundred yards long no more than a mile off Berwick pier, in broad daylight. Bailiffs and other official representatives thereupon went out in a launch to warn the offending fishermen of the serious consequences of their activities, and to announce that further infringements of the Tweed Act would not be tolerated.

Local opinion in Berwick appears to be somewhat divided on this issue. It is asserted that the fishermen are Scots. The situation is undoubtedly complicated by differences in the laws on salmon fishing between England and Scotland. In this connection it is interesting to note that the fishermen of Seahouses, further down the Northumberland coast, have long protested against their exclusion from salmon fishing in their own coastal waters, and have indeed sought signatures to a petition to Parliament for the provisions of the Act to be amended in this respect.

Adam read that report twice, with interest, recognising it to be a very carefully worded and noncommittal statement. On the whole, he was encouraged thereby. Clearly the paper was not committing itself to automatic support of the official line. Clearly too, it recognised that legal complications could alter the picture. And its mention of the Seahouses people's views and efforts at a petition, might be significant. It was hardly to be expected that there would be any mention of the net-destroying raid; whoever was responsible for that would hardly be likely to blazon it forth. But neither was the word poaching once mentioned in the report.

A little more heartened than he had expected to be, since in the end all their efforts must stand or fall by the reaction of public opinion, Adam wended his way down to The Fishers' Tryst.

X

PERHAPS Adam allowed his enheartenment to carry him away, that night. Perhaps the indignation of the fishermen over Sinton's behaviour affected him sufficiently to warp his better judgment. Perhaps it was that he felt partially responsible for the poor accretion to the Fighting Fund, and so for the obvious and urgent need to add to it. At any rate, later that night, at his own insistence, he found himself sitting beside Sandy Logan in the wide stern of a long black coble, being rowed southwards over the dark heaving waters, about half a mile offshore. The lights of Berwick illuminated the sky in front of them. Behind them, the phosphorescence of the long oars of a second coble glowed intermittently; Dand Fairgrieve was on the job, also.

Dand was in fact having quite a day of it. In the agreed rotation, it had been his turn to fish openly that day, and though Logan and Adam had suggested that he should go out beyond the three-mile limit and try operating there, where they were on surer ground legally, Dand had been obstinate, insisting on putting a scheme of his own into practice. He had gone close in to Berwick once more, in fact, but instead of shooting a line of drift-nets had actually shot only a messenger warp and a number of floats. The appearance, of course, above water, had been the same. He had had his reward. After nearly an hour, a boat had duly emerged from Berwick harbour once again—not the official launch, but a fishing-boat, presumably the same one as previously, with hidden markings. It had proceeded to go through the same performance of grapnel-dragging. Its people must have been puzzled, presumably, by the apparent lack of resistance to their hooks—though they had got one entangled with some trailing loose ropes hung from the messenger for that purpose. They had in due course returned to Berwick, to the shouted abuse of the fishermen, whereupon Dand had drawn in the decoy line and shot his true nets—and had the satisfaction of bagging a reasonable haul of salmon thereafter, though with a number damaged by seals again. His crew had been rather pleased with themselves over this. They were out again tonight, at any rate.

The expedition was making for the scene of Tosh's success- ful venture of Saturday night—the back or northern side of Berwick's long and famous Queen Elizabeth Pier. According to Tosh it was not nearly such a foolhardy performance as it might sound. The pier thrust out to sea in a curve for nearly half-a-mile, and being tall, with a high sea-wall surmounting it and no lights other than the little lighthouse at its end, served as an excellent barrier to the lights of the town. In the wide belt of darkness seaward, poaching might go on with little likelihood of being observed. And round the side of this pier, of course, must come any inshore salmon making for the mouth of the Tweed from the north.

The coble, broad-beamed and almost flat-bottomed as it was, swayed and rolled a lot more in the cross seas than did the *Bluebell*. Adam became rather more preoccupied with the salmon that he had eaten for his supper than that which it was proposed to catch tonight. The three-mile trip down to Berwick seemed a deal longer by rowing-boat than under *Bluebell's* engine.

Owing to the menacing series of rocks and reefs that guarded the rugged coast to the north of the harbour, Sharper's Head, Ladies Skerrs and Bucket Rocks, they could not approach the pier from inshore, but had to keep well out until opposite the pier-head, and then turn directly landwards. There was a sandy channel on the north side of the pier itself, leading to an old anchorage known as Meadow Haven. For this the coble made. They were still in the refulgence cast by the lighting of the town, and though probably this would not make them in any way apparent from the land, it formed an uncomfortably bright approach.

"Too darned well lit altogether, for a place like Berwick!" Adam deplored. "An old walled town like that. You'd think it

123

was Blackpool!"

"Aye—that's because it's good Scots lighting," Tosh declared. "They can ca' Berwick an English toon, but it's got to get its light frae the South o' Scotland Electricity Board! Aye, and a deal else, too."

"Uh-huh. It's comforting to ken that, if we get oor heads broken this night, it's to Edinburgh Royal Infirmary we'll be taken, no' to yon English Newcastle!" Logan added, cheerfully.

They were all thankful when they ran into the zone of deep darkness under the lee of the long high pier. Tosh directed the four oarsmen to pull towards a point about three-quarters of the way along, or some two hundred yards from the pier-head light—because the closer they could operate to the end of the pier the better the chances of their catch, for the salmon would all have to round that pier-head to get into the Tweed, even those that had, as it were, cut a corner.

Quietly they drew in to the slanting base of the pier, and clambered out on to the slippery weed-hung stonework. To Adam it was very reminiscent of that first night of all, at the much smaller Airdmouth pier—though this one, with its surmounting sea-wall, seemed to rear up infinitely higher above them. Dand Fairgrieve's coble came in close alongside, and then turned landward a little way to take up its stance about a hundred yards from them.

Swiftly and efficiently, out of long practice, the wear-net shooting procedure went forward, two men rowing out the coble with the nets dropping into the water behind them. Men spoke only in whispers.

The first shot brought in half a dozen salmon and a few trout—two of the salmon good big fish. Elated, the men were starting a second shot, when of a sudden Sandy Logan emitted an urgent sibilant "Ssshht!" and held up his hand. He had ever the best ears of the party.

Promptly everyone froze into immobility—except the rowers, who were too far out already to hear the warning, and went on slowly, deliberately, pulling the coble seawards. At first, nothing was to be heard above the splash and sigh of the waves. Then, clearly if not loudly, voices sounded over and through it. Only a brief exchange—then they stopped and were not heard again.

The fishermen eyed each other. None could say for sure where the voices had come from. Some, whispering, thought that it might have been some of Dand's people, some trick of the wind bringing the sound up this far. Sandy shook his head. It had been too close for that. It could only have come from up on the pier above them; but would voices behind that high sea-wall carry down here to them? Sandy thought not. In which case, the speakers must have had their heads at least *above* the sea-wall. It was considerably taller than a man's height. Which meant . . . ?

"Och, maybe no'," Tosh put in. "Maybe just the way the wind is. Or it could o' been just a couple o' chaps having a bit breath o' air."

"I think we should get the boat in, and away," Adam said. "It's not worth risking anything. We've got some fish."

"Och, dinna be daft, man!" Tosh objected. "A dozen men, scared off by a couple o' voices! We'll never win a Fighting Fund that way. Likely just some folk taking their dugs a wee walk oot the pier before going to their beds."

"That's all very well, but we can't afford to take a chance on it. And getting away, at this business—getting in these nets—takes such a damnably long time . . ."

Sandy Logan intervened. "It could be either way—and it's right enough that we mustna take any mair risks than we can help. Just the same, Adam, though it takes a whilie to get in the nets, it'd take longer for these folk, if they *were* connected wi' the bailiffs, to get away back into the toon to get help. We've time enough to finish this shot, I think. But, look—go you doon to Dand, Adam, and tell him. Say there's folk aboot, and to be ready to quit at short notice. Three blinks o' three on his torch. Same here. Okay?"

Adam moved along the slanting base of the pier, picking his way with care. The water was deep alongside, and one slip on the greasy weed could hurl him in. He wore wellington-boots tonight, which would promptly fill and drag him down, and in the darkness he would never be seen. He had listened to grim tales about the hazards of this business.

He found Dand and his people standing still, silent—and facing not seawards towards him but landwards. Their attitude of tense listening needed no interpretation. Their coble was just dimly to be discerned some way out. Quietly Adam came up to them.

"Folk along there," Dand whispered to him. "Heard them, twice."

"You mean, up on the pier? We heard voices, too."

"No. They're doon on this ramp, we reckon. At the tide's edge."

"They dinna seem to be moving," somebody vouchsafed. "No' coming this way. No' yet, anyway."

"Can you get away quickly?" Adam asked. "Your net . . . ?"

"The coble's near halfway oot," Fairgrieve said. "Second shot. We stopped them rowing. Take us a bit to get the net in."

"Yes. That's the same with us. Sandy sent me down to warn you that we'd heard these voices. Up above. To be ready to quit at short notice. Three blinks of three, on the torches. . . ."

"Aye. I reckon we'll no' finish this shot. We'll get the net back in, right away. Folk up on the pier dinna matter that much, but doon this side o' it's gey tricky."

"Yes. I agree. I'll go back to Sandy and tell him. He's trying to finish his second shot. We did quite well with the first."

"Aye. We got eight, oorsel's."

"Did you, by Jove! This is the place, all right. A pity we've got to move. . . ."

Adam started back towards his own team. As he neared them, he was surprised to find them in an almost identical state and attitude to the crew that he had just left, silent, motionless, and peering—but this time staring in the other direction, towards the seaward end of the pier. Sandy's tall figure, easily recognisable, held up an unnecessary hand for quiet as the schoolmaster came up.

Adam moved slowly close to the big man.

126

"Somebody along there," Sandy whispered. "More'n one. Doon below, this time."

"It's the same with Dand. They've heard people, landward of them. Down on the ramp, too. Dand's packing up. You, too—for goodness' sake! Looks like a trap, to me!"

"Och, well—it's likely no' just as bad as that."

"Have you not got that wretched coble coming in yet?"

"Aye, they're coming back noo. You can see them. . . ."

"Hsst!" somebody warned. "They're coming."

He was not referring to the rowers in the coble. Men were obviously approaching along the ramp from the eastwards. The hollow sound that sea-boots make could be heard above the noises of the water.

Adam glimpsed dark figures in motion. "Two of them," he murmured.

"Three," Tosh amended. "They'll see the bluidy coble."

There was no doubt about that. Though the black outline of the incoming boat itself might have escaped notice for a little longer, the pale phosphorescence aroused by its regularly dipping oars was all too evident.

Suddenly, from in front of them, a voice called, low-pitched but easy. "That you, Sammy? How's it go?"

The poachers glanced at each other swiftly, uncertainly. There was a pause. Then Sandy Logan lifted up his voice.

"No' bad," he said thickly. "No' bad."

There was another pause. No doubt something unfamiliar had sounded there.

"Is it Jerry, then?" the other called again, obviously coming forward.

Sandy took a deep breath. "No, it's no'. Who's that, yoursel'?"

No answer now. The Airdmouth men waited, tense.

Three men, dressed apparently very much as they were themselves, came close, slowly now, most evidently peering.

"Who the hell are you?" a new voice demanded, abruptly.

As Sandy hesitated, Tosh Hogg spoke up. "Who d'you think? We're minding oor ain business. Hoo aboot you doing the same?"

For appreciable seconds there was no answer. When it came, it was not a spoken one. Without a word, apparently by mutual consent, the three dark figures turned about and went clumping back whence they had come.

The Airdmouth men watched until the darkness had swallowed the others. Then exclamation, comment, questioning, broke out. Sandy Logan stilled it.

"Get this net in, fast," he ordered. "Talk aboot it after. I dinna like the sound o' this."

"Och, what's the panic?" Tosh demanded. "They went meek as bluidy lambs. They kenn't what's guid for them, yon boys. They could count, see . . . !"

"There's others," Adam put in, quickly. "Further down. Below Dand's place. If they've got people on either side of us, the sooner we're out of this the better!"

Despite Tosh's proclaimed confidence, all were automatically obeying the skipper's commands, and dragging in the land-based warp of the net. The coble came in with the other end. Its two rowers, their backs having been turned to the pier, had seen nothing, heard nothing, of what had gone on. They clambered out on to the pier, to assist at the hauling. Once more Adam was agitatedly aware of the solid dead-weight and endless-seeming dimensions of these nets.

Salmon began to appear, gleaming and flashing with their own light in the dark water. Adam almost wished that there were none, for each took a little time to extricate from the meshes. He kept glancing along on either side, and upwards. Once, he was almost sure that he glimpsed a dark head high above, outlined over the sea-wall against the night sky. He told Sandy.

The big man shrugged. "So long as they dinna come at us by sea. In boats," he said. "Cobles are gey slow to be getting away. Frae launches, or anything wi' a motor. Could make rings roond us."

This was a new worry for the schoolmaster; he had not considered that aspect of the matter.

"Then what chance have we got?" he demanded. "Even if we manage to get away before they come. With three miles to row back. . . ."

"No' so easy finding us in the dark, mind. . . ."

"But on a launch they'd have some sort of searchlight, wouldn't they? Even in a fishing-boat. *You've* got a spotlight on *Bluebell*. . . ."

Neither of them paused for a moment at their hauling, during this exchange.

"Aye—but it's no' that easy, even then, picking up a dark boat in the open sea. There's a lot o' water, mind. And they'll maybe no' have a launch or a fishing-boat. . . ."

"But they're bound to have. If they're after us here, at all. They're not fools—we've proved that. The boats they used before will be just over there in the harbour."

"Only if they're the bailiffs or the polis, Adam. They're maybe no'. They're maybe just some o' the Berwick boys, oot for a bit salmon on their ain."

"Eh? You think that? You mean—local poachers? Lord—I never thought of that! If . . . damn it—if we could be sure of that, then we needn't worry!"

"Well . . . maybe aye, and maybe no. . . ."

The words were scarcely out of Sandy's mouth when a sudden uproar of shouting and cursing broke out from down the pier. Most obviously it came from the other Airdmouth crew. The noise maintained.

"The baistards are at Dand's boys!" Tosh cried. "It's a fight!"

"Jings, aye!"

"Three o' you—stay here wi' the coble. Get that net in," Sandy directed. "The rest o' you—come on!" And, as an afterthought, "Adam—you better stay here, too."

Sad to relate, the schoolmaster quite ignored that perfectly clear order by the skipper, and went running along the slippery ramp with the others, stumbling and tripping on the weed and uneven stones, aware again of the danger of falling into the black water, but for the moment not caring.

129

It was difficult to see what went on in the darkness under the shadow of that pier, but the impression, as they came up, was one of complete confusion. Men seemed to be struggling together in pairs and groups all along that precarious slope, some upright, some lying on the stones, some even in the water around the coble, wherein stood one man, swaying and staggering, who sought to beat off sundry attackers with something large and round.

The arrival of the four newcomers by no means lessened the confusion, whatever else it did. Sandy, Tosh, and another man merely hurled themselves bodily into the *mêlée*, intuition apparently guiding them as to whom to attack. Their identity was promptly lost in the general chaos. Adam was less gifted in this matter; all the struggling bodies seemed to be the same to him, all merely dark-clad men in long sea-boots. The man in the coble alone seemed to be identifiable as one of the Airdmouth crew, since he was repelling three attackers. Unhappy as he was about that black water, Adam went plunging to his aid.

Fortunately or otherwise, the process of heaping the net on to the boat had by no means been completed, obviously, when the attackers had arrived, and part of the pile of wet netting and rope was still on the stones and part on the broad stern-board of the coble. The connecting-links and folds sagged into the sea—but they provided some sort of handrail and support. Indeed two of the three attackers were clinging on to this one-handedly—which possibly was why they were not making better progress against the sole defender. The third was half-in and half-out of the boat itself. Adam, also clinging to the rope with one hand, flung himself on to the back of the nearest to him, with a splash. In the excitement he did not even notice the cold of the water.

If the general struggle was chaotic, Adam's share of it was not out of keeping. Maintaining a fight with two opponents, all waist-deep in surging water, with feet unsteadily based on slanting weed-hung stone, at the best of times is bound to be difficult and less than fully effective; but when all three

130

contestants are concerned to retain a grip with one hand on a single length of rope, the attempt becomes the more unrealistic, not to say fantastic. A surprisingly small proportion of the energy and venom expended actually registered, in this instance, on any of the antagonists—which perhaps was just as well. Adam felt himself to be several kinds of a fool, throughout—always an off-putting influence in a fight.

Nevertheless, his wild and distinctly frustrating flounderings, wallopings and buffetings, probably performed as useful a function as any produced by the new arrivals, for he served to neutralise two of the enemy, turning their attentions upon himself and away from the coble. And the boat, of course, was of prime importance. He may well have saved it—though its sole defender was no laggard in the matter, of course.

Adam received punishment in the highly confused process—but not in proportion to the sound and fury and general splatter. Inevitably not a few thumps and blows reached him, however small a percentage of those aimed. Worse, much worse, more than once he lost his footing sufficiently to go completely under—which was unpleasant and served to confirm in him a recognition that the first objective of all this was to keep a firm hold on the lifeline of the nets. The fisticuffs and manifestations of hate were very much a secondary consideration. Clearly and fortunately this recognition being shared by the opposition, the situation was more or less regularised.

For how long this comparatively token encounter might have gone on, there is no knowing. A new development, however, altered everything—and in a remarkably short space of time. It consisted of a considerable shouting from directly above, from up on the sea-wall, obviously—a high-pitched and urgent sort of shouting, very different from the curses and grunts and groans resounding from sea-level. As astonishing as the speed at which these warning cries penetrated and then stilled the uproar below, was the effect on all concerned. Both sides took equal heed, and appropriated the warning to themselves. Men disentangled themselves from other men with as eager a unanimity as previously they had hurled themselves at each other. The seemingly hopeless confusion began to resolve itself into two distinct groups, one drawing off to the east, the other to the west. Like oil and water, they separated.

Adam Horsburgh, the least experienced in such affairs, was only dimly aware of all this, his back being turned to the pier. Some perception that the situation had changed quite substantially, however, dawned on him when his two personal opponents, seeming to bear down on him with a sudden new and more united determination, proved to be only concerned to bypass him on the lifeline without actually having to lose hold on its comforting security. Almost lovingly, indeed, they passed him, encircling his waist with their arms in the process— and grunting in mixed pain and reproach at the shrewd digs that he was able to get in with his elbows in the by-going. It was only on turning round to deliver a valedictory swipe at the retreating back of the second man, that Adam perceived that hostilities were apparently in abeyance, and disengagement the order of the day.

After that, everything happened at speed. Dragging himself heavily ashore after his two enemies, Adam found himself all but swept aside and into the sea again by a new tide, that turned out to be Dand Fairgrieve's crew making hastily for their coble and dragging the remaining wet folds of their net with them. Too breathless to protest adequately at this, he was surprised to find himself, in a moment or two, apparently alone on the scene of the battle, his wellington-boots full of water and more or less anchoring him to the spot. He was vaguely aware of lights flashing up above him, and one that shone downwards evidently from the sea-wall, only a little way from his position. Then a large shape came clumping up, from the eastwards, and a great hand reached down and practically hoisted him upright, bodily, from his position on hands and knees on the slippery weed.

"C'mon Adam," Sandy Logan's voice boomed, urgently. "We're getting oot o' this. Quick, man!"

"Can't," Adam gasped. "Got to get . . . water out . . . of my boots."

"Damn that," the other declared vehemently. "Nae time." And exerting all his great weight and strength, the big man propelled and half-carried the schoolmaster on along the ramp eastwards at a lumbering stumbling trot.

It was as well, undoubtedly, that the men left behind with their own coble had managed to get their net all aboard in the interim, and so, after taking in the rest of the crew, were able to row down parallel with the pier. Sandy and Adam therefore had barely half the distance to stumble back, when the boat loomed out of the gloom ahead. Thankfully they plunged down towards it, up to their thighs in the water. The shouting and light-flashing from up on the pier was now incessant and a major offence to the night.

Eager hands dragged them aboard, at the stern over the untidy heap of the soaking net, amongst which salmon still heaved and flapped. Even as they did so, the rowers turned the upthrusting bows northwards, away from Berwick and its pier, pulling on the long sweeps vigorously.

Panting, Adam lay on the nets, water draining from his person. More than once he sought to speak, but could find neither breath, voice nor coherent words to say. Tosh Hogg, untroubled thus, was cursing with a fluency to rival a pre-Reformation anathematiser.

Sandy, after a few moments, cut him short. "Quiet, man," he ordered, pointing to port. "There's Dand." Raising his voice he cried. "Ahoy, Dand—you okay? All your boys get clear?"

"Damn you, you rotten lousy baistards, you!" came back across the dark water from a shadowy boat apparently identical with their own. "Keep oot o' this, d'you hear? Right oot. Bluidy poachers! Keep to your ain water, after this, or it'll be the worse for you! I tell you, if you come back here, we'll get you! Aye, we will. We ken you fine, you damned thieving skunks . . . !" The indignant voice faded as the two cobles drew away from each other and their shapes likewise faded into the night.

"Och, aye," Sandy mentioned, easily. "It wasna Dand, at all. Right uncivil boys, them. . . ."

Adam, swallowing hard, found words of a sort. "For Heaven's sake . . . will somebody tell me what goes on?" he demanded. "What in the name of all that's wonderful is it all about? Who were those people? Who have we been fighting? What happened? Why on earth did everybody break off, like that? Of all the utterly crazy affairs . . . "

"Och, yon were just some o' the Berwick boys," Sandy explained. "Oot for a bit poach on their ain. Seems like we struck on a place they work theirsel's . . . and they werena too keen on sharing it wi' us! You heard them? They werena keen on getting caught by the bailiffs either, of course. That's why they're away off oot to sea, noo."

"You mean, all that noise and light up on the pier . . . ?"

"Aye. Somebody must have gone and told the bailiffs. Some other folk. Brought them along, later. Tom says there was polis in it, too—he saw their hats. Up on the wall. A guid thing the Berwick boys had somebody up on the pier to gie them warning. Saved a lot of trouble. . . ."

"Saved a lot of t-trouble!" Adam repeated. "Lord—what d'you c-call that?"

"Och, yon was just a bit stramash. Nae harm in it. The bailiffs'll no' ken we were in it, at all. They'll just reckon it was a big night for the local boys."

"I was thinking they made a right fuss and bother aboot it, Sandy," Tosh put in. "The guys up on the pier, I mean. The dam' bailiffs. All that noise and lights. I reckon they werena too keen on catching anybody—just warning them off."

"Maybe you're right, Tosh. They're likely no' wanting trouble wi' the local boys, the noo—they got plenty on their hands, wi' us. Aye, you're likely right enough."

Adam swallowed. "P-poaching seems to be quite a, a p-problem, around here!"

"They say it's Berwick's favourite pastime, o' a night," Tosh informed. "But, Jings—I didna ken the back o' the pier was so bluidy popular! We'll maybe have to try a new place, next time."

"Next time!" Adam cried, from between chattering teeth.

"C-confound it, haven't you had enough of this? We m-might all have been caught, tonight. As well as having those t-two nets lost. And broken heads! This whole b-business is folly. I said so before, and I'm all the more certain now. It's got to stop. *I'm* not having any m-more to do with it, anyway! Of all the c-crazy risks to run. . . ."

A battered silver hip-flask was thrust in front of Adam's face. "Here, Adam man—have a slug o' that," Sandy said kindly. "Do you guid. We wouldna want you to be catching a cauld. You're fair chittering. Och, you'll feel better when you're warmed up a wee. Here—let's see those boots off you. . . ."

"I t-tell you, this poaching's no g-good," the other insisted.

"That's right. Drink it doon, noo."

"I've heard tell there's a good bit the other side o' the Lifeboat Station, Sandy—when the tide's ebbing," Tosh mentioned. "Just this side o' the Spittal. Worth a try. . . ."

"Aye, maybe. We'll think aboot that another time, Tosh. Look—yonder's Dand, noo. Sure to be, this time. Rowing north, like us. Ahoy, Dand . . . !"

XI

AN urgent message reached the school the following forenoon, from Jamesy Pringle, requesting Adam's early appearance at the pier, and amounted to another stroke of luck for the fortunate pupils of Airdmouth, who undoubtedly found the entire salmon dispute much to their liking. It was breaking-up day anyway, of course, and a half-holiday was in order. Leaving a joyful pandemonium behind him, the schoolmaster hurried down to the harbour.

He found that Jamesy, showing every sign of agitation and distress, had retreated on to the deck of his own boat at the quayside, before three hatless gentlemen in raincoats, with open notebooks and poised pencils. It was Pringle's boat's turn to do the demonstration drifting out off Berwick that day, and he was now paying the price of a shockingly late start. Sandy and Dand Fairgrieve had long been out at their normal and legitimate fishing somewhere beyond the grey horizon.

Clearly the Press had found its way to Airdmouth. With a sinking heart, Adam viewed the backs of its three representatives. There was no escape for him, however; at sight of him Jamesy's eager relief was so apparent that immediately his tormentors turned to look, and then came purposefully to meet the schoolmaster, clearly aware that here must be quarry worth pursuing. Recognising that he had no time to marshal his thoughts, Adam had to pin faint and fond hopes only on attempts to bridle his tongue.

"*Express*, *Mail* and *Standard*," the shortest of the trio introduced cryptically. "We understand you are the schoolmaster here, sir, and know roughly what goes on? Were you in this attack on the English fishermen last night, sir?"

Adam all but choked. "What . . . what on earth are you talking about?" he managed to say. "What attack? Where? On whom? What nonsense is this?"

136

"The fight at Berwick last night, sir. On the pier. We gathered from this gentleman here, Mr . . . er . . . Pringle, that you might be able to tell us something about it?"

Adam shot a glance of sheerest malevolence at the admittedly shamefaced Jamesy, who was now hurriedly casting off ropes and doing other work that his crew should have been doing—at the same time as keeping his eyes carefully directed elsewhere. "I don't know why Pringle should imagine any such thing," he said stiffly. "Do you gentlemen imagine that I am in the habit of fighting with people on Berwick pier, or elsewhere for that matter?"

That sounded fairly well in his own ears, but seemed to make no impression one way or another on the pressmen. "Were you actually present at this encounter, sir?" the stout one asked expressionlessly.

"My goodness—if you can't ask less foolish and offensive questions than that, you may as well spare your breath! And mine!"

No flicker of either hurt or abasement showed in the reporter's eyes. "We take it that this is all part of the Berwick-for-Scotland movement," the third man mentioned. "Can you confirm that, Mr . . . er . . . ?"

"Good Lord . . . Berwick for Scotland! No, I can't! This gets more and more absurd. I assure you, you're barking up the wrong tree, altogether."

Much to Adam's alarm, all three wrote something in their notebooks there, in shorthand.

"Wrong tree . . ." one of them repeated. "Can you inform us what tree we ought to be barking up, then, sir?"

"No—of course not. Not at all. . . ."

"You are a Scot, Mr . . . er . . . ?"

"I am, yes. But what on earth has that got to do with it?"

"I take it that you believe that Berwick-on-Tweed should be returned to Scotland, sir?"

"Well . . . yes, of course I do. All Scots do, I should think. It is obviously a Scots town, racially, geographically, and in every other way. Part of Berwickshire, not Northumberland. . . ."

Adam stopped—though not in order to give hurrying pencils longer to write. "Look here—what are you putting down there? This has nothing to do with the question. . . ."

"You agree that there *is* a question, sir? And that this village, Airdmouth, is involved? You are just within Berwick Bounds, are you not? Would you care to express your opinion of this question, in a few words?"

"Damn it—I'll do nothing of the sort. You twist everything I say. . . ."

"The fact that it was fishermen who were involved is significant, sir, is it not?" That followed on evenly, without any sort of stress. "English fishermen on the one hand, and Airdmouth fishermen on the other. Would you care to comment on that aspect of the matter? Since you claim that the fight had nothing to do with the Berwick-for-Scotland campaign."

"Look here—that's not what I said. Not what I meant, anyway. I didn't even know that there *was* a Berwick-for-Scotland campaign on! And this fight, you talk about? What makes you think that Airdmouth fishermen were involved? Or English fishermen, either?"

"You don't deny it, sir, do you?"

"I'm not confirming or denying anything. I'm asking for information. You are not the only people that can ask questions, are you? I want to know what all this is about?"

"One of the, er, combatants was taken by a local doctor to the out-patients' department of the hospital late last night," the stout reporter mentioned. "Suffering from injuries received. Er, lacerations. He gave a, h'm, interview to press representatives this morning."

Adam blinked. "You mean, you went and grilled some poor devil in his bed!" he accused. "You fellows are quite unscrupulous!" Despite his shocked tones, however, Adam was thinking fast. If one of the Berwick poachers had been cornered and had talked, then it might be wise for him to change his tactics a little. Bland denials might be worse than some careful and accurate admission about their cause. The injured man had probably extemporised and prevaricated wildly, in an effort to throw everybody off the scent of his poaching friends in Berwick. That would account for the 'English' fishermen—a convenient red herring. The trouble was—what had he said about Airdmouth and the salmon dispute? The fact that the Pressmen were here at all, indicated that he had named the village. There would be no keeping that secret now. Adam took a deep breath.

"I can't tell you anything about fights at Berwick, or injured fishermen's tales," he said loftily. "Any more than I can about Berwick returning to Scotland. All that is rather beyond my depth. But I do know a little bit about the campaign for the amendment of the Tweed Salmon Fisheries Act, which we have started here—and which is probably what James Pringle meant when he put you on to me. And possibly what the injured man has got mixed up about, too. A very different kettle of fish, needless to say."

"Different kettle of fish. . . ." somebody repeated. "Quite good, that." The scribes were all very busy now. "Tweed Salmon Fisheries Act. . . ."

"Hmm. Yes. We believe, and I submit on good legal grounds, that the present Act, passed in London in 1857 and amended slightly in 1859, is both inequitable to the coastal fishermen and unworkable in law. . . ."

"Unworkable in law. . . ."

For minutes on end—while Jamesy's boat headed discreetly away in a south-westerly direction out of the more immediate trouble—the three pencils worked swiftly, as Adam enunciated what he hoped was a lucid, careful and skilfully edited version of their epic struggle against the grasping forces of outdated landlordism and monopoly. He was careful, however, to throw the entire blame on Parliament, and not to indicate that he thought that there was anything very reprehensible in the attitude of the present Tweed Commissioners themselves—who were presumably only doing their duty according to their lights under a thoroughly deplorable statute. He said quite a bit about common law, of both English and Scots varieties. Poaching, needless to say, was never once mentioned.

139

The pencils had flagged rather noticeably during the latter part of Adam's peroration; their wielders were but little interested in legal niceties, it seemed. One of them interrupted.

"I take it that this salmon business is geared to tie up with the Berwick-for-Scotland campaign, sir?"

Adam swallowed. "Lord—are you back to that again! I told you, I know nothing about any such thing. If you can't accept a plain statement of fact, then I'm afraid I have nothing further to say to you. . . ."

"Would you agree that if Berwick was returned to Scotland, there would be no need for your salmon-fishing campaign, Mr . . . er . . . ?"

"No, I wouldn't! It's nothing to do with that. Scots law is actually less favourable to coastal fishermen than English, in this case. It's the Act itself that is at fault."

"But you will agree that if Berwick was part of Scotland, it would be much easier . . . ?"

"Look—I'm not saying another word. All this is merely confusing the issue. I've said quite enough. I must get back to my school. If you'll excuse me, gentlemen?"

"Can you tell us who to go to to get a typical local reaction to this matter of Berwick-for . . . ?"

"You can all go to, to . . . !" Adam managed to restrain his tongue, there, but swung on his heel and stalked off instead. Back over his shoulder, he called, "Good-day to you."

All three had found something else to write.

Adam deliberately kept away from The Fishers' Tryst that evening, lest he get involved in any more crazy poaching expeditions. His heart sank therefore when, having got settled for once into the mood for his novel, with his pencil running comparatively smoothly, the sound of heavy footsteps approached his door.

It proved to be Sandy Logan's steps. He had not come to entangle the schoolmaster in more operations, however—though he was noticeably non-committal on how Tosh Hogg and the boys were filling in their evening. It was to report on Jamesy

Pringle's unprofitable day at sea. Jamesy, it seemed, had gone out to deep water a little south by east of Berwick, and there, just outside the three-mile limit, had proceeded to shoot his nets. They had not been out twenty minutes before, from behind the Farne Islands to the south, a fishery-protection frigate had appeared. She had come straight for them—obviously she had been lying in wait for that very purpose—and her captain had ordered Jamesy to get in his nets and clear out promptly. Jamesy had argued a little, evidently, but when the Navy shouted him down with its loud-hailer and started making threats about arrest and confiscation, Jamesy had done as he was told. It was a pity that it had been Jamesy and not himself, the big man said. Jamesy was a good lad, but not all that bright; he was the least able of the Airdmouth skippers to put up any sort of wordy battle. Sandy himself would have challenged the frigate to a showdown. . . .

Adam agreed that it was a pity. Pringle should have stuck to his position. But of course it was easy to talk that way in comfort here, and a different matter when faced with a warship a hundred times your own size with all the authority of the British Navy behind it.

It was clear, he maintained, what the authorities were up to. They were going to avoid any court action if possible, and intended to make the whole business hopeless and too costly for the fishermen by destroying their nets whenever they fished inshore, and chivvying them off with the might of the Navy when they tried further out. It was a typically mean and backstairs method of getting their own way—relying on the likelihood, almost the certainty, that the fishermen were in no position to force the issue to the courts on their own. But it was significant too, Adam thought, that they were apparently so anxious not to prosecute. It certainly looked as though they were not at all sure of their case. Which was hopeful for the fishermen's cause, in the long run.

Logan conceded that—but pointed out that the length of the said run was important too. In any war of attrition, the advantages were all with the enemy. Ordinary folk like themselves, with their livings to earn, could not keep up this sort of thing for long. They may have shown that the authorities did not want to put the Tweed Act to the test in court—but apart from that, they did not seem to be getting anywhere. They weren't getting forward. And now Jamesy had gone and actually taken a step backwards. . . .

Adam did not contest that. But he pointed out that no irreparable harm had been done. It was Sandy's turn to do the salmon-drifting tomorrow—and the first day of the Easter vacation. They would go out to the three-mile limit, and see if the Navy was still there. That was agreed.

Sandy proved to be not greatly interested in the Pressmen's visit, being more concerned about the Berwick poacher's injuries than about possible reactions in the sphere of publicity. How had the fellow come by such a thing—lacerations, hadn't Adam called it? A decent honest bit of rough-and-tumble like they'd had shouldn't have resulted in anything like that. He hadn't noticed anybody looking badly the worse for wear. Had Adam?

The schoolmaster wondered a little bit about the hero who had been trying to get into Dand Fairgrieve's coble. In his mind's-eye he could still see the sole defender in the boat with something large and round upraised in his hand. It had only occurred to Adam later that night that it had probably been the boat's baler. Thereafter he had preferred to put the matter out of his mind.

He tried to put more than that out of his mind when Sandy departed at length, and he could return to his writing. What on earth had made him imagine that the remote fishing-village of Airdmouth might be a suitable spot for the uninterrupted perpetration of a novel?

It was too early for anything at all to be on Adam Horsburgh's mind, next morning, when the telephone-bell shrilled, during his semi-conscious preparation of breakfast. His consequent barely civil bark into the mouthpiece elicited an unsuitable tinkle of feminine laughter at the other end.

"Good-morning, Adam," a clear voice said. "You don't

142

sound very loquacious this morning. Not nearly so much as you seem to have been yesterday!"

"Eh? What's that? Loquacious . . . ?" the man floundered.

"Eloquent. Vocal. Or is it too early in the morning for more than one-syllable words?"

"No. Not at all. I mean . . . oh well, skip it. It's Miss Scott, isn't it?"

"None other. I just rang up to congratulate you on your manifesto. And to ask after your health. And, possibly to seek just a little elucidation. Oh, forgive me—that's no word to put to a schoolmaster at such an hour, obviously! Just call it information."

"Look—what are you talking about, Miss Scott? Manifesto? Congratulations? I'm afraid I don't quite get you. . . ?"

"Do I take it that you haven't read your morning papers, yet?"

"No, of course not. I haven't had breakfast yet, actually. I . . . well, I had rather a late night."

"Ah—celebrating your triumph? That accounts for much. You weren't actually injured though, were you? In this famous victory over the hated English?"

Adam swallowed. "I'm afraid I haven't a clue what you're getting at, Miss Scott. I gather from what you say that there's something in the papers this morning?"

"Something in the papers! Hark at him! Such modesty! You've hit the headlines, my dear man. Horsburgh the Hammer of the English! The Fighting Dominie, in person. You didn't tell me, Adam, that you were such a militant nationalist."

The man groaned. "Just a minute," he pleaded. "*The Scotsman's* just over on the table. I'll get it. . . ."

"Oh, it's not *The Scotsman*. I don't think it mentions you at all. It's the *Standard* that's most brilliant. But the *Express* and the *Mail* are only a little less ecstatic."

"Oh. I see. Well . . . I did speak to some reporters yesterday. . . ."

"Speak! You were eloquence itself. Magnificent! Especially

143

the bit about the grasping forces of outdated landlordism trampling on the rights of the common man!"

"Good Lord! I say—for Heaven's sake don't believe all that tripe. Obviously they've got everything twisted. They were putting words into my mouth, all the time."

"Oh, but I approve! What you say is so delightfully true. You just strike exactly the right note. Entrenched privilege hiding behind a law that is as inequitable as it is unworkable! That's the stuff! It strikes me that you should stand for Parliament, Adam. Daddy wouldn't have a look-in!"

"Please, Miss Scott—you must let me explain. . . ."

"Nothing to explain, I assure you. It is all explained for you here. Most clearly. Though I'm still not quite clear as to who these dastardly Englishmen were, that you beat up on Berwick pier . . . ?"

"Confound it—that's just a lot of absolute rubbish!" Adam all but shouted. "A complete fabrication."

"Oh, I see. You made that bit up? Like the Russian Army, with snow on their boots. A red herring. Rather clever, that."

"No, no. Nothing of the sort."

"Mind you, I'm all in favour of Berwick coming back to Scotland. Definitely. But, I do think you might have given me an inkling. . . ."

"Look, Hazel . . . Miss Scott. It's no use going on like this. Talking at cross-purposes. Not until I've had a chance to see these wretched papers, anyway. After that I'll get in touch again, and explain. Or, well—I'm going out in a few minutes. Salmon drifting. Less than half an hour, now. But I'll write. That would be best. I'll explain everything. . . ."

"Goodness—why write? Why not come and see me? Come and have a meal. I'm just dying to hear all about it. Straight from the horse's mouth."

"No. Really, I would rather not. I mean, I would rather write. It's a little difficult, you see. At this juncture. About the others. Now, I'll really have to go, I'm afraid. . . ."

"I see. So I'm getting the frozen mitt, am I? Interfering female shown the door!"

"Heavens, no! Nothing like that. It's just that . . . well, the people here, the fishermen, tend to be a little bit suspicious of you. Because of your father, I mean. They are grateful for your help, of course, in getting a market for the fish. But, h'm, they feel that you aren't an awfully good risk. Ridiculous, after what you've done for us—but there it is. I'm sorry. . . ."

"I see. Yes. I see."

"I hope that you understand?"

"Yes, I'm sure I do. I understand, I think, perfectly. Well, then—I must not keep you. Sorry for butting in. Good morning, Mr Horsburgh."

"Look—maybe I didn't put that very well. . . ." Adam stopped as the line went dead after the click of the receiver at the other end.

The man glared at his own instrument. "Damn!" he said. And again, "Damn and blast! Damn everything!" No doubt most of his condemnation was directed against himself. He did not have to be told that he had not done that very well.

He made but a poor breakfast of it, thereafter.

XII

ADAM was late, of course. He had not even time in the end to try to buy any more newspapers; not that the single small general store that served the village was apt to invest in any large supply of extra and unordered copies of the daily offerings of the Press. He was not really averse to putting off inspection of any such, anyway.

Tosh Hogg, however, had brought a copy of the *Daily Standard* aboard with him, and apparently he had been profitably filling in the time of waiting for the belated schoolmaster by reading aloud choice excerpts to his fellow crew-members. Adam's appearance was greeted with grins and considerable cheer.

As *Bluebell* chugged out to sea, Adam almost reluctantly, and certainly distastefully, forced himself to scan the newspaper. He had no difficulty in finding the item in question. It was on the front page, and inch-high headlines trumpeted their message;

BORDER BATTLE AT BERWICK
MIDNIGHT CLASH ON PIER
BERWICK FOR SCOTLAND, FIGHTING DOMINIE SAYS

Late on Monday night, the damped-down fires of repression and patriotic fervour blazed out at Berwick-on-Tweed into open conflict. The age-old tug-of-war for Berwick between England and Scotland has recommenced. Following on years of local dispute and grumbling, enhanced by the statement of the South-East Scotland Regional Planning Committee that Berwick obviously and undeniably should be an integral part of Scotland and the county town of Berwickshire once again, plus the recent conflict between Scotland's Lord Lyon King of Arms and the English Garter King, the issue has at last reached the stage of action. Violent action. So violent that at least one of the

146

disputants is in the local hospital, with other casualties thought to have been secretly removed in boats.

This first clash in a new chapter of an old war occurred on Berwick's long Queen Elizabeth Pier after midnight two nights ago. The full circumstances leading up to the conflict on the pier are not yet clear, but it is known that the fight was between Scots and English fishermen. Local people are asking what the English fishermen were doing on Berwick's pier at that hour?

SCHOOLMASTER SAYS PRESENT POSITION INEQUITABLE AND UNWORKABLE

One of the leaders of militant Scottish opinion is youngish, dark-haired, dynamic Adam Horsburgh, headmaster of Airdmouth Public School. Interviewed by *Daily Standard* special representative, Mr Horsburgh declared that all Scots believed that Berwick should be returned to Scotland, Berwick being obviously a Scottish town, racially, geographically, and in every other way. Mr Horsburgh did not deny that he himself had been present at the fight on the pier, but said that he preferred not to comment on the significance of the English fishermen's presence there at that time. Mr Horsburgh was more forthcoming about the salmon-fishing problem as between England and Scotland, that is clearly allied to the larger question. He claims that the present Tweed Act is as inequitable as it is unworkable in law, and that the provisions relating to fishing off the mouth of the Tweed are particularly improper, denying coastal fishermen their rights and their livings.

"GRASPING FORCES OF OUTDATED LANDLORDISM"

Mr Horsburgh said, "We are challenging the grasping forces of outdated landlordism represented in the antiquated provisions of the Act of 1857. The right of the common man, in common law, must be upheld and vindicated. The Act forbids fishing for salmon in the sea within five miles of low-watermark at Berwick, and *only* at Berwick in all the United Kingdom. Yet Scots law only allows Crown rights in salmon for one mile out to sea. We have been fishing, and will continue to fish, within that area, prepared to put our case, if prosecuted, before any court in Scotland."

"A VERY DIFFERENT KETTLE OF FISH"

Mr Horsburgh said that Scots and English law, as related to salmon, was "a very different kettle of fish". He made it clear that

147

the people of Airdmouth were solidly behind this campaign. This was confirmed by Skipper James Pringle, who said that he was not anti-English but did not mind a fight.

Adam forced himself to read this effusion twice. Hazel Scott's comments and quotation had prepared him in some measure, of course, but not for the deceptive and undeniably clever way in which he had been misrepresented, in which his own words had been used to give a wholly misleading picture of his aims and attitude. Presumably every word quoted against him, he had used—he could not remember exactly everything that he had said—but in hardly a single instance had they been used to convey his own meaning and reaction. He could not deny these phrases of his—but by skilful twisting, taking them out of context, allying them with some conception or premise of his own, the writer of the report had made them appear to tell a totally different story to that intended.

"It's damnable! Utterly unscrupulous!" Adam exclaimed, lurching over to the wheelhouse doorway and waving the offending paper at Sandy Logan. "I wouldn't have believed it possible that anyone could so misrepresent another man's words. His point of view. And deliberately. It's not just that the wretched man took me up wrongly, misunderstood me. This is sheer and malicious distortion, a kind of forgery!"

"Och, it's no' all that bad, Adam," the big man said. "It's maybe a wee thing off it aboot the English—but that'll no' do anyone any harm. . . ."

"But it's all wrong! It makes me out to be some sort of leader of this Berwick-for-Scotland business. A thing I know nothing about, at all! It makes me some kind of wild extremist. Heaven knows what the Education people will think of this! Tying up our genuine and legitimate salmon campaign with this crazy caper . . . !"

"It's no' just crazy, either, man. Berwick *should* belong to Scotland. . . ."

"Of course it should. But that's nothing to do with the salmon-fishing laws. It's not a thing we can do anything about,

148

in this fight of ours. It's just confusing the issue. If we get mixed up in a lot of crankery and high-flown nonsense like this, it could do our cause a lot of harm. Especially if we seem to go in for violence. That utterly idiotic fight on the pier! Why on earth we had to get involved in a thing like that, Lord knows! It all springs from that. It's this poaching. . . ."

"Och, aye—but it wasna a bad fight, as fights go. It's just this joker in the hospital that's the trouble, wi' his yarns. But never mind, Adam—Tosh and the boys discovered a new place, last night. A real good spot, the far side o' the pier, near the Spittal. Nae bother. They got a good haul, too. . . ."

"My God! Not again? Not back to Berwick, poaching . . . ?"

"Och, well—poaching's no' just the right word, at all, Adam."

"I'll say it's no'!" Tosh Hogg declared, coming up. "It's England doon there, is it no? And you said yoursel', Adam, that in England they dinna have this nonsense aboot Crown rights reaching oot a mile frae the shore. Anybody can fish the shore, there, you said—except for this bluidy Tweed Act! Well, then—why no' us?"

"But, damn it, man—that's not our case! That's not what we're fighting about. And we'll get no public sympathy on that line. Quite the reverse. And if the locals are against us—as they've every right to be—we're just going to run into more trouble. Like this." Adam thrust the newspaper at its owner.

"That's no' trouble, man—that's fine. You did a good job wi' that, yesterday," Tosh declared. "A right spread, you got us. Real nice. . . ."

"It's not good work, or real nice! It's an utter shambles!"

"Och awa', man—what mair d'you want? You got half a page, there. Front page, too. And some right juicy bits—aboot the bluidy landlords. I didna ken you had it in you. The boys are real pleased. . . ."

Adam scowled. "Then the boys are as stupid as you are! Don't you see . . ."

Sandy intervened. "Adam reckons the paper took him up a wee bit wrong, Tosh."

"A wee bit . . . !"

"It did you proud," Tosh averred. "What you girning aboot? Did us all proud. We're in the papers, noo. Folk'll ken what we're doing, aboot the salmon. It'll gie those bailiffs something to think aboot. But look, Adam—I'm no' that keen on being called stupid, see! I am no'!"

"Och, he didna mean that, Tosh," the skipper put in quickly. "No, no. Did you, Adam?"

"Well—I suppose not. I'm sorry. Maybe I'm not at my best, this morning. I've already offended Miss Scott, I think. Over the phone. She rang up—about these confounded newspaper reports. I . . . well, I told her that you were all a bit suspicious of her. That you didn't want her having too much to do with it all. She wanted me to go and see her. To tell her all about it. But I said I'd better not . . ." Adam was trying to justify himself before these men—why, he could not have explained.

"Good for you!" Tosh commended. "Choke her off. She's too nosey to be healthy, yon dame. Gie her the works."

"Hogg—I'll thank you to speak more respectfully of Miss Scott!" the schoolmaster said sharply.

"Ooh, aye. You getting sweet on her noo, eh? I kenn't that would be the way o' it. That's aye the trouble. . . ."

"Shut up, you oaf! When your personal comments are required in my affairs, I'll ask for them. . . ."

"You will, will you . . . ?"

"Tosh—yon automatic hauler could do wi' a droppie oil," Sandy said quietly but firmly. "See to it. Adam, away you forward and keep a look-oot for yon fishery cruiser. We'll need to ken in plenty o' time if she shows up."

Both men accepted the reproof without argument or comment. Wordlessly they went aft and forward.

There was no need for Adam to do a lot of searching for the Navy. Almost as soon as, frowning, he had picked his way up to the bows, he saw her. She was in fact almost dead ahead of them, not quite hull down on the horizon, perhaps six or seven miles away, her naval-type top-hamper unmistakable. Undoubtedly Sandy Logan had seen her before ever he sent

150

Adam forward.

Whatever the skipper had said about having to know about the cruiser in plenty of time, *Bluebell* thereafter made no change of course. Straight out, south by east, she bore.

After a little while, it could be seen that the naval ship was making a sort of patrol, up and down, out there, on a beat of perhaps a couple of miles. She did not alter this, nor come closer in, as *Bluebell* headed out—but then, of course, there was no reason for her to be suspicious of every fishing-boat making for deep water.

When Sandy, from chart and bearings, reckoned that they were just immediately outside the three-mile limit and exactly opposite the mouth of the Tweed, he set his boat before the wind, had the red mizzen sail run up, and ordered nets to be shot. These were partly new, purchased from a merchant at Berwick at a wicked price, and partly some borrowed from Dand Fairgrieve. He only shot three, however, on this occasion.

"I wonder how many pairs of naval binoculars are fixed on us, this minute?" Adam said, his ill-humour quite submerged in a rising tide of challenge and excitement—even though he found the more powerful roll of the swell, out here in deeper waters, rather trying.

"What I'm wondering is what her orders are!" Sandy answered, a little grimly. "Yon ship, wi' her knife-edge bows, could chew up my nets a deal quicker than the boys wi' the grapnels. I've just shot the three nets, in case. . . ."

The frigate, however, seemed to be in no hurry to approach them. Possibly she was radioing for instructions, waiting until there might be a catch in the nets, or merely playing cat-and-mouse. There *was* no hurry, of course; once shot, drift-nets cannot be lifted in a few moments.

It was more than half an hour later, with Adam's stomach feeling distinctly queasy as a result of the lazy rolling, before anything happened. And even then, it was not the grey warship to seaward that created the diversion, but a couple of fishing-boats similar to their own, which headed out towards them from landwards. The fishermen watched their approach with

151

interest.

"What d'you make o' them, Sandy?" Tosh asked. "Oor friends wi' the grapnels again? They're no' coming frae Berwick—no direct, anyway."

"No. More like frae Seahouses. Or even Holy Island. Northumbrian boats." Logan said. "Coming up frae the south, that way. I wonder what they're after?"

"It could be that they've been summoned by the frigate?" Adam suggested.

"Why should they? The Navy doesna need any help to deal wi' us, if it wants to."

"No. Perhaps they're just making for fishing-grounds further to the north, then, and passing this way?"

The others did not comment on that. Sandy got out his glasses. "Seahouses boats, the both o' them," he reported.

The watchers did not have to conjecture for much longer. When something less than half a mile south of them, and roughly on the same line, the leading craft suddenly swung round in a semicircle, and cut down speed. Her bows pointing back towards the land, she lay wallowing.

"Jings—she's going to shoot!" Tosh cried. "She's turned with the wind, to shoot nets. Drift-nets. Damn it, they're after the salmon, too!"

"Looks like it," Sandy nodded, rubbing his chin. "Well, noo . . ."

"But . . . it needn't be salmon, need it? Here?" Adam wondered. "They could be fishing for anything."

"Nothing else worthy trying for, here," the skipper told him. "No' wi' a drift-net. No herring here." He pointed. "There's the other one doing the same, further down. They're doing just what we're doing—just ootside the three-mile limit but inside the five." He smiled. "Looks like oor wee bit revolt's catching, Adam man! The Seahouses boys have got smit wi' it!"

"It's those newspapers!" Adam declared. "They've been reading the papers. Reading what we're up to. And seeing us out here, they think they'll try their hand, too."

"Just like the rotten stinkers!" Tosh snorted. "Come creeping oot, when we've done all the bluidy work!"

The other crew members seemed similarly offended by the arrival of their Northumbrian colleagues.

"Och, there's no' that much harm in it, is there?" Sandy said. "If the sea's free, it's free to them, too. It's maybe no' a bad thing, at all. A sort o' united front."

"Ye-e-es," Adam agreed, but with some reservation. "It *could* be a good development . . . so long as they don't spoil our case for us. I mean, do things that would prejudice our case in law. Put the whole campaign in the wrong. Otherwise, it might not be a bad thing. After all, we knew these Seahouses people felt strongly about the position of the Tweed Act. They actually did something about it before we did, with their petition. If we can co-operate with them, map out a line of conduct that we all stick to, and say roughly the same things to the authorities, then the more that come out to challenge the powers-that-be, the better."

"Aye. We could have a bit chat wi' them on the radio—but the cruiser'd be listening-in," Sandy said. "Better to wait. When we've hauled in, we could go over and talk to them."

"The toes o' oor boots would do them mair guid!" Tosh grumbled. "They should stick to their ain water . . ."

"Like you did at Spittal, last night!" Adam cut in.

"Och, to hell . . . !"

"Well, noo—look who's here!" Sandy pointed out. "The Navy reckons it's time it joined in."

Presumably the captain of the frigate had been just as concerned over the arrival of the newcomers as had the complement of *Bluebell*, and had decided that it was high time that he took a hand. The warship was steaming up directly towards the fishing-boats now, the white bow-wave under her tall prow curling superciliously. Clearly it was for the Airdmouth boat that she was making.

"She looks, h'm, extraordinarily fierce and powerful for a fishery cruiser," Adam commented, unwillingly impressed. "All those guns and things aren't really necessary, surely?"

"Och, she's no' one o' the regular fishery boats, her. She's a pukka naval frigate seconded for fishery protection duties. She'll be frae the Forth, likely. They often do that. There's no' enough o' the real cruisers to cover the coast, especially since yon one sank. I'd a sight rather have one o' the proper ones, though. Easier to deal with. We sort o' speak the same language as their skippers. These Navy boys aye sound so snooty. Mind you, I reckon this sort o' job's no' popular wi' them, either."

"Baistards!" Tosh commented, briefly.

"D'you think she'll go for your nets? Plough through them?"

"No' at first. No' till she's warned us off. . . ."

The frigate swept round, reducing speed, and came up slowly well to leeward of *Bluebell*, at the other side from the buoyed line of nets. She seemed very large and potent and lofty, close at hand, with everything about her horribly shipshape and efficient-looking.

There was a loud clicking noise, and then a clipped voice spoke, clear but metallic, over the ship's loud-hailer, managing to sound well-bred, pleasantly casual and thoroughly authoritative at the same time.

"Hullo, hullo, hullo, you chaps. Naughty, naughty! Shouldn't be here, you know. What are you up to? Can you hear me?"

"Ooh, aye. We can hear you fine," Sandy shouted back. "We're fishing, Mister. Maybe you havena noticed oor nets? You'll watch them, will you? We wouldna want them damaged, mind." That was as pleasantly conversational as the other.

"We're watching them, all right!" came back, considerably more crisply. "We don't *want* to damage them, Skipper!" There was no mistaking the hint, there.

"That's fine, then. But you're a wee thing close, for safety. I'd be obliged, Captain, if you'd maybe continue your naval exercises some place further oot to sea. You'll be sort o' scaring the salmon, this close, wi' your great fine warship!"

They could almost hear the gasp of outrage and astonishment from behind the loud-hailer. "Look here—you *did* say salmon? You admit you're fishing for salmon?"

154

"Why no', Captain? You wouldna want me to tell a lee? We're in open waters. More'n three miles oot. You any objection to that?"

"I have, yes. You're a local boat with a local registration. You must know perfectly well that you are two miles inside the restricted area, here. You know that what you're doing is illegal."

"I ken nothing o' the sort. But what I do ken, Captain, is that there's an international three-mile limit. Beyond that, the sea's free. All roond the coast. Everywhere. Same as Iceland, Captain. I'd of thought the Navy would ken that, too! You been on the Iceland patrol?"

"Damn it, man . . . !" There was a brief pause. The voice was no longer casual, pleasantly or otherwise. "Don't come that line of talk with me, Skipper. This is HM ship *Unicorn*, presently detached for fishery protection patrol. My orders are quite clear. No salmon fishing is permitted within five miles of low water without permission of the proper authorities. The Tweed area is a special case, as you well know. Those are my orders."

"Then your orders are wrong orders, Captain, and no' legal. They may apply to you—but they dinna apply to me."

"Are you refusing to obey my orders, man, to get those nets up at once and clear out of this restricted area?"

"Aye, I am that, Captain, wi' all due respect—since you canna enforce them legally."

"My God, can I not! I'm not interested in legalities, my friend. I'm only interested in carrying out my orders. . . ."

"This is where I butt in, I think, Sandy," Adam said quietly, and the skipper nodded thankfully. Not having Logan's enormous lung-power, he picked up the megaphone which had been brought along in anticipation of just such a conversation. "I think that is rather unwise of you, Captain!" he called. "Not to be interested in the legalities, I mean. You may have to be, you know. In the High Court, at Edinburgh. If we have to charge you with malicious and deliberate damage, wrongous arrest, and conduct liable to provoke a breach of the peace!"

He made that sound as sonorous as he could, through a megaphone. "Unless, of course, you would enjoy a court appearance?"

"Who the hell are you?" That came clacking back at him like the snap of castanets.

Adam coughed. "Shall we say I am the Skipper's adviser, in this matter? On the legalities . . . that you're not interested in! Tell me, Captain—have you ever heard of the Sea Fisheries Act, of 1869? And the International Convention on Territorial Waters, of 1883? Of course you have, a naval officer like you. Britain is bound by these agreements with other nations that territorial waters shall extend only for three miles beyond low-water mark. Do you recollect hearing anything about the Tweed being the only area in the world excepted?"

"I know that the Tweed is in a special position. I understand that there is some special Act of Parliament about it."

"An Act which never was sound in law, passed in 1857, and which anyway has been superseded and invalidated by later legislation, especially the International Convention of 1883."

"All that is no concern of mine, sir. My concern is only to carry out my orders. . . ."

"Yet it is you who will have to appear in court, Captain. It's you whom we'll charge. You we'll claim damages from."

"You won't get any damages out of *me*, by George . . . !"

"We'll leave you to argue that with the Judge," Adam said. "That is, if you are so foolish as to go carrying the can for others, who won't risk going to law themselves. For whoever issued you with instructions that you cannot enforce without breaking the law yourself. I'd think twice about it, if I were you.

"I'm not asking advice from you," the naval spokesman declared strongly. "I'm giving you orders, here and now, to get in those nets and leave. Without any more argument. You understand?"

"Yes. And we refuse, of course. Secure in the knowledge that we are within our rights."

"You do, do you! We'll see about that. . . ."

"Captain—will you tell us would you act this way to any foreign boat fishing here? A Dutchman, say? Or a Norwegian? Even a German or a Russian? In defiance of international law?"

"That's nothing to do with it. You're a British craft under British law, I'd remind you. . . ."

"But on the high seas, outside territorial waters, breaking no international law . . . as you are doing!"

"Be quiet, man! Stop it! I'll have no more argument from you. I've met sea-lawyers like you before. Get those nets in . . . or else!"

"I warn you, Captain—any attempt to cut up our nets will result in a legal claim for damages against the master of HMS *Unicorn*, for acting in deliberate excess of his duty. And nets are expensive, remember. Very!"

"Damn you . . . !" There was a noticeable pause. Adam even found it in his heart to be sorry for the frigate's captain, no doubt a young lieutenant-commander, who was only trying to do his duty. For himself, he was hoarse and a little breathless with all this long-range shouting.

The loud-hailer crackled again. "I give you fifteen minutes to get these nets in, and away out of here, Skipper," the voice informed them stiffly. "Otherwise you will take the consequences of disobedience to a naval command at sea."

They distinctly heard the tinkle of the bridge telegraph as the frigate's commander rang for engines. With a churning of white water under her squared stern, the long grey ship surged forward and away, to leave *Bluebell* rocking jerkily in her wake.

"Guid for you, Adam," Tosh chuckled. "You got yon geyser all hot and bothered. I'll say that for you—you're a right powerful talker. Comes o' being a teacher, I suppose. You sound like you ken everything!"

"Thanks," the schoolmaster acknowledged dryly. "Actually, I'm skating on thin ice all the time."

"You got the man worried a bit, just the same," Sandy averred. "But hoo much is he worried—that's the question?

He's away to gie the Seahouses boys the same treatment."

"Yes. I wonder. . . ." Adam nodded.

Clearly enough the frigate was tackling the next fishing-boat. In a minute or two they could hear faintly across the half-mile of water the metallic clatter of the loud-hailer in action once more. Sandy watched through his glasses.

"Aye—they're doing what they're tell't!" he reported. "They're no' arguing. They've started up their hauler. A pity, that. Mind, I dinna blame them. I wouldna have been so brave at defying yon character, mysel', if I hadna had you by me, Adam, to talk law at him!"

Soon it was apparent to the naked eye that the first Seahouses boat was in fact hauling in her nets. The frigate moved on to the next craft.

"Lily-livered skunks!" Tosh declared. "Just like them! Come oot here where they're no' wanted, and then spoil oor stand for us by running away wi' their tails between their legs! I tell you. . . ." He stopped, and pointed. "Jings—look yonder! Mair o' them."

Sure enough, three more fishing-boats were approaching the area from almost due south, fairly close together and coming on steadily.

"Holy Islanders, for sure," Sandy, with the binoculars, reported. "They werena to be left oot. Gosh—it'll be right interesting to see what happens noo."

"Och, they'll just sheer off, like the others. Wi' that bluidy cruiser there. . . ."

"They can see the cruiser noo, well enough, and they havena sheered off yet," the skipper pointed out. "They're tough boys, those Holy Islanders, mind."

"I hope they're not *too* tough," Adam said, "It's a touch-and-go business this. We're walking a tightrope. Too much toughness could be as bad for us as these others packing in. It's tricky. . . ."

The second Seahouses boat was now obeying naval orders and hauling in her nets. The three new craft must have seen that clearly enough, but they still came on, just a little way

158

seaward of the line that the others were on. They passed the frigate at some four hundred yards distance. The first of the Seahouses craft had got about half of its net in.

"If they had good glasses wi' them, they could see all the time that we werena hauling in," Sandy mentioned. "Here they come."

The leading newcomer was definitely swinging in towards *Bluebell* now. The others followed suit. They came close, slackening speed.

"Aye, aye," Logan called, waving. "You Holy Island boys like a bit o' salmon, too?"

"That's right, lad," the skipper of the first boat shouted. "You'll be the lads from Airdmouth, eh? Thought we'd join you. Having trouble with the Navy, eh?" The voice there was rich Northumbrian. Adam was surprised at the notable difference of accent from that of the typical Lowland Scots of the Airdmouth men; after all, the communities were not much more than ten miles apart, as the crow flies.

"Och, the poor man's just trying to carry oot his orders," Sandy told them. "We tell't him where he got off. Real civil, mind. He gave us fifteen minutes, just, to get oor nets in, the boy. That was aboot twenty minutes ago."

"You're not hauling in, then?"

"No fears. We're making a stand on this. We've just the three nets oot, mind."

"That's the stuff! D'you think he'll cut them up? Sail through them?"

"Maybe—maybe no'. We tell't him we'd sue him for damages if he did. It's a toss-up what he does. But we reckon we got him worried. Aye, then—here he comes."

"Right, lads. We'll draw off a bit to the north o' you, and see what happens. Good luck!"

"Thanks. Why no' put doon a messenger, just, and a line o' floats? It'll look like nets—and if he does get nasty, it'll no' cost you much if he chews it up. No use us all sacrificing nets."

"Good idea, lad. . . ."

"And, look," Adam put in, "if you talk to him, keep civil,

159

will you? Put him in the wrong. Hold hard to the fact that you're beyond territorial waters, and he's no authority to move you on. Quote the International Convention of 1883. Stick to that only. Got it? The International Convention of 1883. Tell your other chaps."

"Okay. The International Convention o' 1883. Sure. . . ."

The frigate came steaming up. She swept round landward of them this time in a wide arc, looking very impressive. Past them she surged at speed, the embodiment of grace and power. Then listing over dramatically, she swung sharply to starboard, seawards again.

"The bluidy nets!" Tosh cried. "She's going to cut right through them. Damn and cooper her!"

Adam bit his lip. "I'm sorry," he said. "I'm sorry, Sandy. I didn't really think she would actually do it."

The big man said nothing.

They watched, set-faced. Then abruptly, Tosh raised his voice again. "Jings—she's no'! She's no' going through them. She's missing them. It's a dummy run, that's what it is—a dummy run, just!"

The frigate was in fact sweeping past a few yards beyond the yellow buoy that marked the end of the net-line. The buoy heaved and tossed—but that was all. It was a demonstration, no more.

With expert seamanship, the *Unicorn* swept on in its tight curve, to come back towards *Bluebell*, reducing speed drastically.

"He kens hoo to handle his ship, yon guy," Tosh said, with reluctant admiration. "Throws it aboot like it was a wee scooter!"

"Aye—it's maybe as well he's no' as hot on law as he is on seamanship," Sandy nodded.

Once again the loud-hailer clicked on. "I told you, Skipper, to have those nets in," it said. Adam thought that he sensed a hint of reproach, almost of pleading, to flavour that accusation—but that may only have been his imagination.

"Aye," Sandy shouted back. "And I tell't you we werena going to, mind. You were gey near to my nets yon time,

Captain."

"I'm glad you noticed it! You realise that I could just as easily cut them to ribbons?"

"Ooh, aye—nothing to stop you, Captain. Except what you might call the consequences, maybe! The High Court!"

"I order you for the last time—get them in, man."

"Sorry to disoblige you, sir—but they stay oot."

"Don't be a dam' fool! Your friends along there have had the sense to do what they're told. . . ."

"Och, them! They're no' friends o' oor's. Just English—like yoursel', Captain?" Sandy glanced southwards. "But they dinna seem to be obeying you awful fast, at that—do they?"

Inertia did indeed appear to have overtaken the two Seahouses boats. The first one had her nets in and aboard, certainly, but she was still lying motionless in the same place; the second evidently had stopped hauling altogether, with her nets part in, part out, and was merely waiting. Undoubtedly they were watching the progress of events with interest.

"All right," the frigate captain snapped back. "You've asked for it. I've been very patient. I've got your Registration Number and your craft's name. But I'll have your own name too, Skipper, please?"

"Surely, surely. Alexander Logan, it is. Airdmouth. That'll find me. Och, we'll get yours, easy enough, oot the Navy List. For the legalities, you ken. . . ."

They heard the telegraph ringing again, and the ship slowly moved off, gathering way.

"See you in court!" Tosh yelped after it.

The frigate rounded right back on her recent wake, heading north again. She went up as far as the position of the three Holy Island craft, swept round them, and began to come down the line again. Suddenly there was a muffled boom from her direction, and at her stern a white column of water spouted upwards. The fishermen were staring, wondering, when another boom followed, and another spout.

"Losh—she's depth-charging us!" Tosh exclaimed. "The rotten baistard!"

161

"Yon are no' depth-charges," Sandy declared. "No' the real ones, anyway. A depth-charge is ten times that power, and mair. I ken—I've fired them mysel', in the war. There's another! Yon are just seven-pound charges—just noise and splatter! And another!"

The warship was now driving due south at full speed, just a short way to landward of the strung-out fishing-boats, leaving a trail of submarine explosions behind her, at perhaps fifty-yard intervals. The air shook to the repeated shock of them, the spouts followed each other in quick succession, and a drift of spray hung like mist behind her, glinting rainbow colours in the noonday sun. Highly spectacular the entire performance looked.

"But . . . what's it for?" Adam cried. "What on earth is he doing?"

"I'll tell you in a wee minute," Sandy said, blue eyes narrowed. "When he reaches my nets."

The frigate came abreast of *Bluebell's* net-line. She did not change direction nor slacken speed. Parallel with the nets and the drifting boat she swept, still dropping her explosive charges, and on southwards, towards the Seahouses boats.

Sandy Logan let out a long sigh. "Poor laddie," he said, grinning. "Och, he had to do something, the man!"

Wet by the fine spray of spouting waters, they watched the *Unicorn* drive on past the last two boats, and further still. The explosions stopped soon after she left the last one, but the ship herself neither slackened speed nor turned around. On she went, leaving a broad boiling white wake, White Ensign streaming, authority in every long line of her, the vivid expression of sea-power—but getting smaller every moment. Away and away she swept, her course set deliberately southwards.

"Well . . . !" Adam said. "That was a dramatic exit, anyway! But why? What was the point of it?"

"Just what you said, Adam—a dramatic exit," Sandy agreed. "No more'n that. He couldna just slink off, withoot doing something. His wee bangs sounded real impressive . . . and didna hurt a soul! They maybe killed a few salmon, though.

162

They certainly would drive away any fish frae hereaboots—
which was likely the man's idea."

"Your nets? The explosions wouldn't damage the nets?"

"I dinna think it. No' yon wee ones, at that distance. They'd
be fifty yards frae the nets. If it had been real depth-charges, of
course, it would have been different. . . ."

"So it was all just a gesture! Bluff! He must have been told
not to damage the nets, surely. Or else we scared him off it. It
looks more and more as though the powers-that-be aren't
happy about the whole business. They're unsure of themselves,
that's clear. Especially out here, beyond the three-mile limit.
This is . . . hang it, this is encouraging, you know!"

"Aye, I'll no' say it's no'."

"We've got them licked!" Tosh cried. "Hooray, boys! They've
left us to it. Losh—the boys wi' the telescopes in at Berwick'll
fair be tearing their hair!"

There was modified jubilation aboard *Bluebell*. The sound
of ragged cheers floating down the wind from the Holy Island
boats added to the general satisfaction. The first Seahouses
boat came up to congratulate them, but pointed out that it was
no use for her to shoot her nets again here, after all that
disturbance of the water. She would come out and try it
another day.

After all of which it came as a distinct anti-climax when,
hauling in *Bluebell's* nets, they found only one medium-sized
salmon caught therein—though there was a fair selection of
other fish. All were dead, killed by the shock-waves.

It would be a question of finding the right place out here,
undoubtedly, where the salmon lay, or took their route to the
river mouth. Obviously they had not found it yet. And there
was a lot of sea. . . .

They sailed for home with mixed feelings.

Once again a reception committee awaited *Bluebell* on the pier
as she drew into Airdmouth's harbour. Indeed there was quite
a crowd present. This time, however, it was not composed of
wholly local well-wishers. The dark blue uniforms of the

constabulary were prominent. Tosh Hogg it was who recognised George Hogarth the Tweed bailiff there also. For his part, Adam perceived the presence of at least one of the reporters of the day before.

"It looks like a showdown, at last," he said. "I wonder what's screwed them up to doing something? The cruiser business, d'you think?"

"We'll soon ken," Sandy observed. "They'll no' be here to congratulate us on licking the Navy, I'm thinking!"

As *Bluebell* berthed, and Sandy switched off his diesels, Hogarth stepped forward, with the same Police Inspector as before at his elbow, and the Pressman only a pace behind.

Indeed all the watchers surged nearer, excitement in the air. "Skipper Logan," Hogarth said, harsh-voiced. "I am here to charge you with fishing for salmon in restricted waters, contrary to the provisions of the Tweed Fisheries Act."

"Ooh, aye," Sandy nodded. "A fine day, Mr Hogarth. 'Afternoon, Inspector."

"You can cut out the backchat, Logan," Hogarth snapped. "We've had quite enough of that. This is serious. You're being charged. I have authority to charge you, under the Act."

"Surely. You had last time we met, too, Mr Hogarth—but you didna do it. We've been wondering when you'd get roond to it."

"We have had a radio message from the captain of HMS *Unicorn* that he caught you fishing well within the five-mile limit, this morning. He warned you, and you persisted in fishing. Do you deny it?"

"No. Just as I didna deny fishing a lot nearer Berwick than that, you'll mind, a few days ago. You'll mind that too, Inspector?"

"You were let off with a warning, then. We've been patience itself. You have deliberately ignored all warnings, and openly flouted the law of the land."

"Not the law of the land—just the Tweed Act of 1857," Adam intervened.

"Be quiet, you! I am speaking to the skipper of this vessel,

164

who must bear the responsibility."

"I'd remind you, nevertheless, Hogarth, that this is not a court of law, and any man may speak who so desires," Adam returned quietly. "If you are charging Alexander Logan, you will of course have to charge me also."

The bailiff ignored him. "Logan—you realise, I hope, what you have let yourself in for? Under the Act, I may arrest your boat and confiscate all nets, engines, gear and fish."

"Jings—I'd like to see you try!" Tosh cried out. "Just you try it, Mister!"

"Quiet, Tosh," Sandy said. "Leave this to me. Mr Hogarth will do his duty . . . maybe."

There was an angry murmur from some of the crowd at the back.

The Inspector turned and looked round, frowning. He cleared his throat heavily. Four constables standing nearby stirred.

Hogarth cleared his throat likewise, and glanced at his companion, "You heard the threat, Inspector? I want that noted."

The reporter was writing hard.

"I'm coming aboard your boat, Logan," Hogarth went on. "And I warn you—any resistance or violence, and it will go hard with you. The police are quite capable of dealing with you. They have their orders."

"But you're welcome, Mr Hogarth. And you too, Inspector. Why should there be any violence? We're no' resisting anything."

"We are, in fact, just delighted that we have forced you to take action against us," Adam informed. "Legal action, I mean—as distinct from illegally tearing our nets to pieces with grapnels. We've been hoping for this, from the start."

The bailiff looked at the Inspector, lips tight. He stepped forward, and jumped down into the boat, studiously ignoring the hand that Sandy held out to aid him. A degree more stiffly the bulky and silent police officer followed on.

"May I come too, Skipper?" the Pressman asked, eagerly.

"You may not!" Hogarth barked back, over his shoulder.

165

"Och, yes—come if you want to, man," Sandy nodded genially. "It's my boat yet. Nobody's arrested it so far—nor me neither!"

The reporter jumped down, grinning. "Up Scotland, eh Mr Logan?"

"Och, well. . . ."

"What's that got to do with it?" Adam asked, frowning.

Hogarth stood by the fish-hold, and looked about him. "I want to see your catch, Logan," he said.

Sandy, with a huge hand, wiped the beginnings of a smile off his face. "Well, now," he said. "There's no' that much to show you, mind. . . ."

"Stop quibbling, man. I'm going to confiscate your catch, d'you hear? There will be no argument about it."

"Hear him!" Tosh hooted. "Hear the big fellow!"

"What aboot the boat? And the gear? And the nets? You confiscating them too, Mister?"

"H'mm. I should do—but on this occasion we'll let you off more lightly than you deserve. We'll take your catch only. But I warn you, in future we will not be so gentle. Open up this fish-hold, Logan."

"Och, it's no' worth your while, Mr Hogarth. . . ."

"Be quiet! Open it up."

Sandy shrugged. "Okay. Pe'er. Tom. Open it for the gentlemen."

Grinning, two of the crew did as they were bidden.

Hogarth peered in. He shifted his position, the better to see into the dark far corners. He frowned. "This is empty," he accused. "Where have you hidden your catch?"

"We havena just hidden it. . . ."

"You needn't think that such childish tricks will get you anywhere, Logan," the bailiff told him. "We'll search your vessel."

"Search away," the skipper agreed. "There's a wee salmon in yon box forrard there. You can take that, if you want to."

The other glanced disdainfully at the single medium-small fish in the large fish-box. He spoke a word to the Inspector,

166

who called down a couple of constables to conduct the search. With Hogarth these two looked diligently into every corner of *Bluebell*, to the cheerful commentary of her complement. When they found nothing, the bailiff's ever-darkening frown was black indeed.

"D'you mean to say this is all you caught?" he demanded, pointing at the modest fish in its box.

"Just that." Sandy picked it out and handed it over to his inquisitor. "It's all yours, for your confiscation, Mister. If you wait just a wee minute, I'll wrap it up in a bit paper for you. . . .

There was a titter from the crowd.

Hogarth's and the Inspector's eyes met.

"H'rr'mmm. That'll be about it then, Mr Hogarth," the latter said, heavily—his first major contribution to the discussion.

The bailiff looked down at the fish in his hand, up at the crowd, and far away. His lips moved soundlessly. Then shrugging, he turned to climb back on to the pier. "Let this be a warning to you, Logan," he said. "We'll be a lot harder on you next time—if you're such a fool as to risk it. And if we catch any of you poaching at night . . . God help you!"

"Poaching, man—us? Och, mercy me—what an idea! Can I give you a bit hand up, Inspector?"

"I'd remind you, in front of all these witnesses," Adam put in, "that we do not accept your right to take this fish. We shall hold you responsible for taking illegal possession of it."

Hogarth did not answer. He did not even look round.

Sandy raised his voice after the departing bailiff. "Och, Mr Hogarth—maybe you should ken it wasna us kill't yon fish, at all. It was the captain o' the *Unicorn*. He kill't it wi' all his wee depth-charges. We just sort o' brought it along so's it wouldna be wasted. . . ."

There was a shout of laughter from the pier.

Through it the official procession stalked, with what dignity it could muster, to the waiting cars. George Hogarth well in front and holding the unfortunate fish at arm's length before him almost as though it stank.

167

Somebody started to cheer.

Adam found the Pressman at his elbow. "Could I have a few words with you, Mr Horsburgh?" he asked confidentially.

"By Heaven, you could not!" that man cried. "I had my bellyful of you and your kind yesterday—and this morning! Good-day to you!" And he jumped up on to the pier and set off for the schoolhouse, striding hugely.

XIII

A DAM'S precautions anent not speaking to the Press were, of course, of no avail. Every paper in the land featured the Berwick salmon war next morning, most of the Scottish ones in a very big way. Even *The Scotsman* made it front-page news. The Berwick-for-Scotland tie-up was still generally taken for granted, though the fishing controversy got pride of place. Unfortunately, misconceptions on this issue were as major as they were varied. The most common of these were that somehow the Scots were getting a raw deal, and that it was the English and their law that were at fault. From many, it might be inferred that, if it was not for the English connection, anybody could fish for salmon anywhere without let or hindrance. Wild and curiously irrelevant comments were made by folk who ought to have known better—or, at least, sub-editors' paraphrases of such comments. The Airdmouth fishermen were in general accepted as high-minded patriots— a role to which they had not actually aspired.

It was not all comment, of course. Reportage had not neglected its opportunities. There were highly coloured reports, not all of them strictly accurate or pertinent, from a number of sources. The scene at Airdmouth harbour was variously and imaginatively chronicled, with a marked unanimity of emphasis on the vanquishment of the authorities. It appeared to be taken for granted that the fishermen had indeed managed to catch and hide away a large haul of salmon that the bailiff and police had been unable to find. Somebody had been prevailed upon to give some account of the frigate incident—presumably a Northumbrian. The general picture given was of a large fleet of fishing-boats outnumbered and out-gunned but gallantly defying the angry might of the Royal Navy, the impression being somehow conveyed in more than one North of England journal that it all constituted a great victory for the brave Holy

Islanders in their age-old struggle against the thieving Scots.

Seals got into it too, though the connection was made less than clear. Much was made of the depth-charging, which assumed the proportions of almost full-scale warfare, the reverberations of which had apparently reached land.

It all made spirited and exciting reading, with pictures of fishing-boats, warships, Bamburgh Castle, stretches of the Tweed near Peebles, and curiously, a leering portrait of Jamesy Pringle in his Sunday blues, to garnish it all.

What worried Adam Horsburgh most of all, however, were somewhat less prominent paragraphs at the end of two or three of the features, reporting a crop of night poaching incidents along the course of the River Tweed inland. These appeared to be the work of amateurs and optimists, some of whom had been apprehended in the act by gamekeepers and police, and most of whom appeared thereafter to have become grievously vocal, one as far upstream as Kelso, to the general effect that they were committing no offence, that all the salmon laws had been proved to be invalid, and that honest men could now fish where, when and how they wanted. Grim and stern assurances to the contrary were published by the highest authorities, who with one accord placed the responsibility for this eruption of criminal behaviour squarely on the irresponsible activities of the Airdmouth fishermen.

"The fools! The complete, ignorant and confounded fools!" Adam cried, at mankind in general and these ingenuous sportsmen in particular, and went hotfoot in search of Sandy Logan. That wise man, however, had escaped to sea about his normal daily business, and Adam was left to his own anxieties. The telephone in the schoolhouse rang almost incessantly that morning, apparently at the instance of cranks, fools and sub-editors from as far away as London. To escape them, on this second day of his vacation, he went off to Berwick to consult certain books of reference, mainly legal, in the local library. There, at the end of the Tweed bridge, he ran into a colourful demonstration led by banner-waving, tartan-clad enthusiasts from Edinburgh, demanding of bemused Berwickers whether

William Wallace had died in vain, and was Berwick to remain forever England? When he heard a bearded kilted stalwart declare that the door to freedom was now wide open, and the way thereto pointed by the gallant schoolmaster of Airdmouth, Adam fled forthwith.

The quiet of the library reference room, with its sober serried volumes, seemed a haven of sanity thereafter.

Adam very nearly did not answer his telephone's summons that evening. Only the lateness of the hour made him do so, on the perhaps foolish assumption that it at least would not be the Press again at that time of night.

It was in fact Hazel Scott. Her mood sounded, he felt, rather different from that in which she had telephoned him the day before. There was a crispness that he had not noted previously, nor did he fail to perceive that he was Mr Horsburgh again, not Adam.

"Hullo," she said. "Look, I don't want to be a nuisance, Mr Horsburgh—but I think you ought to know what is going on here. We had salmon poachers here last night, and a little bother—but nobody was caught. But now our keeper has just come in to say that there are actually two gangs of them on the river again tonight. Our river, I mean. One lot has got a couple of vans and nets. The keeper ordered them off, but they just jeered at him apparently, and threatened to throw him into the river."

Adam groaned. "I'm sorry," he said. "It's bad, bad. It's all this Press nonsense. . . "

"Yes, probably. The point is, though, that Daddy's here. He came back from London this afternoon, after reading the morning papers. He is . . . well, a little worked up. And Paterson—that's the keeper—wants to send for the police. I've stalled him off, meantime—told him to get together a few of the estate people. But these poachers seem to be pretty tough, and you can't blame him for wanting police help and protection."

"No, of course not. . . "

"I needn't tell you what will happen if there is a fight with

171

these folk, and the police catch any. On our ground, Daddy being who he is. There's no doubt about the law of the matter here, and they'll make an example of them. It will all be linked up with your campaign, and will be a big black mark against you, I'm afraid."

"Don't I know it! It's the worst possible thing. These folk just haven't a clue what it's all about, and the harm they're doing. Look—would it be any help if I came over, myself . . . ?"

"That's what I rang up to suggest. If you could bring a bunch of your fishermen with you, and deal with those people yourselves. It might save the day. Keep the police out of it. Daddy's swithering about sending for the police, anyway. He doesn't really want them—not on his own property. As local MP he doesn't want to make himself unpopular—doesn't want to lose votes. It mightn't look too good if there were reports of him calling in the police to persecute local poachers. Landlord-oppressor stuff. On the other hand, he recognises that it could help *his* side of the battle about the Tweed Act—just as you do. So I thought if your people could take care of the situation for us, it might do some good."

"Yes. Of course. That's right. I'll be over, just as quickly as I can. With whoever I can collect. Don't let your father or the keeper send for the police, if you can help it. Where do I go . . . ?"

"I'll meet you at the Mains. Linburndean Mains—the home farm. In the steading. It's handiest for the river—you can get cars down closest that way. How soon? It's about seven miles from Airdmouth. You'll have to hurry."

"Yes. Give me half an hour. I'll try to do it in less. But I don't know . . . well, how many of our chaps will be available. But I'll get as many as I can. Try and stall till then. . . ."

It was in fact nearer three-quarters of an hour than half before Adam's car and the old green van lurched into the farm steading of Linburndean in the Tweedside parish of Ladykirk. He had had some difficulty in gathering the men he wanted. It was not that they were all out poaching again, themselves, as

172

he had feared—some were indeed innocently asleep in their beds—but that there was no enthusiasm for going out to interfere with other poachers upriver in order to preserve Sir John Scott's salmon. The fishermen's attitude generally was good luck to the poachers and let Scott look after himself. It was not until Adam had run Sandy Logan to earth, in the Manse of all places, that he was able to get some appreciation of the dangers of the situation to their cause, the Reverend Mr Fraser strongly supporting the schoolmaster. Thereafter Sandy had prevailed upon and rounded up nine or ten men for immediate action, and piled them into the two vehicles. A further contingent was to follow on, under Dand Fairgrieve, when it could be assembled. The drive through the night, over the Lamberton hills, by winding country roads and farm tracks, had been hectic.

It was only a little short of midnight.

Hazel Scott was waiting for them by the corner of a cartshed. She had a young man with her, whom she did not bother to introduce.

"You've been an age!" she accused, to Adam. "I thought you were never coming. It may be too late, now."

"Too late? How d'you mean . . . ?"

"Too late to do any good. The police have been sent for. They may be here—at the House, anyway—by now. There were explosions after I phoned you. On the river. They've started dynamiting the water, the idiots! It was too much for my father. Especially when Colonel Newman phoned about it—from Norhamwick Hall on the English side of the river. He couldn't let it go, any longer. He got on to the Chief Constable. . . ."

"Lord!" Adam cried. "The utter fools! Dynamiting the water! That's fantastic, criminal . . . !"

There was a growl from the crowding fishermen.

"Where are they, Miss?" Sandy asked. "What bit o' the water are they on?"

"There's two lots of them. I don't know whether they're working together. One lot is at the stretch just down from here, that we call the Long Ladder. It's a succession of good pools. The others are at Pate's Bank—or were. By the sound of it the explosions were coming from the Long Ladder."

"I ken it fine," the big man nodded. "We'll away doon, and see these boys."

"Aye, we will!" Tosh Hogg agreed. "Stupid baistards!" One result, at least, of the bad news about the use of explosives, was the swinging of the fishermen's sympathies wholly against poachers who would ruin the fishing for everybody else— including other poachers—by killing everything in the area wholesale. There was neither sport nor fairness in that.

"Will Paterson—that's our keeper—has got together a few of the estate-workers, and they're down there somewhere too," the girl went on. "He doesn't know about you people coming. I . . . I thought I'd better not tell him. It's the police he wanted. He's waiting for *them*. I didn't think . . ."

"Quite," Adam said grimly. "*We* certainly don't want to get mixed up with the police. This looks like being a somewhat confused affair! You don't think that your keeper and his friends will have tackled the poachers on their own?"

"I shouldn't think so. He's already challenged them, you see, and they defied him, threatened him. There's too many of them for our own people to handle. He will just be keeping them under observation, I imagine, waiting for the police. Though the police may be here now. . . ."

"Then we shouldna be standing here jawing," Sandy intervened. "Time we were taking a bit hand. There's mair o' oor chaps coming, Miss. Will you bide here, and send them on after us?"

"No. I'm coming with you. I may be needed."

"This gentleman, then . . . ?"

"I shouldn't think Ronnie—Captain Calthwaite—would be much use," she answered, with marked frankness. "I mean, he doesn't really know the place."

"Aye. Well, Sim does. Eh, Sim—you ken the Lang Ladder, fine? You wait for Dand, and bring him doon. But tell him to watch oot—no' to get mixed up wi' the polis, or this keeper and his bunch. Tell him to give his wee whistle—you ken? Okay? Right, boys—come on."

They hurried out of the steading, leaving the oldest of the fishermen behind, and with the silent Captain Calthwaite tailing along in the rear doubtfully, to follow a muddy farm-track that led southwards towards the river. It was flat ploughland here, but soon they were into sloping open wood-land. There was half a moon somewhere behind a high ceiling of cloud.

It was very dark in the woods. There was only a narrow path, but Sandy led the way without faltering. Having to fall behind him, Hazel turned to Adam, who came next.

"Your friend seems to know the way very well, for a stranger . . . on our property!" she mentioned.

The same thought had occurred to Adam. "It's not so very far from Airdmouth, really," he pointed out.

"Just what I was thinking!" she answered dryly.

They left it at that.

As they neared the river. Sandy swung away to the left, off the path. "The keeper's no' likely to be lying waiting *doon* river o' them," he explained. "The Big Hoose is upstream, so if he's waiting for the polis to come frae there, he'll be that side. We'll approach frae doon the way."

Nobody argued otherwise.

Slipping and stumbling in the darkness amongst roots and dead leaves on a steepish slope, they made their way along eastwards now—with many hists and shushes for silence from forward. Eventually, without any sign of other men, the trees died away before them, and the broad smooth-flowing river lay open. There was a track that followed the riverside. Along this they turned.

"What's the position of the Captain?" Adam whispered to the young woman, when he had opportunity.

"He's a friend of mine," she answered briefly.

"Yes. But I mean, about getting involved in all this? Dodging the police, and so on. Not just his line of country, I should think?"

"He's all right," the girl assured, lightly now. "Don't worry. Ronnie's quite devoted to, to my interests!"

"Oh!" Adam said, and frowned. "I see." He pushed a little way ahead.

They had progressed three or four hundred yards along the bank, and the louder murmuration of the river, where shallows and broken water linked the pools of the Long Ladder, was sounding before them, when suddenly Sandy halted practically in his tracks. There was something of a pile-up behind him, inevitably. His sibilant hiss for silence, plus the abruptness of his stop, prevented anything more than involuntary grunts of protest. Adam, close at the big man's shoulder, peered ahead and down towards the river.

"No' there," Sandy breathed in his ear. "Right ahead. At the side o' the path, just."

Staring, Adam perceived darker shadows against the loom of what appeared to be bushes at the landward side of the track—nothing distinct or clear-cut. There did not seem to be movement of any sort. The bushes were perhaps a dozen yards away. He nodded.

"Half a dozen o' them, at least," Sandy murmured. "They've seen us, too. Watching us."

How he could tell that was beyond Adam.

The girl was at the skipper's other side. "What are they doing?" she whispered. "Are they a guard, for the poachers? Sentries?"

"Too many for that. They didna seem to be doing anything. Just waiting and watching. I'm wondering if they could be the polis?"

"I . . . I don't know."

They all stood there, staring. So, presumably, did the unidentified men ahead. Neither party moved.

"It may be your keeper and his people," Adam suggested, beneath his breath. "Sandy says there are half a dozen of them."

"I suppose it could be. . . "

"How far are we from where the poachers are working?

176

This Long Ladder?"

"We're just at the tail of it, now. It extends for a couple of hundred yards. The pools and runs. They could be anywhere along there."

Still they stood. So did the others. The ridiculousness of the entire situation was not lost upon Adam at least.

"What are you going to do?" Hazel asked.

"Better get back and roond them, I reckon," Sandy said. "We dinna want mixed up wi' the wrong folk. We should of come in from the other side, after all." He turned. "Pass the word back, boys—we're backing oot. The way we came. And quiet mind."

"There's mair o' us than them!" Tosh protested in a stage-whisper. "Let *them* get oot o' it. We dinna need to turn back for them!"

"Aye, we do. We want to settle this business withoot trouble. That's what we're here for, is it no? To keep the polis oot o' it. And this keeper, too. The only ones we want any words wi' are these boys on the river. We'll move back."

"This is bluidy daft!" his mate grumbled, but obeyed.

Adam was about to give his support to the skipper's decision when he perceived that this was unnecessary; everybody had begun to edge their way slowly backwards. Almost at the same moment, he glimpsed movement ahead. He paused, peering. Yes—he was sure of it. The others were moving too—and backwards likewise, in the opposite direction.

Turning, he hurried after his own party. "Look, Sandy—they're packing up, too," he said. "Moving away. Same time as we did. I saw them."

"Jings!" Tosh exclaimed, "Whatna circus, right enough!"

"Will we move forward again, then?"

"No," the big man decided. "We'll carry on as we're doing. They maybe just moved back a bit behind yon bush. We'll work up through the wood again, and doon a bit higher up. Beyond them. We'll have to be real quiet. It's a tricky game this we're playing, mind."

So they climbed up into the trees again, roughly back on the route that they had come, treading softly. At one pause, to listen, Hazel spoke in Adam's ear.

"I like your big fellow," she whispered. "Knows his own mind, and takes charge. No to-ing and fro-ing. That's the way a man should be."

"You think so? I must remember that . . . !"

"Quiet!" Sandy said. "We'll go doon again, now—at a slant. We're a good bit past where they were."

A large clump of evergreens of some sort blocked their way, parallel with the river. Sandy had paused, to ask the young woman how far it extended, when he stopped in mid-phrase. Clear for all to hear, a stick cracked nearby—from the evergreens in fact, in front of them. There was a rustling and scuffling, a grunt or two, and then almost at their very feet, barely seen but distinctly perceived, somebody parted the bushes and emerged therefrom. He was followed by another, and another. The party above stood as though turned into trees.

The newcomers came on. The foremost had only a few feet to climb before he all but collided with Sandy Logan. They heard his gasp as he came to an abrupt halt.

"Goad!" somebody behind him said, simply.

There was a few moments of strained silence. There was no backing out this time. The two leaders were little more than a yard apart. Sandy at length cleared his throat.

"Aye, then," he said, warily non-committal.

There was no response to that.

As the silence became uncomfortable, Hazel Scott spoke. "Is that you, Will? Will Paterson?"

There was no reply to that either.

"They're no' wearing polis caps, anyhow," Tosh Hogg observed, *sotto voce*, from the rear.

"No," the girl agreed. Her voice, though still low-set, sounded very clear. "I think, you know, that these people have no right to be here. On our land."

"Aye," Sandy took her up. "The same lot as we saw back there, I reckon. Who are you, boys?" The question was put quite mildly.

He obtained a reply this time. "Least said, soonest mended, maybe," the foremost man told him.

"Nae names, nae pack-drill!" somebody else added, from behind.

Sandy rasped a hand over his chin. "Aye, maybe," he conceded.

"Have you been poaching salmon?" the girl asked, bluntly. No answer.

"I think you should leave this to me, Miss," Sandy mentioned. "Look, you boys—we dinna want trouble. But there's mair o' us than there is o' you." He kept his voice low. "You been after the salmon?"

"Who're you that's asking? You're no' Will Paterson. And you're no' the polis. . . ."

"Ho—so you're local, eh? You ken the keeper. Then you ought to ken better than to dynamite yon water."

"Hell—yon wasna us! Losh, no! We were just having a bit haul wi' a wee net. Nothing serious. We wouldna do a thing like that." The words came in a flood now, urgent but soft-spoken. "They're doon there still. Them that did it. Gathering in the dead fish. You can see their torches, behind these bushes. They're no' caring who sees them."

"Who are they, then? These others?"

"Goad kens! They're a right gang o' them. Doon frae Edinburgh, likely. Coorse boys, yon. We had a bit word wi' them, as we came by—but they gien us a flea in oor ears! When we heard the explosions we packed up quick. We didna want mixed up in that sort o' thing. We just thought we'd have a bit fun—like it said in the papers. Aboot it no' being against the law to take a bit salmon, see. . . ."

"That's nonsense," Adam intervened. "That only refers to salmon in the sea. You've not read it properly. . . ."

"Leave that the noo, Adam," Sandy said quickly. "Look, boys. We want quit o' these dynamiters. All o' us. Wi' as little trouble as possible. You're local—so you ken the harm they're doing. The polis have been sent for, more's the pity. Naebody wants them mixed up in this. Will you give us a hand?"

179

"Eh? You mean, us? But . . . who're you, then? Yon's Miss Scott, is it no'?"

"Never mind that. We're frae Airdmouth. Fishers. We're giving Miss Scott a hand, to clear up this before the polis come. We're no' against a bit o' decent honest poaching—but this is different! Are you wi' us?"

"Well . . . aye, I suppose so."

"Och . . . maybe, then."

"Good. That's fine. We'll get doon at them, then, withoot wasting any mair time."

Adam swallowed, and stared at the young woman beside him. He was surprised to find her laughing softly but with every appearance of enjoyment. "This is . . . this is extraordinary," he got out.

"Rum do, I must say!" came almost apologetically from the rear, in the accents of the Brigade of Guards—the silent Captain Calthwaite's first contribution to the evening.

"Aye, then. Doon through these bushes. And quiet, mind."

Once through the belt of evergreens, there was no need for further searching. Below them, in fact, was a scene of great activity. The people down at the river were not caring about secrecy or even discretion. Lights were shining everywhere, some on the water, some on land. Adam was shocked—though it was presumably logical that folk who were not afraid to advertise themselves by making loud explosions were not going to be chary of using a few electric torches. He counted nine lights.

Just how many men were down there was not easy to say. There could not be less than a dozen, and there were probably more. The majority seemed to be wading about in the shallows between the pools, many of them waist-deep; others, on the bank, obviously were dragging in a net. A substantial gleaming pile of silver glowed beside the path, and lesser gleams reflected the flashlamps' rays elsewhere, as the stunned and dead fish were handled.

"Look at that! It's just murder!" Hazel declared hotly.

180

"Those are some of the best pools on the entire Tweed—wrecked, ruined!"

"They've got some fish there, losh!" Tosh exclaimed. "Hundreds o' quids worth. Yon's big business, all right!"

"It's criminal folly . . ." Adam began, but Sandy cut him short.

"Aye, that's so. But, look—we'll away doon and talk to them. *I* will, anyway. Try and make them see some sense. The rest o' yous just sort o' move roond behind me in a circle. To cut them off. We'll do it the decent way if they'll let us—get them oot o' this quietly and leave the fish behind. If they'll no', we'll learn them a bit lesson so's they dinna come back in a hurry. There's mair o' us than them, I think. But we'll have to be quick aboot it—before the polis turn up. Okay?"

"Aye, Sandy—sure."

"We'll gie them the works!"

"I'll come down with you, Sandy," Adam put in. "Explain the law of the thing to them, if necessary."

"I dinna think that lot'll be right interested in the law, Adam. They'll be mair concerned wi' hoo many o' us there are! You stay here. All o' you—move up quiet while I'm talking. Let them see you. You stay here wi' the lassie, Adam—there may be some rough stuff."

"No, look here . . . !"

"You don't need to think . . . !"

Adam and the girl made their protests simultaneously.

"Och, peace, peace! I'm away doon, noo. Some o' yous be ready to get in the water, after them. And mind, if it comes to a fight—watch oot and no' kill anybody!"

Sandy strode down towards the centre of the activity below. With the loom of the wooded bank behind him, to shadow him, he got quite close before a shout proclaimed that he had been seen. Swiftly a number of torch beams concentrated upon his large figure. He raised a hand, and his great voice.

"Listen to me, you boys," he called. "We dinna like folk that dynamite the water, aboot here. It spoils things for other folk, see. We're no' standing for this. We've got you surrounded. If

181

you ken what's guid for you, you'll get oot o' this double quick, see—before the polis arrive. . . ."

"Shurrup, you!" a hoarse voice interrupted. "Who the hell d'you think you are?"

"Pitch him in the river!" somebody shouted.

"Aye—scrag him! He's another of them keepers."

"I'm no keeper—and I'm no' shutting up either, for any gang o' city corner-boys!" Sandy asserted—but in the same almost conversational tone. "We're local, see—and there's plenty o' us. Plenty to give you boys your needings. Gaffing or netting the odd fish is one thing—but blowing up the river's another. Noo—we're giving you a chance to get oot o' this withoot any trouble—but you'll leave yon fish behind you. And you'll no' come back, see."

"You talk too much, big boy!" the hoarse voice said, and closed on a sort of snigger. A slight figure, its slenderness accentuated by the long dark jacket and almost skin-tight trousers, moved forward, silhouetted in the light of the torches. "A wide-mouth, eh? We ken how to deal wi' guys like you— eh, boys?" Despite the aspect of youthfulness about that slim padded-shouldered figure, with the immature giggle at the end of each hoarse phrase, there was something distinctly and potently menacing there, undeniably.

"Dinna be daft, laddie," Sandy advised, standing his ground. "I tell't you—the polis'll be here any time. You've got a chance to get oot. . . ."

"We're no' worried for the mucking polis, clever guy! The polis canna do anything to us for taking salmon—d'you no' read the papers? No more, they canna. Yon law was a dud, see. These guys from the fishing-village showed that. Real smart guys."

"You're all wrong, my wee mannie. You couldna be wronger! *We're* your smart guys frae the fishing-village—that's us. We're the Airdmouth fishers—and we're here to stop you and your kind ruining oor fight for us. It's only in the sea that you can take salmon, free—a mile oot to sea. Here on the river it's private, like it's always been. You could get six months each for what you've done here. . . ."

"Away and scrag yoursel'!" the other declared, impatiently. "Better still—we'll do it for you! Eh, boys? You think because you're the size o' a haystack you can run us aroond, eh? Jeeze—time you learned different!"

That undoubtedly was a popular suggestion with the rest of the gang. Men had been climbing out of the river all this time.

Logan's supporters had not been wholly inactive, either. They had spread out singly and in little clusters, indistinguishable against the background of the evergreens, and had begun to move downwards. Adam, all ears for what was being said below, had stayed where he was, the girl and a few others with him. As all the signs of imminent and violent action multiplied, he began to edge forward also. Suddenly he found that his arm was being tightly gripped.

"Don't, Adam!" Hazel Scott whispered urgently. "That man—look at his hand. He's got a knife there, I'm sure. He's dangerous. Don't. . . ."

Certainly the slender character in the drape suit seemed to be moving forward in a curious fashion, sidelong, crabwise almost, with one hand evidently behind his back.

"All the more reason to see he doesn't get at Sandy . . ." Adam began, when his other arm was grabbed.

"Over there! See him—creeping roond!" The man at the schoolmaster's other side was not one of the Airdmouth people, but one of the newcomers whom they had picked up.

Looking where he pointed, Adam was just able to distinguish a dark crouching figure working round by the river bank, obviously to get behind Sandy, threat in every line of him, and carrying some sort of stick or club.

"Yes. Time we took a hand," Adam jerked, and shook off the girl's hand.

He was forestalled, however. Tosh Hogg had noticed the creeping man also. His yell, of mixed warning, challenge and sheer glee, incoherent but entirely eloquent, sounded loud and clear as he launched himself downwards like a missile.

"Stay here," Adam ordered the young woman. "Calthorpe

or whatever he's called will look after you." He raised his voice. "At them, boys! Come on—down at them!"

The fight by the riverside, though it held some superficial resemblance to that other struggle of a few nights before, under the Queen Elizabeth Pier of Berwick, in fact bore no real relationship to it. Even Adam Horsburgh, inexpert in these matters as he was, did not fail to recognise that. This was serious. Not that the other had been a mere sham or pretence; it had been a good fight of its kind, a conventional and suitable method of emphasising a point of view, between men of similar background and outlook, with little or no personal animosity about it, and considerable satisfaction for many if not all. Here, however, no such limiting factors prevailed. The combatants represented entirely different and hostile ways of life and thought. Each group undoubtedly despised the other. Malice was here, resentment, hatred even.

Adam hurled himself at the other side's spokesman. Sandy Logan was there before him, however—as indeed was another of the Airdmouth party, who was thereupon quickly attacked by somebody else. Preoccupied with the horrible possibility of knife-work, Adam dodged round this scrimmage, peering to see if he could glimpse any gleam of steel. He did not see anything of the sort—but he did perceive another man bearing down on the group, upraised stick in hand, and mouthing profanities. At this newcomer's legs he flung himself, in a rugby tackle, and together they crashed to the muddy ground.

Rolling over and over, they struggled, seeking to jab at each other with fists, elbows and knees. Adam quickly realised his advantage. The other was trying to cling to his club, which was of little or no use to him at such close grips; moreover, he was wearing heavy waist-high fishing-waders, which obviously hampered his agility. Adam was getting in three blows to the other's one, and heard the satisfying grunts and gasps of punishment taken. Recognising that the prime requirements of the situation demanded the swift if temporary incapacitating of as many as possible of the enemy, he abruptly arched back his

184

body away from the other, to give him room, and before his opponent could use the opportunity to bring his stick into action, he drove forward his right fist with all his strength, to contact the man's solar plexus. With a combined sob and yelp, the fellow doubled up, winded.

Quite pleased with himself, Adam struggled to his feet. He was turning away to look for another target, when, on second thoughts, he stooped and picked up the stick from his writhing victim's limp grasp, and hurled it out into the river.

He saw a man climbing out of the water. This seemed to offer another quick and easy victory. Dodging struggling couples in the way, he rushed to the bank, caught the man while he was still off balance, and with a stooping uppercut toppled him backwards over the edge. Great was the splash thereof.

Unfortunately Adam's own impetus was hard to check. Also the bank was sloping and slippery. Feeling himself to be falling, he sought to twist round and fling himself straight down, still on the bank, rather than to topple forward into the river. He was only partly successful. Most of him came down on the bank, but one leg went into the water. He slithered. Clutching desperately, he managed to grab a root that held, his second foot now in the water. Spread-eagled thus, he scrabbled.

Glancing up, he saw a huge and menacing figure above him, curiously shaped and seemingly much larger than life-sized. He was shrinking back when he realised that it was Sandy Logan—but not only Sandy. The big man had another twisting struggling figure clutched to him and held high. Even as Adam peered, the second silhouette was launched bodily out into the river—clearly the slender drape-suited spokesman for the opposition.

The schoolmaster was about to call out mixed congratulation, identification of himself, and a request for a hand up, when the splash of the falling man first drowned his voice and then the thudding of heavy feet at the other side of him turned his head. A man was running up, with another close behind him. Both clutched sticks in their hands. Adam changed his cry to a shout of warning for Sandy, who had turned away. His call was choked off abruptly, as a savagely lashed out boot-toe took him on the side of his brow.

Brilliant light, and then complete darkness, silence, enveloped Adam Horsburgh.

XIV

ADAM probably was only fully unconscious for a very brief interval, but the period of semi-consciousness that followed seemed to him, afterwards, to have lasted a long time. In it he was vaguely aware, in an impersonal and not unpleasant way, of the struggle going on around and about him, of other people exerting themselves and suffering noisily, with nothing required of himself at all. He had a great throbbing in his head, admittedly, but so long as he did not move it, or open his eyes, or do anything aggressive like that, it did not trouble him too much. Just where he was he did not know, nor feel to be particularly important; at least he was neither in the river nor scrabbling on a steep bank.

It was the sound of whistles that brought him approximately to his senses. Only the police made a habit of blowing whistles. At first, he thought that he was under the cliffs of Airdmouth again, and then back below Berwick pier—indeed all these nocturnal battles had become somewhat confused in his mind, for the moment. The urgency and insistence of the whistling and allied shouting presently penetrated the haze of his perception, and unwillingly he opened his eyes.

Even so, it took him a little while, blinking and gazing around him and seeking to hold his splitting head together, to decide what was happening. The whistling seemed to be coming from across at the other side of the river, here at least two hundred yards wide. There were bright lights shining from there, too—car headlights again, undoubtedly, blazing across to light up the scene at this side.

Closer at hand, and thus illuminated, confusion reigned, with men exchanging blows or locked together, on their feet, on the ground, or in the water. But even to Adam's bemused brain it was evident that the fighting was only half-hearted now, temporising rather than furious, preoccupied with that embarrassing light and whistling rather than with wrath any more. Men were seeking an excuse to disengage. Some had already broken away. Adam, getting unsteadily up on to his hands and knees, perceived something of this.

Then Sandy Logan's powerful voice rang out, over-topping all other sounds. "Scram, boys!" he shouted. "Scram—everybody! All o' you. Scatter! The polis are here. They're this side, too. Further up. The others are calling them doon. Scram, while there's time. Watch oot for yon keeper and his boys. He's just up the track, there. I heard him yelling . . . to the polis. Scatter!"

Clearly this invitation was just what most of the combatants were waiting for. With remarkable unanimity men disentangled themselves from whatever involvement they were in, and sought to remove themselves from the vicinity, none hindering the other. Most headed singly or in small bunches into the dark cover of the evergreens and uphill. Those in the water went splashing downstream, heading in to the north bank. It was surprising, considering the savagery of the initial engagement, that no litter of the fallen seemed to be left behind on the field of battle, Adam Horsburgh himself appearing to be the last on the scene.

Even that unfortunate, dazed as he was, could now hear that some of the whistling was coming from upstream and on their own side of the river, punctuated by shouting. The knowledge got him to his feet, somehow. He stood swaying dizzily. He found that he was quite a few yards in from the river's edge— though undoubtedly he was very wet.

"That you, Adam? You okay, man?" Sandy's voice came again, from not far away. "Feeling better? I had to just aboot drag you oot the river. Come on—time we were oot o' this."

Adam found no words. Keeping on his feet was as much as he could manage, meantime.

"Something wrong?" The big man came pounding up. "Losh—your head! I didna see that. Thought you were just winded, maybe. Is it bad, Adam? Look—can you walk . . . ?"

The schoolmaster was trying to produce an answer to that

when hurrying lighter footsteps heralded Hazel Scott.

"Adam—are you hurt?" she cried. "I've been looking for you, everywhere. Somebody said you'd gone up the hill. Oh, Adam—your brow! Your brow's cut, bleeding . . . !"

"It's . . . it's nothing," he managed to assure, if thickly. "Just a kick. . . ."

"A kick! My goodness—the brutes! The cowardly mean brutes . . . !"

"He'll no' die, I reckon!" Sandy said. "Look, Miss—we'd better get him oot o' this, pretty quick—if we dinna want catched. Come on, Adam man."

With the skipper and the girl each taking an arm, they all moved up towards the bushes. Adam wanted to assert that this help was not really necessary, but somehow his customary eloquence had deserted him. After two or three false starts he gave it up, concentrating on putting one foot before another.

They were just into the blessed cover of the evergreens and out of the flooding light of at least four cars' headlamps on the English side of Tweed, when a new outbreak of shouting, in front of them and not upstream, brought them to a halt. It was not far off. Sandy snorted.

"That's Dand—the great muckle sumph! He's arrived, ower late—and he's letting the world ken he's here! Gosh—that's an awfu' noise! He'll bring every polisman in the county doon on him! Look, lassie—I'll have to get him to shut up, some way. It's Dand Fairgrieve, one o' oor skippers. . . ."

"It's all right. I'll manage Mr Horsburgh fine, myself. Off you go."

"You're sure? He's maybe best wi' you, anyway. If the polis was to come on him."

"Yes. I'd tell them the truth—that he was helping to get rid of these rotten gangsters. . . ."

Adam spoke clearly, each word by itself and distinct.

"No police," he said. "Don't want involved with police. Dangerous."

"Sure," Sandy agreed, hurriedly. "Well, I'm off. Get him to the cars, Miss—quick's you can."

"No. His brow needs attention. Must see to that first."

"But . . . we canna wait. And his car's there. . . ."

"You people get away in it. I'll bring him over to Airdmouth, later."

"Not at all . . ." Adam said, frowning.

"Okay, Miss. Guid luck, then. And . . . you're a guid lassie. Adam was right aboot you, all the time." The big man went hurrying off.

"This is . . . dam' silly!" Adam declared—though he wondered whether he could still keep upright and moving if the young woman took her surprisingly strong support from his arm and shoulder.

Hazel did not answer. She was listening—listening to the varied noises of the night, judging, weighing chances. Below them, there was a considerable commotion now, at the river bank, with shoutings to and fro across the Tweed. It seemed that the police were now in possession of the battlefield—empty, presumably, save for a net or two and a great heap of salmon. Would they come up the hill, beating out these woods? And where was Paterson the keeper, now?

"I think, you know, we should change direction, Adam," she said. "Keep along this way. Parallel with the river. Towards the House. And then down. I don't think they'd look for us behind them. There's somewhere there that we could hide, for a while. Though I don't see why we should, really. Hide, I mean. With me, you'd be all right with the police. . . ."

"No," the man said strongly, obstinately. "No police."

"All right. Whatever you say. This way. Mind that root. Can you manage, Adam? Is it very bad?"

"No. Getting better," he lied.

That wooded slope, in fact, represented nightmare to Adam Horsburgh ever after—despite a due appreciation of the solicitous young woman at his side. She placed herself below him, the better to support him—and any pretence that he did not lean on her heavily, metaphorically and actually, was soon dispensed with. The fallen leaves that thickly coated the ground were slimy, and the soil beneath slippery; roots ran and coiled everywhere; brambles clutched and tree-stumps projected; and as for the trees themselves, they seemed to jig and dance before him, deliberately to place themselves in his way even as he sought to avoid them. His head did not help by opening and shutting, opening and shutting, and sense of balance, like sense of direction, had more or less ceased to function. Adam did not hear people crashing about in the woods around them, nor the shouts of men, did not even perceive the glow of headlamps to the south or the flickering lights of electric torches nearer at hand; he had too many weaving lights of his own to cope with. Slight concussion can achieve that sort of result.

After a little, Hazel guided and eased him downhill again. Pausing when they reached the waterside track once more, she darted glances right and left. There were many lights to the left, but none seemed to be actually pointing in their direction, and she could glimpse no figures near enough to be seen. Across the track a dark square shape loomed against the vacancy that represented clear space above the river. Over to this she hurried her charge.

It was a timber boathouse. Apparently the door was locked, for the young woman groped about on a ledge below the rusticated eaves, and produced a key therefrom. Opening the door, hastily she urged Adam within, and reversing the key shut the door and locked it from the inside. She heaved a sigh of relief.

"Thank the good Lord for that!" she said sincerely.

It was dark in there, with visibility only just sufficient to reveal the south side open to the river, the U-shaped wooden platform that went round the walls, and the boat moored on the black water at their feet. A dank earthy smell permeated the place, and bats fluttered around, brushing them with their wings, before escaping out into the night. Adam made no complaint.

"We'll be safe here. We'll sit in the boat," Hazel decided. "If, by any chance, anybody did try to force their way in, we could push out into the river and get away. There are oars in the boat—and no other boat nearer than the House, to follow

191

us. See—hang on to this, and I'll get in first and help you down. You'll be all right?"

"Yes," he said—though climbing down into a swaying boat was for him a terrifying conception. With her aid, however, and by sitting on the edge of the platform first, he achieved it without the feared downfall. Thankfully he collapsed on to a thwart, as the boat heaved and dipped, and his breath came out of him in a long quivering sigh. "Much . . . obliged," he muttered.

She stood in front of him for a few moments, panting a little. Then she knelt down on the floorboards beside him. "Have you a match?" she asked. "I'm going to have a look at that brow of yours. Yes, I am. We've got to risk a light, for a moment—but you could hold up my coat behind us, to shield the flame from the other side of the river. We don't want anybody over there noticing it in here."

"No need," the man grumbled. "Be all right. Just a knock. . . " He groped in his pocket for a box of matches, nevertheless.

"There's blood all over your face," she declared. "Don't be silly." She was stripping off the suede and lambskin half-length coat that she wore over jumper and jodhpur breeches. "Can you hold this behind me, while I strike a light? You'll need both hands, to hold it out properly."

Adam did as he was told. And doing it, some comparatively unimpaired portion of his bemused mind recognised that here was a situation that, at another time, he might have given a deal to organise. The pity, the sad pity, that he was not in a state to do justice to the possibilities. With an arm resting across each of the girl's shoulders, and holding her coat up high behind her to shield them both, inevitably the two of them were in very close proximity indeed, faces only an inch or two apart, her hair in fact tickling his nose. And when she lit the match, and told him to put his head down so that she could examine his brow, it was naturally to find his face now equally close to a most adequate and delightfully outlined bosom, the articulated heavings of which were, he believed, not wholly an illusion of his own unsteady senses. The fact that Adam could

192

thus at least appreciate the mistiming of opportunity was perhaps confirmation of Sandy Logan's assertion that his injury was not likely to be fatal. He did not protest when she used up another of his matches.

"There's a horrid gash, going right up into your hair," she reported, shocked. "The brutes! It's laid quite open. It must be horribly sore?"

"Er . . . well," he said, seeking to collect his thoughts. "I've a sort of headache." He still held her coat up.

"A headache!" Gently she disengaged. "It'll have to be attended to, anyway. It really needs pulling together—two or three stitches. If you're not to be marked for life. I can't do much here, but at least I can clean it up a bit—bathe it. The river water is reasonably clean—better than the mud that's round it just now, anyway."

"Don't bother," he said. "It will be all right. . . ."

"Do stop being difficult and . . . obstinate!" she exclaimed. "What's the use of saying it'll be all right? You could have blood-poisoning in that, as easy as anything." She shook her head over him. "This is where I should tear a strip off my maidenly petticoat and bind you up like all the best books say—undeserving as you are! The trouble is, I'm not wearing a petticoat. Nor anything else really suitable. Isn't it a pity? Have you a reasonably clean handkerchief?"

"Well . . . not awfully. I . . . well, I live alone, you see."

"So I'm told. I suppose you mean by that, that—oh well, never mind. You'd better give it to me, just the same. I have one, but it's very small. I'll use it as a pad, and yours to tie it on. Can you lean over the side, a bit . . . ?"

So Adam had his wound bathed and cleaned, gently but firmly, in the cold Tweed water—that Tweed with which he had become so curiously involved. Once, in the process, the girl paused, as hurrying footsteps beat on the path outside. But they passed, and she resumed her ministrations.

"It's started to bleed again," she reported. "That's good, of course, It will help to clean it—wash out any dirt. Am I hurting you much? You're quivering, trembling."

193

"No. It's just . . . well, I suppose cold. Wet." That was not really true. He did not feel especially cold. He had been trying to control that shivering for a while.

"Mercy—you're soaking wet! All over," she cried, feeling his clothes. "I didn't know that. You must have been in the river? Look—put this coat of mine round you. It's fine and warm. . . ."

"No. No—I don't want your coat. I'm not really cold at all. You need it yourself. . . ."

She insisted on putting it round him, but he took it off and gave it back to her. Eventually she came and sat on the thwart beside him, and draped the lambskin coat partially over them both. To maintain it in position somebody had to hold it there, and since the hunched man made no attempt to do so, Hazel Scott put her arm round his shoulder to keep the thing in place.

So together they sat in the darkness, very close, and gradually the man's involuntary jerks and shivers died on him. For a while they did not speak. The sound of voices still came to them, but more faintly now and of a different quality, seeming to be callings-out to keep in touch rather than angry shoutings. The pair in the boathouse thought their own thoughts.

Out of the jumble and confusion of his own, Adam spoke, at length. "You . . . you are very kind to me, Miss Scott."

"Amn't I!" she agreed. "I don't know why I do it."

"No. After what must have seemed like my rudeness to you. Over the phone that time, I mean. I didn't mean to be rude. . . ."

"I am glad to hear that," she said gravely.

"I was in a difficult position, you see—standing between you and the fishermen. They were very suspicious of you. Because you are your father's daughter. Despite what you had done for them, about selling the fish. They won't be suspicious any more, though, after this. You heard what Sandy Logan said?"

"I was suitably gratified. But, look—I don't think you should be bothering your head about all this, just now. Better just relax."

"But I want you to understand. I am grateful—very grateful

for all your help and support. You have been very good, kind. And tonight . . . now. . . ."

"You are feeling better, I take it? Do you think that you ought to be talking away like this, just the same? You must be recovering, I think!"

"I suppose so, yes. No harm in talking a little, anyway."

"You might, of course, say things that you regretted afterwards! In your present fevered state, Adam. Much safer to deal with me over the telephone, don't you think? Or by letter? You said before, didn't you, that you'd rather write? Not an awfully good risk—wasn't that the phrase?"

He groaned, and would have gripped her arm—only, it was round his shoulders, so he had to grip her leg instead. "You see—you *don't* understand! I didn't mean to offend you— you're the last person I'd want to offend. All that stuff in the papers, too—about outdated landlordism and entrenched privilege. That was all wrong—taken out of context. I was referring to the Act—the Tweed Act as it was passed in 1857— not to you, at all, or even your father. . . "

"That's fine," she interrupted. "I thought it was a wonderful phrase, really. But you *are* recovering, aren't you? I mean, if your improvement goes on like this, we can hardly remain huddled up together in the dark much longer, clutching each other this way! Can we? I'd be running into danger, I fear!" And gently, she detached his hand from her thigh.

"Oh . . . !" After the brief exclamation, she had him plunged into profound silence, now, as he strained away from her to his own side of the boat. The coat all but fell from his shoulders in the process, so that the girl had to replace it carefully. She did not withdraw her arm—which, since it was not elastic, entailed her moving along the thwart after him, just a little.

So they sat, and it was the young woman who spoke first, and in a perfectly conversational tone of voice. "You are a bit of a mystery, you know, Adam," she said. "You can hardly blame a girl, can you, for not knowing quite where she is with you? After all, people like you don't usually turn up in little remote country schools. And then get involved in illegal and

195

violent crusades of this sort."

He did not comment on that.

"I mean, you don't seem just cast for the part. Airdmouth hardly strikes me as any stepping-stone to greater things. You haven't been there very long, I discovered. Oh, yes—I've been making discreet enquiries. What made you come in the first place? Not so that you could conduct a salmon war?"

"No. I came looking for peace!" With something between a snort and a moan, he said that. "Peace—that was what brought me to Airdmouth, heaven help me! Just peace and quiet!"

"You mean . . . you were running away from something?" Her voice had changed, now. "Hiding yourself? That was the obvious thing, of course. But then, to involve yourself in all this excitement and publicity! It doesn't seem to fit."

He hesitated. Then she felt his shoulders shrug. "I wasn't really running away—though perhaps that *could* describe it, in a way. I am writing a novel, you see. Or I was. The present tense seems a little out of date!"

"A novel! You're a writer?"

"Not really. Not yet. Would-be, shall we say. I wrote one, once. A novel—a slight thing, just a who-dun-it. It was published, but wasn't very successful. And I don't wonder. But I felt that I could do better. I had all sorts of big ideas. My publishers, strangely enough, encouraged me. But I could never get down to it. I was in a big school in Edinburgh. And mixed up in all sorts of what are called extra-mural activities. It was no good. Things got in the road. I had to get away, to somewhere where there were no distractions, and not a great deal of work. I . . . well, I was idiot enough to think that Airdmouth filled the bill!"

"Goodness—but this is exciting! A novel. And here I had you lined up as a mystery-man with a lurid past! A man running away from something—a wronged wife almost certainly, possibly drink or drugs, or, or . . ."

"Sorry—nothing spectacular like that. Not even the wife."

"Tell me about your novel, Adam. The story. What is the theme? It is not a who-dun-it, this time? Is it historical? Tell me

196

about it."

And since no writer ever born could resist that sort of request, Adam Horsburgh told her. Needless to say, in the process he told a keen-witted young woman a great deal more than the mere outline and background of his story. She listened and nodded and prompted, and forgot the part that she was playing—if any woman can forget such a thing entirely, where a man is concerned. And he forgot gangsters and policemen and his fishermen friends, his splitting head—even the arm about his shoulders. For too long that story had been bottled up within him, seeking to be born in words—a thing not good for any creator, any originator.

Once started, of course, as well halt the dark Tweed itself at its flowing past that boathouse. A man was only talking, and a woman only listening—but between them they were forging something, links stronger than either of them knew. Or did she know, perhaps?

Some time later, some unspecified and unnoted time, after Adam had come to a gradual and natural halt, the young woman had asked questions on one or two points, and they had sat in silence for a little, they made a move—reluctantly on the man's part, at least. If there had been any sounds from the surrounding woods over an appreciable interval, other than the accustomed murmur of the water and the hooting of owls, they had not noticed them. The glow from the headlights of cars had long since vanished.

The move was out on to the river, for Hazel pointed out that the House and her car were almost half a mile away, and it would be infinitely more easy for Adam to cover that distance sitting in a boat than stumbling through any more benighted woodland. She would not hear of him taking an oar, saying that rowing would be quite the worst exercise for somebody in his state—which was possibly true enough—and that anyway she often rowed this boat alone—which was probably less likely. At any rate, she handled the oars well, and if progress upstream was slow, the current could be blamed. Not that the man noted it.

They drew in to a timber landing-stage beside another and larger boathouse, directly under the square looming mass of a great Georgian mansion. A few lights shone from the serried ranks of windows. It seemed distinctly blatant, to Adam, this landing on the very doorstep of the huge house, but after all it was Hazel's home. That thought depressed the man considerably, and he was very silent as they landed and picked their way up moss-grown stone steps, along a gravelled terrace that crunched horribly underfoot, and round the side of the house. His companion, however, was entirely cheerful, if solicitous for his progress, offering an arm that he claimed no longer to need. At one point, indeed, she laughed, and nodded up towards a lit window on an upper floor at the end of the south front.

"Poor Ronnie!" she said. "Ronnie Calthwaite. He's off to bed. Very sensible of him, I must admit."

"He's . . . he's staying with you?" Adam had forgotten the Captain.

"Oh, yes. He often does. I'm afraid I've not been a very good hostess to him tonight, have I?"

"Well. . . . He, h'm, he might at least have waited up for you! But . . . your father? Won't he be worried about you? By this time?"

"Not he! I've got him well trained not to worry about me. Ronnie too, I suppose. You're not a worrier, are you, Adam?"

"Ummm. I, I don't think so."

"I hope not," she said. "How's the head now?"

"Better. Only, I wish the ground wouldn't heave about so!"

"Never mind. Only a little way now—to the stable-yard. Just round the back of that range of buildings ahead. The car's there."

In the spacious cobbled stable-yard with its wide arched entrance and clock-tower, impressive if somewhat grass-grown and empty-seeming, the cream sports car shared a large garage with a mature but gleaming Rolls, a gold-painted vintage Bentley—no doubt Calthwaite's—and a mud-spattered Landrover. The sight only engendered further gloom in the visitor, with his own humble Morris Minor in his mind's eye. Agitation took over, however, when the girl not only switched on her headlights, there in the garage, but after the loud clangour of the self-starter, insisted on revving up the deep-throated engine in a long series of challenging roars, as though deliberately letting all rural Berwickshire know what was afoot.

"It will let Daddy and Ronnie know that I'm safely round about," she explained, in answer to Adam's protest. "They can go to sleep now, with an easy mind."

Drumming off through the echoing archway and down the tree-lined drive, the man meditated, while his spirits unaccountably continued to sink.

"I wonder what's happened to the dynamiters?" his companion said, swinging out and to the east at the open lodge-gates. "I do hope that they all got away—but with very sore heads and other parts, naturally. At least they left the salmon behind, and their gear. It will be a complication if any of them were caught. I don't think they'll come back, though. Do you?"

"I hope not. But these days, I'm prepared to believe in the absolute folly of any- and everybody! Anything can happen. Somehow, we'll have to try to get it over to all the great ignorant wooden-headed newspaper-reading public of this land that nothing has changed as far as angling is concerned—river fishing. That it is only sea fishing that we're fighting about. Nobody seems to have grasped that."

"I think, you know, that you'll have to make another of your announcements, Adam," the young woman said. "I mean, a deliberate one, this time. A Press statement. I'm sure all the papers would just jump at a statement from you, and give it lots of publicity. You could prepare something, making it absolutely clear and simple for all to understand. Pointing out that all this indiscriminate poaching and nonsense is just ruining your campaign. Calling on all sympathisers with the, h'm, downtrodden and underprivileged masses, to hold their hands for the time being, and let you Airdmouth people fight your battle with Parliament and rampant landlordism in peace! Something like that? Phone all the papers with it, tomorrow?"

"M'mmm. Well . . . I suppose something of the sort might help. I wish I could keep out of it, though. . . ."

"A bit late to wish anything of the sort, is it not?"

"Look—isn't it time you turned north? Towards Airdmouth? You've passed two or three road-ends already. The one we came down was a good bit before this."

"My dear man—you'll get to Airdmouth in due course. First of all you're going to Berwick. To the hospital, to get that head stitched."

"By George, I'm not! Not to that place. There have been stories enough out of there. I believe reporters lurk round that hospital like vultures waiting for bodies. I can just imagine the results if *I* turned up there, with a damaged head . . . !"

"All right, then—it will have to be Doctor Macnair."

"But, look—you can't rout a doctor out of his bed at this time of night just to do a little first-aid! It can perfectly easily wait till morning."

"No, it can't. That brow needs attention. Now. Doctor Macnair may not enjoy it—but he'll do it. He's our family doctor, and brought me into this sad world. And he's an angler, and appreciates our water."

Evidently these constituted sufficient grounds. Presently, in one of the old grey houses of Berwick's Castlegate, a tousle-headed elderly man, dressing-gowned and silent, dealt in somewhat tight-lipped if efficient fashion with Adam's head while, after a casual announcement that there had been a slight accident, Hazel Scott chattered away cheerfully about irrelevant matters. In only a few minutes they were escorted to the door, with some very brief instructions as to elementary treatment for slight concussion, and some white tablets rolled up in a screw of paper—for which services the physician was rewarded with a dazzling smile from the young woman and a reminder to come along and have a go at the river one day soon. Entrenched privilege had its conveniences undoubtedly.

Both young people were rather silent on the run up the coast to Airdmouth. The village was in complete darkness when they arrived, only the red gleam of the pier-head light piercing the

200

gloom. A scrap of white paper was tucked partly under the door of the black and unwelcoming schoolhouse on its little peninsula by the fretting sea. They examined it by the light of the headlamps. It was a note, reading:

All back safe and with nothing worse than wee scratches you are the worst Adam and hope you are all right. The polis were that pleased with getting the fish I don't think they got anybody else we led them a bit dance to let the city boys away so thats all right. I like your lady friend shes a right improve on her father.

SANDY

"H'mmm. Sorry about that," the man said. "These chaps— well, they don't always put things awfully well. But . . . thank you for bringing me home. And for all your kindness, Hazel. . . "

"Aren't you going to ask me in for a moment?"

"Well . . . no. Not tonight, I think." Adam was quite decided on that point. After glimpsing something of Linburndean House and all its massive magnificence, the present comparative squalor of his own bachelor establishment weighed heavily on his mind. "I left in rather a hurry. When you phoned. Everything is . . . well, a bit untidy. Another time, perhaps."

"Goodness—as though that mattered! Anyway, you ought to be put to bed, with a hot drink. . . ."

"I am perfectly capable of doing that for myself, thank you." That was probably stiffer than he meant it to be.

"Let me at least see your novel, Adam. The manuscript, as far as you've got."

"I'm sorry. There's really nothing to see, at the moment. Just a few loose sheets, and a lot of scribbled notes. Nothing."

"Oh . . . sometimes you are the most obstinate, stubborn man, Adam Horsburgh!" the girl exclaimed, in sudden exasperation. "Utterly immovable. And selfish. And . . . and a great boor into the bargain! Goodnight to you!"

"I'm sorry . . ." he began again, as she jumped back into her car, and slammed the door. "But—well, that's the way I am, I suppose."

She did not press the self-starter at once, however, but sat there in silence. He could not see her expression, in the pool of darkness behind the headlamps' glare.

He moved over beside the car. "I would not like you to think me ungrateful. Unappreciative. Of everything," he jerked. "I'm not. I'm . . . I'm *too* appreciative, perhaps. That's the trouble. . . ."

"You have a strange way of showing it, then, Adam," she answered, but no longer hotly.

"Perhaps. I am different from . . . well, we belong to rather different worlds, you know."

"We can't all be authors, writers!" she gave back, quickly.

"That is not what I meant at all, of course. It was background I was referring to—social background. Perhaps I don't react in just the way you're used to."

"Lord—am I never to be forgiven for being a wicked landlord's daughter?"

He gave it up. His head had been throbbing badly again since the doctor's ministrations, and the tendency to tremble was coming back. All this was beyond Adam Horsburgh that night. He sighed. "Anyway—thank you for . . . well, for being yourself, tonight," he said.

"That is the nicest thing you've managed to say!" she told him, with a small laugh. "I'm away, before you spoil it with something else!" She started up her engine. "Go in, now—and take care of yourself. Get those damp clothes off. Make a hot drink, and take your tablets. Don't forget them. And don't be in any hurry to get up—in the morning. I'll give you a ring about midday, to see how you feel. Oh, and Adam—if you really are grateful to me for, for anything, there's something you could do for me. Apart from looking after yourself, I mean. I want to come out in a fishing-boat with you, one of these times when you are salmon-netting and defying the State. Will you arrange it for me? I can't feel that I'm really taking part in this thing until I've done that. You will, won't you? And remember your Press statement." She brushed a couple of fingers lightly over his hand that gripped the side of her car to steady him. "Goodnight, Adam."

The man watched as the headlights' beams swept round over the sleeping village and climbed away up the steep hill beyond until they were lost behind the towering enclosing cliffs. Then he went into his house. He switched on the light, and gazed distastefully at all the muddle and disarray that he saw. He saw much more than just the superficial mess of it, too. His eyes strayed to the table over by the window that looked out to sea, where the litter of his papers all but hid his typewriter. He frowned, even though it hurt his head the more. The fool, the utter and benighted fool that he was! He, to come here to write! First to hurl himself into a damned ridiculous battle that was no real concern of his—and then to fall helplessly, hopelessly, for Sir John Scott's daughter, of all people. With his eyes open, against all reason, warning, suitability and common sense!

Adam Horsburgh was entirely sorry for himself.

XV

ADAM'S long lie the next morning did not materialise. He was awakened, feeling light-headed, a little sore and distinctly sour—though, almost reluctantly he had to admit to himself, better than he had expected to feel—soon after nine o'clock, by repeated knockings at his door, supplemented even by faces peering in at his windows. Since the faces seemed to be those of complete strangers, not local folk, he was grumpily tempted to turn over again and ignore them; but the sight, from a corner of his bedroom window, of a couple of men with large cameras taking photographs of the schoolhouse, was too much for him. Aggrievedly he dragged himself out of bed to face the clamant demands of this new day.

It was the Press that seemed to have invaded Airdmouth. Every paper in the land, apparently, had sent its quota of reporters, photographers and special correspondents. Eager for stories, pictures and personal angles, they thronged the village and pier, besieging houses, almost mobbing anyone who ventured into the street, cornering even the children in search of human interest leads. All the fishermen, at the first hint of the invasion, had slipped discreetly out to sea, leaving their womenfolk to cope with the situation as best they might. And the schoolmaster, of course; the battling schoolmaster of Airdmouth.

The first sight of Adam's rash appearance in his own open doorway, haggard and with his head dramatically bandaged, of course, brought a rush to the schoolhouse from all quarters. The photographers took priority, some crouching, some climbing high on the garden wall, all issuing urgent and frequently contrary instructions as to posing and expression. Adam unwisely sought to ignore them all—with no doubt disastrous results photographically. Unshaven, with hair unbrushable because of the bandaging, and with old tweeds and silk neckcloth superimposed over pyjamas, he was hardly looking at his best.

The reporters—and there were a surprising number of women amongst them—only allowed the picture people a very short innings before they surged forward, notebooks out. Questions came thick and fast.

Adam tried to counter the barrage, if not to shout it down, but found the effort quite beyond him and his sore head. He held up his hand, and eventually achieved a sort of quiet.

"Look—I don't know what's brought you all here this morning," he said, frowning as the words seemed to stab through his head. "I can't say I'm pleased to see you. But I realise that you've got a job to do. Also the fact that you can help the cause we're fighting for here—if you'll write a bit more accurately about it all than you've done hitherto! I'm prepared to make a statement. In fact, I was going to do so, anyway. But I haven't prepared it yet. I was up most of the night, and I'm just out of bed, as you can see. . . ."

"What were you doing, during the night, Mr Horsburgh?" somebody asked.

"How did you come by a broken head, sir? Was it the English gave it to you?"

"Or the Navy? Did the depth-charges do that?"

There was considerable laughter.

"No. Of course not. I fell. That was all. Slipped on a muddy bank, and fell. Cut my brow. But, see here—I'm not answering a lot of questions. Give me half an hour to make up my statement. Then come back."

"Are any of your boats out challenging the Navy just now, Mr Horsburgh?"

"How many depth-charges would you say were fired at your, sir, that time?"

"Were any of the boats actually badly damaged?"

"I don't know what you're talking about." It was obvious that it had been yesterday's high-flown reports on the frigate incident that was mainly responsible for this sudden united descent on Airdmouth. "I've told you—I'm answering no questions. Not just now. Come back in half an hour, and I'll have something to say to you."

"Who's paying for this fight, Mr Horsburgh? You've had a lot of losses. Who is putting up the money?"

"When do you appear in court, sir?"

"Go away! I'm saying no more. If you don't leave me in peace, you'll get no statement at all."

"Mr Horsburgh—perhaps *I* could be a help?" a sweet girlish voice suggested, and a somewhat less girlish figure dressed as for the Twelfth of August, in vivid checks, tweed hat and everything but gun and shooting-stick, insinuated itself to the front of the throng. "I could help you with making up your statement. You can't be used to that sort of thing. I could lick it into shape, for you. . . ."

"Hey, Maggie—come off it! We know your kind of licking!"

"Give it a miss, Maggie!"

Her fellow scribes were good-humouredly against any such idea, most evidently.

"No thank you, ma'am," Adam said. "I'm quite capable. . . "

"Let me at least come in and make you a cup of tea, while you're doing it, Mr Horsburgh. Poor dear—you haven't had your breakfast!"

"Tea! My God—tea, and Maggie Knockatter!" somebody exclaimed.

"Rum's more like it! Where's your hip-flask hiding, Maggie? Hips crowding it out, eh?"

"Watch her, sir—she's poison!"

"Keeps it down the front, nowadays. More space. . . !"

"Half an hour, ladies and gentlemen," Adam insisted, and managed to get his door shut in the faces of the ribald company, and locked too—but not before a couple of folded newspapers had been thrust in with him.

Wearily he moved across to his writing-table. On the way he glanced at the papers. The first was the *Daily Standard*. Splashed across its front page were banner headlines: SEA FIGHT OFF BERWICK. FULL STORY OF BATTLING FISHERMAN DEPTH CHARGE OFFENSIVE BY NAVY. Groaning, Adam looked at the second paper. It was the *Northern Post*, of Newcastle, and seemed to be more up to date than the *Standard*. Its headlines shouted: RIOT AT BERWICK MEETING. TEMPERS RISE AS SCOTS AGITATE. DISGRACEFUL SCENES. COUNCILLORS MANHANDLED.

Adam sat down in his chair heavily.

Reading the *Post*, it appeared that there had been a big-scale public demonstration held in Berwick's largest hall the previous evening, by supporters of the Berwick-for-Scotland movement, with an overflow meeting in the street outside. Well-known personalities had come down from Edinburgh and Glasgow. Fiery speeches had been made. Everyone clearly linked up the salmon war with this semi-political campaign. Differences of opinion amongst the audience had led to blows, two Berwick Town Councillors who had indicated a contrary attitude on the subject had been roughly handled, and the police had been called in. The *Post* quoted much substantial comment—all of it rather noticeably on behalf of the establishment—deploring in strong terms this folly, and berating the unscrupulous illegal salmon-netters who were obviously making enormous profits out of fishing in these troubled waters. Cheek by jowl with this main story was a lengthy series of brief reports about salmon poaching outbreaks on the River Tweed, right upstream to its headwaters in the Peeblesshire hills—though curiously enough the Linburndean affair was not mentioned—and sundry respectable and influential citizens called upon the police to take the sternest measures to put down this shocking lawlessness and violence, that could so easily ruin valuable fishing-rights and the innocent sport of many. A footnote pointed out that the annual value of fishing-rights on the river, apart from the commercial fisheries at the mouth, amounted to many hundreds of thousands of pounds. Were the irresponsible activities of a few dissident coastal fishermen to imperil this national asset?

The *Standard* concentrated on the two-day-old frigate incident. Whom, under the heading of Our Special Correspondent, it had found to give what it declared to be the first eye-witness account of the Battle of Berwick Bay, was not disclosed, but it was patently a man of rich and varied imagination. He concentrated on the depth-charging, exaggerating it out of all recognition into an inferno of shot and shell in which the gallant fishermen battled for their very lives. Without actually stating that there was more than one warship involved, the impression given was rather of an embattled fleet engaging a few tiny rowing-boats. An interesting side-issue was the quoted protest, from Edinburgh, of the President of the Nature Protection Society at the outrageous damage undoubtedly done to the well-known and innocent seal population of this Farne Islands area by the bloodthirsty *battue* on the part of ignorant and uncaring naval authorities. A petition and subscription-list was being organised forthwith to ensure that there would be no repetition of like barbarities against such a lovable and harmless national heritage.

There was a very different account, in this paper, of the Berwick-for-Scotland meeting, indicating the presence of *agents provocateurs* from Newcastle, but Adam dared read no further lest his head split right open. Moreover, time was passing. Sighing, he reached for his typewriter.

Knocking was resounding upon his door before he was finished, of course, hardly assisting his composition. Less well armed and equipped than he would have liked, he returned to face the fray.

"I have three main points I wish to make," he told the waiting throng. "The first is—and I would be glad if you would stress this—that our campaign here refers only to the Tweed Fisheries Act of 1857, and to that part of the Act which includes fifty square miles of open sea at the mouth of the Tweed, and forbids salmon fishing there. We believe this to be contrary to Scots common law, as well as to international law beyond the three-mile limit. That's all that we are fighting about—sea fishing. Nothing is altered, nor is hoped to be altered, about river fishing. All these outbreaks of river poaching are not only nothing to do with us, but are definitely hurting our cause. I appeal now to all those who sympathise with our

208

struggle, or who think they'd like a bit of free salmon, not to endanger that struggle by engaging in river poaching. Not just now, anyway. Give us a chance. . . "

"Mr Horsburgh—would you say that English law is being unfairly imposed on Scots, here?"

"No. That is my second point. This is nothing to do with English law, as such. It is just a bad Act of Parliament. In fact, it hits the English fishermen at Seahouses and Holy Island and so on, just as badly as the Scots. As you know, they have started a petition to Parliament against this Act down there, too. We felt that more active and practical steps were needed, to bring the matter before the courts in Scotland. So we have deliberately challenged the Act, by fishing in the waters it prohibits, trying to force the authorities to take legal action against us, to get a final decision."

"And have they not done so, sir?"

"Not so far. But two days ago, after the incident out beyond the three-mile limit, they did charge Skipper Logan of the *Bluebell*, on return to harbour and confiscated our catch of one salmon! So now they will have to do something about it. We believe that in a court of law it will be proved that we committed no offence by fishing beyond the three-mile limit, or even probably beyond a one-mile limit. In which case the Act will have to be amended. . . "

"How many depth-charges would you say were set off against you, Mr Horsburgh?"

"They weren't real depth-charges at all—just small explosive charges. Merely for making a noise. It's ridiculous to suggest that they were real depth-charges, or that there was any danger. It was just to scare away the fish, I think—just a demonstration. The frigate commander was in a difficult position. . . "

"You wouldn't say that he grossly exceeded his duty?"

"No, I wouldn't. I don't see what else he could have done, when we refused to haul in our nets—since he obviously had been told not to arrest us."

"Is it your belief, Mr Horsburgh, that if Scotland had a

209

Parliament of her own, all this could never have happened?"

"I haven't said that, have I? Though I think it is probable. But that is not the point, really. And that brings me to my third point. That this fight of ours is totally unconnected with the Berwick-for-Scotland business. I want you to make that very clear. It is totally unconnected. To link the two up is just to complicate our difficulties. I'm personally in favour of Berwick returning to Berwickshire and Scotland—but that is purely incidental. I didn't even know that there *was* a Berwick-for-Scotland campaign going on when we started this fight. Please underline that. Let's get this struggle finished first . . . "

"But, Mr Horsburgh, is it not true that the very fact that this matter of the Tweed fishing, including the mouth of the Tweed, has to be settled by Scots law, and in Scots courts, not English, proves that Berwick should be in Scotland?"

"I dare say it does. I'm not arguing against it. But, as I say, that's not our case. Now, look—there's one final thing I want to say. Somebody asked about who is paying for our fight. The answer is that *we* are. The fishermen themselves. All the salmon that is being caught is being sold for a Fighting Fund, to help recoup our losses in nets and gear, and to pay for legal costs to come. None of it is going into anybody's pocket. This is important. All that stuff about making enormous profits out of fishing in troubled waters is just so much nonsense. Every penny goes into the Fund."

All the pencils were writing hard, now—save the tweed-clad lady's. "Mr Horsburgh, you haven't told us how you hurt your poor head? Really and truly, I mean. I'm sure it was most exciting. . . ."

"I did tell you—I fell on a slippy muddy bank."

"Oh, you don't expect us to believe that!"

"I do, ma'am . . . "

"Were you at this Berwick meeting, last night?"

"No, I wasn't. I didn't know that there had been a meeting until I read that paper this morning."

"Do you belong to Airdmouth, sir?"

"You live alone here, Mr Horsburgh. I take it you are not

210

married?"

"Is the local Member of Parliament in favour of your fight?"

"Are you interested in politics . . . ?"

"Look here, ladies and gentlemen—you've had my statement. All of it. That is all I have to say. I'm not answering indiscriminate questions—or any questions at all."

"But, Mr Horsburgh, won't you tell us . . ."

"No, I won't. Not any more. I've a sore head. I haven't had any breakfast, I was up most of the night. . . ."

"Doing what, I wonder, Mr Horsburgh, dear?"

"Minding my own business, ma'am—as no doubt you were doing too! Only, I was probably less practised about the business—hence my sore head! Good-day to you all!"

There was a shout of laughter mixed with protest, in which Adam managed to get his door shut.

The schoolmaster did not laugh, however, as the people outside dispersed. That was hardly the sort of statement he had intended to make. And what those folk out there would make of it in tomorrow's papers, he preferred not to contemplate.

Hazel Scott telephoned soon after midday. Adam assured her that he was feeling better, fine in fact, and looking after himself; that he had made his Press statement—however, it might be mauled and travestied; and that he had not yet been able to see Sandy Logan about arranging a trip for her in a fishing-boat. She told him that all the dynamited salmon left behind by the gangsters was going to Berwick in the afternoon, to Sinton, and that if the Airdmouth people had any fish ready to dispose of, it would be a good opportunity to add it to the Linburndean consignment and get the full market price. Adam, though he had starkly decided that morning that he was hereafter going to see as little as possible of the young woman, for everybody's sake, weakly agreed that this was too good a chance to miss, and since the fishermen were all away at sea, he would himself bring such salmon as was stored in the kirkyard crypt and meet the Linburndean vehicle somewhere well away from Berwick.

So, two or three hours later, the old green van and the Land-rover met in secluded rendezvous amongst woodland near Mordington—and though it had not been Adam's intention, another few minutes saw the green van left in the trees, and Airdmouth fish transferred to the back of the Landrover and man to the front, on their way to Berwick. So much for resolutions.

Adam, feeling only too conspicuous with his bandaged head, in that grey old town, hid himself in Woolworths while Hazel went down to Quality Street alone and sold the salmon. There had been quite a substantial accumulation of fish waiting in the crypt, almost all of it poached, of course, and the girl, later, was able to hand over the usual bundle of soiled and bent notes, to the value of over seventy pounds. Thereafter they had tea, and since Adam was still obsessed with the thought that he was far too recognisable in Berwick, the young woman suggested that the dark of a local cinema would be the answer to that—if his sore head would not suffer? He said that he ought to get back, that his novel was being shockingly neglected, that though he had told the minister to explain to Sandy Logan about the salmon being gone, he ought to see the fishermen just as soon as they got home from the sea. He went to the cinema, nevertheless.

He enjoyed it, too, head or none—though he might have been unable to pass any very detailed test as to the contents of the programme, afterwards.

On the way back to his van in the woods, he learned that Sir John Scott had been reasonably content with the outcome of the previous evening's cantrips, and quite thankful that none of the poachers had actually been caught—in the interests of public relations and votes. He was not saying much to his daughter about the authorities' tactics against the salmon fishers—though he was off to Edinburgh today, to Saint Andrew's House, undoubtedly on that business, and was dining with the Secretary of State—but she had gathered that they were very worried at the way things were going, and that Hogarth the bailiff was in trouble for having charged Logan over a three-mile-limit offence rather than with a one-mile infringement. Adam consoled a somewhat guilty conscience with the thought that the obtaining of this information possibly justified the way that he had spent the evening.

He did not ask what Captain Calthwaite might be doing.

They parted amongst the dark shadows of the woods again, Adam taking his departure somewhat abruptly. But though he left Hazel sitting there in her car, looking after him with what expression was not to be perceived, something of her presence went with him, part challenging, part mocking, part comradely and wholly devastatingly attractive to that man, all the way back to Airdmouth. Halfway there he found himself to be singing, despite the ache it produced in his head—and promptly cursed himself for a fool and worse, a weakling and a man of straw. Song returned and persisted, however. It must be something to do with the kick at his head, he decided—he was just a little light-headed still.

He was a terrible singer, too, was Adam Horsburgh.

XVI

THERE followed a period of inaction, of waiting, for the Airdmouth crusaders; one of those irritating interregnums wherein everything seemed to hang fire. This did not apply to all related issues, unfortunately; thanks to the highly diversified and unanimously resounding and prominent Press reaction to Adam's omnibus statement, all sorts of associated and quite irrelevant activities went ahead with vigour and gusto. The Berwick-for-Scotland movement went from strength to strength, with the old Border town in a permanent ferment. A Save-the-Seals campaign grew almost overnight, uniting nature lovers from Land's End to John o' Groats. A Society of Free Fishermen was formed, in London curiously enough, whose objects were not crystal clear but which started an enthusiastic inaugural meeting with the singing of The Red Flag. Northumberland County Council issued a dossier to show how much money they had pumped into Berwick-on-Tweed since they took over in 1929, plus the assertion that the Berwickers had never had it so good—the main effect of which seemed to be a clamant volume of protest in the Newcastle papers that Berwick should be thrown back to Scotland forthwith as an expensive luxury and a liability. The Lord Lyon King of Arms reiterated that heraldically Berwick still came under his jurisdiction, that he was considering the position of the ancient Scottish kingdom of Strathclyde, which of course went down as far south as Lancaster. The Icelandic Foreign Minister pointed out, in New York, the typical two-faced and deceitful attitude of the British Government over territorial waters.

Yet all the while, in Airdmouth, the fishermen waited. They waited, first and foremost, for the charge against Sandy Logan to be proceeded with, for the arrival of the summons to appear in court; but no summons came, no sort of follow-up to the charge was made. It was maddening, but no doubt all part of the authorities' war of attrition. How long a free citizen could be left with a charge hanging over his head like this, Adam tried to find out from legal friends in Edinburgh—but got little satisfaction. Apparently it was for the Procurator-Fiscal, as the public prosecutor was called, to decide whether a case could or should proceed to court, and it seemed that he had six months in which to make up his mind—a pleasantly leisurely interval, which could be quite otherwise for the unfortunate who happened to have been charged. It did not appear even to be necessary to inform the accused whether or not he was going to be proceeded against.

Not that Sandy Logan fretted or ate out his heart over the threat of the sword of justice hanging above his head. The delay, however, did affect the fishermen's activities. Since the powers-that-be were evidently unhappy about this three-mile limit charge, it obviously would be folly to give them a better case to fight by risking another charge in the one-mile belt, so that demonstration fishing near Berwick was inadvisable meantime. As for further efforts out beyond three miles, there was not a lot of point in it, now; that gesture had been made, produced its charge—and, anyway, there were precious few salmon to be caught out there it seemed. As for the more profitable night poaching, this was clearly contra-indicated during this waiting period; almost certainly that was what the opposition was waiting and praying for—a false step that would deliver the Airdmouth men into their hand as criminals. Undoubtedly the entire coastline was being watched each night with hawk-like eyes. Sea poaching did not in fact cease—but it was done with marked discretion, much to Tosh Hogg's disgust. Dullness and frustration reigned. Adam saw the danger of the entire campaign petering out in inertia and boredom—just as the enemy planned. Something must be done to restore to themselves the initiative. But what?

Despite all Adam's brain-racking and pestering of legal acquaintances, to try to force the issue, the business was brought to a head quite otherwise. The Airdmouth boats had set out as usual, some ten days later, for their normal daily seine-netting in deep water beyond the horizon, when the fishermen were distinctly shaken to observe, to the south of them, no fewer than seven large Norwegian deep-sea craft, drift-netting in the forbidden Tweed waters, between the three- and five-mile limits—salmon fishing most obviously, openly and unchallenged. Going to investigate, they had got but little change out of the Norwegians, who were using the latest equipment and extra long series of drift-lines with fully a score of nets to each messenger. Lined up in file thus, they presented a wall of net nearly two miles long. Certainly, if salmon were there to be caught, this was the way to catch them.

On Sandy Logan's advice the Airdmouth boats put back to harbour. This was a new situation that seemed to call for specific action. He and a few other fishermen were up at the schoolhouse, interrupting Adam again at his novel, to inform him of the development, when the telephone bell rang. It was Hazel Scott.

"Listen, Adam," she said, speaking urgently, without the usual persiflage. "Something important has happened. My father has just had a phone call from Edinburgh—from Saint Andrew's House. I took it, at first—and when I heard that it was from the Sea Fisheries Department, I put it through to Daddy, but listened in myself. They're in a bit of a panic, up there. It seems that there are some Norwegian fishing-boats fishing off the Tweed now. . . ."

"Yes. I've just heard. Sandy and the others are here now, telling me. They were on their way out to the fishing-grounds when they saw them. Seven of them. Norwegians. Fishing quite openly, for salmon. I suppose they must have read about it all, in their papers, and come to try their luck. . . ."

"Maybe. Well, they're in a flap about it, obviously. The Fisheries people, I mean. They don't want to have to take action against these boats, and cause an international rumpus. Whoever it was that was phoning Daddy said that it would have been better, now, if the case had been proceeded with straight away—against Sandy Logan, obviously—and they had got a decision before this happened. He said it will look very

216

bad if Logan is sentenced for doing something that they let the Norwegians do. He was wondering if they could somehow decoy the Norwegians away for the time being, on some technicality—not be tough with them, or arrest them, or anything, nothing that they could complain about—and at the same time rush forward this Logan case in the Sheriff Court, and get a decision . . . ”

“The dirty dogs!”

“Yes. It’s a lousy trick. Daddy’s just gone off to see the Fiscal about it all. He’s worried, I could see. I don’t think the Fiscal was happy about the whole business, anyway. Look, Adam—somehow, surely, you can turn this to your advantage?”

“By George, we’ll try, anyway! If we were to go out there now, beside the Norwegians, and fish. If a few boats went . . . surely they’d have to do something about us. We want to force their hands, now. Yes—Sandy’s agreeing. He says we’ll go out right away. If we can force the authorities to take action against us again, but not the Norwegians—we’ve got them in a spot. Or if they do tackle the Norwegians too, we’ve still got them—for there’ll be a great hullabaloo about international law being set at naught, and so on.”

“Yes. Splendid! Listen—I’m coming over. Right away. This time I’m taking no excuses or refusals. Don’t dare sail without me! I’ll be over in twenty minutes.”

“Well, but . . .”

The receiver at the other end slammed down before anything more could be said.

All the fishermen agreed that every available Airdmouth boat ought to go out to the three-mile Tweed area right away. Men were sent hurriedly to change over the nets from seine to drift. Sandy telephoned fishing-interests that he knew of at both Seahouses and Holy Island, informing them that foreign craft were fishing the Tweed’s mouth and urging any boats that could be mustered to go out there and fish likewise.

Hazel Scott arrived, her cream sports car roaring down the steep zig-zag cliff road, at impressive speed, before the quite lengthy net-changing procedure was finished. Dressed in slacks and a Faroese heavy-knit fisherman's jumper that despite its voluminous and non-clinging lines seemed only to emphasise the excellence beneath, with waders and oilskins over her arm, and her chestnut hair tied in a scarlet headsquare, she made an eye-catching figure. Taking a woman to sea was anathema to the older fishermen and assuredly productive of bad luck, but after the girl's assistance to them, even Sandy was not bold enough to refuse her passage, face to face. The wolf-whistles of the younger men seemed to indicate a different point of view. She went aboard the *Bluebell* with Adam.

Four other Airdmouth craft followed *Bluebell* out of the harbour—Dand Fairgrieve's, Jamesy Pringle's, Heck Scott's and Jock Thomson's boats. They made quite a display in the mid-forenoon sunshine, as they turned southwards in line ahead. As they rounded the headland and came in sight of Berwick, Adam wondered how many field-glasses and telescopes were trained upon them. The seven Norwegians lay to their nets, evenly spaced out in a long chain, south by east of them.

As they drew nearer it was evident that these foreign vessels were much larger than their own, probably three times as heavy, big ugly craft all dull brown paint and littered gear, but powerful, seaworthy and tough.

"Baistards!" Tosh commented, but almost automatically rather than with his usual conviction. The Scots fishermen were used to seeing these vessels in the North Sea and Hebridean fishing-grounds—but seldom operating so close inshore as this.

"Och, they're doing us a good turn, these boys," Sandy reproved. "Even if they dinna ken it themsel's. Dinna frighten them away, Tosh, wi' your glowers!"

"It's no' me that'll frighten them away," the mate returned, glancing forward balefully to where Hazel sat decoratively on the edge of the fish-hold.

"Och, wheesht!"

The odd Norwegian fisherman raised a hand as the Airdmouth boats passed down the long line of vessels and nets, but by and large they were ignored. Sandy decided that, in view of this great barrage of net, the best place for his boats was slightly to the south and a little landwards of the foreigners— for these were not quite so close in to what he calculated was the exact three miles from shore as they might have been; moreover, the chances were that most of the salmon would approach the mouth of the river from the southern side. So, strung out at something of a tangent to the others, the local boats went about and proceeded to shoot nets.

Hazel was interested in everything, and Adam explained the process quite professionally to her—until Tosh Hogg's sardonic glances rather shut him up. Thereafter they settled down to the business of waiting. The young woman had brought a handsome pair of field-glasses with her, and Adam borrowed Sandy's set. Together, sitting on the fish-hold cover, with their backs against the winch, they surveyed the scene as they swayed and rolled to the swell.

They scanned the Berwick coast, the sea to north, south and east, and their Norwegian neighbours. For a long time there was nothing to report. The girl commented that it was very pleasant—but a lot less exciting than she had anticipated.

Then the Norwegians began to haul nets. Everyone in the Scottish boats was concerned to see what sort of a catch they had. There seemed to be quite a lot of glinting silver in the nets of the nearer boats. This large-scale co-operative effort was undoubtedly the way to get the fish, providing a solid wall of netting that they would not easily avoid. A couple of rifle-shots cracked out from the north of the line, and then another nearer at hand. That would be seals being dealt with summarily.

Presumably the Norwegians were reasonably satisfied with their catch, and not too upset by the seal menace, for they re-shot nets in the same position.

Adam heaved a sigh of relief. "I was afraid that they might have had enough—have considered it wasn't worth it," he said. "We want them to stay right there."

Three boats arrived from Seahouses. As they came level with the Scots craft they made shouted abusive comments on the foreign invasion. They seemed indeed to be going on, presumably to give the intruders a piece of their mind, when Sandy called out to restrain them, pointing out that this was just what was needed to force the authorities' hands. They should be welcoming these Norwegians, not abusing them. Sandy preferred to shout all this between the boats, rather than to use the short-wave radio with which they were all equipped, in case the foreigners were listening-in and understood English.

A little doubtfully the Seahouses craft turned, and took up fishing positions near by.

It was soon after this that Adam spotted, through Sandy's powerful glasses, away on the north-eastern horizon the distinctive upper works of a warship. Tension grew perceptibly at his announcement.

Tension was succeeded by other emotions, however, when after a time it became clear that the warship was not approaching. It was not departing, either. In the same position, or nearly so, it remained, hull-down, with only its top hamper visible from the lowly level of the fishing-craft. Undoubtedly it was merely watching. Hazel it was who, after a while, noticed another similar silhouette against the southern horizon. This too seemed to be stationary. The Navy was on the job—but holding its hand.

Indignation and disappointment waxed in the Airdmouth boats. For how long the warships had been hiding there, they did not know—possibly before even they themselves had arrived. It seemed, however, that they were not going to interfere. Because of the foreigners, only too obviously. It was galling and infuriating. How the Norwegians must be chuckling.

"They can't have thought up any excuse to decoy them away," Hazel commented. "I'll bet a lot of people in comfortable official armchairs are biting their nails just now—or tearing their hair!"

"I'd like to tear their hair for them!" Adam gave back. "Britannia rules the waves—but only against her own folk!"

"Nobody coming oot frae Berwick, either," Sandy pointed out. "They're all deaf, dumb and blind this day!"

220

When the Airdmouth boats hauled nets, they were at least cheered by the best catch yet to come their way. There was a certain amount of seal damage, and Heck Scott's *Fair Maiden* had a seal entangled and a net ruined. But even so there was a lot of salmon. *Bluebell* alone had twenty-three good fish, averaging perhaps ten pounds, besides a number with bites out. So, like the Norwegians, they stayed where they were, and shot nets again.

The afternoon was as uneventful as the forenoon. The frigates kept their discreet vigil miles away. The only vessel to emerge from Berwick harbour was a small coastal tanker going north. The Norwegians hauled in again, but did not do so well this time. They shot once more, however, still in the same position. A helicopter flew fairly low over the scene of operations, about three o'clock, back and forwards, providing a diversion—but it did no more than that. The consensus of opinion was that it was taking photographs, probably to establish the registration numbers painted on each boat.

After another couple of hours, Sandy ordered the nets in again. Like their Norwegian neighbours, none of the Airdmouth boats had done so well as formerly. Still, it was a better catch than on any previous day at sea, and *Bluebell's* total haul was now reckoned at fully three hundredweights. Even at Sinton's poorest prices, that should fetch nearly £70. Of the other four, Jamesy Pringle had done better still, and Heck, at the end of he line, poorest of all and with most seal savaging of fish and nets.

The Seahouses people were being slightly less fortunate further south.

It was decided to call it a day, since patently no official interference was forthcoming. The question was—would they be met by Hogarth and the police on their return to harbour, intent on confiscating this catch that was worth £250 at least? Angry men declared vehemently what they would do, in such event, in terms not carefully censored for a lady's ears—much to Hazel's glee.

As *Bluebell* led the way homewards, along the line of Norwegian craft, Sandy hailed their skippers to ask if they were going to continue to fish, if they would still be at it tomorrow? The first two produced no answer other than uncomprehending waves, but from the third answered somebody who could speak English.

"*Ja, ja*," came back to them thickly, across the water. "Fish ver' goot. We here stay. But no goot bloddy seals!"

"Sure, Mister. Aye, aye. You will be here tomorrow, then? More fishing?"

"*Ja, ja*—tomorrow. Sure, tomorrow."

"Good. Fine. See you tomorrow, then . . . "

No crowd awaited the boats' return to Airdmouth harbour, at any rate. The usual old man or two and scattering of vociferous youngsters reached the pier by the time that they tied up, but there was no sign of bailiffs or police. They were getting the catch ashore when Sandy Logan's wife, a buxom fresh-faced woman, came bustling down to announce, happily, relievedly, that a policeman on a bicycle had arrived at her door in the early afternoon, to tell her that the charge against Logan would not be proceeded with, this time.

If poor Mrs Logan had expected cheers and rejoicing to greet her news, she was disappointed—and undoubtedly surprised.

"Eh?" her husband said. "No' proceeded with, Meg? You mean—just nothing?"

"Aye. That's what he said, Sandy. The charge'll no' be proceeded with, this time. To tell you."

"But, Meg . . . "

"D'you mean to say—that was all?" Adam demanded. "A mere message, like that, by a man on a bicycle? No reasons? No apologies? No letter, even?"

"No, Mr Horsburgh. Should there ha' been? The man was nice enough. . . ."

"But, damn it—this is fantastic! They charge you, like a criminal, in front of a great crowd, Press present, accuse you of this and that offence, confiscate your catch, treat you like dirt, then keep the threat of judgment hanging over your head for weeks—then this! A casual message of dismissal! Lord—

we'll see about this!"

"It's disgraceful!" Hazel agreed. "It was bad enough before, keeping Sandy hanging on like that, not knowing where he stood. But shrugging the whole thing off this way. . . ."

"If there was no case against you, they shouldn't have charged you, in the first instance," Adam said. "But having done so, publicly, aggressively, and they find that they can't go ahead with it, make it stick—then the least they could do would be to retract and apologise, as publicly as they accused."

"Och, well," Sandy shrugged. "I suppose they dinna just look on things the same way as we do."

"Why not? We're free citizens of this so-called democracy, aren't we? The same as they are. Why should one citizen get away with publicly traducing the name and reputation of another, and not even have to take it back when he can't substantiate it? Just because he's supposed to be acting in the name of the state? If the state makes a mistake, it should have to admit it, like other folk. There's a principle at stake here— and I'm going to do something about it."

"Guid for you, Adam! Gie them the works!" Tosh agreed heartily. "But . . . what can you do, man?"

"I can telephone the Procurator-Fiscal. And the Chief Constable. For a start. And the Press. I think the newspapers will be interested in this!"

"Aye, the newspapers, right enough . . ."

"It's significant, though, isn't it—that they *have* withdrawn this charge?" Hazel put in. "After the way they were talking on the phone this morning. Daddy went to see the Fiscal, remember. He must have advised that the case was unlikely to stand in court. About the three- to five-mile ban, at least. I think . . . I think, you know, Adam, that this silly irritating incident is important. I think, in fact, it means that you have won! Yes, won! It may seem a poor, unexciting way for victory to come about, admittedly—but the fact remains. They daren't take you to court."

"That's right—the lassie's right," Sandy nodded. "They didna dare interfere oot there today either. Man, Adam—I reckon we've beat them!"

Adam was silent, brows furrowed. The fishermen stared at each other, nonplussed, uncertain. This was not the way that any of them had foreseen victory, or an end to their campaign—this feeble, barely noticeable retreat on the part of the authorities.

"Och, to hell!" Tosh growled. "It's just a bluidy trick, likely . . . ."

"No," the girl insisted. "This is it, I'm sure. It may seem nothing much—but it is vital, I feel certain. The turn of the tide. I know something of how the other side works. How it thought and felt about the whole thing. After what I listened to this morning, I'll swear that this decision to drop the charge means victory for you. They may wrap it up—try to make it seem like generosity, giving you another chance, and all that. But the fact remains that they didn't want to be merciful. They wanted to make an example of you, and stop this whole business. They've climbed down, instead. It may not seem a very important thing to you—and the bad manners of it all are what is bound to strike you. But, away back, away up high somewhere, I'm sure this means that a decision has been taken—and this is just the first distant echo of it."

"That's all very well," Adam said. "It may be as you say. They may have recognised that they can't win in court. And that international repercussions would make it inadvisable to interfere with foreigners fishing out there—and therefore with us, when foreigners are present. And so they're just going to do nothing. Masterly inactivity. But that's not good enough. That's not what we've fought for. That still leaves us technically criminals every time we fish the so-called mouth of the Tweed. We want the Act changed. That's what we set out to do—to get the Tweed Act amended. Until we can make them do that, we can't say we've won."

"But isn't that bound to follow, eventually?"

"Not necessarily. They could just do nothing. They're good at that. No—we've got to force their hands. And . . . and I think I know how to do it. With the help of our good friends of the

Press!"

"What are you going to do, Adam?"

"I'm going to do a lot of telephoning, to start with. You too, Sandy."

"Eh? Me . . . ?"

"Yes, you. Or travelling if you prefer it. Though you've hardly time. You'd have to go all over the place. To all the fishing-villages. To Burnmouth and Eyemouth, and St Abbs and Cockburnspath. To Seahouses and Bamburgh and Holy Island. Tonight. All the sea fishermen, both sides of the Border. Get them out there, tomorrow, while the Norwegians still are there. And I'll get the Press. We'll make a day of it—and we'll make this thing stink so high that even London will have to do something about it. London, where they make and unmake Acts of Parliament . . . !"

"Jings, man—you've got something now! We'll show them!"

"That's the stuff—time we took the bluidy gloves off!"

"We'll get the boys oot—up and doon the coast . . ."

"I'm off to phone the Fiscal. And the Chief Constable. Then the papers."

"And I'm coming with you," Hazel cried. "I want to hear this!"

"You get busy, Sandy. . . . "

Adam's telephoning to the Fiscal and the Chief Constable was not productive of much satisfaction or result. The former was cool, polite, and very careful as to what he said—and when he discovered that he was talking, not to Logan's solicitor but to the notorious schoolmaster of Airdmouth, cagey indeed. He admitted that decisions as to whether prosecutions should go forward to court were his business, but that he was not in the habit of explaining the reasons for his official decisions to all and sundry. There was no question of apology or retraction being either called for or suitable. The normal procedure had been carried out, and the matter was closed, as far as he was concerned. He suggested that Mr Logan should consult a qualified solicitor if he was in any further doubt, and wished

225

his caller good-evening, civilly but firmly.

The Chief Constable was harder to reach, but rather more forthcoming. He was sorry if Mr Logan and his friends were offended at the method of receiving the good news. No actual onus lay upon him to send the information, at all—but he had thought it courteous to let Mr Logan know as quickly as possible, once a decision had been made, and he had sent a constable right away. The confiscated salmon was still in cold storage, and would be restored to its owner if he made application. He hoped that this incident would mark the end of an unhappy business, and that there would be no further need for a great deal of police time to be wasted on avoidable misunderstandings of legalities . . . especially when he required all his available men to deal with this shocking and quite phenomenal outbreak of night poaching, of which Mr Horsburgh no doubt had heard . . . !

Adam did rather better with the Press. He telephoned first the Chief Reporter of *The Scotsman*, and was much encouraged by his reception. He recounted the day's doings, and made very clear what he and the fishermen thought of the official attitude and reactions, concentrating on the two issues of the curt dropping of the charge, and the failure to interfere with the Norwegian fishing-boats. He was asked one or two shrewd and incisive questions thereafter, which seemed to leave no doubt that here at least the facts of the case, and the important issues that lay behind it all, were understood and appreciated. Considerably cheered, he went on to tackle the other major newspapers.

It was a formidable and lengthy task—but all were most definitely interested in what he had to say, even if some of the asides, enquiries and rejoinders tended to shoot off the main track into unprofitable byways. After a very little of it, Hazel, who had at last gained access to the schoolhouse, and had been standing by listening, wandered off around the house, to the considerable distraction of the telephoner. Presently, however, the smell of frying bacon in some measure reassured the man. The telephonic marathon was in due course interrupted with

226

an authoritative summons to supper—and thereafter Adam's preoccupation with the consistently sympathetic and even enthusiastic Press reception helped considerably to overlay his embarrassment at a poorly stocked larder, less than dainty tableware, and general domestic inadequacy. The young woman undoubtedly kept a strict watch on her tongue, and accepted as a silent compliment to her cooking Adam's hearty if absent-minded demolishment of the last scraps of all that she had prepared.

It was late before he was finally finished with the Press, and later still before the cream sports car went roaring off up the Airdmouth cliff-road. It was only afterwards that Adam Horsburgh became uncomfortably aware that he had perhaps been a little off his guard, latterly. Also, the house seemed to have been tidied up in alarming fashion. However, troublesome as these thoughts were, they tended to be submerged in a rather more pressing concern. What were the Airdmouth skippers and fishermen going to say, tomorrow morning, when they discovered that somebody had as good as promised passage in their various boats to a fair proportion of the newspaper reporters of Scotland?

XVII

UNDOUBTEDLY, Airdmouth had never known such a morning before. Even that day after the dynamiting episode was outdone. Not only did the Pressmen and the photographers reappear in large numbers, from an early hour, but innumerable other visitors and spectators arrived also—presumably as a result of the fishermen's efforts at rousing the neighbourhood the previous night, and of newspapermen's gossip in Edinburgh and elsewhere. Parked cars occupied every foot of the not very ample open space of the cliff-side village, and stretched away up the zig-zag climbing road—so that when Hazel Scott arrived soon after nine, she had to leave her own car right away on the cliff-top. Added to the bustle and stir on land, was the sight of a steadily increasing fleet of fishing-boats assembling just outside the harbour. By the time that Adam and the girl reached the pier, there were no fewer than eleven of them lying there, Scots boats from Eyemouth, Burnmouth and as far north as Cockburnspath, waiting for the Airdmouth craft to lead them out to the fishing-grounds.

Adam's guilty feelings about the Pressmen largely evaporated when he found them in more or less undisputed possession of the Airdmouth boats. Even women, in two instances, had wormed their way aboard, and the fishermen, looking embarrassed and self-conscious admittedly, appeared to have abandoned the struggle. A certain amount of lip-smacking, and a faint aroma of malt liquor, perhaps indicated that passengers had come prepared for all eventualities, including subtle persuasion.

Sandy Logan, imperturbable and genial as ever, did not even suggest that it was all Adam's doing. He merely wondered how so comparatively few newspapers could employ, or afford, so many minions, and hoped that they would not all be sick. At Adam's expressed wonder that they were apparently contemplating putting to sea with all this lot aboard—six on *Bluebell* alone—the skipper grinned, and informed him *sotto voce* that they would in due course transfer the bulk of them to the boats waiting outside the harbour—and have some fun in the process perhaps. Technically, of course, the fishing-boats were not licensed to carry passengers—but as technically, probably, the Board of Trade would find good reason for not getting involved in this fray.

Tosh Hogg sulked in *Bluebell's* wheelhouse, frowning blackly at all concerned, his comments unprintable but by no means muted.

A police patrol-car arrived on the scene as the last of the nets—which had had to be cleaned and dried since yesterday—were being loaded, but its occupants showed a marked interest only in the parked cars and kept studiously away from the harbour.

The five boats eventually left port to the ringing cheers of apparently everyone but the policemen. Adam counted nineteen extra passengers altogether, and hoped that they were all genuine journalists. He consulted a rather older, soberly dressed man, looking like a bank-manager, who admitted, almost reluctantly it seemed, that they all were, approximately. He revealed also that he was the representative of *The Scotsman*. Adam decided that it would be wise to keep him, at least, in the *Bluebell*, since that was the paper which could be expected to make most impact on influential opinion.

Sandy Logan had a quiet word over the radio with the waiting flotilla at the harbour mouth, so that when they came out, the Airdmouth boats were able to run promptly alongside some of these others and unload a good proportion of their passengers. There was considerable outcry at this, pleas that it was dangerous, objections at being parted from friends and photographers, the ladies skirling loudly. But it was pointed out that they were at sea now, and must do as they were told by skippers of vessels. The transference was completed under protest but without mishap, indeed with some hilarity, and *Bluebell*, with now only the middle-aged reporter and his photographer in addition to her normal crew, plus Adam and Hazel, moved to the head of the long line of sixteen craft, and led the way south-eastwards.

It was a relief, to Adam at least, to see, as they rounded the headland, that the seven Norwegians were still in position off the three-mile limit. It almost looked as though they had kept up their fishing all night.

The Scotsman representative had with him most of the morning's papers, and he passed them over to his hosts to study. Adam could not be disappointed with the results of all his telephoning. Without exception the Berwick salmon war was given prominent if not foremost placing, with head-lines which left no doubts as to where lay the sympathies of the news-editors at least. NELSON'S BLIND EYE FOR THE NORWEGIANS; SEA-DOGS KEPT ON THE LEASH THIS TIME; FOREIGNERS FISH WHERE BRITONS MUST NOT; AIRDMOUTH CHARGE FIZZLES OUT; and AUTHORITIES BACK DOWN OVER SALMON, were typical. The journalist pointed with dignified satisfaction to a leading article in his own paper, which was headed GOVERNMENT'S PREDICAMENT, and which stated in restrained but unequivocal language, that without entering into the finer legalities of the matter, it was clear that the situation that had developed off Berwick was a bad one, and of no credit to the responsible authorities. It was quite improper, surely, that British fishermen should be prohibited from fishing where foreigners were not interfered with. If the dropping of the charge against Skipper Logan meant that this had become apparent to the said authorities, then clearly the legislation under which the charge had been made was direly in need of amendment. This entire issue went far higher than the powers and interests of any local Fishery Board or Tweed Commissioners, and if the provisions of the Tweed Act of 1857 were inoperable, without causing grave international repercussions, as seemed probable, then Parliament ought to take prompt and remedial action to bring the Act into line with reality—and not least, with equity for the local inshore fisher-men, whose campaign appeared to the man-in-the-street to be

230

both well-founded and overdue.

The *Standard* also had a leader, in rather different terms, claiming curiously that foreign trawlers were taking the bread out of the mouths of Scots fishermen, aided and abetted by a government at Westminster too timorous either to protect its own people or to assert British fishing-interests adequately off Iceland and elsewhere. The Tweed Act should be scrapped forthwith, and Berwick returned to Scotland.

The *Bluebell's* complement, if somewhat mystified by this last, were distinctly cheered.

Cameras were busy on all the boats as they drew level with the Norwegian line. What the Scandinavians thought of this extraordinary armada was not to be known. To reassure them that no sort of enmity was indicated, Sandy Logan hailed one or two of the vessels, enquiring whether they were still getting fair catches, and sounding generally affable. He obtained a certain amount of rather doubtful waving in return, and the announcement from their friend in the third-last craft that the fishing was ver' goot were it not for the bloddy seal, mine Got!

It was disappointing that there was no sign of the lurking warships today, to point out to the Pressmen.

So many boats salmon fishing at the one time was quite ridiculous, of course, from a practical point of view, however impressive as a demonstration. The most effective arrangement would have been to add the sixteen craft and their nets to both ends of the already two-mile long line of the Norwegians, thus forming a barrier of nearly five miles right across the mouth of the Tweed—effective from the point of view of catching fish. That however would have invalidated much of the impression of great numbers involved, from the shore at any rate—the effect of a mass demonstration. Moreover, if the authorities *were* forced and provoked into taking action, as was hoped, it would be as well to have most of the boats reasonably close at hand, not too far scattered. Sandy, who seemed to be accepted by all, without question, as commodore, decided therefore that the boats should be grouped in lines of five or six, roughly parallel with the Norwegians, one line slightly landwards, as

231

before, and the others seawards, so that the foreigners were well and truly sandwiched. He issued his instructions over the radio accordingly.

The resultant manoeuvring was not carried out with entire clockwork precision, but at least the impression of many boats and much activity was dramatically maintained. All this kept the Press interested, as did the subsequent shooting of the nets. Thereafter, however, excitement soon flagged. As the boats slid and tilted and rolled in idleness on the long swell, public relations began to sink. Soon the radio was crackling with increasing frequency in *Bluebell's* wheelhouse, bringing reports of plunging morale, requests to be put ashore, and general distress at sea. The fishermen were on the whole not very sympathetic—though Sandy Logan was more concerned than he admitted, and Adam knew some little fellow-feeling.

The sighting of more fishing-boats coming up from the south created a welcome diversion. These proved to be five reinforcements from Seahouses and four more from Holy Island. Almost more welcome than their supporting presence was the news which the latter brought, that they had plainly seen, on the way north, a couple of frigates lying well out to sea, and apparently more or less stationary. This word, passed around the fishing-fleet, had a definitely enlivening effect.

Finding somewhere for the newcomers to shoot their nets, reasonably near at hand, was difficult. Drift nets take up a lot of space, at least longitudinally, and fouled nets are a fisherman's nightmare. There were now no fewer than thirty-two vessels concentrated in a comparatively small area, and the problem of sea-room was beginning to weigh on every skipper's mind. Moreover, the Seahouses people said that there were some more of their craft to come. Sandy confessed to Adam that he was beginning to wonder whether they had not been just a bit too enthusiastic, last night, in their invitations. A good show was very nice, but this might be getting out of hand. If the wind was to change, or the Norwegians got nasty, or somebody did something daft . . . !

Hazel Scott, with her glasses, was again the first to spot the

Navy—in *Bluebell*, at least. The two warships appeared to have taken up approximately the same positions as yesterday. They gave no impression that they were likely to be any more active, either.

This news had barely passed round, in the interests of morale, before somebody else pointed out that boats were coming out from Berwick. These proved to be two launch-type craft, heading apparently directly towards them—and one of them looked very similar to that launch in which Hogarth and the police inspector had made their first sally, three weeks ago.

"Good!" Adam commented. "It looks as though we've stirred up something, at last. They could hardly ignore this lot indefinitely, without making themselves the laughing-stock of the country."

"But what can they do?" the young woman asked. "They can't charge or try to arrest over thirty boats and crews! There's no point in them coming out and pointing out that we're all committing an offence. And they're certainly not going to come and tell us that they're going to let us off again, that everything is all right and we're forgiven."

"No-o-o," he agreed. "Admittedly, I don't know just what they *can* do. But I do know this—that if they do nothing, make no sort of response to this demonstration, after all the publicity, and with the Press here—then they've had it. They'll never dare to try to enforce this ridiculous Act again. They've got to do something—or else throw in the sponge."

To the disappointment of all, however, as the newcomers drew closer, they were seen to be crowded with very unofficial looking and unseamanlike figures, most of whom seemed to be equipped with large cameras. Perched on the short foredeck of the first launch, indeed, was what appeared to be either a television or a movie camera, complete with two operators. This was obviously nothing more than a second instalment of Press and observers in hired craft.

As the launches came near, a great deal of shouting arose, partly from Pressmen exchanging greetings, questions and friendly abuse, and partly from anxious and irate fishermen warning the newcomers to keep clear of their nets. This tight-packed concentration of netting was no place for joy-riders.

Sandy Logan began to get seriously worried when, a little later, three more boats were seen coming out from Berwick, and glasses revealed them to be crowded likewise with sight-seers of one sort or another. Utter chaos could so easily ensue if anyone was to play the fool, or even be stupidly careless.

A radio message from Dand Fairgrieve, whose *Ladybird* happened to be the end boat of the inner line, informed Sandy that one of the launches, in passing close to him had shouted to his passengers that Berwick was in a great state of excite-ment, that the entire town was in a ferment about the demonstration, and that little work was being done, with most of the population congregated on the seafront, gazing in their direction. A naval battle seemed to be anticipated. Sandy was about to reply sardonically that it looked as though the Navy was going to disappoint, when, glancing out of the wheelhouse window seawards, he paused. The two frigates were no longer hull-down beyond the horizon, but fully in sight and clearly steaming towards them. Moreover, they now had a third vessel in convoy. She looked like a fast motor-torpedo-boat. Sandy switched off his radio, a little abstractedly.

Soon all eyes in the fishing-fleet were concentrated on the approaching warships. Tension rose perceptibly as the distance between rapidly lessened. Even seasickness loosened its grip.

Hazel turned to Adam. "Well—this seems to be it!" she said. "This is what you wanted, isn't it? What you've worked for. How do you feel now, Adam?"

The schoolmaster moistened his lips. "Just a little bit fluttery about the stomach," he admitted. "It's . . . well, it's just that those ships look so damned efficient and impressive . . . "

"I wonder whether Royal Naval stomachs ever flutter?" she commented. "I suppose it's possible. If so, I'd imagine that the sight of thirty defiant fishing-boats, and their nets, spread out in front of them, and every newspaper in the land there to watch, might just conceivably set up some little palpitation."

"True," Adam conceded. "Er . . . thanks."

234

No hesitancy was apparent in the naval approach now, at least. The three grey-hued warships, White Ensigns streaming, paint-work gleaming, swept up to the concentration of small craft in imposing, not to say arrogant style. Slowing down, they swung round in line just short of the most seaward group of fishing-boats. By the nature of things, they were fully quarter-of-a-mile away from *Bluebell* and the Airdmouth line, with many craft intervening. The *Unicorn* was seen to be one of the frigates, but she was lying second to another, HMS *Cockatrice*.

There followed quite a lengthy interval wherein nothing happened—save that somebody shouted out that three more fishing-boats were approaching from the south, the Seahouses reinforcements presumably. The inaction and comparative silence was not a little unnerving.

"Biting his dam' nails, and trying to ken what to do next!" Tosh Hogg jeered. But Sandy shook his head.

At length the loud-hailer of the *Cockatrice* click-clacked warningly, and a stern voice spoke—and despite the distance, everyone on *Bluebell*, and therefore on all the other boats, could hear the measured authoritative words perfectly.

"Ahoy there! All skippers pay attention to me," it rang out metallically. "You are in breach of navigational regulations. I order all craft to haul in nets and disperse from this position. At once."

There was a pause, as people looked at each other. Nobody could answer that, from *Bluebell*, the distance being too great for intelligible shouting. Presently a scattering of cries and shouts and even boos did break out from amongst the boats, but nothing coherent. As it happened, the craft nearest to the naval ships were the latest arrivals, the Holy Islanders.

Again the stiffly severe voice echoed across the water. "I demand immediate compliance with my orders. Otherwise I shall take active steps to enforce them. I shall move you forcibly, with your nets. You are obstructing navigation. At all times, by law, the rights of fishing are subservient to navigation. You are obstructing free passage to the port of

Berwick-on-Tweed. You will remove from this position at once."

Standing beside Sandy Logan, Adam heard the skipper's breath catch. "What's this?" Adam said. "What's he talking about? What does he think we are—school children?"

The other shook his head, slowly. "Man," he said, "this is . . . och, it's a pity, that's what it is. Aye, a right pity."

"Eh? You mean . . . ?"

"I mean that he kens what he's doing, this boy. *I* ought to have kenn't, too. I blame mysel', for no' thinking of it—I do that. He's got us, right enough. Navigation's a superior right to fishing. Always has been. If a naval ship reckons fishing-craft are an obstruction to navigation, he has plenty authority to move them away oot o' it. And if they winna go, then he can take what steps he reckons necessary, just . . . and there's no comeback. No claims. He's the boss."

"Mr Logan—would you mind repeating that, please?" *The Scotsman* representative, notebook in hand, had moved up. "The bit about navigation. A superior right, did you say . . . ?"

"Och, another time maybe, sir. . . "

"Confound it—this is fantastic!" Adam cried."It's just a shabby trick. They daren't tackle us under the wretched Act, so they're just doing this to throw their weight about! It's quite irrelevant to this whole issue. . . "

"It's maybe all that, Adam man—but he can *do* it! He can plough right in amongst us, with yon cruiser bows o' his, and chew up oor nets into bits o' rag. And we couldna do a thing aboot it."

"He wouldn't dare!" Hazel exclaimed.

"Would he no'? No' for illegal fishing, I'll grant you. But for refusing to move, as an obstruction to navigation, blocking the entrance to a port, he's got every law in the book behind him. We havena a leg to stand on—and every skipper in this fleet kens it."

"But, my goodness—it's a trumped-up charge! We're not blocking anybody's access to Berwick. Nobody's trying to get in to Berwick. And if they were, they could get round us, easily

236

enough. There's plenty of sea!"

"Aye—but that's no' the point, man, If the captain o' a naval vessel, on duty, says we're an obstruction, then we are an obstruction. That's the way o' it!"

"D'you mean to say, then, that we're going to tamely pull in our nets and clear out? After all we've done. At this stage!"

"Mr Logan—I want to get this right. This naval ship is not really interfering with your fishing, but claiming that this lot of boats constitutes an obstacle to navigation? Is that . . . ?"

"Och, wheesht, the both o' you. Somebody's hailing him. Wi' a megaphone. Can you hear what he's saying?"

Somebody on one of the Holy Island boats was indeed shouting back at the *Cockatrice*, but since he was facing seawards and a fair distance off, it was impossible to distinguish his words. All that they heard was the answer from the warship, which came out thereafter with staccato crispness.

"That is no concern of mine, Skipper. It is my duty to see that free navigation in these waters is not interfered with—and I intend to see to it. There are over two dozen boats and their nets blocking the seaway to Berwick. They must disperse—and without delay."

"Damn the hectoring yap-yapping busybody!" Adam fretted. "I wish to goodness I could talk back to him! I tell you. . . ."

His words were drowned in Sandy's great voice. "Tosh—haul nets!" the skipper called. "Get them in."

"Sandy! You're not going to do it? To obey him?" the schoolmaster demanded. "You're not going to turn and run—now! You, of all people!"

"Man—listen," the big man said, as he saw the automatic hauler start to turn, and his men take up their hauling positions, cursing but obedient. "We brought all these other boys oot here. They came because I tell't them. D'you ken what you want me to do? There's near on ten thousand pounds worth o' nets lying oot here, this minute. Those ships could write the lot off in ten minutes. D'you want me to take on responsibility for the loss o' all that? All these boys' property? If it was just

237

oorsel's. . . ."

"Hurry up, there!" the loud-hailer commanded impatiently. "Some boats have started pulling in—some haven't. Get cracking, all of you. I'm not waiting all day!"

"Oh, you great loudmouthed bully!" Hazel cried, hotly. "Of all the unsporting rotten tricks!"

"I still don't believe he'd do it—cut up your nets," Adam declared. "I think he's bluffing. Like the other chap did, last time. Especially with all the Press here to report on it."

"Maybe aye and maybe no. But he'd have to do something, mind. After yon last time, he couldna just go off wi' his tail between his legs. He *can* do it. He'd have the law behind him, this time. And I reckon he would. He's a senior man this, too, to the boy we had before—you can hear that. They've sent somebody that can take decisions—probably a full Captain. Anyway, I'm no' taking the risk. The others look to me for a lead. I canna do it, Adam—no' to all these boys. It's no' even just their nets. It's their certificates. We've all got to have skipper's certificates, for these boats—and they can take them off us. It's too much to risk. . . ."

"I see. All right," Adam said, levelly now. "I've no right to ask it. But . . . we've got to do *something*, Sandy—not just tamely lie down under this. All of us. Suppose . . . could we not slip free of our nets, somehow? Just this boat, I mean? Get round and through the rest, to go and talk to that Navy man?"

"What for? What's the good o' it?"

"To parley. Offer something. Talk to him. It's terrible not to be able to say a word, like this—to speak back. . . ."

"What could we say to him, Adam man? What have we got to offer?"

"Could we not say we'll do something to meet this thing about navigation? Say we'd clear a passage right through the middle of our boats. A lane. Free of boats and nets."

The skipper shook his head. "He wouldna listen to that. He wants us oot o' it, altogether. And he can put us oot. He'll no' be content wi' anything like that."

"But we can at least offer it. It's reasonable. It wouldn't

238

make such a total surrender—even the attempt at bargaining. And it would surely give the Press something to write about. To counter the bad publicity. To say that our offer was rejected. We've got to think of the effect of this on public opinion. We've got to put the Navy in the wrong, somehow."

"He's right," Hazel substantiated. "Adam's right, Sandy." The girl turned to the Pressman. "Isn't that the case? That if we offer to make a channel right through the fishing-boats, a wide channel and the Navy refuses and insists on us all packing up— then the newspapers would have something to go on? They would be able to show that we weren't really obstructing anything, and that it was all just a dirty trick? Wouldn't they?"

"Well . . . h'mmm." The journalist blinked a little. "We're not really here to take sides in the matter, of course, Miss. Just to report. But . . . well, I think there's no doubt whose side our sympathies are on—most of us, at any rate. Personally, that is. And I think if such an offer as you suggest was refused by this naval commander—it would weigh quite heavily. Against the Navy—or whoever's giving the Navy its orders. I don't think there's any doubt about . . ."

"You see, Sandy!"

The skipper nodded. "Right, then." He raised his voice. "Tosh—cut the messenger, and hitch it to yon big float. We're moving."

"Aye, aye, Sandy. You've got some sense in your heid at last!"

Only the first of the *Bluebell's* series of nets was inboard— with not a single salmon in it. The hauling was stopped, and a large red float lying in the bows was attached to the end loop of the incoming net, two coils of the messenger hitched round it, and the rest of the messenger-line itself chopped through with an axe. *Bluebell* swung free, and Sandy switched on the diesels.

All around them boats were at some stage of the protracted business of drawing in nets—the Norwegians included. Most skippers were being distinctly slow and apathetic about it, and at sight of *Bluebell* cutting away from her gear, many of them

239

halted the process, to await events.

Sandy steered his craft carefully and skilfully through the maze of boats and nets and floats, on a zig-zag course seawards.

The loud-hailer was not long in registering disapproval. It clacked out curt commands to get on with the hauling-in more quickly, and ordered Sandy, by his registration number, to get back to his nets.

Bluebell continued to thread her way towards the warships. The boats that she passed began to cheer her progress.

A sudden loud series of blasts on the *Cockatrice's* siren made everybody jump. With a threshing of white water at her stern, the frigate turned closer to the line of the first fishing-boats, her tall sharp prow now pointing directly and ominously at them. The other two naval vessels did likewise. The cheering died away.

Bluebell was almost through, now. Sandy picked up his megaphone, and shouted at the full pitch of his lungs towards the warship. "Ahoy, Captain—a word wi' you, please."

"I'm not here to argue," came back at them. "I'm here for one purpose only—to ensure free navigation. Get back to your nets."

"Just a wee," Sandy persisted. "You'll no' deny us a word, surely? No wi' forty or fifty newspaper-reporters listening, sir?"

There was only a brief pause. "That's nothing to do with me. There's nothing to talk about. D'you want me to clear these nets away by force?"

"No, no—we do not, sir." *Bluebell* was now within comfortable hailing distance of the frigate. "Hold your hand—we're willing to clear a passage for you. Aye, we are."

"Are you? Then get cracking about it, man."

"Sure, Captain. But you canna just haul in quarter o' a mile of heavy net in a couple o' minutes. It's slow work. . . ."

"You've had twenty minutes to do it, already. And many of your craft have stopped hauling, I see. I warn you, all of you, I'm losing my patience fast, by God!"

240

"Look, Captain—no need for all o' us to move," Sandy called. "We're willing to clear a passage right through our fleet. A wide channel. We'll move the boats in the middle, oot the way. Give you plenty room—a fine wide lane. For your navigation. And the rest o' us can go on fishing, as we've every right to do . . ."

"You'll do nothing of the sort, my man!" Swiftly that was snapped back. "Every boat fishing here will up nets and get out of it. Right out. You're causing a gross obstruction on this seaway, and it's to be cleared. Those are the orders I've been given."

Adam Horsburgh grabbed the megaphone. "So that's it, Captain!" he shouted. "You had your orders to clear us before ever you came? Eh? Before you knew whether we were obstructing anything, or not! In other words, this is a put-up job! A fake! I'm sure the Pressmen present will note the fact . . ."

"Be quiet, whoever you are! I only deal with skippers. And I'm in touch with my headquarters all the time."

"Is that so, Captain!" Sandy took back his megaphone. "So it's no' your fault? Just the folk who sent you. We're no' blaming *you*, mind . . ."

"Silence! That's enough. No more of it. All nets must be in, and every boat away from this area, in ten minutes. Every boat. That's my last word. You've got precisely ten minutes. Then we move in amongst you. And that's a promise! I'm leaving this loud-hailer, now. D'you hear? There will be no more talk." As though to underline the finality of that, the instrument choked off in a sort of bark.

Sandy sighed, shrugged, and turned to Adam. "I kenn't that would be the way o' it," he said. He stepped back into his wheelhouse, and put *Bluebell's* engines into forward. Then he switched on the radio. "Attention all skippers," he spoke into the mouthpiece. "Logan calling, in *Bluebell*. Nets in, and disperse. Nae mair fishing the day. Away hame. Message ends." And he switched off.

Adam's glance met that of the young woman, and for

241

moments they gazed at each other, wordless. At last he spoke, as the boat surged back towards its jettisoned nets.

"Battle lost!" the man said, shortly, bitterly. "Beaten at the last—by a lousy trick!"

She shook her head. "Lousy trick—yes. But not beaten yet, Adam—surely? All isn't lost, because of this. The situation remains as it was, doesn't it? You've proved the Act at fault, and unworkable . . ."

"Yes. But proved it to whom? In the end, this whole campaign depends on public opinion. It's only public opinion that the Government is afraid of, active public opinion—not the rightness or otherwise of our cause. And this—this will be written up as defeat. The Navy has cleared us off. Legally. We've obeyed—showing ourselves to be in the wrong. The public won't differentiate between one reason and another. They're not interested in finicky details—don't know or care about the finer points of the law. The fact that it's navigation law, and not salmon fishing that's beaten us, won't register— I'm prepared to bet on that. By and large, nobody will note that. Our *Scotsman* friend will probably do his best for us. But what will the headlines say tomorrow? '*Navy Drives Salmon Fishers off the Sea! Salmon Demonstration a Flop!*' That sort of thing. And that will be that. The authorities will heave a sigh of relief, and do nothing. Masterly inactivity again. And our campaign fizzles out."

"I think that is too gloomy a view, Adam . . ."

Gloom undoubtedly permeated that concourse of fishing-boats, as everywhere the nets came in. Whether any salmon were caught therein now seemed scarcely relevant. *Bluebell* threaded her way back to her own nets, amidst her silent fellows, recovered the large float and end of the messenger, and recommenced hauling. Everywhere fishermen's faces were set as they worked at the nets, and cursed as they worked—and Press pencils scribbled busily.

Ten minutes was just about long enough for most of the boats—though not for *Bluebell*, of course. The period of grace ended with the *Cockatrice* hooting again on her siren. By that

242

time many of the craft were moving away, others were stowing their nets or pulling in the last of their gear. The two frigates and the torpedo-boat moved forward promptly but slowly, carefully—and there was now ample space for careful manoeuvre around the remaining boats.

Tosh Hogg shook his fist at the naval vessels, but otherwise compliance with orders was complete.

The Norwegians, with their longer lines of nets, and *Bluebell*, were the last to leave. What the foreigners thought of the entire proceedings was not to be known—nor what their further action would be; meantime, they obeyed like the rest.

No more announcements nor commands issued from the naval vessels. By the time that Sandy Logan started up his engines again, and turned his prow northwards, the great assembly of boats was already widely scattered and dispersing fast, the Norwegians directly seawards, the English southwards, the Scots northwards and the Berwick pleasure-craft homewards. Only the three grey warships moved about, slowly, back and forth over the area that had been so full of boats, seapower triumphant.

They made a very silent company in *Bluebell*, on the way home to Airdmouth.

XVIII

IT was Hazel Scott, as they entered harbour, who perceived amongst all the clutter of cars that thronged the village and its approaches, the tall and imposing outline of the Linburndean Rolls. It stood out like a wolfhound amongst terriers, down near the pier-head. How it had managed to get that far, through the crush, could only be guessed. It was not difficult, after that, to distinguish its owner, pacing up and down the pier itself. Sir John Scott appeared to be alone—though a couple of policemen stood not very far away.

"Oh," his daughter said. "M'mmm. I wonder, now . . . ?"

Adam said nothing at all, but his jawline set.

Bluebell was the last of the five Airdmouth boats to berth. Pressmen were streaming up from the other craft, into the village, making for telephones probably. Sir John seemed to be calling briefly to each group of them as they went past. He could be seen to actually wave one couple away that came back towards him, however.

The *Scotsman* representative touched Adam's elbow. "May I use your phone, Mr Horsburgh? In your house?" he asked. "There's still time to get something brief into the late editions of our evening paper, the *Dispatch*. I, h'mm, might manage to put this business into better perspective than . . . well, than some of them. It might help tomorrow's reactions, perhaps, if the *Dispatch* treated the story the right way. Your way, I mean. Not that I can promise, of course. . . ."

"Go ahead," the schoolmaster nodded. "You'll find the back door's open. And thanks for trying, at any rate."

The reporter and his photographer were the first to clamber up on to the pier. Sir John threw a word to them, as he came forward to stand looking down into the boat.

"Don't go too far away, you chaps," he said, easily. "I'd like a word with you all in a minute. I'll give a few toots of my car

244

horn when I'm ready. I'm Scott, the local Member."

"Jings!" came fervently from Tosh Hogg, staring up.

Adam, Hazel and Sandy exchanged quick glances.

Sir John smiled down at them all. "Well," he said. "Had a good trip? You're back rather earlier than was expected, aren't you? Saved me a wait, though."

Hazel looked up at her sire, steadily. "What are you here for, Father?" she asked. "Have you just come to gloat?"

"Gloat?" he repeated. "Oh come, my girl—that's a bit forthright, even for you, isn't it? I mean, you can't expect everyone else to take quite such a rosy view of all this as you seem to do! A good catch, Skipper?"

"No, sir," Sandy answered shortly.

"A pity. Still, all the more left for the next time, eh? Coming up, my dear?" Her father reached down a hand to assist Hazel.

"I'll manage," the girl said, ignoring his hand, and clambered up the rusty iron ladder nimbly enough.

"Well, young man," the baronet said, as Adam climbed after her. "You've been pretty busy, one way or another, since last we foregathered!"

"Quite, sir."

"I must say, you haven't allowed much grass to grow under your feet. A fast worker, eh?"

"I wouldn't think so, sir—not particularly." Adam looked back and down. "Are you coming up just now, Sandy?"

"Och, there's no hurry, Adam man. . . ."

"Yes—come away, Skipper," Sir John said. "All of you. What I have to say to the Press will be of interest to you all, no doubt. Very handy, you know, you having all these newspaper-johnnies on hand, like this."

"Father—what have you come here for, just now?" Hazel demanded. "You never do things without a very good reason . . ."

"Like my daughter! Beware of that, young man—there's a motive behind her every word and look. You'll find out. But thank you, my dear—I'm glad you have such a high opinion of me . . ."

245

"It's just *because* of these Press people, isn't it? You heard we had them all with us, and thought it was a fine opportunity to get at a big lot of them at the one time?"

"I won't deny, Hazel, that the convenience of the arrangement occurred to me. But that was a secondary consideration. I really came along to witness our conquering hero's return!"

"I think that's in pretty poor taste, myself," his daughter said. They were walking up towards the village, now. "I wouldn't let him speak to the Pressmen, Adam," she declared, turning—for Adam tended to lag behind. "It's not fair that he should use them for *his* purposes—after you've got them all together."

Adam shrugged. "It's a free country—sometimes!" he said.

"Precisely. You can't stop me, my girl—so don't you try. Besides, the Press will be very interested to hear what I have to say. More than sometimes, I fear! We'll get on with it right away, shall we?"

They had come up with the Rolls Royce, and Sir John, opening the door, pressed the melodiously autocratic horn a few times. Already a number of the reporters were hanging about, waiting, and others now came hurrying. One or two photographers took the opportunity to snap a few pictures of the scene.

"D'you want to listen to this, Adam?" the young woman asked, low-voiced. "I'm sorry. I . . . well, I'm sorry about it."

"I think I'd better," he told her. "I might be able . . . well, to correct one or two wrong impressions, possibly."

"Yes. Of course. But it's not a very pleasant proceeding for you. Or for me . . ."

Sir John came back from the car, and posed beside his daughter for a couple of photographers. He insisted on Adam being in the picture also. He was very much the master of the situation.

When an adequate crowd had gathered, fisherfolk and sightseers as well as journalists, Sir John raised a hand for silence. "I shan't keep you long, ladies and gentlemen," he began pleasantly. "But what I have to say is, I think, worth passing

246

on. A lot of nonsense has been written and spoken about this salmon-fishing dispute, as I think you will agree. This is not just more hot air. I am glad to say that I can state something definite, at last. I have not made any public statements hitherto, for the very good reason that there were too many people making statements already. But that isn't to say that I wasn't extremely interested. As Member for this constituency I have, of course, been much concerned about it all from the first."

"And you're one of these Tweed Commissioners yourself, aren't you, sir—appointed under this disputed Act?" somebody put in.

"H'mm. Yes, I am. That is still another reason for my interest. A third, more personal still, is that my daughter here has taken quite a'h'mm, prominent part in the proceedings. Almost from the beginning, I am given to understand." He reached out to pat Hazel's shoulder—and she shrugged off his hand with a quick frown.

"Miss Scott seems to have been fighting on the other side, however—doesn't she, sir?"

"Eh? Other side? God bless me, sir—what sort of talk is this? Other side from whom? Not from me, surely? You wouldn't divide a family, would you? Father and daughter? No, no—the fact that I have kept pretty quiet doesn't mean that I have been entirely inactive, my friends. Quite the reverse, in fact. I've been constantly and quietly working away behind the scenes. It doesn't do for a Parliamentarian to get mixed up in challenges to the law, and violent excitements of that sort, however sporting. But there are things that can be done, you know, less spectacularly. I have been in constant touch with the Secretary of State for Scotland, right up to an hour or so ago. And I am happy to be able to tell you, gentlemen, that this whole matter looks like being most amicably settled. The Secretary of State has now agreed to advise the Prime Minister to appoint an official investigation into the provisions of the Tweed Act, with especial reference to those sections relating to salmon fishing in the sea. I think that you may take it that there will be no more trouble on that score."

247

Smiling broadly, Sir John reached over to pat his daughter's shoulder once more. He reached round her back even further, and patted Adam's also.

There was a period of almost complete silence, broken only by the sigh of the waves on the rocks and the unending screaming of the gulls. Pencils stopped their scribbling, as it gradually dawned upon the writers what had just been declared. Then a great buzz of talk and exclamation broke out, and the gulls were drowned out quite, in shouted questioning.

As for Adam Horsburgh, his mind refused to accept what his ears had heard. He merely stared ahead of him, unseeing, frowning. Even the young woman's sudden and fierce grip on his arm barely registered.

Sir John raised his hand again, but geniality itself. "I need hardly say how much pleasure it gives me to make this announcement," he went on, when he could make himself heard. "And, by the way, ladies and gentlemen—it's quite official. The Secretary of State has given me full permission to make it public. As you will all realise, an investigation of this sort is never ordered until there is very good reason to believe that it is entirely necessary. I think that you can take it, therefore, without prejudging the findings of the committee of enquiry, that the Tweed Act will indeed be amended, and this spirited campaign therefore crowned with well-deserved success!"

A spontaneous cheer actually broke out from the assembled Pressmen—an unexampled demonstration that seemed even to surprise themselves.

Adam's mind was beginning to function again. Was all this true, genuine? It must be true, surely? It couldn't all be a trick? Not in the face of all this publicity. Scott could never eat these words. If this *was* true . . . then they'd won! Won their battle. Done what they'd set out to do. Won . . . despite today's debacle with the Navy. Somehow . . .

"Adam!" Hazel was crying. "D'you hear? It's all right. Everything's fine! They're going to do it—amend the Act. You've won! Won—d'you hear?" And she threw her arms

248

around his neck and kissed him.

That set back the man's brain-work again, quite considerably.

Cameras clicked, and photographers shouted for a repeat.

Smiling broadly, Sir John pulled down his waistcoat, and patted his paunch this time, with every appearance of assured satisfaction.

"Any comment to make, Mr Horsburgh?" somebody shouted, amidst laughter.

Adam sought to collect his erratic thoughts. "Er . . . well, it's very nice," he said, lamely. "Very nice indeed. The news, I mean. I'm afraid I'm all at sea, at the moment . . . "

There was more laughter at this involuntary sally.

Adam found that his elbow was being plucked—at the other side from the one that Hazel had grabbed. He turned to find the *Scotsman* representative standing there, a scribbled paper in his hand.

"Mr Horsburgh—I thought you'd be interested to hear this," he said, low-voiced, "I've just been talking on the phone to my Chief Reporter. He tells me that the opposition to your campaign seems to have folded up. At noon today, the Secretary of State issued a statement. It said that the Government is going to set up a Committee of Enquiry into the Tweed Act . . ."

"Yes. I know. We've just heard all that, from Sir John Scott."

"Oh, you have? Did you get any details? Did he indicate why? Why this sudden collapse?"

"No. No—I haven't quite been able to grasp that, myself."

"I asked my chief. He said that the Procurator-Fiscal had sent in an official report saying that he cannot undertake to prosecute any further infringements of the Act as it stands at present. As far as sea fishing is concerned. That, together with the fuss about the Norwegians and international opinion, and the need to damp down this Berwick-for-Scotland rumpus, seems to have done the trick. But it was mainly the Fiscal's report, I think."

"I see." Adam's glance had lifted—and he found Sir John Scott's gaze upon him. And the baronet's change of expression, from the satisfaction of a moment or two ago, was as striking as it was almost ludicrous. If ever a man's eyes betrayed his confident pose, in sheer alarm and anxiety, it was at that moment, as he obviously wondered what the journalist was whispering to the schoolmaster. The sight came as quite a shock to Adam—and had the effect of clearing his mind quite extraordinarily.

Was it a trick, then, after all? Was this whole thing fraudulent? No—the news from *The Scotsman* confirmed it. Yet there was something wrong, here—something that was false. Adam's mind was working swiftly, logically, at last. It was Scott's satisfaction that was false. Then . . . of course! He had made his statement, as though it was all largely his own doing, as though he had been on the side of the campaigners all the time, quietly. He was fighting to get as much credit out of the thing as he could—hurrying to be on the winning side. And afraid that this journalist was bringing news that would show him up in public as a fraud. Here was a man who needed to be on the winning side—always. Because he *needed* popular votes. To keep him in Parliament. A politician, in fact!

Adam's met Scott's gaze then, directly, and for a long moment they stared at each other. The moment of truth, perhaps. The younger man let his breath go in a long sigh. They had won, all right. He read that, without any doubt, in the other's eyes. And, sighing, he knew some pity now, some compassion, for the older man, to quell the suddenly rising surge of indignation and contempt at him for trying to steal the credit and the applause. What did it matter, when they had won? That man had his own battles to fight, and on murky shifting sands indeed as a battleground. Perhaps politicians got less sympathy than they deserved? The men who must always come down on the right side of the fence.

Adam's compassion switched to the young woman whose father this was, and he knew a great flood of tenderness for her. Humbled pride was a sore business, and she was one of the proud ones. Undoubtedly her pride was being humbled here and now. He reached out a hand to squeeze her shoulder, and she turned to face him, tight-lipped, tense. She knew her father too, indubitably.

Adam cleared his throat, and raised his voice. "Ladies and gentlemen—our friend here, from *The Scotsman*, has been telephoning. He confirms what Sir John Scott has said, and can add that the Fiscal's decision that the Act was unworkable helped to swing the issue. I am sure I speak for all the fisherfolk when I say that we are very happy about this . . . and, h'mm, greatly indebted to all who have helped us in our fight." His glance at Sir John was very brief. "There is just one point that I might make. It seems that the Secretary of State's decision was issued to the Press at noon. Over four hours ago. That is, an hour at least before the naval commander out there issued *his* ultimatum! It appears therefore that our naval friend was, in fact, thrown to the wolves. The authorities who sent him out, and gave him his instructions how to deal with us, suddenly changed their minds—and didn't even trouble to let him know. He won his victory, poor chap—but he was an hour late with it! I'm sorry for that officer. Perhaps he lacked the Nelson touch, after all—he should have turned a blind eye to unpleasant orders. He deserves our sympathy, I think—not our blame. I hope that you will all make that clear in your papers."

In the laughter and ironical cheers that greeted this, the young woman looked from her father to the speaker. "Thank you, Adam," she said quietly. She had not missed either his gesture or his side-tracking.

He shook his head, and called out once more. "Now, everybody—I want you all to acknowledge the real hero of this business—Skipper Sandy Logan! Without him, nothing would have been achieved. He's trying to hide, back there—but being the size he is, it's not very easy. . . !"

It was the fisherfolk's turn to cheer, now, and willy-nilly Sandy was pushed forward.

The big man was gravely embarrassed. He mumbled something to those around him, before he hesitantly found his

251

powerful voice. "Och—I'm no' one for making speeches and announcements," he declared. "No' me. I'm just an ordinary fisher-chap . . . that likes a bite o' salmon, noo and then. I didna do a thing—bar give Adam there a bit hand. Aye, and keep Tosh Hogg frae committing murder sometimes! Adam was the one that did it all—Mr Horsburgh, I should say, the school-master. He thought it all up, and kept us at it. We're right grateful to him, the lot o' us. And to the lassie, too—Miss Scott. She was a right help. And bonny, too—which aye counts for a lot! Except wi' Tosh, maybe! Aye—well, that's the lot. . . ."

Out of the applause, a woman's voice rose, the dulcet but penetrating tones of the formidable Maggie Knockatter. "You haven't any announcement to make, by any chance, Sir John, about your daughter?" she asked coyly. "No sort of romance building up, or anything?"

"Hey, Maggie!"

"Keep the party clean, Knockatter . . . !"

"Why ask me, my dear lady?" Scott answered. "I haven't an earthly idea. I'm just the father, I'd remind you—the last who would be informed if there was anything of the sort in the air. . . ."

"Father! Look—this is insufferable!" Hazel exclaimed, flushing scarlet.

"I agree," Adam said stiffly, jerkily.

"I think, then, that closes the interview, ladies and gentle-men," Sir John declared, pleasantly firm, in the saddle once more. "I'd say you've had your money's worth, haven't you? And you will all be in a hurry to get back to your papers, I've no doubt. Good-day to you all. Good-day. No, madam—no more questions. Not one . . ."

Adam looked after the retiring Pressmen, rigidly keeping his eyes in that direction. Her back to him, Hazel stared out to sea. Neither of them had anything to say.

Sir John Scott, looking from one to the other, shrugged. "Well, that seems to be about the lot," he observed. "By and large, I would say, a pretty satisfactory outcome to the whole affair."

"You . . . *you* stand there and say that!" his daughter flung back at him, though without turning round.

"Why not, my dear? A little give and take on both sides— that's the way most things get done. The whole art of good government, in fact."

"You . . . you hypocrite! You realise, don't you, that Adam could have blown you sky-high at any time? With your shameful pretence that you had been for us all along!"

"Of course he could! But he didn't—being a sensible man. I think he may go far, your Adam—for sensible men like him don't grow on every bush! He didn't—for what good would it have done him? After all, he was in a difficult position, too. Blowing up his prospective father-in-law wouldn't have helped anybody! Fathers-in-law still have their importance—so long as they're prospective!"

"Father!" Hotly, she turned now. "Oh—you're hateful! How could you! Adam—pay no attention to him. He's just mad, because he's lost and you've won!"

"Dear me—have I said something wrong?" Sir John asked, innocently. "I must have taken you up wrongly, a couple of nights ago. I think. Didn't you say . . . ?"

"Adam—this is crazy! Don't listen to him. He's . . . he's a politician—that's all. He'd sell anything, for public support. This is his way of keeping you quiet—to keep you from giving him away. He's trying to sell *me*!"

"Well, I'm damned—you little minx! After all you said about this novelist fellow. . . ."

"Oh—to think I have to call you Father! I won't listen to another word!" And twisting round, Hazel Scott left them there, and went running away up the village street.

Sir John turned to the appalled young man, actually smiling. "Well, Horsburgh—this is where you do your stuff, isn't it? I've done all *I* can. Up to you, now."

"Eh . . . ?"

"Don't stand there goggling, man. After her. You'll be a poor fisherman if you can't land her satisfactorily, now! She told me, the other night, that she was afraid you'd never get round to popping the question. Had to do what I could to bring things on, you know."

"But . . . look here, sir . . . this is utterly impossible!"

"Why? D'you love her, man? Or don't you?"

"I . . . yes, I do."

"Thank God for that, at any rate! I was beginning to wonder. You were cooked, anyway, of course. I could see she'd decided on you a week ago—so you hadn't a chance. But she reckoned you'd take a bit of bringing up to scratch. Thought you probably had some outdated notions about mating up with a wicked landlord's daughter, and all that. Tommy-rot of that sort. Well, I think I've untangled that one for the pair of you. Done my best, anyway. Lord—what are you waiting for, man?"

Adam swallowed, his glance turning away up the road. "I don't know what to say," he got out.

"D'you mean to me—or to her? Say nothing more to me— and Lord help you if you don't know what to say to Hazel, for I won't do any more of your courting for you! Off with you, now, for Heaven's sake—before she reaches that abominable car of hers. Though, mind you, I think she'll not run all that fast. Not once she's out of sight. And look Horsburgh—be sort of nice to her, will you? She may not think it, just now—but I'm fond of that little wretch!"

"Yes, sir," Adam Horsburgh said—and began to run.